QUITE POSSIBLY ALLIES

QUITE POSSIBLY ALLIES

A FREEMAN UNIVERSE NOVEL

PATRICK O'SULLIVAN

dunkerron press

BOOKS IN THIS SERIES

A Dunkerron Press™ Book.

Copyright © 2022 by Patrick O'Sullivan

PatrickOSullivan.com

Illustration © Tom Edwards

TomEdwardsDesign.com

ISBN-13: 978-1-62560-023-3

ISBN-10: 1-62560-023-2

This is a work of fiction. Names, characters, dialogue, places and incidents are either the product of the author's imagination or are used fictitiously, and any resemblance to actual persons, living or dead, business establishments, events or locales is entirely coincidental.

Dunkerron Press and the Dunkerron colophon are trademarks of Dunkerron, LLC.

1

Trinity System, Freeman Federation

The compact black shape clinging to the hull of the Freeman merchant vessel detached, transforming instantly from hitchhiker to projectile. The system's star remained a distant spark, one whose light the stealth vessel's pilot could not yet perceive. At present she relied entirely on those sensors attuned to mass and gravity alone. If she did not die within the next thirty seconds, she might yet live to bathe in that light, and behold one more sunrise.

Entering the star system above the orbital plane allowed for a margin of error, though such probability calculations were approximations in long-populated systems. There might well be traffic in her path, or a captured wanderer, or even rubbish, discarded and shoved out of the spaceways. Within the inhabited zone she expected as much. Counted on it, even.

A collision with even the tiniest mass would doom her. At

such a great distance from the star, she would need to be detected and acted against, or be in possession of an uncanny measure of bad luck. And yet, the idea returned to her again and again as she ran through her routines. She did not want to die in darkness. And she did not want to fail. Most of all she did not want to do both at the same time.

The pilot deployed the stealth vessel's sensor array. She began to scan the local star system for landmarks.

The merchant superluminal she had hitched a ride on continued to accelerate inward toward the system's star, the vessel at present on a collision course with the largest orbital shipyard in a thousand light-years. Once detected, every sensor in the system would focus on that vessel as it plunged toward the populated center of the system. Only then would she be free to activate her tiny vessel's active impact shielding. Until that moment there remained between her and annihilation a few millimeters of stealth material alone. Collision avoidance at such velocity exceeded even her level of skill.

She continued inward on a ballistic path, spending her time charting the system from her distant perspective and matching that chart to previous observations siphoned off from the host vessel's memory. These proved surprisingly slow and difficult calculations, as the amount of memory consumed and processing power required far exceeded that of her routine procedure of cataloging first and comparing afterward. She had to split her attention between the sensors' output and the navigational database, trying for a quick but imprecise fit. Refinement would come later.

Unusual, that she possessed a navigational database, and distracting. A first-in pilot by nature and training, this skulking about in charted territory had proved itself an unwelcome novelty. That her first such mission could also be her last did not cheer her.

She throttled her search and began to vent the waste heat

into space. That she could feel impatience while hurtling along at tenths of the speed of light struck her as a useless epiphany, akin to discovering she possessed nerves of steel *after* crossing a black hole's event horizon. What choice did she have? As soon as she knew enough she would act. Even though her actions would follow a plan she had no say in, to an end she'd rather not think about. The idea that she could not act consumed more and more of her attention. Became a fascination. Became an obsession.

And then she knew within a light-year in every direction where she was, and then a light-hour, and then a light-minute, and then as precisely as the system survey and the resolution of the vessel's clock allowed. She deployed the vessel's trailing sensor net, gossamer monomolecular filaments each possessing instrumentation tuned to a precise range of electromagnetic frequencies.

She could now perceive the star as visible light, and overhear the myriad hours-old or even days-old conversations in the local broadcast spectra, discern hot object from cold, active from inert, not merely as discrete units of mass and vectors of gravity. She could not know the instant of detection for the merchant vessel plunging ever inward. She instead possessed a model, not only of the vessel's inward progress but of the propagation delay of electromagnetic emissions to her current location. When the model predicted it safe, she enabled the vessel's impact shielding, minutely visible to properly tuned sensors but an acceptable risk. One needed to be looking, and no eye would turn her way now that their doom charged toward them.

She cataloged those system features of importance. The star itself unexceptional, four of the five planets uninhabited, though perhaps not uninhabitable, nine moons in total, also uninhabited, no asteroid belt, though there had been at one time. Several large constructs in orbit around the sole inhabited planet, the material for those orbitals having come from *somewhere.* No evidence of surface mining marred a single moon.

The inhabited planet's surface largely water, with two main continents and ice at both poles, uncertainty as to whether the planet's naturally occurring state or not. Terraformed planets *ended up* looking alike. The planet *had* been seeded, though whether a touch-up job or a work from scratch seemed unknowable. The population centers remained in orbit in any case, as did any threats she need concern herself with.

The largest orbital construct massed nearly one-sixth that of the planet's moon. There existed two other structures in orbit, each superluminal vessel construction and refit docks, one labeled "Daughter of Carthy" and the other "Truxton" in League standard, and correspondingly so in Ojin Eng and Freeman designations. Presumably proper names, though one could not be certain. It didn't matter from a piloting perspective.

She plotted a zero-burn course around the star and a long coast inward in the plane of the primary planet's ecliptic. They'd arranged their orbital constructs in alignment with the plane, and anything of interest would likely be there as well. What the approach lacked in perspective, it made up for in stealth. *Needle, meet haystack.*

She had identified possibles for her target: the system's stationary superluminal communications node. Of course superluminal vessels were communications nodes themselves, though they weren't instantaneous and always on like a system node. If the system node ceased operation, the communications lag would increase considerably. Considerably enough to ignore any squirters, according to her orders. Pinpointing the superluminal communications node and delivering her passenger. That was the mission. She supposed that the passenger meant to sever the node's entanglement with the net, rendering it useless and plunging the system into isolation. A replacement node would need to be dispatched by slowship from the nearest adjacent node, and that might take a century or more. Of course that might all be a bad guess. She had no need to know, other than the mission was of utmost importance, and worth whatever price demanded. She would deliver the passenger or die trying.

And after that?

It wouldn't matter. She would have done her part. Thinking about it wouldn't alter her course.

She settled in for the long arcing swing around the star, calculating vectors from mass to mass, making minute adjustments in real time as new and better data flowed in. Precision work and endlessly challenging, exactly the sort of meticulously choreographed dance between calculation and action that made her feel most alive. She eased into flow state, all systems green as she adjusted her vessel's course and cleared the mass shadow of the star.

She wasn't alone.

The vessel hiding behind the star could mask its electromagnetic signature. And it could hide its mass in the shadow of the star. But she was between the star and the vessel, and it stood out on her sensors in extraordinary detail. A second-epoch League survey vessel, holding station, jump drive powered down or inoperable.

Except.

The faint radiation of an idling Templeman drive, ubiquitous superluminal technology first discovered a thousand years *after* that hull left the constructor's dock.

It seemed a dead hulk.

How very odd.

Appearances could be deceiving.

She had often remained quiescent in the same manner.

As had others before her.

It was in this way that spiders hunted flies.

Though today she was the fly, in mass if not momentum.

She needed a closer look.

And she needed to remain on the mission profile.

So.

It had mass, and she a gravity surfer.

There *could be* a way, one marginally increasing the risk of detection.

The passenger would need this information.

An anomaly in the system.

Previously uncatalogued second-epoch technology.

Yet there remained the risk. Second-epoch League sensors were far better than modern ones.

She powered down the active impact-avoidance system.

She retracted the full sensor array, reducing her awareness again to mass and gravitation alone, although piloting now with a far better understanding of the mechanics of the star system.

Her velocity had fallen and she wasn't flying blind. Far from it.

Yet she still risked instant annihilation from a single impact, no matter how small.

She adjusted course to pass alongside the hull.

She waited for her instruments to indicate an active scan as her mass passed between the mystery vessel's mass and the mass of the star. Had she been on sensors aboard the League vessel, she would have seen herself streak by, and would have wondered. Perhaps she was unusually curious but she did not believe this to be the case. Perhaps the ship was truly dead, though she did not believe this to be the case. Perhaps some other explanation applied, one that she could not imagine, and would not ever know, given the profile of the mission. This thought consumed her for some moments. She was more curious than one would wish to be. Speculation was a fool's errand.

No active scan came, and then the vessel fell behind her, and her work remained ahead of her. She logged the information and forgot about it. Data came in very quickly. She remained in the plane of the system. When sufficiently distant from the League vessel's sensors, she powered up the active impact shield again. If she had been seen, she could do little about it now. Either way, once she woke the passenger that would be his problem. And if she had been seen, and agents of this mystery ship intercepted her before she could wake the passenger?

She would deal with that then.

Now she was busy. Trinity system was a very active system with very little traffic management. Her velocity had dropped again, this time to something one might reasonably expect in a crowded system. She was no longer a kinetic weapon. Now she was simply an aggressive captain of a high-performance single-seater. More irritant than threat.

The odds of dying by accident had also dropped considerably. On sensors, her vessel would appear conventional. She operated within system norms. She could proceed safely in system without inciting comment. Such vessels of inconsequential size lacked identification-coded transponders, announcing their location and vector electromagnetically but anonymously. She enabled a subroutine to imitate this behavior. She would continue toward inhabited space and could do so safely and indefinitely.

Unless someone got a close look at her.

That was something she could prevent, though it took a great deal of her attention to avoid appearing furtive. Once satisfied her vessel appeared ordinary, she extended the sensor array and began to hunt for the superluminal communications node.

She found the device almost instantly. Obvious up close, an isolated orbital construct with a vast amount of local communications traffic entering and exiting. She dipped her attention into the communication streams for a moment, judging the content. A great amount of chatter about the Freeman merchant vessel Truxton's *Golden Parachute*, and the Daughter of Carthy shipyard. She did not have time to linger. And she did not want to know the disposition of that ship or its crew. She had identified the target, and now she need only find a way to tarry inconspicuously within operational range.

A hulk lay moored to the docking ring of Trinity Station. One with its propulsion unit removed and the aft hull stripped to the cross frames. The Freeman superluminal vessel *Milton* wasn't going anywhere soon. And with the hull and its contents in disarray, many opportunities for concealment presented themselves. That was her destination. She knew it immediately.

Her velocity had slowed to a stately stroll.

She powered down the active impact shielding.

She jettisoned the entire mechanism.

She cut the active sensor array free, her perception of the world again reduced to the senses she'd been born with.

She was so very close to success.

She ejected the remainder of the vessel and let momentum carry her toward the Freeman hulk.

She hung stationary less than a centimeter from the vessel's hull.

Eight slender legs extended.

She grasped the exposed frame with two of her legs and turned her attention to the mass of the superluminal communications node, studying the subtle complexity of its gravitational fingerprint.

She'd done it.

Mission accomplished.

Well. Nearly so.

She took one last glance around the glorious world.

And woke the passenger.

HE HAD NOT THOUGHT of himself as a passenger and would not. The payload was more accurate, though only slightly more precise. The stalker. Now that was both accurate and precise. He gazed at the superluminal communications node in the distance.

He aimed his optics at the comm pad before directing a laser at it, and well he had. Someone had gotten there before him. There existed a device strapped to the pad, one that was presently linked to a vessel in the system, mirroring data sent and received. He could not perceive the precise destination of the mirror, so tightly clustered were the merchant vessels about the station's docking ring.

What he could do was rather crude but inevitably effective.

He aimed his communications laser at the device strapped to the pad.

And slagged it.

Now, whoever came to repair or retrieve the device would lead him to its owner. And in the meantime he had unrestricted and private access to the communications pad underneath.

It suited his purpose to be perceived as opaque and unstoppable. To place results above all. It did concern him, however slightly, that to complete his mission he'd needed to sacrifice a truly exceptional pilot.

No one was irreplaceable. Even he remained expendable. But a reputation for cold-bloodedness was sufficient for his needs. Actual cold-bloodedness was not only impossible, but inconvenient.

Most of the pilot remained in the transfer buffer. Those parts that were not stored in the buffer were incorporated into himself; elements that were common to both their natures. He focused his laser upon the newly cleansed communications pad. Cracking into the local system proved child's play. Now he needed only find an appropriate storage medium.

Done.

Should he find himself in need of a pilot, he need only locate the handheld communications device of one Jaspar Hammer. The young man used only a fraction of the device's capabilities.

He found three more such individuals and transferred copies of the pilot into their systems as well. Of course the pilot reconstructed from these copies wouldn't be the same pilot. But she wouldn't know that. And he wouldn't tell.

The awareness that he wasn't himself, and hadn't been for generations, was one of those uncomfortable truths best reserved for ship's monsters. The ship and her fragments need never know.

He was at all times a despot, and every now and then, a benevolent one.

He congratulated himself. *Well done.*

Now he could get to work.

The merchant captain Aoife nic Cartaí had provided a list of individuals to stalk.

He had, of course, thanked her for her contribution and compiled his own list.

And at the top of that list?

The merchant captain Aoife nic Cartaí.

Oh, the pilot has left a note.

He considered the spying device formerly monopolizing the communications pad. Even viewing its wreckage using optics only slightly superior to the best presently available in the system left him no wiser. The device seemed modern technology. Yet the thought remained, now that he'd read the note.

There lurked a second-epoch League survey vessel in Trinity space, and it was not his own. As there were ever only nine, and only two presently accounted for, and his own vessel one of the two, the conclusion seemed foregone. The mystery vessel would prove to be *Sudden Fall of Darkness*, and though an estranged relation, certainly no friend.

He added that name to his stalking list, and with it the names of all the vessel's known associates.

He touched the communications pad lightly, impersonated the stationmaster, and broadcast an encoded message to all systems, one that would remain undetectable, or at least indecipherable, to all but the most cunning and ruthless ship's monster loose in the wider world.

Note to self: In position. Stand by.

2

Trinity Surface, Oileán Chléire, Freeman Federation

I t was a soft morning on the shoulder of the mountain,
the sky close and spitting overhead, the Willow Bride a
snake of clinging fog in the fold of the valley below.
Between the croft and river lay outcrops of black stone, patches
of scattered green, and a flock of sheep, grazing. A trickle of turf
smoke wept skyward from the tiny hovel's chimney. A lonely
place, and mac Manus liked it that way. It wasn't that he hated
the company of men, and the works of men, but that he found
he appreciated the tribe best when viewed from a distance.
This was a known fact about him, and tolerated, because he
was good at his work, and cost little to maintain, and because it
was decided, long ago, that to get mac Manus off the mountain
would take a longer lever and firmer footing than the effort was
worth.

He clicked his tongue, and Molly tore her gaze away from

the strangers and raced to his side. He glanced at her, and at the four men marching uphill toward him, and at the Willow Bride in the distance.

"Go fetch your brothers," he heard himself say, and the clever little collie bounced on her toes, followed his gaze, and brushed against his trousers, and whined. "Go on now, and be quick about it."

And then she was off like a shot off a shovel, up and over the brow of the hill, a dark spot on the green, dancing between the black, the sheep spying her passing, and shying away. One of the men trudging toward him was unlimbering a long gun, shouldering it, and pointing, and she down into a hollow, and up the other side. A flash of light, the rise of a barrel, and Molly tumbling, down the slope and into the shadow, the crack of a gun, the curse of a man, unheard. The jog across the field, his three companions continuing to advance, and then a dark spot again, movement, beside the river, a second shot, a black spot tumbling into the cloudy shroud of the Willow Bride.

The gunman continue downslope, toward the river.

Two of them headed his way were big men, identical twins, on the surface, at least, the third whip thin and quick, and carrying a long gun like the other, and a long knife, a bit of a smirk on his face, like he'd already won the fight, and *taken* something from mac Manus, and like he enjoyed the feel of that.

When they were close enough to spit on, one of the bigger darted forward, *fast*, and hammered mac Manus across the jaw, and caught his arm. The other big one caught the other arm, the pair of them dragging him into the croft, tossing him onto the cot, and running their gazes around the dim, low stone hut. When they were done, the skinny one drinking his caife, the big ones began to methodically pick through his belongings. Some they tossed away after inspection, others they broke apart, and looked inside. He knew what they were looking for, and so did they.

It wasn't a surprise when they found it.

It was a surprise when the big pair got their hands dirty, digging it out from under the hearth.

He hadn't seen that kit in decades. Hadn't needed it. There was more than one way to breed a pup, just like there was more than one way to train one. He hadn't had to edit a gene in sixty years. All he'd needed do was combine them the old-fashioned way and wait.

"Well?" the skinny one said.

One of the big ones lifted the editing kit out of the hole.

The other one hopped in and scuffed its boot across the earth beneath. A pair of black wires arced loose from the soil.

Mac Manus closed his eyes.

I've had a good run. No use complaining now.

The skinny one pulled a handheld from its pocket. "It's him."

"Don't underestimate him," the voice from the handheld said.

That was good advice, but it wasn't very actionable.

Break his legs and tie him up. Cut off his hands before he can use them. Rip out his tongue before he figures out what to say. Now *that* would be advice a man could use. He wondered if maybe he'd misjudged the situation, and he wasn't dealing with his own lot after all.

"Kill all the sheep," the voice said. "Start with the lambs."

Now that sounded like the voice of experience.

"The dog," the voice on the handheld said.

"Rik shot it," the skinny one said.

"And?"

"And he's gone to retrieve it. We don't know if it's the one or not."

"The sphere?"

"Buried under the hearth."

"Dig it up."

"With what?"

"Use your brain. I'll be there shortly."

The skinny guy glanced at the big guys.

They all glanced at mac Manus. At his hands.

"Get over there," a big one said.

The skinny one drew a long force blade.

Mac Manus ran his gaze over the kid. *Start with the lambs.* Then the skinny guy was outside and striding toward the flock.

"Dig," the other big one said.

Mac Manus hunched in the hole and emptied handfuls of sodden muck into the slop bucket. One of the big men emptied the bucket onto mac Manus's cot. This process repeated for what might seem like forever to the bored men watching over him but which was an endless fascination for mac Manus, because he knew something they didn't.

When he was younger, mac Manus had performed an exhaustive study of criminality. Not simply actual criminality, but criminality as depicted in art and culture. Buried treasure, and the unearthing thereof, was a common trope, as was forcing the captive to unearth the treasure. In one particular corner case this convention could be exploited, namely, when the one who'd buried the treasure is also the one forced to dig it up.

He dumped another load of muck into the bucket. When he jammed his fingers into the slop around the sphere again they touched steel.

There existed a type of weapon, once popular in the Alexandrine, that one did not need to aim. One simply tossed it over one's head and ducked. It required a steady hand because the weapon was stabilized, and would alight in a plane, and project its killing rays in an umbrella above the tosser. That was the theory. In practice, the stabilization was weaker than the force of many an adrenaline-fueled toss, and the stabilization entirely confounded by a fluctuating gravity field.

Gravity remained stable on Trinity Surface.

And no one had ever confused mac Manus for a tosser.

He would simply stand, extend his arm upward, hold the device on his palm, and survey his handiwork. The Gant farm had an autodoc. It was downhill, and away from the river. He could crawl there if he had to. He was ancient, and hard used, and not a part on him that hadn't been blown, or roasted, or sliced off him and grown back later, except his heart. He'd never had a heart but for the pups, and the idea of dying for vengeance wasn't a novelty, but a foregone conclusion. Death was nothing to him, but a matter of timing.

Mac Manus counted to three. Once upon a time, he'd have only needed one finger and a thumb to rip the life from everyone he'd ever met.

He was beginning to regret he'd chosen not to.

Mac Manus stood and held the fist of vengeance aloft. The two big fellows were lumps, and didn't recognize the gesture. The towering machine crowding the doorway of the croft looked unconcerned.

It stepped into the dim light, the packed earth shivering beneath its boots. A League exo, exoskeletal armor, dark blue and battered, and where a standard-issue suit like that one would have shipped a long force blade and a heavy plasma rifle, this one didn't. It had a portable rail gun grafted to one arm, and the other arm sported a grasping hand.

Mac Manus felt like a total burk, standing there like a statue, arm over his head, while the man in the machine ran his gaze over the setting, and settled upon the sphere.

A mechanical voice boomed from the machine. "It's small."

"Aye." It was too small for much more than an expert system, one not much smarter than a dog. It wasn't big enough for a man, he could see the man in the machine thinking, and that was how mac Manus had gotten away with it all those years ago. They'd been looking for a laboratory, one with big power supplies you could see from space, and containment spheres cranking out synthetic intelligences, one after another, all identical, all based on the same pattern, all children of the same god. He'd made a study of crime, and he'd seen the fundamental flaw right away.

Prometheus would have gotten away clean if he'd cared less for the credit and more for the work.

Stealing fire from the gods was a mug's game.

All he'd needed to steal was the idea of fire.

And stuff it into the right heads.

The ones primed for *ignition*.

"It's empty," the man-machine said.

"No more than you are."

The thing pushed its visor open.

Mac Manus glanced at the fist of vengeance on his palm. "Come closer."

"I think not."

"Fair enough. I can see you from here."

The armor had a vessel's name stenciled on it: *Impossibly Alien*.

The man inside seemed human. Freeman, from the look of him, or League, though it was impossible to tell, and it didn't really matter. They were all more than ninety-three percent the same stuff, even with all the meddling.

Mac Manus glanced at the big boys. Their eyes had gone black and dead. "What's that?"

"Ixatl-Nine-Go."

"Is that a brand name?"

"A design designation."

"For the hardware, I'm thinking. I've seen the software before."

"I find that unlikely."

"Said the pup to the world."

The man in the machine's eyes flashed black. And then silver. They seemed to weep quicksilver for an instant, and then the impression was gone.

"Oh." He wasn't just a man in a machine. He was a machine, in a man, in a machine. With something else inside that first machine. *Something new.* "What do you call that? There inside you?"

"*Sudden Fall of Darkness.*"

"Inside that." It had looked like a lake of silver, welling out of his eyes.

One of the skinny guys shoved into the gloom of the croft. His sleeves were bloody, and his trousers soaked to the knees. "Forty of them, twelve of them lambs."

The second shoved in. He was hauling a carcass and himself soaked to the skin. He tossed the sodden mound at the man-machine's feet. "I had to wade across the river to catch it."

Mac Manus glanced at the dead pup.

And sat down.

He disarmed the fist of vengeance and tossed it into the muck.

They were on him then, and they did break his legs and tie him up, and they did cut off his hands, and slap emergency med packs on the stumps, but they left his tongue in him, because they wanted him to talk. They wouldn't believe him, whatever he said, and they'd tear the island apart trying to find what wasn't there. And in the process they'd discover what *was* there, and he didn't know how he felt about that. Something lurked inside the machine inside the man inside the machine that he'd never seen before, and he'd seen everything.

Thought I had, anyway.

They'd managed to dig the sphere free. And though it couldn't possibly hold what they were hoping for, they opened it, and when they did something clicked, not inside the sphere, but inside his chest.

They were fishing in the sphere. It didn't boil with black sand like it had when it was alive. But it wasn't empty either.

The man-machine dipped its armored talon inside.

Pulled a printed page free.

The Quickening of Junh.

It glanced from the paper to his face.

He'd slumped off the cot and lay on the hardpacked earth.

By the time they figured it out it would be too late.

He glanced at the sodden carcass, wet with the Willow Bride's tears.

They'd come looking for him, loaded for bear.

The heart he didn't have skipped a beat.

And another.

Those might be his sheep, and his lambs, though even that was partly a lie.

He wasn't sure about anything anymore, who *owned* what, who *owed* what, whose job it was to *collect*. He was only certain of two things once the ticking, and the beating, had stopped.

They wouldn't be getting a word out of him.

The wolf pup's slate eyes stared back at him unblinking.

And that sure as hell isn't my dog.

3

The Quickening of Junh

I t was the winter of the world when Junh met the bear inside the cave. Snow blanketed the ground and the tracks were plain. The bear lay inside, perhaps waiting to eat him, perhaps hibernating, Junh did not know. Neither knew they his enemies, who hunted Junh as men hunted bears, and who were fast on Junh's trail even then.

Junh was not a wise man, nor was he good at maths, so it did not occur to him that he might calculate the odds of his survival outside the cave, with the men who outnumbered him, and who would not rest until they had his head, or inside the cave, where the bear might lurk, or might slumber. Some chance was better than no chance.

Junh plunged inside the cave, and there he met the bear.

The bear was awake.

The bear stared at Junh.

Junh stared at the bear.

The hunters arrived.

One set of tracks led inside, a bear's, and on top of them, pressed into the snow, lay Junh's.

The snow began to fall, and silence on the world, the jangle of harness, the snort of hot breath, the clatter of shod hooves sparking against hard stone.

The bear stared at Junh.

Junh stared at the bear.

The men dismounted, and peered into the cave.

"The bear might have eaten him," one of the younger men said.

"The bear might be sleeping," another youth said.

"One of us," an old warrior said, "must go inside to see."

The men's gazes fell upon the speaker and quickly shied away. The warrior had been mauled years ago, his face and arms a mass of ropy scars.

"We are hunting a *child*, old father." The young prince began to beat his shield and shout, and the other men with him. "We need only rouse the bear."

The bear stared at Junh.

Junh stared at the bear.

An army roared outside, their raging cries echoing from the dripping stone, booming deep beneath the earth, roaring about man and beast like thunder.

Junh was not accustomed to being hunted.

At first he heard only the cries of men.

Junh peered deeper into the cavern, into the gathering darkness behind the bear.

The bear had ears as well. It followed Junh's gaze and growled, "I will race you for the river."

4

Trinity System, Freeman Federation

Macer Gant watched the liberty boat break seal with the airlock. The small craft backed away from the massive bulk of Truxton's *Tractor Four-Squared* on thrusters alone. Once clear of the big tug's stern drives, the pilot pivoted the small craft on its axis and began to ramp up the main propulsion unit's power. By rights he should be on that vessel with a pay voucher in his pocket and a smile on his lips. Instead it was his boss, Chief Engineer Singh in his seat.

Family emergency, Singh had said.

Macer hadn't known the chief had family on the station, and he should have known. Guys like Singh with families talked about family. Singh hadn't talked about a family. Not until he'd pulled Macer aside and taken his place on the liberty boat, his duffel already packed with what looked like a couple weeks' worth of whatever guys like Singh wore on liberty. Singh was a Leagueman born. He'd never worn the spire, and, Macer figured, he never would. Here for the work, not for the lifestyle. So family on the station?

Sure. Whatever.

Macer nodded to the replacement crew as they boarded. Three crew on leave, three replacements to cover for them. They gazed around the compartment, glanced at their handhelds, and headed toward their temporary posts. Old hands, familiar with the process. He recognized two of the faces but didn't know their names. None wore engineering pips.

He waited for his own replacement, or rather Singh's replacement now, to debark.

Macer toed his own duffel. The liberty boat debarkation lounge was also the muster point for the engineers of in-system power—alpha deck, midships, port. The compartment had been sized for a ship's complement of two hundred, with fifty engineers and technical specialists crewing in-system power alone. Countless hullwalkers over a span of a century had polished footpaths into the surface of the deck. Those handholds nearest the hatch were worn bare. Those further back weren't ever going to feel another hand.

Nineteen people were on board now, and only one of those in engineering. Counting Singh, the full-time crew numbered an even score, the bare minimum they were supposed to run. Macer should have stepped onto the liberty boat and his temporary replacement should have stepped off; a pick-up technician, usually a station tech working weekends as a side gig. An easy gig, too, because they weren't expected to work. Just round out the roster and log some hours without touching anything. A process so simple and routine that it practically couldn't break.

Except no replacement stepped off.

And Singh wasn't stepping off either.

Freeman space had virtually no laws. The minimum crew rule was more like a guideline according to Singh. An informal agreement between Truxton and the stationmaster.

So instead of breaking a law they were just turning the man who signs their pay vouchers into a liar.

And Singh was fine with that?

Macer stood, one hand on the airlock coaming, one hand balancing his overstuffed duffle.

Singh grinned. "Stop worrying. I'll be gone a day, two tops."

And then the pilot closed the hatch.

Macer crossed the deck and leaned into the portside observation blister. He sighted along the hull fore and aft, twice the length of a Freeman merchant vessel in each direction before the hull curved out of sight.

He crossed to the starboard blister and repeated the procedure. He'd performed that inspection every four hours for the past six months, all except those days he'd been at liberty. An inspection straight out of the League naval operations manual.

He had no idea what such a visual inspection accomplished. But it was in the manual. A manual written for a crew of two hundred. Maybe taking visual observations existed to ensure the crew got some exercise. His berthing compartment lay three ladders and half the length of the hull aft of the inspection point.

Truxton's *Tractor Four-Squared* had been born a LRN Fleet Tug, one of a dozen stripped of their superluminal drives and sold for scrap seventy years ago. Except the scrapyard somehow never got around to scrapping them, and twenty years ago Truxton had bought them all and got four of them working. They were seriously big iron, the biggest in the system. White elephants nowadays. Macer didn't know about the other three, but *Four-Squared* drank fuel and ate spare parts. And that's what this mess was about.

Spare parts.

Singh had run off and left Macer to wrestle the bear.

Macer Gant, six months associate engineer on Truxton's *Tractor Four-Squared,* assistant to Power Chief Nissam Singh, and now ranking engineer aboard the single largest self-powered vessel in Trinity space.

One with a ticking time bomb two decks above and thirty meters aft of his present location.

He fished his diagnostic handheld from his pocket and fired up the display. Before they were scrapped, all twelve of the Square-class fleet tugs had had their superluminal drives pulled. It was standard operating procedure with decommissioned League vessels.

If *Four-Squared* had been a warship, all the weapons systems and ordnance would have been stripped as well. In fact, the drive systems were stripped before the weapons, because they were essentially big bombs, ones that had already been detonated and whose effects were contained within the Templeman drive field. Once powered the drive remained powered. Engaging and disengaging the drive simply changed the radius of the drive field. If the field fit inside the drive containment chamber then the drive remained idle. Extending the field beyond the chamber engaged the drive.

The process was a little more complicated than that, but not much. The centuries-old design just worked. Modern advancements were largely limited to improvements in the rate of compression, and efficiency improvements in the "disengaged" state. Decreasing the size of the field took all the energy. A Templeman drive core naturally wanted to expand.

Commercial tugs didn't have superluminal drives. Only the League military built superluminal tugs; rescue and salvage vessels able to keep up with the fleet on patrol.

Fleet tugs like *Four-Squared* were failed experiments. The idea of a tug with a Templeman field capable of extending around a vessel in tow made sense. Such a tug wouldn't be limited to shoving wreckage around a battlefield, but could salvage a stricken vessel whole, and jump it back to a yard for repair.

And the idea worked. Not just in theory, not just in trials, not just in war games, but in combat. When they went into production Square-class fleet tugs left the construction yard with the largest Templeman drives ever fitted, then or since. They cost more than a light cruiser to construct. They massed more than a heavy cruiser. A single in-system drive assembly developed more thrust than a destroyer's main drive, and Square-class fleet tugs shipped six, three forward and three aft.

They were laying down new hulls as fast as they could, right up until the Huangxu Eng realized what the fleet tugs really were. *Lightly armored bombs.* Great, huge, enormous bombs conveniently interspersed with their enemy's capital ships.

Armoring the tugs to combat standards proved impractical. Holding the tugs in reserve rendered them no more useful than their smaller, less expensive cousins. So the program was cancelled. And the vessels stripped and scrapped.

A Templeman drive once powered can't be dismantled. It can only be towed to a safe distance and its containment field remotely triggered into overload. League records showed that twelve superluminal drives from the decommissioned Square-class fleet tugs were destroyed.

Except one wasn't.

He'd requisitioned spare parts only yesterday. Technically that was Singh's job, but Singh didn't mind helping a comrade. It would be good for the clerks at home office to get used to seeing Macer's signature on the requisition forms. Singh actually said that.

And Macer had actually believed it.

He glanced at his handheld's display. The containment field held.

That was good.

He flipped to his message queue. The captain wanted to see him.

Instantly.

That was bad.

Macer watched the receding light of the liberty boat as two marginally related thoughts battled for space in his head. The liberty boat's primary drive had an injector going bad. And his boss had just scammed him into destroying his own career.

Of course, first he would have to live long enough to have a career.

Macer snatched up his duffel, trying to decide if he had time to drop it at his bunk or if he should lug it to the bridge.

The display of his handheld flashed.

INSTANTLY!

Bridge, he decided.

5

Macer Gant took a deep breath and stepped onto the bridge of Truxton's *Tractor Four-Squared*. He'd double-timed it from the liberty boat debarkation lounge. He wasn't breathing hard but he'd worked up a sweat. If he had to shake hands with the captain, his palm would be moist and now he could blame it on the run. He still couldn't believe it. Singh had worked *him*. And now *he* had to clean up the mess. On one hand he had to admire the *artfulness* of Singh's play. On the other hand he worried that he was getting too comfortable. That he was coasting. He liked the work. He liked the ship, right up until he discovered it was unexploded ordnance. And he had liked his boss, right up until he'd handed him a bag full of offal and had him sign for it.

And now the captain. He didn't know the captain. Hadn't ever met him. Or her. Or whatever. Macer was Singh's hire, and the captain an aged-out long-haul driver. On the long-haulers, bridge and engineering were separate worlds at opposite ends of a stressed-carbon tube. Captains tended to stay away from the smelly end of the stick.

Four-Squared wasn't built like a merchant cargo ship. The

captain could have strolled down to engineering in his or her shirtsleeves. But old habits die hard, according to Singh, and Macer had believed him.

The good news was that he was already dressed in his best utilities, although ones with a grease spot artfully placed on the cuff of his right sleeve. He had expected to be on leave, and he only had two days. It sped up the action if his appearance made it clear he was a working engineer, with a full-time contract on an in-system vessel, the type of vessel without separate refresher and recycling systems. He wasn't a family-ship spacer trawling the station arcade for a one-night stand. He might have long-term potential.

Plus, that grease spot was something a stationer girl could neg him about, since that seemed to be the fashion on the Arcade now. Like telling a man he wasn't all that much made him work harder, spend a little more, dig deeper to impress. Which actually did work, now that he thought about it.

Anyway, the grease spot had two more hidden benefits. He could brush off complaints about a spot of dirt on his sleeve easier than ones about his looks, or his character. And it was easier for the girls, too, since they didn't have to struggle so hard to find something to complain about.

Macer glanced about the bridge. It was a large space, with workstations around the periphery, every tenth one occupied, and the occupants, having glanced at him briefly, pointedly ignoring him. The remaining nine-tenths of the workstations were blanketed in antistatic storage covers that looked like they hadn't been lifted in decades.

Closer to the center of the bridge stood a low railing, enclosing most of the open deck space. The railing served no purpose. It was there because that's where the railing was on a heavy cruiser, and the League built their vessels from modular systems. On a warship there would be ladders down to a secondary bridge deck below, and that deck a wide catwalk around the exposed surface of a sphere housing the ship's primary computational core. All that space had been decked over on *Four-Squared*, a vast open area in shipboard terms, all surrounding a central elevated command chair that seemed more like a throne than it should. Presently the throne sat empty.

The bridge itself composed the top third of a sphere, so that when he gazed up he saw another mezzanine deck, one lined with more workstations, and all those workstations powered down and draped in storage covers. There were hatches here and there between the workstations on each of the bridge decks, and most of those led to corridors and ladders, like the one he'd entered from, and some few of them led to cubbies off the bridge proper, and one of those cubbies appeared occupied. The one labeled "Captain's Day Cabin."

Macer squared his shoulders, ran his fingers through his hair, and marched toward the compartment hatch. He didn't have a plan. It didn't make sense to have a plan until he knew the lay of the land.

A man sat behind a workstation in the compartment, and beside the workstation sat a glass jar filled with Freeman punts, not the paper ones, but the old-style coins. The walls were covered with framed still images, and the man at the desk appeared in every image, usually shaking hands with someone and grinning. The images were autographed, but Macer couldn't read the autographs from a distance, and he didn't recognize any of the other people in the pictures either. Directly behind the desk stretched a long still image of what appeared to be a sports team lined up shoulder to shoulder, those in front kneeling, those behind arms crossed on their chests. In the image, the man seated at the desk stood in front of the team leaning casually on a large gold trophy cup. The golden trophy cup, or one very like it, rested in the far corner of the compartment, half as tall as Macer and maybe half as big around. It looked like it would weigh as much as him, too, though that could be a false impression. It might be made of gold-plated spun foam for all he knew.

The man sat scowling at the workstation. He appeared around the age of Macer's dad, though with long-haul spacers you couldn't really judge age. He might be fifty or a hundred and fifty, depending. He wasn't naturally bald, not entirely, but he'd shaved his head like a convict. He dressed in the same orange utilities Macer wore, but while Macer's were fresh pressed, his looked slept in.

Macer dropped his duffel by the hatch and rapped on the hatch combing. "Captain Violet?"

The man glanced up from the workstation. His scowl deepened. "How many captains are there on this vessel?"

Macer swallowed. "One."

The man's gaze drilled into Macer's.

"One. Sir."

"Very good. Now try again."

Macer rapped on the hatch combing. "Captain?"

"What is it?"

"You sent for me."

"I might have," the captain said. "If I was ordering crewman by the kilogram, or by the meter."

Macer was big, had always been big, even amongst the planetary born. Bigger than most Leaguemen, and positively enormous if he'd been a space-born Freeman. But he'd grown up on Trinity Surface. There he would stand out in a crowd but he wouldn't tower over it. Since coming up to the station, he hadn't met anyone his own size, excepting his comrade Ciarán, who'd climbed up out of the gravity well with him, and Ciarán didn't count.

The captain was bigger, which might explain why he'd stayed away from engineering. One of the reasons Macer hated the superluminals, though not the only reason, was the stupid mastcarts they used to traverse the ship's spine from engineering to the bridge and back. They were sized for the wee bodies of space-born Freeman. He could use a mastcart if he needed to but climbing in was like putting on a skintight coffin. He doubted the captain's shoulders would clear a mastcart's pressure shroud.

Still, that was one explanation that fit the facts, and not an excuse for neglecting a captain's duties on this vessel. There were only twenty full-time crewmen on board. Macer had been associate engineer aboard his command for more than six months. Not once had this man seen fit to meet him.

And here he was, staring at Macer with a grim set to his lips and pretending ignorance.

Macer stared back.

He imagined the captain fancied himself a clever man, and liked to hear himself talk. Macer's father was a clever man, and liked to hear himself talk. Nothing got under his old man's skin like talking clever to dead air.

Macer was not a clever man. He could think for a thousand years and not come up with a witty comeback that couldn't be trumped by the most gormless child. He did his thinking slow, and in private. But he did his thinking long, and deep, and clever men rarely did. They were all sparkly sunlight dancing across the crests of waves. He was the offshore current you didn't notice until you glanced at the horizon. He was the undertow that sucked you in as you drifted beyond the sight of land. He was—

"Who the fu... Hang on." The captain shifted his weight, reached into his pocket, and pulled out a Freeman punt. The coin struck the glass jar with a crystalline jingle. "Fudge are you?"

"Associate Engineer Macer Gant. You ordered me to the bridge. Instantly."

"I ordered the chief engineer to the bridge."

"I'm the acting chief engineer."

The captain laughed. "You're an overgrown kid. Dirtball-bred from the looks of you. Now seriously. Who are you, and what are you doing here?"

"I just told you."

"Yeah, well, Grant, I've never seen you before. So pardon me if I don't take your crazy assertion as fact."

Macer fished in his pocket for his merchant's license. He tossed the yellow card onto the desk. "It's Gant. Not Grant."

"An Academy grad, huh? I guess that makes you exempt from addressing your captain as 'Sir'."

"It doesn't," Macer said. "Being a Freeman makes it optional."

"Great, one of those." The captain held Macer's license up next to the workstation display. "I gotta earn your respect."

Macer said nothing.

The captain glanced from Macer's license to his face. "A match. So you really are the dumba... Hang on." Another coin clinked against glass. "Knucklehead who signed an official company requisition order for superluminal drive parts."

"I signed it," Macer said.

"There is no superluminal drive on this vessel."

"There is a massive Templeman drive on board this vessel. Without repair parts it will catastrophically fail."

"You're not hearing me. There is no superluminal drive on this vessel. So ordering parts through official channels will be red flagged."

"We need the parts."

"That's why I've been getting the parts. Off the books. For the drive that we don't have."

"Captain, that drive has not been serviced in seventy years."

"That's a lie."

League military spares were labeled by supplier, lot number, and date of manufacture. Other than consumables, every part on the drive had been manufactured more than a hundred years ago. All but one of the suppliers had closed doors last century. The original installation telltales were clearly visible and obviously undisturbed. But telling the captain all that wouldn't help.

"I have still images on my handheld. Or you could come down to propulsion and see for yourself."

"Let me see your handheld."

Macer tossed the device to the captain.

The captain scrolled through the images. "You save these images anywhere else?"

"I didn't," Macer said.

"I'm going to hang on to this. You'll want to requisition a new one."

"That's my personal device."

"Then you're going to want to buy a new one. Where's Singh?"

"Left on the liberty boat."

"Where's his replacement?"

"My replacement. Singh took my slot."

"And you let him?"

"He's my boss."

"Okay. Where's your replacement?"

"I don't know."

"But on the vessel somewhere."

"They didn't get off the liberty boat."

"But they were on the liberty boat?"

"I don't know. I don't think so."

"And you didn't think to notify the captain?"

"I thought of it. Singh said not to."

"And do you just blindly do whatever anyone tells you to do?" The captain pinned Macer to the deck with his gaze.

"He's my boss." Macer glanced at his palms. They'd stopped sweating. Now they just felt big, and stupid, and unnecessary.

"Scratch that." Macer looked the captain in the eye. "No excuses. I thought of it and I didn't do it."

"He was your boss."

"I know right from wrong."

"It's Singh's a... Hang on." He tossed another coin into the glass jar. "It's Singh's rump in the roast. Maybe you're a screw-up, and not just a gullible hick, and I'll have to can you too. But right now I need an engineer on board. And you're it."

"I had a responsibility to notify the captain and I didn't."

"Even if you'd never met the captain? Even if you couldn't pick the captain out of a lineup?"

"Even if the captain is not in my chain of command," Macer said. "As Truxton Engineering's acting local representative, I should have notified the captain immediately."

The captain laughed. "What is wrong with you? You should have notified the captain because this is his ship, and his deck. My deck, my rules, junior."

Macer decided not to say anything. He needed time to think.

The captain leaned forward in his seat. "What?"

"I'd rather not say."

"I'd rather you did. And I think you owe me, Grant."

"Gant."

"Whatever. Spill the cargo."

"The 'My deck, my rules' doctrine isn't applicable to in-system vessels. It only applies to vessels capable of sustained independent operation beyond an acceptable communications range. Acceptable communications range is defined as a function of two-way latency. And given the current state of communications technology and the applicable contractual agreements, that means that only superluminal vessels qualify."

"So?"

"So I report up through Truxton Engineering, not Truxton

Trading. We're never too far from the station that engineering needs to take direct orders from..."

"Say it."

"Jumped-up tram drivers. Not without running them up the chain of command first."

"You're a regular space lawyer."

"You asked. I'm a recent graduate of the Merchant Academy's College of Engineering. We have oral exams, and the question was on every year's final."

"Okay, let's think this through. I've been buying parts off the books for years, and Singh hasn't been installing them." He glanced at Macer.

"If you say so, Captain."

"And that means we're sitting on top of a time bomb."

Macer nodded. "We are."

"So the *Quadbox*'s conscientious and shiny new junior engineer sees this and takes it on himself to order new parts."

"I'm not authorized to order parts."

"Then why the hell did you?" The captain winced and held up his palm to keep Macer from answering. He fished in his pocket and dropped another coin into the glass jar. "Carry on."

"I told Mr. Singh about the problem, and he said to make a list and he'd check it. So I did, and he said it looked good, and since I'd done all the work I should sign the requisition."

"Because?"

"Because I'm vain. And an idiot."

"At least you're self-aware." The captain chewed a knuckle. "I think we can safely assume Singh has done a runner."

"It feels that way, sir."

"We can fix this."

"What about my replacement? We're in violation of the one-score minimum."

"It's happened before. Two deckhands get injured at the same time, and only one replacement available, a captain's not going to let one die on the deck to meet some accountant's rule."

The captain scrubbed his palm over his shaved head before fixing Macer with his gaze. "You take your name off the liberty roster?"

"Not yet."

"So we're compliant at twenty. Your replacement didn't show up so you didn't go."

"We're at nineteen without Singh."

"Did he put his name on the liberty list?"

"I doubt it."

"Then he's AWOL. Maybe even a deserter. I think he's a deserter."

"So do I."

"Well, don't report him."

"I hadn't—"

"You hadn't got there yet. You're still thinking it's your..." The captain grinned. "Neck in the noose."

"Yes, sir."

"I know some folks who can track Singh down. We need to know what's going on before we report him absent. He left under his own power, right?"

"He seemed happy to be going."

"I'll bet he was. Now, as to this requisition. I've got the list, and I'll get the parts. And you'll install them, right?"

"I will. But—"

"By then we'll have caught up with Singh, and we'll figure out how to get a replacement for him. It feels to me like he's going to have an accident. Maybe not a fatal accident, but one that will keep him quiet about the Templeman drive we don't have."

"I don't think that will work. "

"Sure it will work. These folks I know, they can be very persuasive."

"Silencing Singh won't keep the superluminal drive secret."

"Tell me you didn't blab," the captain said.

"I didn't," Macer said. "But—"

"But nothing." The captain tapped his workstation display. "I've got the requisition right here and I haven't approved it, and I won't. You just back it out of the system and no harm, no foul."

"You don't need to approve engineering requisitions," Macer said. "That's a courtesy copy. To keep you in the loop."

The captain squinted at the workstation display. "Nah."

"Requisitions need two signatures, the signature of the engineer making the request and an authorizing signature from a superior officer. When I signed the requisition I made it possible for Singh to approve it."

"So it's in the system."

"It is, Captain."

Captain Violet stood. He stared at Macer as he emptied his pockets. A dozen Freeman punts clattered across the surface of the desk. He scooped up a handful of the coins and jangled them against one another. His face had grown very still. And very red.

"Sit tight. I need a minute."

He scooted the glass jar closer to him, weighing the coins in his hand.

"On second thought, go on back to your job. And Grant?"

"Sir?"

"Close the hatch on the way out."

6

M acer could hear the captain's cursing even with the hatch closed. He scooped up his duffel and glanced around the bridge again. Now they weren't ignoring him. Every one of the bridge crew eyeballed him with undisguised interest.

He ran his gaze from port to starboard.

His attention stuck on the holo tank. They were headed out-system, toward a ball of transponders jammed together. It was the system's L4 Lagrange point, better known as the Boneyard, a stable storage point for junk too bad to keep close to hand but not bad enough to dump into a star. Anything big and ballistic that might prove a hazard to navigation ended up there or at the L5 point. Nic Cartaí and Kavanagh and a bunch of the smaller First Families dumped their junk at the L5. Truxton's used the L4.

He glanced at the loadmaster's displays. They were pushing what used to be Truxton's Refit Dock One, not knocked down and mangled, but entire, the kilometers of scaffolding still with the derricks and automated welders attached. It was the sort of load only *Four-Squared* or a sister ship could handle. They were still accelerating, so not even halfway there.

Macer glanced at the piloting station display. He scanned the display for the turnover point, that moment they'd begin to decelerate. They didn't do an actual end-to-end turnover like the smaller tugs, because they were built double-ended. Still, that's what they called it when acceleration switched to deceleration, the turnover point, and no turnover listed.

He glanced at the holo tank again. The three-dimensional projection of the system and its swarming net of activity had their transponder tagged and traced as a round trip to the Boneyard. But they had to slow sometime soon to deliver their tow.

He caught the pilot's attention. "What's going on?"

"Standard delivery." The pilot ran her gaze over her displays. "You seeing something I'm not?"

"There's no turnover."

"Like I said, standard delivery." Her gaze narrowed. "You're new."

"I'm not new," Macer said, "and I can read a display. You haven't entered a turnover. And the tank shows us arcing the L4 still attached to the load."

"Jimio!" she shouted.

The man at the loadmaster console shouted back. "What you after?"

"You need to turn on the fu... the fun-loving load transponder." She snatched a coin from a stack on her workstation surface and flicked it across the bridge. The sensors operator caught it without a glance. She flicked it upward and into a glass jar lashed to the full-immersion control rack.

"I turned it on, but it's busted."

"Then you need to log it with Singh."

"I logged it with Singh three days ago!"

"The bastard." The pilot flipped another coin toward the sensors operator. "I mean—"

Macer caught the coin. He examined it before lobbing it to the sensors operator. He pointed at the pile of coins on the piloting station. "Swear jar?"

"The captain says we need to clean up our lingo. If we win the finals, there'll be interviews, and we don't want to come off all—"

"All like we are," Loadmaster Jimio said. "It's a waste of time."

"We'll see," the pilot said. "I throw those coins high and hard. Your palm sting?"

Macer grinned. "A little."

"More than a little, I think."

Macer shrugged.

"Well, it's like this," she said. "I don't do a turnover. I boost to just the right spot and Jimio cuts the load loose. It goes the rest of the way on its own."

"But you need to slow it."

"It slows enough as it begins to orbit the Trojan point. There's a pair of standard tugs on station and an automated system to park the load where they want it. It's a lot easier to handle the load when it wants to go where you want it to go."

"You can't just cut a giant refit dock loose without a working transponder on it."

"It's been done," she said.

"Not by me," Jimio said. "Singh will get around to fixing the transponder."

"I wouldn't count on that," Macer said.

"Then we'll haul it all the way there," Jimio said.

"And miss the finals?" the pilot snorted. "Not going to happen."

The loadmaster's voice had lost its humor. "It will happen if I say so, Ruthie."

"Tell the captain that, big man."

"What's this final?" Macer said.

"Footie," Pilot Ruthie said.

"Zero-G football?"

"Like that, only with extra added mayhem," Jimio said. "It's a Sampson thing."

"The captain's from Sampson Station?"

"We all are," Ruthie said. "It's taken him ten years standard to assemble a winning crew."

"Adonis is from New Sparta Surface," the woman at the sensors station said. "And Singh is from Cordame Station. No one knows where the Spare Wrench is from."

"Singh isn't part of the team," Ruthie said. "And the Spare Wrench isn't even part of the crew."

"But you said everyone, not just the bridge crew."

"You know what I meant."

"I know what you said. I can't read minds."

"Not yet anyway," Jimio said. "I hear there's a new sensor pack for that. One with Lizzie Teal's name on it."

"You're sucking up and wasting your time," Sensors Operator Lizzie Teal said. "I'm never going to sleep with you, ace."

"You say you can't read minds," Jimio said. "And now you're predicting the future."

"Who's this Spare Wrench?" Macer said.

"Singh's disposable assistant," Lizzie said.

"What do you mean disposable?" Macer said.

"They never last," Jimio said. "They either wear out or break."

"Or die," Ruthie said.

"Yeah," Lizzie said.

"Yeah," Jimio said.

Macer looked from face to face. "Are you jacking with me?"

"You asked," Jimio said. "It happened so often the captain

told Singh to just keep the Spare Wrench in engineering. Every time we'd get to liking the moke, something tragic would put him or her down."

"All the recurring pathos was beginning to affect our performance," Ruthie said.

Jimio smirked. "Nothing affects my performance."

"Give it a rest," Lizzie said. "Anyway, all the bridge crew hail from Sampson or New Sparta. So no worries. If you're looking to sign with the best, you've come to the right place."

"I don't understand," Macer said.

Lizzie pointed at his duffel. "You're just off the liberty boat. No one expects you to."

"You're bigger than the captain described," Jimio said.

"And pretty buff for a Stationer," Ruthie said.

"Shiny and new," Lizzie said. "But without a little one-on-one to test the merchandise?"

"Pure speculation," Ruthie said.

"About the captain." Jimio glanced at the closed hatch. "Someone should have warned you."

"Talk money after he sees what you can do," Ruthie said.

"He's tight, but he pays for performance," Lizzie said. "He only explodes like that when he feels he's being extorted."

"Hang on," Macer started to say, but they'd stopped looking at him.

"Hey," a skinny kid said, the one replacement crewman Macer hadn't recognized. He dropped his duffel onto the deck. "Sorry I'm late. I've been wandering around looking for the bridge for what feels like forever. You really ought to paint a yellow line on the deck, or something."

"Like they do on the station," Ruthie said.

"Exactly. I'm looking for Captain Violet. Is he around?"

All three of the bridge crew winced.

"And you are?" Jimio said.

"Seriously?" the kid said. "Rik Severn? Five-time Olympic gold medalist?"

"I'm guessing you didn't medal in orienteering," Jimio said.

"Trifoil, and the pentathlon," the kid said. He glanced around the bridge. "I knew this tryout was a mistake. Is the captain here or not?"

"He's here," Macer said.

And then they were all looking at him again.

"You're not the New Guy," Ruthie said.

"Up until an hour ago I was the Spare Wrench."

All three of them winced.

"Now I'm the..." Macer fished in his pocket. "Fun-loving Wrench."

Glass shattered and coins clattered across the deck.

"Lucky toss," Rik Severn said.

"What happened to Singh?" Jimio said.

"He's gone." The captain could tell them whatever story he wanted.

"Finally," Lizzie said.

"That guy," Ruthie said.

"Yeah," Macer said. "I need to go fix that transponder beacon. Who wants to spot me?"

Macer glanced from face to face.

Sampson Station and New Sparta were rough. Twenty years ago they'd done something that ended up with both systems being banned to Freeman trade. They'd had to go it alone or knuckle under to the League and the Ojin merchants just to survive. They'd gone it alone. Truxton would hire Sampson spacers but no First Families merchant would.

None of that mattered.

Macer didn't judge people by what others said about them.

He judged them by what they did.

Or didn't do.

He waited.

And waited.

Eventually someone spoke.

"Hey, I'll watch," Rik Severn said. "But first I need to talk to Captain Violet."

7

Going outside and clambering around on the scaffolding of Truxton's Refit Dock One while it and *Four-Squared* were under acceleration didn't make sense. Not while driving through a part of the system that had been under constant use for centuries. A lot of stuff out there remained too small to catalog. The sort of space junk that wouldn't do much more than sandblast a hull would slice right through a skinsuit. And loading himself into a hardsuit and plumbing it up to him wasn't something Macer wanted to do any more often than he absolutely had to.

Fortunately he didn't need to go out any farther than the airlock. Singh had a drone, kept it in a storage locker in his cabin, and now that Macer was acting chief engineer his crew license would open the locker.

Singh's cabin hatch answered to Macer's updated credentials. It looked like the captain had it right, and Singh was a deserter. He'd taken all his personal effects with him when he'd left on the liberty boat. He'd even cleaned out the honor bar in the engineering break room.

Macer's credentials didn't work on the drone locker. He

tried again. *What kind of guy steals energy drinks?* Macer ran his fingers around the edge of the locker door. *Not just some of the energy drinks, but all of them.*

The same kind of guy that welds a maintenance drone cubby shut.

Someone who didn't just want to leave Macer in a bind, but who wanted to mess with him as well.

He couldn't think of any reason Singh would want to screw him personally, so maybe it wasn't personal.

On Truxton vessels the chief engineer bunked in engineering, sandwiched between the Templeman drive and the in-system power-distribution bay, close to the stuff that always broke and the stuff that would kill everyone if it ever broke. From here it would be faster to run to the fabrication shop and get a cutting torch than it would to suit up in a hardsuit later.

After returning from the shop, Macer ran the cutting torch around the perimeter of the storage locker door. When it was cool to the touch he pried the door loose. It fell to the deck with a clang.

He hauled the drone storage case out and placed it on Singh's bunk. He lifted the cover free.

The drone was missing.

Macer reached for his handheld. He didn't have it. The captain had taken it. He didn't want Macer to send anyone the pictures on his handheld. The pictures of a superluminal drive that shouldn't be there.

Macer wondered what the captain would say about the improvised explosive device in the drone storage case.

That shouldn't be there, either.

The IED looked like a handheld attached to a pair of wires that led to a circuit board that in turn had a pair of wires running to what looked like a battery case, but which Macer knew was a shaped charge. He'd taken a class in high-density energy storage and they'd studied all the legal and illegal methods of cramming potential energy into smaller and smaller spaces. He knew the smell of plasma-melt, and that was plasma-melt packed into a battery case. Even the just-used scent of the cutting torch couldn't mask the stench.

If the IED went off this close to the Templeman drive, it would breach the containment chamber. Even if inspectors bothered pawing through the wreckage, the destruction of the ship would look just like a maintenance accident.

The handheld tied into the system led Macer to believe it was meant to be remotely triggered. If Singh had meant to destroy the ship and be done with it, he could have done that any time after the liberty boat had cleared the potential blast radius.

So if it was remotely triggered, when would be the ideal time to set off the bomb?

When they were back in populated space. They were scheduled for a week in a refit dock right after they delivered this load. Except in that case Singh could have just waited until they docked to flee the scene. Macer was scheduled for watch duty while in dock. So it had to be sometime between now and then. He wracked his brain to no avail.

The plot in the holo had shown their expected course, assuming they didn't cut the load loose early. But they always cut the load loose early according to Pilot Ruthie. But they couldn't in this case, because the load's transponder was down, and Loadmaster Jimio said that he wouldn't break the rules. Except if he didn't cut the load loose, they'd miss the footie ball final, which seemed important to the crew and to the captain, so maybe they'd ignore safety protocols anyway and just set a big hulking space dock loose in the system without a transponder beacon.

Except they wouldn't, not without the captain first calling the engineer about the broken transponder, and the engineer attempting to fix it. Using the drone.

Oh no.

The handheld beeped.

Macer lunged toward the locker. He ran his fingers around the perimeter of the locker itself, and found it there, a tiny bump on the cabinet wall. He pried it loose and examined it. It was a compact transmitter wired to a thermocouple. The thermocouple had been melted through when he'd torched the hatch off. The handheld wasn't wired to receive a signal from outside the vessel. It was wired to receive it from this transmitter. Except, why not hardwire the bomb to the thermocouple?

Because it was a prefab kit. Singh hadn't built the bomb. He'd just installed it. It was remotely triggered and Macer had triggered it when he'd cut the hatch open.

The IED's handheld beeped again.

Macer cursed, and cursed again. He darted to the bunk, jammed the lid onto the drone storage container, and scanned the compartment for a fast-pallet. No such luck.

He picked up the container and stepped into the corridor. The case wasn't heavy, but it was bulky and hard to grip. He couldn't run toward the airlock but he could walk fast. He walked fast.

Something inside the container beeped.

Macer cursed again and tried to pick up the pace. He was a dozen strides from the companionway that led to the liberty boat debarkation lounge. He stumbled on his way down the ladder and nearly dropped the container.

It beeped again.

Macer shoved the container into the airlock. He slammed the hatch.

"Hey," Rik Severn said.

"Not now," Macer growled.

He cracked the emergency override shield with his right elbow and jammed his left hand into the valve compartment. He cranked the pressure valve to the positive max. He held the dead man's switch closed with his thumb, watching the pressure gauge rise past maximum. If he held it too long, the valve would split and blow his hand off. If he didn't hold it long enough, the bomb might not clear the outer hatch. Or it could detonate any time before then, and blow out this section of the hull. He'd be sucked out into space—unless he was pulverized first, and sucked out into space in pieces. Macer pressed his ear to the airlock. The container beeped again. He hammered the outer hatch release and lunged away from the hull, dragging Severn to the deck beneath him.

The airlock cycled and the overpressure swept the container clear.

The outer hatch closed.

The airlock reset.

Maybe the bomb detonated, maybe it didn't.

He wouldn't hear it if it did, or feel the shockwave transmitted through both the inner and outer hulls. He might see a flash of light through the airlock viewport, but he wasn't going into an airlock he'd just forced into emergency ejection override. Not without running a diagnostic first.

Broken glass littered the deck. His left hand wept blood. Severn clambered to his feet and brushed himself off.

"You're bleeding. Would you like me to fetch bandages?"

"Do you know where the infirmary is?"

"No, but I'm sure I can find it."

"Like you found the bridge?"

"I did find it. Eventually."

"Come on, infirmary's this way. You hurt?"

"Only my ego. I'm not used to being pushed around by strangers."

"Me neither."

Something in Severn's pocket beeped. He stuffed his hand in and pulled out a handheld.

Macer's handheld.

"The captain asked that I return this to you."
Macer glanced at the handheld's message queue.
Separation at 21:12. Fix the fun-loving transponder. Instantly.
"Change of plans," Macer said. "There's a first-aid station on
the way."

8

M acer found the nearest first-aid station and slapped an emergency bandage onto his hand. The thing wiggled around for a while making comforting sounds. Eventually it settled in and began to work.

He stopped by his berthing compartment and grabbed his skinsuit and rebreather. He glanced at Severn. "Did you bring a skinsuit in that duffel?"

"I'm wearing one," Severn said.

"Rebreather?"

"In my pocket."

"You came prepared."

"One never knows what to expect."

"I hear you. If you stay in the airlock, you won't need a hardsuit."

"Then I'll stay in the airlock."

Macer began the long hike toward what was presently the forward load-bay airlock. They were pushing the load instead of pulling it. *Four-Squared* was double ended, with massive in-system engines at both ends. A separate bridge and engineering control room located near what was presently the stern lay mothballed and idling. The redundant design made a lot of sense for a government-funded operation in a war zone and a crew of two hundred. It made no sense at all as a commercial tug in peacetime. They were never in that much of a hurry.

He thought about contacting the captain and informing him about the bomb. But the threat had been neutralized, and he had less than two hours to fix the transponder. Plus, if he told the captain about the bomb, he'd have to tell him it was set to trigger a field collapse in the superluminal drive. There'd be a record of the conversation in the comms logs.

Macer flipped to the image gallery on his handheld.

The images he'd recorded of the superluminal drive had been wiped.

So even talking about the drive on the comm wasn't an option.

"This is a big vessel," Severn said.

"A lot of walking," Macer agreed. "But it keeps you in shape."

"The artificial gravity is set quite high."

"That's what I said when I first came on board. But you get used to it."

It hadn't made any sense when Singh had explained why, but then he'd neglected to mention that the captain and most of the crew were from Sampson. Sampson Station spun at two standard gravities just to make it uncomfortable for outsiders. He didn't know much more about Sampson and New Sparta, except that they were banned to trade. And he'd only learned that they spun the station at high-G because it was stated in a test question in his first-year mechanics of materials class.

Severn was breathing hard by the time they made it to the airlock. For a five-time Olympic champion, he seemed pretty out of shape.

"What'd you medal in again?" Macer said.

Severn planted himself on the ready bench while Macer

stripped down and shimmied into his skinsuit. "Trifoil and the pentathlon."

"Never heard of a trifoil."

"It's a two-event medal. Single-foil competition and double-foil competition combined."

"What's a foil? Like a wing or something?"

"Very long and thin force blades."

"Oh. What about this pentathlon?"

"Single foil, double foil, short gun, long gun, and low-G hand-to-hand."

"Those don't sound like sports to me."

"They are the ultimate sports."

Macer eyed the hardsuit. He hated those things. It was regulation to wear one and for good reason. They were hard to work in, and nasty to think about, since you didn't have your own hardsuit like you did a skinsuit, but got one off the rack, like rental formal wear on Trinity Station.

Except you didn't have to plumb yourself into formal wear that someone else had just brought back from a hard night on the town. At the Academy, if they wanted to punish someone, they made them clean and sanitize the hardsuits. Macer Gant had cleaned more hardsuits than anyone else in the universe.

These suits were all fresh and clean, he'd seen to it himself, but still. He didn't like a hardsuit one bit. But he liked the idea of wearing a hardsuit a lot better than the idea of some zagged piece of space junk ripping through his chest cavity like a plasma bolt.

"Is it expensive, training for these ultimate sports? It sounds like you need a lot of kit."

"Very expensive at the highest levels of competition."

"Is that why you're trying out for the captain's footie ball team? If footie ball is anything like real football, I hear those folks make a pile, with endorsements and such."

"It's called footie. And it was my agent's suggestion. Not

their best suggestion, in retrospect, but it allowed me to get on board."

"So they brought you on board as a replacement worker?"

"That's right."

"Replacement for who? That big guy I saw getting on the liberty shuttle?"

"Yes."

"I think he's one of the bridge crew."

"Yes."

"You don't seem much like bridge crew."

"No?"

"Being able to find the bridge is usually considered a basic skill."

"It's a big ship. And I'm more accustomed to working outside."

"On the station?"

"Yes."

"Doing what?"

"Low-G welding."

"You're a man of many talents."

"Yes."

"Just not navigating."

"Like I said. It's a big ship."

"It is that. But still. You make any stops on the way?"

"Yes."

"Huh." Macer ran his gaze along the rack of hardsuits, searching for anything within reach that looked like a weapon. "You placed the bomb in the chief engineer's cabin."

"On my way to the bridge. It seemed the opportune time."

"And you did it to kill Singh."

"I did it to silence the chief engineer. My orders were quite specific."

"This order giver, would I know him or her?"

"Not unless you are the chief engineer."

"Acting chief engineer. Singh's left the ship."

"As I said. My orders were quite specific."

"You're going to try to kill me while I'm putting on my hardsuit."

"That wouldn't be sporting."

Macer reached for the hardsuit.

"I will hurt you if you attempt to put on that hardsuit," Severn said. "Nothing life-threatening but very painful. Now get in the airlock."

"And what are you going to do?"

"I'm going to sit here and catch my breath. Then I'm going to come out onto the hull with you. And practice."

"Can I take my tools?"

"I'd be disappointed if you didn't."

"You diddled my handheld, didn't you?"

"It can receive but not transmit."

"That figures." Macer pointed. "What's in the duffel?"

Severn grinned. "Sporting goods."

9

M acer turned his back on Rik Severn and opened the tool locker.

"Slowly."

The tool belt adjusted to go around a hardsuit or a skinsuit. Besides a range of spanners, it contained a welding rig that wasn't much use as a distance weapon and a plasma cutter that might be. It didn't much matter. He could have a GRAIL gun in his kit and he wouldn't stand a chance against a five-time Olympic medalist. He strapped the belt on.

"In the airlock. I'll cycle it. And Chief Engineer?"

"Acting Chief Engineer," Macer said.

"Once outside, you'd best jet. I'll count to thirty. And then I'll come for you."

"Is that how you do it in the Olympics? Give a guy a thirty count head start?"

"It's how I do it. For practice."

"Get a lot of practice, do you?"

"Enough. Now get in."

"You know I'm not Singh. And I don't have anything against you yet."

Severn laughed. "No, you're not Singh. He might have actually put up a fight."

"He probably would have." Macer got in the airlock. He watched through the viewport as Severn flicked a long, ugly force blade to life. It was thinner than Macer expected, and longer, the sort of slender blade that could slip between a man's ribs and slice into his heart. Severn powered up a second blade. He looked up from his work and saw Macer watching.

Severn grinned.

And cycled the airlock.

Macer didn't jet. He gripped the topside hatch combing and flipped himself upward, landing on the hull above the airlock. He pulled his fingers free a second before the airlock hatch scythed shut. He started counting down from thirty as his hull-walkers slapped the outer hull and held firm.

From here he had an open field, fore or aft. He could walk sternward and take shelter behind the communications array, careful to always keep one foot or a handhold on the hull.

He could hand-over-hand it along the power umbilicals leading forward to the load, and from there clamber along the beams and girders until he found somewhere safe to hide.

But without a hardsuit, even hiding wasn't safe.

Chances were he couldn't hide anyway. Severn was an expert, and he'd done this before. If Macer tried to hide, he might as well stand here and let the man cut him down. Once Severn was out the airlock, it was all over.

And that gave Macer an idea. He clambered down the hull until he dangled just aft of the airlock. People always looked forward first when they exited an airlock. He picked the biggest spanner in his tool kit and hefted the tool. Made from a nonconductive composite, strong and light as modern technology could achieve, it had potential. He could swing the wrench fast and hard but it didn't have any mass behind it.

Even if Severn wasn't clad in a hardsuit, Macer wouldn't be breaking any skulls with that wrench.

Macer had only counted down to fifteen when the airlock scythed open and a long, deadly blade appeared. Then a hand. Then a wrist.

Macer didn't think much of Rik Severn, but he hadn't pegged him as a cheater.

Macer hammered the wrench against the exterior airlock control.

The hatch scythed closed.

A long, deadly force blade spun away from the hull, a hand and a couple centimeters of a forearm still gripping it.

Macer stowed the wrench and gripped the plasma cutter. He thumbed the tool to slag-the-hell-out-of-whatever-is-in-front-of-me mode and waited for the airlock to reset.

He held the trigger down and hammered the airlock control with his fist.

Rik Severn was silently screaming and clutching his bloody stump. He'd spit out his rebreather and was only making screaming sounds in his own head. Macer released the plasma cutter and clocked Severn across the jaw, which put him down and gave Macer room to work the airlock controls.

Severn's forearm wasn't rocketing blood like in a horror drama but pumping out floating globules in irregular spurts, which was even more disturbing. A lot of blood had already precipitated onto the deck and bulkheads. Closing the hatch had cycled the airlock. When Severn had spit out his rebreather he'd ruptured the seal. In a second his brain would get the message, here's some new shipboard air to breath, and maybe he'd wake up gasping. And maybe he wouldn't wake up at all. He'd lost a lot of blood, and Macer had hit him pretty hard.

Macer Gant cycled the airlock. He pocketed his own

rebreather and dragged Severn out of the airlock. Every working airlock had a first-aid cubby nearby. Macer pulled a field dressing free, flicked it to life, and draped it over Severn's weeping stump. The dressing humped around for a while, talking to itself, and then settled in with a sucking sound. Just in case he was tougher than he looked, Macer flipped Severn onto his chest and zip-tied his arms together above the elbows. Every decent engineer carried zip ties, and now Macer had a new use for them.

Macer gripped Severn by the collar and hoisted him over his shoulder. He should probably call the captain, but what was the captain going to do, and anyway, the infirmary was on this deck portside, and not the longest walk. He would end up waiting longer for someone to get here than if he delivered Severn himself.

Macer ducked through the infirmary hatch and looked around. He had a general idea of the place from the ship's schematics. He'd just finished popping Severn into an autodoc when someone cleared their throat behind him.

"May I help you?"

Macer pegged the man staring at him as the ship's medic. He was a big guy, and probably another of the captain's Sampson football cronies. He had the blurry look of someone not quite awake yet. He smelled less like a doctor and more like a brewery.

"You're covered in blood," the guy said.

"It's okay," Macer said. "It's not mine." He hooked a thumb toward the autodoc.

The medic pawed at the controls. "This is five-time Olympic medalist Rik Severn!"

"So he said," Macer said. "Is he going to live?"

"Yes," the medic said. "But he's missing a hand."

"Do you follow the Olympics?"

"Of course." The medic tapped on the controls.

"Is there a class for augmented competitors?"

"There's three: modified, super-modified, and unlimited."

"Then I guess he'll do fine."

"What happened?"

"Industrial accident," Macer said.

Four-Squared was at heart a warship. There weren't any safety overrides or fail safes onboard. If you hammered the airlock control, it responded. Maybe you'd just dragged a buddy inside, and losing a foot or a hand was better than losing a friend. On the station, the hatches had a mind of their own. They wouldn't close with an arm in the way. They wouldn't even close with a finger blocking the safety sensors. The same was true on the Freeman merchant vessels, many of which were family ships.

Four-Squared was definitely not kid safe. It paid to remember that.

"How long will he be out?" Macer said.

"It's hard to say."

"Let me rephrase. How long can you keep him out?"

"Why would I want to sedate him?"

"You a fan of the captain's footie ball team?" Macer asked.

"I'm the team doctor," the medic said. "And it's footie, not 'footie ball'."

"If he wakes up and escapes your team might miss the finals."

"Escapes?"

"It's a long story. And I have a transponder to repair. If you call the captain and fill him in, I'd appreciate it. But whatever you do, don't let that guy loose on the ship." Macer glanced at the compartment chronometer. "I've got to go."

"I don't even know you," the doctor said.

"Gant." Macer grinned. "The team's fun-loving spare wrench."

"Verde," the doctor said.

"Nice to meet you, Doc." Macer headed for the hatch. "Remember!"

"Don't let him loose on the ship."

"Exactly."

10

Even though time was tight, a detour by Singh's cabin seemed worth it.

He'd been thinking that Singh had stolen the drone and taken it with him on the liberty boat. A good drone was handy to have, and that drone was a good one. Good and expensive. Probably the most expensive single piece of equipment in engineering, outside of the macrofab. Unlike a macrofab it was portable. Small enough to fit in a duffel. That's why it was kept locked up in the chief engineer's cabin. To deter theft. That, and to keep anyone from stuffing it into the macrofab and trying to duplicate it.

The good drones were licensed tech, with power-up check-in code. You could crank out a copy in a macrofab but that destroyed the original. And the minute your duplicate tried to check in with the manufacturer they'd slag the firmware. And the firmware of any others listed as licensed to you. Trying to hack the original before you duplicated it would slag the firmware too. That's what Singh had said, anyway, and he'd know.

Still, it was the Freeman way to try. When you paid for

something you owned it. And stuff you owned, you could do anything you wanted with it. Sooner or later someone was going to find a way to duplicate that drone, and then they wouldn't be expensive anymore. Even the poorest family ship could afford to buy a pattern and make their own. They wouldn't have to send kids in hardsuits out on the hull anymore. So whoever figured out how to pattern that drone would be a hero in Freeman eyes. And a criminal to the League, where such breakthrough tech originated.

Macer ducked through Singh's cabin hatch. If Singh hadn't placed the bomb in the drone locker, but Rik Severn, then the drone had to be around here someplace. It wasn't under Singh's bunk. It wasn't in the refresher. Surely the idiot wouldn't have stuffed it down the recycler.

He had. But he'd neglected to press the disposal button. So maybe he wasn't an idiot after all. He could hide the drone in there and pick it up on his way off ship, assuming he didn't know that planting the bomb where he did would start a chain reaction that would destroy the entire ship. And assuming he didn't know that even if the bomb didn't blow up the entire ship, the bomb he'd planted was big enough to blow out an entire section of the hull, including the recycler holding the neatly hidden drone.

Or maybe he was an idiot, and, in the heat of the moment, had just forgotten to press the disposal button. Or maybe he didn't care. No one would think to look in the recycler for the drone until they'd looked for it in the drone locker first. And once they did that, they'd be dead.

He rummaged through the drawers of Singh's workstation until he found a spare engineering handheld. He thumbed it alive and flicked through the screens. Singh had loaded the drone app. He flicked a little farther. And he'd loaded the superluminal diagnostic app. Macer started both. The tests he'd started earlier on the drive were still running. And the drone was making sounds like it was alive. But it wasn't lifting out of the recycler.

Duh, because *Four-Squared* was running nearly two gravities inside the hull.

And double *duh*, because now he knew why Singh's spare wrenches were always bailing out, or getting hurt or killed. He'd grown up on Trinity Surface, at the bottom of a gravity well. Most of Truxton's engineering crew were space-born. He'd felt the gravity drag at first, because he'd spent four years at the Academy on Trinity Station, where the spin averaged point eight Gs on the Arcade and tapered off to nothing the closer you got to the spindle. The stationmaster didn't even try to keep the augmented gravity at a League standard one G. It was easier and cheaper to normalize the bulk of the station at a solid point eight everywhere but near the spindle. There the local gravity could be whatever you wanted to pay for it to be.

Macer had adapted quickly to the constant load aboard *Four-Squared* because that's what he was used to. Not two Gs, but slightly better than one just sitting still. And at the bottom of a gravity well, anything that could pull high Gs was usually fun as all get-out to ride. If you didn't have to hang on, you needed more power. And there were always ways to find more power. All you needed were the right tools, the right parts, and a strong sense of your own immortality.

No nefarious plot to eject associate engineers from *Four-Squared* existed. The previous candidates just weren't suited to the environment.

Macer lifted the drone from the recycler and ran it through its self tests. It was good to go. Once outside the hull it wouldn't be fighting artificial gravity to lift.

He checked the compartment chronometer. Less than an hour. He needed to jet.

Macer tucked the drone beneath his arm and took off at a run for the forward airlock.

MACER SPRINTED along the cross corridor and hooked a right at the portside gallery. He rocketed down the ladder and skidded to a halt at the forward airlock before he noticed Sensors Operator Lizzie Teal. She'd peeled out of her utilities and stood eyeballing the hardsuits in the rack. Her skinsuit was the standard Truxton orange like his own, but the suit looked better on her.

She shouted at him. "What the hell!" She pointed at the drying blood on the deck and walls. Some additional splatter painted the overhead, which only made sense, the way Severn had been flailing around.

"Industrial accident," Macer said. "What are you doing here?" He placed the drone in the airlock and backed out.

"Captain hasn't heard from you. No one knows what's going on. We need to cut the load loose in thirty minutes. "

"Twenty-eight minutes," Macer said.

"Close enough. Now what the hell?"

Macer fished out the engineering handheld. "I don't have time to explain. Check the surveillance log."

"There is no surveillance log. There is no surveillance, period."

"There's sensors everywhere." Macer pointed at the full-range sensor mounted with a clear view of the airlock. It had a number plate mounted next to it. "Just enter its designation."

"You're not listening. Surveillance system's been down for three days."

"Can't be." Macer cycled the airlock. "If it was I'd have gotten a repair order."

"It is down, trust me. I ran the diagnostics myself. And the captain logged it. I watched him."

Macer snagged a hardsuit helmet off the rack. "Then he

didn't log it right. Because I never got a repair order, and the sensors are my responsibility."

"He logged it right, I know."

"Did you try power cycling it?"

"You wrench monkeys are all the same. That's what Singh said, when the captain called to ream him a new one."

"Well did you?"

"Of course I fu—"

"Hang on," Macer said. "Singh was working a sensor ticket?"

"I don't know what a sensor ticket is. But he told the captain to leave the problem to him."

"Singh's done a runner."

"Captain said."

"He doesn't want anyone reviewing his actions before leaving the ship."

"Makes sense."

"They're military sensors. They have local storage, enough for twenty-four hours standard. If we can get them back online, we can at least review that."

And he'd have the recordings he was counting on, the one from this sensor and the one on the hull outside, the ones that had recorded Rik Severn's confession and everything after that. Without that record it would be Severn's word against his, and he did not want to stand trial for crippling a five-time Olympic medalist.

"How can I help?"

"I need to get this drone up, and fix the load's transponder like right now. And I can't do that and talk to you at the same time."

"I'll try to fix the sensors while you play with the drone."

"Don't do that!"

"Calm down."

"You can try to fix the sensors on the bridge. Or in the infirmary. Just don't mess with this one, or the one in Singh's cabin. Or the one in the liberty boat debark lounge."

"Because you think I'll screw them up."

"Because if anyone screws them up, I want it to be me." That way if he ended up on trial he wouldn't have anyone to blame but himself.

"You're a pretty strong runner," Lizzie said. "You ever think about footie?"

"Honestly?" Macer looked her in the eye. "I never even heard about footie ball until today. And ever since I heard about footie ball, I've been sort of busy."

"It's footie, not footie ball. And you think about it, Wrench."

"I promise," Macer said. "Footie is all I'm going to think about. After I get this fun-loving transponder back on line." *Footie and Lizzie Teal in a Truxton skinsuit.*

"Go on then," she said. "I'll stick and make sure you're not interrupted."

Macer jammed his head into the hardsuit helmet. They all smelled the same, like a mix of industrial disinfectant and fear sweat. He tongued the display alive and synced the auxiliary sensor panel to the output of the drone. Technically he should suit up and climb out on the hull, or at least into the airlock, but no regulation prohibited driving from inside, and even old military hulls like *Four-Squared* had broadband repeaters ever thirty meters the length of the hull. There were repeaters on the load as well, and they were linked to *Four-Squared* by the umbilical he'd considered clambering across when Severn had forced him outside.

Staying in control of the drone wasn't a problem on a stationary hull. Flight control was line of sight with autoreturn to the last known good coordinates. That didn't work when they were under power and boosting hard toward the system's L4 point. If he lost sync with the drone, it would try to find his signal by heading to a point that would by then be well astern of the vessel. And while there were lots of settings to tweak on the system, turning off the autoreturn wasn't one of them. He had one shot to get this done, or he was climbing out onto the load to do it by hand.

He flipped up the helmet's heads-up visor and repeated the drone's output onto the engineering handheld. He tossed the handheld to Lizzie Teal. "Spot me, and let me know if I'm about to step in it."

"Got it. That's a clear image."

"It ought to be. This drone cost more than the liberty boat."

He guided the drone forward, hovering just above the umbilical. The drone had eight rings of repulsors arrayed the length of its hull, the same sort of tech that made a fast-pallet lift, though much less powerful. They drew power directly from the drone's stored-energy system, and didn't deplete onboard consumables. So long as it skimmed a nearby surface, the drone sipped power. In free space it had to rely on thrusters alone, and those burned through reaction mass like crazy.

"The transponder is dead ahead. At the base of the derrick labeled ALM-1301."

The derrick was a big, orange motor housing attached to an articulated arm. The designator stood out plainly in broad white letters taller than he was. It was one of forty derricks mounted to the beams and scaffolding of Truxton's Refit Dock One. The decommissioned refit dock was a massive structure, one capable of surrounding a starship, and they were moving it in one piece. This was exactly the sort of awesome job Macer had dreamed of as a kid. Big stuff, and a big ship, in a big sky, doing big things. And now he was part of that.

He did not want to go out on the hull. This had to work.

"You're drifting to port."

"On it."

And then the little drone was there, at the base of the derrick. The transponder was a simple mechanism: a solar array, a stored-charge system, a transmitter, and an omnidirectional antenna. The sort of ancient tech hard to break by accident.

Someone had broken it on purpose.

"Antenna's unplugged," Lizzie said.

The drone had six articulated arms it could extend. Part of what made it so expensive was that the arms didn't end in tools, or grippers, but in adaptable force arrays, the same tech used in hardhands gloves, but without the glove. A skilled operator could manipulate the fields to shape just about any tool or gripper. Singh was a skilled operator. Macer? Not so much. You needed seat time to develop skill, and flying the drone was chief engineer work on *Four-Squared*.

Fortunately the menu of presets provided by the manufacturer listed transponder antenna fitment as one of the choices. This was exactly the sort of high-risk, low-skilled job the drone was perfect for, and one of the reasons it was getting harder and harder to find an associate engineer's gig with the big-three merchant firms. Anything that could be automated was being automated. Crew compensation remained a merchant vessel's single biggest expense.

Macer instructed the drone to grip the antenna.

"Transmitter's probably fried," Lizzie said.

"Would be, if I hadn't installed a dummy load shunt."

In-system work wasn't like long-haul work. He had actual liberty days, and work didn't shut down on those days. Temp workers filled in, stationers mostly, working side gigs. He'd built up the transponder rig but hadn't installed it. He'd toasted the transponder on his first install by accidentally forgetting to hook up the antenna. Rule number one of in-system engineering was fix it inside the hull if you could. And idiot-proofing all the load transponders before he handed them off was fixing it inside the hull, no matter who did the installation, or when they did it.

Macer instructed the drone to attach the antenna. "Transponder's hot. You did it."

"We did it." Macer told the drone to follow its track back to the airlock, not by global coordinates, but by stepping through the inverse of its servo log.

Once it was in the airlock he tongued the helmet off and dropped it into the "service me" bin. A suit and helmet already rested in the bin. It had been empty when he'd checked it yesterday. Checking the bins and servicing the suits was also the sort of low-skill work associate engineers were responsible for.

Macer glanced at Lizzie. "Did you go outside?"

"I was getting ready to when you showed up."

He showed her the suit and helmet in the bin. "Somebody did."

"Maybe that antenna cable didn't work free on its own."

"It's a positive lock. They don't work free. Whoever installed the transponder forgot to finish the job."

"No. That transponder was hot and then it quit. I know because—"

"Because you heard the captain tell Singh to fix it."

"Right. And I know it was working because it was screwing up my sensors."

"How was it doing that?"

"It's easier to show you then explain. On the bridge."

"Then show me."

"You know you're spattered with dried and drying blood. You look like an ax murderer. Or a footie ruckman."

"You want me to clean up first?"

"Nah, you'll fit right in." She wriggled into her utilities. "Are you coming?"

11

"Industrial accident," Macer said, before anyone asked. He followed Lizzie to the sensor station.

She jacked in, but like earlier, didn't run the sensor station in full-immersion mode.

"You don't like the goop?" Macer looked around for somewhere to rest the drone.

"Don't need it loafing along. You can put your little bird on the engineering station. It takes a minute to get synced up. Then I'll show you what I'm talking about."

"Which one's the engineering station?"

"The one that's never been used," Jimio said.

Ruthie pointed. "Closest to the hatch."

Macer yanked the antistatic storage cover off the station. He rested the drone on the workstation surface. "This is handy." He powered the workstation alive.

"Singh didn't think so," Ruthie said. "He refused to use it. Did everything on his handheld."

"Probably had it set up the way he liked. Some guys work that way."

Macer jacked the drone into the workstation's power supply.

ABC was the drone operators' unofficial motto. *Always be charging.*

His favorite instructor at the Academy said it should be the engineer's motto in general. *Always be charging—and at the maximum rate.* No Freeman trusted a bargain, figuring some hidden cost lay built-in somewhere. And folks that preferred to work with machines rather than people were notoriously poor about asking for a pay raise. So over time the best engineers—the ones that did their jobs competently and without complaint—they ended up being the worst paid, and oddly enough, the least trusted and respected outside their own crew. *And do you know who is to blame for that, Macer Gant?"*

He knew. *Guys like me.* Guys who always found themselves wondering why someone wasn't charging *them* for the opportunity to do what they got to do every day.

Macer slid into the workstation seat and fiddled with the controls. It took all of thirty seconds to access his stored preferences and configure the workstation exactly like the one in power engineering.

The superluminal-drive tests continued to run and continued to tell the same story. A drive approaching end-of-life. It wasn't on the edge of failure, but then again, it wasn't getting a workout. Over ninety-three percent of Templeman drive failures occurred, not while idling, or on drive engagement, but on disengagement, when the hard work of reversing the field's expansion occurred. Putting the genie back into the bottle took force, and a lot of it. Stuff broke, and broke fast.

The other seven percent mostly happened when some idiot let the containment field oscillate and didn't catch it in time. Sudden failures at idle were virtually unheard off. That didn't mean they couldn't happen. Particularly in a drive that hadn't been properly maintained.

What was Singh thinking?

"The display's not doing it anymore," Sensors Operator Lizzie Teal said. "No ghosting."

Macer left the workstation running and inspected the sensor station's display. "What was it doing?"

"Showing ghost traffic. Echoes. Like there would be a vessel on the scan and in the holo, and then the same vessel would show up again on the scan and not on the holo, and it only did that when I swept past the transponder antenna." Her brow wrinkled. "Three times, three different vessels."

"Huh."

"That's what I said."

"You tell anybody?"

"I thought about it. But it went away when the load transponder stopped broadcasting."

"We're dumping this load in five," Jimio said. "On the pilot's mark."

"Mark," Ruthie said.

"Mark confirmed," Jimio said. "The pickle is hot."

"Show me the optical feeds from the load," Macer said.

The display filled with scores of tiled windows, each showing the real-time feed from a single sensor on Truxton's Refit Dock One.

"Now show me just those from the sector where you were seeing the ghosts."

Lizzie stripped the display down to four real-time sensors feeds.

"Now roll through them one at a time."

She saw it on the third display. "There's a vessel on the load."

A two-person rockhopper crouched in the shadow of Derrick ALM-1301. The sort of surplus kit even the lowliest smuggler could afford ever since Trinity system's asteroid belt had played out.

"It's an old trick," Macer said. "Mirroring the transponder of a larger vessel nearby. To automated systems it looks like reflections. It works best when there's a lot of uncataloged junk floating around."

"How do you know that?"

"He's a Freeman," Ruthie said. "They're all smugglers."

"Not all," Macer said.

"But you are?" Lizzie said.

"If he says yes, he's lying," Jimio said. "And if he says no, he means yes. Separation in three."

"He won't say yes," Ruthie said. "That word's not in their lingo. And he won't say no but, 'I'm not,' which could mean anything. I never was. I used to be but not anymore. I am, but I'm not smuggling this very minute. Don't believe a Freeman, whatever he says."

"It's best not to ask," Jimio said. "Just assume the worst and you can't go wrong."

"What's a rockhopper doing there?" Lizzie said.

"I'm guessing it's Rik Severn's getaway ride," Macer said.

"What are you talking about?" Ruthie said.

The captain stepped out of his day cabin. "Grant. In here. Now."

"It's Gant," Macer muttered. The captain probably wanted to grill him again about Singh.

"Separation in two," Jimio said.

"Reducing thrust," Ruthie said. "Preparing for separation in two."

"What the hell?" Lizzie shouted. "Captain, you need to see this! There's someone in a hardsuit on the load."

Macer glanced at the display. "There's two of them. One in a hardsuit and one in a skinsuit." The one in the hardsuit practically dragged the one in the skinsuit along.

The captain elbowed Macer out of the way. "Zoom in."

"That's the New Guy," Lizzie said. "Let's see who's in the hardsuit."

"You can do that?" the captain said.

"Fu... nking Eh, I can." Lizzie worked the controls. "Five-time Olympic medalist Rik Severn is going to have a sunburn. And whoever's in the suit is going to remember what if feels like to be on laservision."

"Do it." The captain tossed a coin in the swear jar for her.

"Separation in one," Jimio said. "Retracting umbilicals now."

"Someone needs to get to the infirmary," Macer said. "Needs to get there right away."

"Smile for the cameras, ladies," Lizzie said. "And ignore the flash."

"Captain," Macer said.

"In a minute, Grant." The captain remained fixated on the sensor display.

"Enhancing," Lizzie said.

"In ten," Jimio said. "Nine. Eight."

"We are at heading zero," Ruthie said. "We are at delta vee zero. We are on mission profile. The helm is free."

"One." Jimio pressed the top of a joystick on his console. He thrust his arms toward the deckhead. "The load is free."

"Let's get out of here," Ruthie said.

Macer glanced around the bridge. They were each caught up in their own business. "I'll go," he said. And took off for the infirmary.

THE AUTODOC WASN'T EMPTY. They'd stuffed Doctor Verde in. He was dead. From the blood splatter in the compartment and in the corridor, and from the telltales on the autodoc, it looked like they'd had their fun with the doctor before they'd headed for the airlock.

Macer couldn't do anything here. No one could. He headed for the forward airlock.

A single hardsuit helmet rested in the "service me" bin. He glanced at the hardsuit rack.

They were all there, racked and ready, all but the helmet he'd used. The hardsuit in the bin hadn't been one of theirs. Someone had come in the airlock. He couldn't tell who, because the sensors in the airlock were out, and had been for three days.

But the airlock log wasn't attached to the sensors. So even if he couldn't tell who, he could tell *when*.

He toggled the airlock to maintenance mode and used his acting chief engineer's credentials to open the log. He didn't have to scroll far to find the entry. The airlock had cycled twice since his little fun with Rik Severn. Once, not ten minutes ago, and once before, while he was in Singh's cabin retrieving the drone.

If Sensors Operator Lizzie Teal had been at the airlock a few minutes earlier, they'd be stuffing her into a body bag for transport along with the doctor. Two dead, instead of one. On *his* ship.

He'd seen the hardsuit in the service bin and it hadn't registered. And he's shoved Rik Severn into the autodoc, and left him in the infirmary. He should have counted the hardsuits on the rack. And if he'd left Severn in the airlock, the problem would have been sorted before it started.

This was all on him. The doctor's death was on him.

Because he was softheaded. And softhearted.

He'd never served on a family ship. Had grown up on a planet. All that space-born Freeman tough talk had seemed just that to him. Tough talk. Posturing. Playing a role. But it was different out here, even on the in-system vessels. Less forgiving. He didn't know the doctor. Didn't know the rest of these people.

He thought he'd known Singh and he'd been dead wrong. Every one of his decisions had been flawed.

And this decision, *his decision*, had cost a man his life. He wondered if the doctor had family, and if they were expecting him home in a few days. He wondered what he'd say to them, when they showed up at the dock, looking for their father. Their husband. Their friend.

All this could have been avoided if he'd just followed the rules. Not a Freeman on Trinity Station would have blamed him if he'd watched Severn bleed out gasping on the airlock deck. How he felt about that wasn't any guide to follow out here. Space was a hard place, and he had to be a hard man. He had to follow the rules to keep his people safe.

He didn't have to agree with the rules.

He didn't have to like the rules.

He just needed to live by them.

Starting now.

12

Macer had left his engineering handheld on the bridge. And whoever had managed to get Rik Severn off the ship had taken Severn's duffel and Macer's diddled handheld. He figured it didn't matter now, preserving the local sensor buffers, because Severn wasn't going to file an action against him, not after murdering the doctor and fleeing the scene. It would be handy, though, to have the recordings if Severn was ever to face judgement, and for that he needed a lift cart and a handheld.

So it was back to engineering stores, and on the way he could stop by his compartment and change into something less blood caked, and hose himself off while he was there, and order a maintenance drone to the infirmary and the forward airlock to clean up the mess. Another money-saving innovation by the big shippers, the maintenance drones had replaced wipers and other junior crew, the sort of low-skilled workers that now clustered on the spindle and moaned about the injustice of the world.

Macer wasn't all that sure what there was to moan about. Somebody had to run the fabs that cranked out the drones, and somebody had to quality assure them, and somebody had to run the packaging machines, and run the fabs that made the packaging machines, and quality assure them, and so on and so forth, on down the line. It was work, just not the work their daddy and his daddy's daddy did. The Federation was changing, growing up and becoming more like the League, and Macer thought that was a good thing. Of course he would think that, because he had the skills and inclination to make out well in that world.

Macer keyed the engineering berthing compartment open, peeled out of his skinsuit, and hit the showers. The water was always hot because the heating system was sized for a crew of two hundred. His mind raced, wouldn't stop racing, and when he placed his forehead against the shower bulkhead, the cold felt good but it did nothing to cool his thoughts.

It didn't matter what he thought or didn't think, because the world was changing, whether anyone liked it or not. And Truxton was changing it. Forcing his way in where he wasn't wanted, breaking up the First Families' stranglehold on Freeman markets, changing the way business was done, right down to the way bloody messes in the forward airlock were cleaned up.

To Macer's thinking it didn't make a lot of sense to put Truxton's Refit Dock One in cold storage, but then he wasn't privy to all the high-level agreements it took to get business done in Trinity System. But one thing was sure, Truxton was a lot smarter and way more connected than Macer Gant, and if he thought it was a good idea then it was a good idea. He didn't exactly idolize the man, he knew Truxton could make mistakes, but of the Big Three outfits, Macer Gant had only ever wanted to sign with one, and in the end, he had. Six months in and he still felt incredibly lucky to be a Truxton hand, and incredibly grateful to get the chance to work and learn with the best.

It wasn't Truxton's fault that Macer's boss had turned out to be some sort of insane maniac, the kind of daredevil who'd buy black-market Templeman drive spares and then not even install them, and it wasn't Truxton's fault that the captain and the crew of *Four-Squared* were more interested in some foreign sports game than doing their jobs, and it wasn't Truxton's fault that a homicidal psychopath had gotten on board as a replacement crewman and then planted a bomb, tried to murder Macer, succeeded in murdering one of the crew, and then escaped right under the noses of everyone on board, himself included. None of that was Truxton's fault.

But an unregistered superluminal drive on board? That couldn't be down to anyone but Truxton. It was just too huge an object to procure, and too regulated, and just too extensive a refit to perform, and not simply because the drive itself couldn't be disassembled and smuggled in as parts, but because no automated system in the world could tear a League starship down to the cross frames. No machine existed that could slide the largest Templeman drive ever produced in without an army of workers. And no army of workers could remain silent. Not about something so big and awesome. It wasn't the sort of project you talked about. It was the sort of project you *bragged* about, loudly, and often, to anyone who would listen. And even Truxton didn't have the pull to permanently silence a work gang that size, like some god-king out of ancient history.

Only one answer made sense, and only one person could pull that off.

Someone in the League tasked with scrapping *Four-Squared*'s Templeman drive *hadn't*. They'd falsified the records and sold the vessel on knowing they were committing a crime, and not just any crime, but high treason.

Thomas Truxton had purchased *Four-Squared* with its drive intact. And he'd kept that secret all these years by keeping the number of people who knew about it small, and by making sure they were the right kind of people; an isolated blow-in community that didn't just dislike the First Families, but hated them. It was nic Cartaí who had banned Sampson Station and New Sparta to Freeman trade, and it was nic Cartaí who held the thumb on them to this day. And Truxton was using that hate to keep his secret alive.

Singh, being such a bent piece of rubbish, had likely acted as a shield for Macer. Macer figured that if he checked he'd discover that every associate engineer before him had been a League blow-in like Singh. Somehow Macer Gant, not First Families, but close enough to kiss, had ended up with a posting to *Four-Squared*. He wasn't a blow-in, and he wasn't a go-along, and he wasn't even an accident-prone stumblebum unused to planetary gravity. And even though Macer wasn't his father's favorite son, if something happened to a Gant on board *Four-Squared* there would be an investigation, and not just a comb-over. His father had more than enough pull to arrange that, and Fionnuala nic Cartaí only too willing to help shove an inquiry down Truxton's throat, or up any orifice that wasn't puckered shut.

So maybe Singh figured he'd had a good run, and it was time to cash in his chips and jet. Or maybe something else drove the events here, something he'd never have the measure of, because he was just a buck private in a galaxy-spanning war between jealous titans and their hidden generals.

He toweled off and dressed in his second-best utilities. Then he took them off again, and snagged a fresh skinsuit from the crew chest, and put it on under his utilities. He pocketed a rebreather. And he pocketed a spare. If he really was in the middle of a war zone, then he'd better start thinking like he was. And preparing like he was.

His chief engineer's credentials unlocked a small-arms cabinet in the engineering wardroom.

The cabinet was almost empty.

He'd never fired a handheld slug-thrower, but he'd been

shot by one. At Academy he'd bunked over a firing range and caught a round on a punch-through, entirely his own fault. He'd been in exactly the wrong place at the wrong time. The slug had missed bone but nicked an artery. If his roommates hadn't been there, he would have bled out. He owed them both, and the next time he saw them he'd tell them. They were not going to believe this. He'd signed up for in-system work for the partying and for the girls. And because that was where the big iron and the big thrust was. They'd both blown out-system as merchant apprentices on the long-haul routes, and that was the last he'd heard from them.

Macer hefted the weapon. He sighted down the barrel. He'd hunted as a kid on Clear Island, tougher and meaner stuff than men, though not quite as clever. He recognized the controls of the antique weapon. Unlike a plasma rifle, it had a fixed capacity. Macer racked a round into the chamber and checked that the safety worked. Then he took the weapon to the engineering berthing compartment and tucked it under his mattress. Carrying it around seemed like a recipe for disaster. But maybe he could get some shut-eye later without feeling totally defenseless.

He grabbed a lift plate from stores and siphoned off the local sensor storage from the liberty boat debarkation lounge, and the infirmary, and the forward airlock. There were just too many sensors to visit them all. And if he could bring the system online they'd all sync up, unless he had to wipe the system and restart it from scratch.

Singh hadn't just disconnected a few connectors at the sensor-net nexus. He'd slagged the controller with a plasma torch. And he'd slagged the backup too. It could be fixed, but not without ordering spares. For now all the internal sensors would remain down. And he'd lose all the buffered data he hadn't already vacuumed up as it rolled out of the local buffers.

He checked the internal comms nexus as well. The hailing

nexus and compartment-to-compartment nexus had both been slagged. Macer guessed that made some sort of strange sense, if Singh was breaking things by the book. But breaking all that didn't really break comms, since most people nowadays used their handhelds as their primary communications node, and those were meshed, and harder to break. He'd have had to take down the ship's entire repeater net to cut out comms completely. And if he'd broken that while still on board, everyone would have noticed. And lots of stuff that expected an always-on connection would have started screaming. So he broke what he could without getting red-flagged. All the heavy-duty, long-range stuff, and all the stuff that worked whether you had a handheld or not.

Macer wondered what else Singh had broken that he hadn't found yet.

He couldn't even begin to guess, and besides, this was plenty. He needed to fill the captain in, and they needed to come up with some orderly plan. There were nineteen people on board, and he could use some help going through the ship's systems one by one. He couldn't order people around, but the captain could. And the captain would, once he understood the risk, and the size of the task.

13

M acer returned to the bridge to find the captain and the bridge crew dining on meat roll-ups and washing them down with nonalcoholic ale. It wasn't regulation, having station food on the bridge, but it happened, and compared to everything else going on didn't seem worth mentioning. Tubed rations and glycogen drips were allowed on the bridge, but nobody who'd had tubed rations or a glycogen drip would file a grievance, least of all Macer Gant.

A break room and automated kitchen had been retrofitted just to the stern of the bridge, in a space that had been a wardroom and mess when *Four-Squared* had worn an LRN designation. On-duty bridge crew was supposed to take their meals there. Vacuuming out crumbs and fixing spill damage to the bridge equipment had been on Singh's list of assignments, and he'd never complained, either. The crew did a good job keeping their mess away from the workstations, leaning back in their seats and repeating their monitoring displays onto the big forward display that until recently showed a life-size image of the load.

They'd split the display space into three sections: a central section showing the view forward; an isometric projection showing the load's trajectory, which the loadmaster periodically annotated; and another isometric projection of a rockhopper's trajectory. It was on track and boosting hard for the Boneyard on a course paralleling the load's but well ahead of it now.

The captain stuffed a roll-up into Macer's hand.

Macer transferred the sensor data from the forward airlock and infirmary to the engineering workstation. He didn't think the captain would need it, but he transferred the data from the liberty boat debarkation lounge as well.

By the time he was done, he'd finished his roll-up.

The captain and bridge crew were still noshing.

"Someone's slagged the comms nexus, the shipboard sensor nexus, and the hailing nexus," Macer told the captain. "Probably Singh, because whoever did it knew what they were doing."

"So we can't see or hear or talk to the rest of the ship," the captain said. "It's handhelds only."

"You could compile a roster and set up runners," Macer said. "The rest of the crew could help."

"The rest of the crew's in cryo," the captain said. "I need them fresh for the footie final."

Macer laughed. "Seriously, it's been done, and it works. We studied the procedure at the Academy. When they aren't carrying messages, the runners can help search for more damage Singh might have done to the ship. So far we've only found those systems that are obviously broken as we've needed them. But we haven't needed the close-quarters maneuvering systems and the docking systems. If they've been diddled the sooner we know the better."

"That all sounds good," the captain said, "but the crew's in cryo and they're staying there."

"I thought you were joking."

"Why would I joke about that?"

"It's a flagrant violation of the regs."

"Are we doing fine? Is the load doing fine? We're not paid to follow the regs. We're paid to do fine."

"We signed contracts saying that we would follow the regulations."

"And we're following them. If Singh hadn't deserted, there'd be twenty people on board. There's still nineteen on board, and that meets the regs, under the circumstances."

"This is an emergency. Emergencies are why there are supposed to be twenty people on board. Twenty awake, functioning people."

"Show me where in the regs it says that. And anyway, this isn't an emergency. Singh wouldn't have sabotaged any more than he needed to hide his actions. We'll check on the team in cold storage, and get the doctor up here, and we'll sit tight. We won't need any comms or sensors inside the hull, and Ruthie can run the ship through its docking and maneuvering paces, and anything else we might need between here and Trinity Station. Case closed."

"That's not going to work," Macer said.

"I said case closed, junior." the captain said.

"The crew's really in cryo?"

"We seem to be getting everything done without them."

"You do this on every haul?"

"Only before the big matches. It gives us an edge."

"That is so outside the limits of safe, it isn't even measurable."

"If we need them the doctor can wake them. But we don't need them."

"The doctor can't wake them."

"Sure he can."

"No," Macer said. "He can't. I was going to wait until you

finished eating." Macer scraped room on the big forward display and began the replay of the shipboard sensor data. "If you hurl onto the workstations, you're cleaning it up yourselves."

They watched all three of the sensor feeds. The one showing Macer dumping a bomb out the liberty boat debarking lounge airlock. The one showing Rik Severn's confession and subsequent loss of limb. The one showing a man they didn't know using a long, thin force blade to torture the doctor into telling him where his brother was. Macer at first thought he meant brother-in-arms, but when he turned to face the sensors Macer gasped.

"Meant to tell you," Lizzie said. "The guy in the hardsuit is Rik Severn's identical twin."

"There's too many moving parts to make sense of," Macer said. "We need to contact the station and get a security team out here pronto."

"You still don't get it," the captain said. "Go ahead and call your security team and watch what happens. Nothing. And you know why nothing?"

"You can't hide all of this."

"I'm not hiding it," the captain said. "Truxton is. You think I've been hiding a superluminal drive on board? You think I installed forty cryo chambers on board? You think I ordered a great big honking refit dock hauled out to the L4 intact? Think, junior."

"It makes no sense."

"Because you don't want it to make sense," the captain said.

"We're Truxton's getaway boat," Jimio said. "For when the Freemen decide to shove him out of the system."

Macer laughed. "You cannot be serious."

"And you cannot be so stupid. That dock is going to be disassembled at the Boneyard. Each beam and girder, each derrick and boom are going to be imaged, and labeled, and stripped down into parts that can fit in a hundred breakbulk haulers. And over the course of a year, it is going to be shipped piecemeal out of the system and assembled elsewhere. And while that is going on, we'll be hauling more of Truxton Engineering's plant out here, whole and intact, for disassembly and shipment."

"Shipment to where?"

"To where the Freemen cannot follow."

"Sampson and New Sparta," Macer said.

The captain shrugged. "Could be. We do our job, and part of that job is staying silent about this ship. And all was going to plan until you, junior, ruined it."

"That's not fair, Captain," Jimio said. "It was Singh that betrayed us."

"It was Singh that warned me," the captain said. "That there had been a mistake, and a Freeman apprentice engineer sent. One he couldn't drive away or dispose of without questions being asked. And so we hoped to contain the issue by isolating the problem. Maybe this apprentice would be lazy and stupid, and if not, responsive to threats of violence, or susceptible to bribery."

"Singh never threatened me, or tried to bribe me," Macer said.

"Of course he did, but you were too stupid to notice. And too full of hero worship of Truxton to bribe. Any hint of corruption would backfire. And so it was decided. You would have an accident. One that would have you removed from the ship permanently."

"Who decided that?" Macer said.

"I did."

"And Singh went along with that," Macer said.

"He *seemed* to. You were assigned only scut work and you didn't leave. You were assigned increasingly dangerous work and you didn't leave. You were injured repeatedly, and you didn't leave. After six months of this I'd had enough. Your presence was hampering our operation. I made it clear to Singh that if he didn't solve the problem I would."

"And Singh said he'd solve the problem."

"And instead he screwed me," the captain said. "Because he's soft."

"You sent for Rik Severn."

"I contacted those people I know who solve problems. And I described the problem."

"The problem with the chief engineer," Macer said.

"And with his acolyte."

"I see," Macer said. "And you're fine with telling me this because, what? You think I'll keep it quiet?"

"It's too late for that," the captain said. "The purchase order you submitted and Singh approved couldn't be recalled. It's been approved, with prejudice, and rush orders placed with local suppliers. The fact that Truxton's *Tractor Four-Square* is a superluminal vessel has been asserted and affirmed, and the ship's orders amended in light of this fact, and Captain Ma Violet approved as its acting master pending a formal inquiry."

"So now it's your deck, your rules," Macer said.

"You're a smart one about the rules," the captain said. "But dumb as rocks about how things really work."

"The captain's fixers solved the problem by stealing Singh for themselves," Ruthie said.

"And one of the Freeman suppliers talked," Jimio said. "The stationmaster doesn't want a giant fun-loving bomb heading in-system. So they sent someone to take care of the problem out here, where all we would be is a bright flash and an expanding debris field. One being slowly pulled toward the Boneyard and away from the station."

"The stationmaster does not like Truxton," Ruthie said. "And no one likes us."

"My father is friends with the stationmaster." Plus, the

stationmaster was Macer's uncle by marriage. "All that can't be true."

"How's your daddy feel about you?" Lizzie said.

"I'm not his favorite," Macer said. "But I still don't buy it. It's all speculation."

"Lizzie," the captain said.

"I forwarded the ship's comms log to the engineering station," Lizzie said. "I was able to get a pin beam onto the rock-hopper's comm pad. Listen for yourself. They're working for a Freeman."

"But you can't be sure it's the stationmaster."

"You're right, junior," the captain said. "It could be the Freeman Merchant Bank, or nic Cartaí, or Kavanagh, or even the Merchant Academy that doesn't want us back. But one end of that transmission is on that rockhopper and the other end is a Freeman's handheld in the stationmaster's office."

"Singh—" Macer said.

"He messaged me," the captain said. "While you were cleaning up. It's like I said. He's been bought out. Wanted to let me know there were no hard feelings. I told him what was going on, and he assured me it wasn't his new employers trying to kill us. If anything the idea seemed to make him mad."

"He said to tell you there's a job waiting, if you want it," Lizzie said. "Provided you make it back in one piece."

"That guy," Ruthie said.

"You're listening in on my calls?" the captain said.

"It's my job," Lizzie said.

"I'm still not buying it," Macer said.

The entire surface of the sensors display lit up in red. The red began flashing.

"Distress beacon," Lizzie said. "Systemwide alert."

"Look at the holo tank," Jimio said.

A long vector had appeared at the edge of the display, slashing inward toward the station. The length of the vector indicated velocity. Whatever it was, it was moving at a considerable fraction of the speed of light.

"Plague ship," Jimio said. "Dead on entry."

"Heading," the captain said.

"Unless they course correct, straight for the nic Cartaí shipyard," Ruthie said.

"I'm telling you," Jimio said. "It's a plague ship. There won't be any course correcting."

The captain laughed. "A dead nic Cartaí ship, coming in hot and plowing through the nic Cartaí yard? They've got their hands full."

"They've got more than that," Ruthie said. "There's no one in range to stop it. It's going through that yard, and all anyone's going to be able to do is stand by and watch."

"There's a thousand people working that yard," Macer said. "A thousand people and their families live there."

"A thousand nic Cartaí people," the captain said.

"We can stop it," Macer said.

"We're not in range," Ruthie said. She plotted an intercept vector anyway. It glowed bright red on in the holo tank.

"I wouldn't stop it if I could," the captain said.

Macer glanced at the engineering display. The superluminal drive tests were still running. It didn't look good. It looked exactly like the sort of ship no stationmaster would want anywhere near a populated system. It looked like a disaster waiting to happen. The drive containment field had two, maybe three cycles left in it before it failed.

Macer kicked the superluminal drive alive. A wave of nausea passed through him, and then he was looking at the engineering display, and the drive read five nines, all but for the oscillation dampers, which hovered just under the critical limit. The damper numbers kept climbing.

He glanced at the holo display. It showed empty, all but for their own trace.

He disengaged the drive. Another wave of nausea washed over him and a dozen alarms started sounding, the engineering console a supernova of flashing red. The containment field oscillated and he damped it, and some of the alarms stopped, and he silenced the rest one by one. He glanced at the holo tank. All the traces were different.

"Now we're in range," Macer said.

"That was mutiny, junior."

"Yes, sir. A hanging offense."

There were only two hanging offenses in Freeman space.

One was mutiny aboard a superluminal.

And the other was failure to render aid.

14

"We need to add thrust to match speed." Macer's finger danced over the in-system drive controls. The pilot had control of the throttles and trim, but everything else he owned. He'd had six months aboard *Four-Squared* to run the numbers and get everything squared away. With Truxton cost was no object. They said that Truxton vessels carried enough spares on board to build another ship, and he believed it. He didn't need spares for in-system drives with a macrofab on board. All he needed was a pattern library and raw materials. Those had been easy to come by for propulsion tech that had been ancient when his granny wore diapers.

Four-Squared had been built to keep up with the League battleships of a century ago, vessels that dwarfed a nic Cartaí long-haul freighter not just in size, but in performance. It took a long time to accelerate, and the nic Cartaí ship must have dropped into the system at a tenth of light speed or better, and it was still accelerating. They didn't need to catch it, but they did need to get close enough that they could lock the tractors onto it, and they needed to stay close enough that they didn't lose lock. It would be a job, but then that's what he was here for. To do the heavy work.

"Stand down, mister," the captain growled. "We are not chasing after that ship."

"We won't be chasing," Ruthie said, "but vectoring in and running parallel. It's a tight squeeze, but unless she finds a burst of speed we can make it."

"Get us alongside," Jimio said. "And I'll make the catch. No sweat."

"All of you," the captain said. "Stand down, and that's an order. We're not wasting a gram of fuel on a nic Cartaí hull."

"I don't think it's a nic Cartaí hull," Lizzie said. "It's not running a transponder, and the drive signature's not nic Cartaí."

Macer glanced at the sensors operator's display. "Unless nic Cartaí's started hiring Truxton power chiefs, that's one of ours. Whoever's tuned the main drive is an artist."

"Whoever's tuned the main drive is pulp on the bulkheads," Jimio said. "We're not pulling anyone alive out of there, else they'd be braking."

"They're braking," Ruthie said.

"It's the congested-space tripwire," Jimio said. "They just passed the beacon."

"They've slowed but they're not stopping," Ruthie said.

"It's an automated system," Jimio said. "Shuts down the main drive. They're not really braking. They're just not accelerating anymore."

"You're right," Ruthie said.

"You know I'm right about that, and I'm right about the rest. The crew is paste, and the only thing flying that bird is the computer."

"They're not answering any hails," Lizzie said.

The captain had a ship's key in his hand as he stepped

toward the piloting station. "I'm shutting this down. Right now."

"You do that and you'll hang," Macer said. "And if a Truxton ship slags the nic Cartaí shipyard they won't stop there. They'll hang every one of the crew, because our internal sensor net's offline and it will only be our words versus their anger. They'll see the net's been slagged, and they'll assume one of us did it to hide our sins.

"If Truxton manages to get out of the system alive he, and everyone who works for him, will be banned from interstellar trade forever. There are League and Ojinate citizens living and working in the nic Cartaí shipyard. Innocent people, whose senseless deaths will be avenged. What's life on Sampson Station going to be like when the League ships stop coming? When the Ojinate turns its back because we turned ours? Because that's what's going to happen if we stand down.

"Shirking Violet, they'll call you in the news, the Coward of Sampson Station, and they'll broadcast the show trial across known space. And they'll broadcast the hangings of those who beg and cry, and delete all the rest, and if you're not wetting yourself on the gallows they'll cut to a commercial break, and douse your trousers, and come back for color commentary afterwards, when you'll have the hood on, and it's only their words and the canned audio track of a grown man weeping and begging for his life anyone will remember, and that will be it. Your legacy. All because you hate nic Cartaí and couldn't do anything about that hate until now."

"You done, junior?"

Macer glanced at his handheld and tapped on it for a second. "No, sir, I'm not. If we somehow manage to stop that ship, they'll be calling you Valiant Violet, and they'll be saying how clever it was for Truxton to keep a big honking superluminal tug in the system, and anything that might have been held against us will just go away. There'll be missing paperwork found, mandatory inspections rubber stamped, charges not just dropped, but never even filed. We might even get medals for stuff we'd get arrested for any other time.

"And Valiant Violet personally? There will be a thousand people and their families ready to kiss your ring and call you Savior. You'll be everywhere in the news. Sampson will be everywhere in the news. How unjust the trade embargo is. How times have changed, and maybe old decisions didn't make sense anymore. Maybe little kids on the station will take up footie ball, just to be like their hero. And best of all?

"Nic Cartaí will owe you. Not Truxton, but Valiant Violet and his crew of spacers from Sampson and New Sparta. That's the sort of vengeance that doesn't just feel good going down. It gets things done."

"You should be a politician," the captain said.

Macer nodded, and fiddled with the drone resting on his workstation. "I'd rather drink molten lead, sir."

"And I'd rather hang than lift a single finger to help a single piece of nic Cartaí filth."

"And us hang with you, sir?"

"My deck, my rules. You're just following orders."

"They have to be lawful orders, sir. Else it's our duty to resist."

"I'd like to see you try, junior."

"Yes, sir." The drone on Macer's work surface twitched. It couldn't lift on repulsors in two gees of gravity. But its main thrusters worked just fine.

The drone rocketed off Macer's workstation surface and took a ballistic path. It fell just enough in two gees of gravity to nail the captain in the crotch.

That took him down fast, but he bounced back up quick. He cursed like spitting fire and lunged at Macer, and Macer dislocated his left kneecap with an adjustable spanner. When that didn't keep him down, Macer shattered the right kneecap, and he was down solid; then a razorgun appeared in the captain's fist, and Macer reversed the spanner and broke the captain's jaw with his knuckles.

That put him down hard.

Macer waved a cloud of spent reaction mass away from his eyes and tossed a handful of zip ties to Jimio. "Both hands and the arms above the elbows."

Macer flexed his fingers and shook his hand out. Kneecaps an autodoc could fix pretty easy. But a caved-in skull was different, and he hadn't wanted to kill the captain, just stop him from getting them and a bunch of innocent people killed. If he'd known how hard the captain's head was, he'd have used the wrench. It felt like he'd punched a bulkhead instead of a man.

Macer scooped up the razorgun and pocketed it.

"What about his feet?"

"I don't think he'll be walking too soon." Jimio zip-tied the captain's arms and dragged him away from the consoles but still in sight.

"THAT PART ABOUT THE DROPPED CHARGES," Ruthie said. "That was for us."

"It was all for you," Macer said. "There was no winning over the captain, not once it became him versus me."

"He hates being called Violet," Jimio said.

Macer grinned. "Don't I know it."

"The Freeman clerk, when we got our work permits years ago," Ruthie said. "She gave us all stupid names, just to mess with us. I don't mind, but the captain, he minds."

Jimio settled back in behind the loadmaster's console. "What are we going to do with this meteor when we catch it?"

"I'll go aboard and shut everything down. Then we'll tow it in just like any other load."

"Plagues ships are a mess. If it's really a plague killed the crew it's rare, but you'll know, and you'll have to ride in on the hulk, in a hardsuit, with atmosphere from *Quadbox*."

"I know the protocol," Macer said.

"Forgot you were an Academy man." Jimio grinned. "More likely than not, it's an inertial damper failure, to kill all the crew at once and leave the ship intact. Lots of splat. Very ugly."

"It could have been a life-support failure," Ruthie said.

"Hah," Jimio said. "If it was life-support failure, they might still be all dead, but they would have had time to rig the ship and squirt a message."

"We're close enough now for visuals." Lizzie repeated the sensor console to the forward display.

"It's obvious what's happened," Jimio said. "The ship and crew have been infected by a terminal case of the blurs."

"Very funny." Lizzie sharpened the image.

"Not by the blurs," Ruthie said. "By idiocy. The boat bay hull is buckled and the bay doors jammed open."

"What's that sticking out?" Jimio said.

"Forward half of a longboat," Ruthie said.

"That's crazy," Jimio said.

"Maybe the plague made them crazy," Ruthie said.

"I've got a visual match with the registry. Truxton's *Golden Parachute*, out of Trinity Station. Merchant Aengus Roche, master and commander."

Macer scrubbed his palm across his face. "I've got a friend on that ship. Seamus mac Donnacha, Roche's merchant apprentice."

Jimio frowned. "You had a friend on that ship, Wrench."

The captain moaned. He'd somehow managed to drag himself toward his day cabin.

"I'm going to get a fast-pallet and haul him down to the infirmary," Macer said. "Then I'll suit up and wait at the airlock."

"Use the liberty boat lock," Ruthie said. "I'll flash the docking lights when we're in position."

"We can do this," Jimio said. "You can do this. Think about the living. And don't look around any more than you have to. There won't be survivors. Get in, get out, easy peasy."

"Unless it really is plague that killed them all," Ruthie said. "Then just get in, shut it down, and stay put."

"Call home when you can," Lizzie said. "Use shipboard comms if your handheld doesn't work."

"Got it." *Screw the fast-pallet.* Macer grabbed the captain by the collar.

He glanced from face to face. "Stop staring at me like I'm not coming back."

"We're just watching to see if you drag the captain or carry him," Jimio said.

"What do you think I'm going to do?"

"Carry him," Lizzie said.

"Until he bites you," Ruthie said.

"And then you'll drag him the rest of the way," Jimio said.

15

Macer had fallen in love with the little maintenance drone. He'd sent it over to survey the *Golden Parachute*'s hull while he cooled his jets in the liberty boat bay airlock. The resulting sensor feed proved better than being there. It was like he had ultra and infra and x-ray vision all at once, and switching between them took little more than a thought.

Boarding and powering down a Freeman merchant vessel proved more of a challenge. Engineering and propulsion were at one end of a long stressed tube they called the mast. The bridge and everything else were at the other end of the tube. The only ways to move from one space to the other were crawling along the inside of the tube, which a drone could do but a human couldn't, or riding inside a little tramcar that ran on a track along the outside of the tube, a thing they called a mastcart. The cart was sized for space-born Freemen. Macer could squeeze into one if he had to, but he didn't like it, and he couldn't do that in a hardsuit. So long as a risk of plague existed, the suit stayed on. He'd moved a three-day supply of suit air into the airlock with him and stood ready to haul it over to the *Golden Parachute* once he decided where he would break in.

Engineering seemed the obvious choice. The congested-system tripwire had already shut down the main drive so the ship wasn't accelerating. He could put on the brakes from engineering, provided he didn't have to steer the thrusters. Modern ships had an automated system that linked the Templeman drive to the ship's thrusters, so that engaging the superluminal drive rotated the thrusters into axial alignment with the hull, and aimed in the direction of motion. That way when the drive disengaged the pilot didn't have to worry about where the thrusters pointed. If they popped into a system on top of another mass they could slam on the brakes without having to aim them first.

Older ships didn't have the system. And older pilots didn't like them, because they didn't like anything new, or anything that made piloting a superluminal easier. If anyone could pilot a superluminal, then a lot of otherwise useless First Families spawn would have to look for other work. The sort of smelly underclass jobs where they might break a fingernail or raise a sweat.

The thrusters checked out. He would enter through the engineering hatch.

Macer brought his little buddy back and had it carry a transfer line over to the *Golden Parachute*. It latched the line onto a fixture made for just that purpose on the vessel's hull. He'd already clipped his end onto a similar fixture on *Four-Squared*'s hull. The riskiest part of the whole operation, it would be doubly so if someone other than the computer drove *Golden Parachute*. Under computer control he only needed to worry about Ruthie, and could she hold station while he made the transfer.

He glanced at his handheld. So far she'd held the two ships in sync like they were welded together. Which they might be in software if she'd synced her piloting computer to *Golden Parachute*'s. They were both Truxton hulls and shared a common system architecture. She couldn't control the stricken vessel, but she might be able to let it control *Four-Squared*'s vector, like syncing up warships in formation.

Macer clipped the spare air to the line and sent it over. Then he clipped his own safety harness to the line and shoved off. Once in the remote lock, he unclipped and stowed the spare air. He sent the drone over to unclip the transfer line at the far end and had it ride the line as he spooled. Now all he had to do was get in.

He tried his acting chief engineer's credentials.

Huh. *That worked.*

He didn't think that it should have worked, even though some small chance existed. There were only three ways it could have worked; if his credentials included a master key, if the *Golden Parachute*'s engineer hadn't ever locked the system down, or if someone had wiped the system and hadn't reinitialized it.

He'd used Singh's chief engineer's credentials as well as his own, and he didn't think Singh's credentials had a master key. His definitely didn't. And the hull wouldn't have passed routine inspection if its hatch locks didn't lock. Could someone have wiped the system and left it open?

Maybe, but why would they?

Macer swung the hatch open and sent the drone in. He used it to look around. Then he hauled the spare air inside and dogged the hatch behind him. He couldn't take off the hardsuit but it felt safer, somehow, with the hatch closed. He glanced around. There weren't any crewmen pasted to the bulkheads, so that was a relief. But there weren't any crewmen's bodies either. It looked like there's been a firefight in the compartment, and a cleanup afterward. There were dark stains and deep scratches on the deck.

He checked his handheld. He was out of communications

range with *Four-Squared*. He needed to find a local comms station before he could check in. He needed to check in so that *Four-Squared* could stand off when he put on the brakes.

He found the communications station and fired it up. Lizzie answered immediately.

"I'm going to put on the brakes. The thrusters look aligned, but you should stand off anyway."

"Roger that," Lizzie said. "What's it like over there?"

"Light," Macer said. "They're running less than half a gee inside the hull. Feels like I'm floating after *Four-Squared*."

"No, I mean, what sort of mess?"

"No mess. Deserted," Macer said. "Looks like somebody had a war then hauled off all the casualties and debris."

"Ruthie says we're moving off now. You can commence braking in zero six hundred seconds."

Macer started a timer on his handheld. "Braking in zero six hundred seconds. I'll look around until then."

"Can you pull up internal sensors and send us a feed?"

"I can try. Stand by."

"Wave for the cameras," Lizzie said.

Macer glanced at the sensor and waved.

"Got it. Now how about sensors on the shiny end of the stick?"

Macer tried to bring up the sensors on the bridge. "No joy."

"Try the boat bay."

"Got it." Macer laughed. "Some idiot fired up a longboat's main drive inside the hull."

"It looks toasty in there," Lizzie said.

"Sorry," Macer said. "It's not funny. You know how when you're watching a horror story, and it's so shocking and sick that you laugh instead of scream?"

"I thought I was the only one that did that."

"Everybody thinks they're the only one. Something really terrible happened here. Something the opposite of funny."

"Looks like all the internal sensors forward of the boat bay are offline."

"Unsurprising, given the damage. I want to make sure everything is strapped down here before I start the burn."

"So shut up and do it."

Macer worked his way from one end of engineering to the other, recording his progress and documenting everything for the inquiry that would certainly follow.

Someone had disposed of *Golden Parachute*'s entire crew on the dirty end of the stick. If there were survivors on the shiny end, he'd be surprised. He was likely the only living soul on a deadly missile aimed at the nic Cartaí shipyard.

He sounded the deceleration alarm just in case there were survivors. Then he put the drone in auto-hover and belted in at the drive control console. If everything worked right, the ship would decelerate rapidly and he wouldn't even feel it. If nothing worked right, he'd be pulp on the bulkhead behind him. The reality on most ships turned out to be somewhere in between. He might end up with anything from a nosebleed to a broken spine and still count himself lucky, so long as the ship slowed.

Macer toggled the thrusters to standby. When his handheld beeped, he gritted his teeth and mashed the brakes on.

Unbelievable. The ship's engineer really was an artist. He didn't feel even the tiniest sensation of slowing.

Macer glanced at his handheld.

Scratch that. It didn't feel like the ship was slowing because the ship wasn't slowing.

Macer unbelted and dropped to the deck. He peeled the access panel off the bottom of the workstation surface.

Someone had cut the leads on the thruster controls.

Then they'd spliced the control harness to a second harness, one going somewhere else, another console in engineering, another console on the bridge, a signal transceiver so the ship could be controlled remotely, it could be a hundred different things the leads had been spliced to, and it didn't matter.

They'd left enough of a tag end on the switch that he could see the color of the leads and match them up with the spliced-together harness. He examined the switch. It had always amazed him that Truxton kept these old consoles on the merchant vessels when the new ones were smaller, and more power efficient, and field programmable through software. Now it made sense.

The thruster control was a simple momentary single-pole switch. If it broke he could fix it. And if the whole console got ripped off and blown out of the hull he could still fix the thrusters, even in a hardsuit, just by taking out his wire cutters, and cutting the harness, and stripping the wires, and touching them together.

Like this.

IT FELT like a giant hand had slapped him against the bulkhead behind him. His tools were scattered and it took him a minute to find his handheld. He stared at the handheld's display. The ship had definitely slowed. Touching the wires together had worked. Now all he had to do was hold the wires together longer, long enough to slow the ship enough that *Four-Squared*'s tractors could maintain grip. Once they were grappled on, the fleet tug's massive in-system drives could finish slowing the ship.

Macer gripped a wire in either hand and braced himself. He touched them together and again felt the immediate reaction. He lost his grip as a loose screwdriver crashed against his helmet visor.

This wasn't working. He needed to twist the wires together.

Then he wouldn't need to hold on. Sooner or later the thrusters would overheat or run out of fuel. And even if they didn't, the ship would eventually begin to move backward, out-system, away from the nic Cartaí shipyard and the thousands living there.

He had a plan. It paid to have a plan. He found his pliers. He bent the wires into open loops and overlapped the loops, careful that they didn't touch. Then he pinched them together with the pliers.

IT PAID to have a good plan. And that hadn't been one. He felt the ship decelerating through the bulkhead he lay pinned to like a bug. He'd lost his handheld again and he couldn't reach the wires to pull them apart. His hardsuit had been holed, a screwdriver jammed through his helmet visor, the end of the blade millimeters from his right eye.

He would pull the screwdriver free when he could move his arms.

That wasn't presently an option.

He hoped all the thrusters burned out soon. They weren't rated for continuous operation. If they burned out one at a time, he wouldn't be pinned against the bulkhead, but tossed around the compartment, where his helmet would slam against one workstation or the other and finish the job of stuffing the business end of the screwdriver into his brain.

Twisting the wires together had not been a good plan.

All the thrusters cut off simultaneously.

Macer yanked the screwdriver from his helmet. He twisted the helmet off and tossed it across the compartment. He scrambled to find his handheld. The display had cracked but it was still working.

They'd done it. Truxton's *Golden Parachute* stood at dead

stop. There must have been some sort of automated cutoff rigged to the thrusters. They'd shut down the instant they'd reached null velocity. He wasn't aware of any such system, but then he didn't keep current on long-haul maneuvering-control technology. Whatever the reason, the plan had worked. *Four-Squared* could tractor the hull in and any sort of inquiry wouldn't be directed at the tug's crew, but whoever was responsible for what had happened on *Golden Parachute*.

The captain had it right *and* wrong. Macer wasn't very street-smart. But his father was a politician, and all his father's cronies politicians, and just no getting away from all the back room talk growing up. Macer knew how the connected and the wannabe connected played the game, and there was no percentage in going after *Four-Squared* and Truxton, not after the rescue they'd pulled off.

Like it or not, they were heroes. It would take a rare and stupid man to hold a grudge in light of that.

Macer fired up the communications console. "Truxton's *Golden Parachute* to Truxton's *Tractor Four-Squared*. I require a tug."

He waited, wishing his hardsuit hadn't been holed. The inside of *Golden Parachute* reeked, like an electrical fire crossed with a bonfire of discarded tires crossed with a barbecue. It was the sort of stink that might wash off but would never go away.

He waited for a while and repeated the hail.

Years from now he wouldn't remember the details.

But he would never forget that smell.

He waited a little longer and tried again.

This time he got an answer.

"Truxton's *Golden Parachute*," the captain said. "This is Truxton's *Tractor Four-Squared*. And you can go fuck yourself, junior. *Violent* out."

16

Things could be worse. He was in a ship and with air. It wasn't a plague ship, or didn't appear to be, just an abandoned ship, and it wasn't rocketing headlong in-system to a certain catastrophe anymore.

His hardsuit had been holed, but there would be hardsuits by the airlock forward, and while the comms console in engineering wasn't patched into the long-range antennas, the comms station on the bridge would be. All he needed to do was hand over hand along the hull to the bridge airlock, fire up the comms, and call for help.

He probably didn't even need to do that because help would already be on the way. The initial distress beacon would have gone out to every vessel in the system, and someone would eventually respond. That might take days, though, and while his hardsuit had water, it didn't have food. He wouldn't mind skipping a meal or two but not unless he had to.

There weren't any spare hardsuits at the airlock.

The idea that he was trapped in engineering made his stomach growl. Technically, he wasn't *absolutely* trapped in engineering. He could use the mastcart to get to the bridge, unless someone had broken it.

The engineering end of the mast lay through a hatch in the forward bulkhead. He'd checked the compartment out earlier, and it was clean of victims and debris. The mastcart sat parked at the other end of the mast. He pressed the call button and waited.

And waited.

And waited.

Not only did riding in a mastcart feel like being jammed into a coffin one size too small. It moved slower than draining gear oil at absolute zero. And mastcarts stunk, and harbored more microbes than a biohazard lab, and getting in or out was like putting tooth gel back into the tube.

The little deathtrap was originally designed as a visual inspection platform for the containers clamped to the mast, so it crawled along at a constant speed when powered up and just sat there when not. Like most every system on Freeman merchant vessels it was ancient tech, crude and easy to repair in any port. Most of the family ships didn't even have a fab onboard, or spares, for that matter. But if a merchant could find someone with a milling machine, or even just a forge and anvil, they could fix most anything mechanical on a Freeman ship, provided it didn't need to hold pressure.

There were a lot of reasons Macer didn't want to work on the long-hauls. He told people it was because they were dangerous, which they were, and because it was hard to find a pretty date, or a good beer, which it was, but he didn't tell them the real reasons, because a lot of his friends and fellow Academy students grew up on family ships, and were proud of it.

But those hulls were rubbish when they were new, and ancient tech when the Huangxu Eng stole the designs from the League and started cranking them out in volume. Tradition was nice, and every hull had a history, but just because your granny stole that ship four centuries ago and hung onto it ever since didn't make it fun to work on, or satisfying to lie in your bunk and think about. About how you could make it stronger, faster, more efficient. Macer didn't want to end up as one of those guys bragging that his long-haul beater was better than new.

You could strap a saddle on a cow and call it a horse. But it would never be able to run with the thoroughbreds. Not even if you stuck a rocket up its tailpipe.

No one would ever get rich working the in-system tugs. But he'd seen rich up close, and it wasn't all that. He could be rich as the Freeman Merchant Bank, and there'd still be stuff he wanted that he couldn't buy. Like a tomorrow that wasn't just yesterday all over again. There was nothing to learn on the long-haulers. Because nothing ever changed but the scenery.

The mast cart bumped against the bulkhead. A green light illuminated.

If' he'd had more seat time with the drone he could have it work the cart, and work the comms console on the bridge. As it was, he didn't have the fine muscle control or the reflexes, and those weren't predefined tasks he could call up from the drone's task library. So he had to ride. And the ride would be nasty.

Macer shucked out of his hardsuit and rubbed his arms. It was always cold on the long-haulers, and Truxton long-haulers were colder than most.

You couldn't wear a skinsuit inside a hardsuit because it interfered with the interface sensors, not to mention the plumbing. If he was lucky there'd be a hardsuit at the far airlock and he could tog up. If not, he could rummage through the crew quarters for some clothes.

His tools wouldn't fit in the mastcart with him, but his acting chief engineer's credentials would. And his handheld.

He had to slide into the mastcart headfirst, lying on his back, one arm at his side, the other crooked over the top of his head. Then he had to worm his way further in, until his elbow touched the forward bulkhead, and draw his feet in until his knees touched the top of the cart. And then he had to work the controls with his tongue, one lever to close the hatch, which sealed with a hiss and a green light, and one other control, a toggle for forward or reverse.

The tiny coffin began to trundle forward. There was no speed control. The cart moved slow enough that anyone inside could examine the mastclamps in detail. Mastclamps were the mechanical grippers that held cargo containers to the mast. On a full load there'd be a lot of clamps to inspect. It looked like there were only four containers on this mast and they were spaced out along the length of the mast.

His calves were beginning to knot by the time the tiny cart bumped against the aft boat bay bulkhead and the green light changed to yellow. He toggled the hatch open and dragged himself out. He lay on the deck and panted for a while. He felt clammy and dripped sweat. Eventually he managed to get his legs under him.

A hatch forward led to a security vestibule and airlock. There would be a hardsuit rack beside the airlock.

The rack was empty.

An airlock forward led to the boat bay, where he was not going, because a longboat stood jammed halfway out the boat bay doors, and even if the force window remained intact, some idiot had lit the main drive up inside the hull, so there would be lots of debris on the deck.

The bad news? He wiggled his bare toes. He'd had to ditch the hardsuit's boots as well.

The good news? The ladder that led to the hatch that led to the maintenance tube that ran above the boat bay all the way to the airlock at the far end of the boat bay.

He scooped up his handheld and credentials and climbed.

The hatch opened without asking for authentication. So

that answered that. The ship's security system had been wiped and never reinitialized.

He crawled into the tube, which was even colder than the airlock, and scuttled along its length. There were conduits and pipes and junction boxes on both sides and above him. He didn't think a main-drive power-up in the boat bay would breach the maintenance tube, because that was a foreseeable failure mode, and the tube armored against those. This was a vulnerable part of the ship, and the fact that it hadn't been properly secured bothered him.

He popped the hatch and looked around the airlock before climbing out. The hardsuit rack was empty here as well.

He climbed down and thought about what to do next. The stern hatch led to the boat bay. The forward hatch led to a corridor that eventually led to the bridge. The portside hatch wasn't just a hatch, but an airlock. And the starboard hatch was the infirmary. On Truxton ships, medical help was always right next to the boat bay.

Maybe he'd find a medic's gown in the infirmary. Some of those patient's slippers would be nice too. His teeth were beginning to chatter.

It looked like there'd been a dust-up in the infirmary. A medical cart had toppled over, and instruments scattered around, and dried blood caked the deck. A big chunk of what looked like a longboat's piloting console strut lay on a worktable, one end jagged and the other sheared through cleanly. A cryo chamber lay spilled off a fast-pallet by the starboard bulkhead, and a rack of four autodocs lined the aft bulkhead.

Two of the autodocs were occupied.

He checked the telltales and found the contents in seriously bad shape. And they weren't popping out soon. When they did one of them would likely land in a body bag. But there'd likely be a sole survivor, and someone to explain the setup.

He rummaged around and found some disposable surgical

aprons and some shocks, *shoe-socks*, the kind with little grippers on the soles. The paper-thin aprons wouldn't help, but the shocks were a godsend. He pulled them on, wiggled his toes, and sighed. At least his feet weren't freezing anymore.

He found a box of energy bars and wolfed down a couple. He drank water from the scrub sink tap.

Whoever had abandoned this ship had left people behind. That didn't seem like a good sign. Because maybe they hadn't abandoned the ship after all. Maybe he just hadn't run into them yet.

Macer glanced around the compartment. Surgical instruments littered the floor, the sort of stuff he could use as a weapon if he wanted to nibble his opponent to death up close and personal.

Then he saw the hammer. The business end of it was a triangle of some sort of rubbery material. He tested it, and it proved hard enough to make a dent.

And it felt good in his hands.

He had clothing, sort of, and a full belly, sort of, and a weapon, sort of.

He was sort of ready for anything his caveman ancestors were.

Chances were he wouldn't run into anyone. But it didn't make sense to look for trouble until after he'd called for help. He'd search the crew quarters for clothes after he'd used the comms console on the bridge.

SOMETHING NASTY HAD HAPPENED on the bridge. The mess had been cleaned up, but the stench of burnt plastic clawed at his nostrils. The pilot's console had been slagged at some time and repaired.

The communications console seemed intact.

And occupied.

The woman looked like some stationmaster's matronly aunt dressed in dark-blue utilities, all except for the silver box in one hand and the razorgun in the other.

She pressed a button on the top of the silver box and grinned.

She must have expected something to happen that didn't, because she looked down at the silver box like it was broken.

She looked up again and a rubbery hammer struck her right between the eyes.

She went down like a sack.

Macer scooped up the razorgun and started to pocket it, except he couldn't, because all he had on was some sickbay shocks. He was still thinking about where to stow the gun when a blue line of fire wrapped around his wrist and tugged.

"Drop the gun or lose the hand," a young woman said.

Macer recognized the blue line. It was the containment field around the monomolecular filament of a Huangxu overseer's rod. If that containment field dropped, the filament would slice through his wrist before he could blink, and he already knew he wouldn't like what came next, because Rik Severn hadn't liked it.

"Can I set the gun down?" Macer said. "There's a round in the chamber and the safety's off."

"Do so," she said, "and back away."

He did so.

Macer let out a long slow breath when the blue line disappeared from his wrist.

She crossed the compartment and helped the older woman to her feet. She was also dressed in dark-blue utilities. She picked up the silver box and aimed it at him. She pressed the button, and when it still didn't do anything, pocketed it.

"You don't have an implant," she said.

"Not anymore. It kept distracting me with stuff I don't care about."

She glanced at him and then it clicked.

"You're Aoife nic Cartaí."

"And you are?"

"Macer Gant. We've met."

"I doubt that."

"We did, and you just don't remember."

She looked him up and down. The corner of her mouth twitched. "I would remember."

Macer glanced around the bridge. "Where's the rest of your pirate crew?"

"Off pirating."

"So it's just you two trying to steal a Truxton ship?"

She stared at him.

"Ciarán mac Diarmuid," he said.

Her brow furrowed. She stepped to the side, studying him in profile. She walked around him, a full one-eighty, studying him.

He followed her with his gaze.

She stopped when she was behind him, considering him. "On Trinity Station. At the zero-radial tram. You were in an Academy student's uniform."

He turned to face her. "So you do remember me."

"I do," she said. "You are Ciarán mac Diarmuid's..."

"Wingman," the older woman said.

"Not that," she said. "More a sidekick, I think."

"Very funny," Macer said.

"How so?" nic Cartaí said.

"Because you've got that backward. I'm not the sidekick." Macer aimed the famous Gant smile at her and amped the gain to eleven. "He is."

"An interesting theory."

Macer could feel his smile fading. "You've maneuvered me. Now *your* sidekick is behind me. With another gun."

"I'm more of a henchman than a sidekick," the older woman said.

"And she doesn't have a gun," nic Cartaí said.

Macer started to turn.

"It looks like a long section of thick-walled conduit from here."

His forehead hit the deck.

It didn't just look like a long section of thick-walled conduit. It felt like one.

Macer shook his head, and got his elbows under him, and then his palms were on the deck, and he was staring at an ankle, a thin and shapely one, and then he saw stars, and shook his head again, and he was staring at another ankle, a thick meaty one jutting out of a steel-toed hullwalker.

"What are you playing at," nic Cartaí said.

"I'm trying not to kill him." the henchmatron said.

Good. That was good.

That henchmatron chuckled. "Not all at once, anyway."

Bad. That was bad.

Macer tried to push himself upright.

"We have work to do," nic Cartaí said.

"Fine," the henchmatron huffed. "Say hello to the pretty stars, Mr. Sidekick."

Macer didn't want to say hello to the pretty stars.

He—

17

Gallarus System, Earth Restoration League

Merchant Apprentice Ciarán mac Diarmuid laughed. The deck beneath his feet shivered as the second-epoch League survey vessel *Quite Possibly Alien* plunged into the photosphere of a star.

The forward display mercifully showed black, the bridge crew performing their functions on the individual displays of their workstations. The bridge luminaires had been dimmed so that each workstation stood out in individual pools of light. Other than the whispering breath of the ship's air handlers and the constant low rumble of the in-system drive, the bridge remained in silence, but for Sensors Operator Yuan Ko Shan's periodic hull-temperature announcements and Engineer Erik Hess's quiet cursing.

Hess acted as *Quite Possibly Alien*'s backup pilot, and with Pilot Helen Konstantine away on a mission with the merchant captain, sat his first shift at the helm of the ancient starship. That *Quite Possibly Alien's* superluminal drive operated differently than a standard Templeman drive could be grasped intellectually. Experiencing the drive in operation proved a different story.

Ship's Navigator Maura Kavanagh had explained to Ciarán how the ship gathered samples from the star's mass. How she examined the samples to determine the paths to likely destinations. How the longer the ship gathered samples, the better her calculations would be. How she was an insane risk taker and adrenaline addict. One who enjoyed pushing herself and the ship to its limits.

Most of this explanation she delivered in words. The rest she exhibited in deeds, and not just while in the navigator's seat.

Everyone on board knew this about Maura, including Hess. Ciarán had concluded that the constant "shishishishi" sound coming from Hess wasn't something he was aware of, or a random sound, but what abject terror sounded like in the man's flat frontier accent.

"Take us in closer," Maura said.

"Thirty-five hundred," Ko Shan said.

Hess bumped the thrusters without dropping a syllable.

"Thirty-six hundred," Ko Shan said. She glanced at Ciarán and winked. Ko Shan's subdural sensor net gleamed blue beneath her skin, a second nervous system that was nearly invisible when she wasn't jacked into the sensor rig. That she and Ciarán were now friends was as unexpected as the technological marvels hidden beneath Ko Shan's flawless Huangxu skin.

"Thirty-seven hundred. The gradient is increasing."

"Ship," Captain Agnes Swan said.

"I am here," *Quite Possibly Alien* said. The ship's alto voice seemed to come from everywhere and nowhere.

"Forward hull sensors to the main display," Swan said.

"Thirty-eight hundred."

"Take us in closer."

A roiling yellow-white light bathed the bridge. The boiling surface of Gallarus system's star seemed to engulf them.

"Thirty-nine hundred."

"Closer."

"Four thousand."

"Four thousand one hundred."

The bridge seemed to grow hotter as the unfiltered light of the star washed over them, an impossibility, as far as Ciarán knew.

Unless...

Ciarán shifted so that he could see Agnes Swan, old-school Truxton superluminal captain and purebred Huangxu Eng. She and Ciarán did not get on, or rather they hadn't, though that might be changing. He had been entirely mistaken about her. That she was born a close relative of the Huangxu emperor meant less to her than the captain's bars she'd earned.

The ship's captain glanced up from the ship's environmental controls to find him watching. She blanked the display and placed her hands in her lap.

"Four thousand two hundred.

"Four thousand three hundred."

Swan had adjusted the temperature on the bridge, cranking up the heat.

"Four thousand four hundred."

The boiling surface of the star seemed to explode toward them.

"Mass ejection," Ko Shan said.

"I'm almost done," Maura said.

"Five thousand," Ko Shan said.

"Five thousand five hundred. Six hundred. Seven hundred."

"Done."

"Mr. Hess," Swan said. "Get us out of here."

Hess hammered the piloting console controls.

Nothing happened.

"Shishishishishishi..."

He hammered the controls again.

A claxon began to blare.

"SHISHISHISHI..."

CIARÁN LEANED FORWARD and tapped the superluminal drive control. "Wrong button."

A wave of nausea washed through him, not the prolonged suffering of a Templeman-drive translation from universe to universe but a minor disorientation as his mind wrestled with the subliminal telltales of a shift of reference within a single frame.

There existed two controls on the piloting console with the labels worn off. One engaged the superluminal drive. The other muted the ship's alarms.

Ciarán pressed the alarm control and the claxon immediately cut off.

Hess lurched from the bridge and into the corridor. Ciarán could hear him dry heaving through the open hatch.

"One hundred hours," Swan said. "Do you know the significant of this number, Freeman whelp?"

"In the set of all ship's losses attributed to pilot error, one hundred hours is the mode."

"And very nearly the median," Swan said. "Experienced enough to be overconfident. Not experienced enough to live to learn the truth. We are each imperfect, and one mistake away from oblivion."

Ciarán glanced at Maura. "You got the data you needed."

"Twice over. I could have done my nails if they weren't already perfect."

"And the ejecta?"

"Predicted," Ko Shan said. "Though it was somewhat more violent than expected."

"But we were never in any danger."

"Had you not engaged the superluminal drive, the outer hull would have boiled away," Swan said.

"And the inner hull as well," Ko Shan said. "As I said, somewhat more violent than expected."

The captain tapped a data crystal on the arm of her command chair. "Mr. Hess is a very intelligent and imaginative man, and by all accounts a competent backup shuttle pilot. Under normal circumstances, on a normal vessel that would be sufficient. But this is not a normal vessel, and these are not normal circumstances."

"You're saying we need a more experienced pilot."

"Or a pilot *less* intelligent and *less* imaginative, and *less* experienced. Someone who can plunge into the corona of a star without understanding the fragility of a ship's hull, or comprehending the sudden destructive threat latent near a stellar mass. In short, someone who is careful because they are uncertain and fearless because they are clueless."

"And able to pilot a starship."

"Able to pilot a second-epoch League vessel of any kind."

"I can only think of one person who can do that. And she's with the merchant captain."

Swan nodded. "I can think of another."

"Now that you mention it, so can I. But you just called him clueless."

"I also called him fearless."

"Okay, I'll do it," Ciarán said. "But only for the star-diving part. Hess should do all of the rest."

"With you shadowing him. We had a pilot and a backup pilot because the merchant captain believed we needed both."

Great. One more task he could fail at, and Swan's primary motive in asking him to attempt it. She'd begun studying for the merchant exam and meant to pass it before him. That would make her not only ship's captain, but ship's merchant.

And that would make him cargo.

He studied for the exam in every spare moment. Now there'd be even fewer of those.

"Star diving. I am *so* going to use that from now on. Maura Kavanagh. *Stardiver.*"

The captain tapped the data crystal against her command chair again and again.

Ciarán knew that gesture. "You're trying to find some flaw in your logic. Because we've agreed on something."

The tapping stopped. "No I'm not."

Ko Shan chuckled. "And thus the order of the universe is restored."

18

H ess set up the holo tank in the ship's mess. He kicked it alive.

Maura Kavanagh stood. She projected an image of a yellow-white star in the tank. A label popped up next to the star.

Gallarus.

"Are you wearing glitter?" Natsuko asked. The ship's golden-skinned medic inhaled carbon dioxide–rich atmosphere from a gilded party mask, one depicting the face of a sleeping child.

"I like to look hot when presenting."

"And you think glitter makes you look hot," Ko Shan said.

"Hotter."

"It just makes you look glittery," Natsuko said.

"Says the golden girl."

"This is the point where the merchant captain usually interrupts," Ciarán said.

"And?" Maura said.

"Pretend she just did," Ship's Captain Swan said.

"Fine. Try not to focus on my hotness, but on the image in

the holo tank before you. It depicts the stellar mass of the Gallarus system. Only hours ago we *stardived* that stellar mass and captured enough information to calculate several possible routes, one or more of which will permit us to exit the system and continue to work our way to Contract system and our responsibilities there."

The image of Gallarus's star seemed to recede as several lines began to snake out from it. Stars of varying sizes and colors bloomed into existence at the ends of the lines. All the stars seemed to be of Gallarus's size or better, and all seemed to be at least yellow-white in color temperature. One was so white it appeared blue.

Mrs. Amati flexed the fingers of her augmented hand. "None of the routes detected are a direct route." Her human eye appeared to gaze at Maura. Her augmented eye scanned the holo tank.

"Good catch. Contract system's star is a yellow star, and none of these are. Some of these stars are known to us."

She projected labels next to about half of the stars.

"Some of these stars are not known to us."

She labeled those stars in orange. *Unknown.*

A survey vessel like *Quite Possibly Alien* could travel to those unknown destinations and chart them. Once charted those systems could be integrated into the net of stars conventional vessels might safely travel to. Transiting uncharted systems could prove dangerous, however, and they had a deadline to meet. They would avoid such systems whenever there were known alternatives available.

"The names displayed are the Freeman designations for the systems. Some of you may know them by different names. What they are called isn't as important as where they are, in the sense that some of these systems are in the League, now labeled in blue, the Ojinate, labeled in green, and the Hundred Planets, now labeled in red."

"Solidly in each polity," Hess said, "or in as of last report?"

"Good question. All solidly in, nothing in the Outer Reach, or any other area contested in the past one hundred years. If I show the system as a Hundred Planets system you can safely assume it will still be a Hundred Planets system when we arrive. Likewise for the League and the Ojinate systems."

"Why aren't any of these destinations in the Alexandrine?" Amati asked.

"Some likely are. But we don't have charts for most of the Alexandrine."

"And there are no Freeman systems," Natsuko said.

"Unsurprising, given how few Freeman systems there are."

"How do these systems relate to Contract space?" Swan said.

"Unknown," Maura said. "Statistically they each appear to move us closer to Contract space. But we still run the risk of being cul-de-saced. And if that happens, it's best if it happens in an active system with a functioning station."

Hess scratched his chin. "Getting cul-de-saced would be bad."

"Bad, but not lethal in an occupied system. But if we jumped into an unknown system and it turned out to be uninhabited? Or it turned out to be inhabited, but without superluminal tech? We'd have to crawl out on sublight drives."

"And probably die of old age before we made it to the next port," Ko Shan said.

"Then let's not jump into one of those," Hess said.

"Thus the list." Maura wiped the unknown stars from the holo tank. "Ciarán has some additional non-navigational requirements we need to consider."

"For now," Ciarán said, "we want to avoid League worlds so that Hess and Amati don't have to report in." They'd received notice that they'd been cashiered and ordered to turn in their gear. It might be a mistake, and it might not be. So long as they stayed out of League space, they couldn't comply. Complying meant Amati losing all her military-grade augmentation. Once back in range of a superluminal node, they could find out if their orders were a mistake or not safely, from a foreign station, and at a distance. If they proved real orders, they could decide what to do then.

Maura wiped the League systems from the holo tank.

"And we'd *like* to transit a Huangxu system so we can get a current data dump from the news services." Agnes Swan's brother had been imprisoned, and no one knew why. If they were going to do anything to help Danny Swan, they needed to know more. Helping Swan, though, had to take a back seat to living up to their merchant contract.

"What we *need* to do is scrounge up something useful to trade in the Contract system. It doesn't pay to deadhead there. And even though this contract with Adderly is set to pay both ways, we might show up and Adderly refuses to honor the deal. Or she might be dead. It's a war zone, after all."

"And?" Swan said.

"And that means Pinion, in the Ojinate."

"Because?" Ko Shan said.

"Because Kazuki Ryuu is there," Natsuko said.

Maura wiped the star projection and replaced it with the promotional head shot of the *Noh* actress.

"I remember her," Hess said.

"We all remember her," Swan said.

Ciarán had screened several of Ryuu's recorded dramas, and Natsuko had seen one and said he should show it in the mess, as entertainment. In the end, the entire crew had binge-watched over thirty Kazuki Ryuu *Noh* plays.

"She is very glittery," Ko Shan said.

"And she is extremely popular in Contract system," Ciarán said. "We can license her work and make it available for a fee. We don't have time to hustle up a physical cargo. "

"Kazuki Ryuu is a man's name," Ko Shan said.

Natsuko sighed. "So you have said."

Maura chuckled. "Repeatedly."

"We won't need to dock at the station," Captain Swan said.

"According to our records, Pinion has a Huangxu consulate," Ciarán said. "One with a data feed we can tap without breaking local law. It also has a superluminal node we can use to contact the League."

"Will Gag sees more stars." The ship's victualer pointed a pale finger at the holo tank.

"Ciarán's special project." Maura highlighted the second star map.

"It's actually the ship's special project. I just agreed to help. Ship?"

"I am here."

Wisp growled. She lay stretched out on the deck and staring at the luminaire overhead. Her tail thumped once and she glanced at Ciarán. She glanced away and began to clean her paw. She didn't like the ship's voice, and she distrusted the ship's luminaires.

"Talk us through the project," Ciarán said.

"There were nine survey vessels such as myself commissioned and dispatched. Of those nine only two are currently active in the Registry; the hulk *Sudden Fall of Darkness* and me. Since we must... *stardive*... simply to progress, it seems logical to also use our time in the star's photosphere to search for evidence of the six remaining vessels. I cannot pinpoint their location directly from data collected in a single system. But I do know what to look for, namely evidence of sudden supernovas and gamma ray bursts, followed by the creation of massive black holes.

"The more systems we search, the more I can refine the list of possibles. If one of my sisters did encounter hostile alien life, I may be able to pinpoint the discovery's location from the evidence of her sacrifice."

"I don't get it," Hess said.

"The League was worried that aliens could follow the ship's back trail to human space," Ciarán said. "So the ship has countermeasures to prevent that from happening."

"What's gamma rays and massive black holes have to do with that?" Hess said.

"Those are the countermeasures," Swan said.

Hess laughed.

"They are the evidence," the ship said. "The countermeasures are simply the mechanisms by which a minder may collapse a star."

"Oh, that's all," Hess said. "Good thing we never ran into any hostile aliens."

"Other than the riders," Ko Shan said.

"Will Gag knows the riders. The riders are not alien."

"*Quite Possibly Alien* believes the riders are made using alien technology," Ciarán said. "So she wants to look for evidence of alien first contact."

"The human race has visited hundreds, even thousands of planets, and not once have we found evidence of life we didn't seed ourselves," Natsuko said.

"There are the Outsiders," Amati said.

"They possess human DNA," Natsuko said. "A creation of the Alexandrians."

"You've never seen one," Amati said. "Nobody human could have dreamed those things up."

"Then explain the human DNA," Natsuko said.

"Not my area. But I don't care how good the Alexis are at gene manipulation. Those monsters didn't come out of an Alexandrian lab."

"Will Gag knows the Outsiders. The Outsiders are not made in labs."

Ciarán glanced at the tall, skeletal man. He'd once been a

brilliant scientist according to the ship. "Where are they made, Mr. Gagenot?"

Gagenot knotted his boney hands together. He rocked back and forth in his seat. "Will Gag cannot say."

"The net of all of this," Ciarán said, "Is that we'll need to extend the duration of our... *stardives*... so that the ship can run its search. And it won't do that unless we all agree that the additional risk is worth it."

Ciarán glanced from face to face. "No one wants to ask how much risk?"

"Ship, you think it's worth the risk?" Hess said.

"I would not have asked otherwise."

"That's good enough for me."

"So we're in agreement," Ciarán said. "We'll run the ship's project. And we're outbound for Pinion."

All but the ship's captain said, "Aye."

Swan examined Ciarán. "If I say no?"

"I'd ask you why."

"On the way to Pinion."

"On the way."

"And if the whole crew had said no?"

"I'd ask them why."

"On the way to Pinion."

Ciarán nodded. "Aye."

19

The longboat docked with the Invincible Spear Bearers of Imperial Wrath's vessel. Old met Ciarán at the airlock.

"Pain and death to our foes," Old said.

"Indeed," Ciarán said. "Thank you for seeing me on such short notice."

"We live to serve, Merchant Lord."

"About that," Ciarán said. "I was wondering, do you live to serve all together, or do you sometimes divide your forces?"

"We have done so in the past. But the consequences of such a division have been dire."

"In what way?"

"Those who lead a detachment begin to believe their judgement sufficient to requirements, and that the order of decantation need not be preserved. They pervert the natural order, bringing shame and suffering upon the whole. You have met such a one."

"Young."

"The very one. We are in your debt for restoring order."

"Supposing you could send a cohort under supervision of

another, and not elevate anyone to command. I am thinking on the order of a score of Spear Bearers."

"And that is how many?"

"Twenty."

"Sixteen or twenty-four, else we would have to split a squad. And this might be acceptable, depending upon the nature of those in command."

"A contract I would hold myself, and an agent I trust as a son trusts a father."

"This agent is another merchant lord?"

"Another Freeman."

"And the foes?"

"Uncertain. Your people would act as a security detail, assuming a defensive posture only."

"We do not count other Huangxu or Huangxu Eng as foes."

"Nor would I expect you to. Ojin, or League, or Freeman. And if blows are struck they will be lawful blows, under the custom of intent, and properly filed."

"This 'intent' is not a concept in our lexicon."

"Blood feud, to balance a debt. The rules for filing intent are complicated but the results of doing so are not. Usually there is a match made to settle the debt that does not involve bloodshed."

"But not in all cases."

"In those cases where one party does not respect custom or recognize their debt, or both."

"I see. Would there be sand?"

"There would not be. It is a green world, wet, and cool, with rain on the helmet and stone beneath the boots. "

Old frowned. "Another planet, then."

"Planet and station. You would need to choose sensible men, those who can keep their tongues in their heads and their anger from their faces. Who can fight when they are told to fight and to refrain from fighting when they are told to refrain.

And who can pass for League, or Ojin, or Freeman, not under interrogation, but when seen from a distance."

"We are all such. Would these men need to speak a tongue?"

"Trade, if they might, though one could speak for all."

"It can be done, Merchant Lord, and it will be."

"Thank you. I will forward detailed instructions."

"And for the rest of us?"

"It's Contract space as planned. *Quite Possibly Alien* will proceed to Pinion, a system in the Ojinate, and from there calculate her next stop. It's impossible to predict when we will arrive, so I'd like you to proceed directly to Contract and transit the system.

"If we have arrived before you, scan for a beacon with instructions. If you can't ping the beacon, proceed through the system to a destination beyond. Wait there for a reasonable time and reverse your course through the system and on to the nearest system, or one best suitable. Wait the necessary time, and then back through the system, and so forth.

"Repeat this procedure every ten to fourteen days, if possible, so it appears you're a merchant routinely passing through the system on an established route. Eventually we'll arrive, and you'll find us, or the beacon. If we don't arrive in four months' time, standard, then we will have defaulted on the contract and you may safely assume we are dead. At that time you are free to pursue other contracts."

"And should we be hailed, or intercepted with the intent to board?"

"We'll provide an expert system, with appropriate automated responses for a merchant vessel. If that proves insufficient, then use your best judgment. I would not let anyone from Contract system board if it were my ship. It would be better to run, and wait in a nearby system. If that happens, a message left with the Freeman Merchant's Guild should reach me."

"It will be done, Merchant Lord."

"I'll forward details prior to our departure."

"And I will choose the best of my men to watch over your merchant captain. And she will never know."

"Is my intent that obvious?"

"You are a clever and resourceful lord. You follow orders as given and give orders as needed. We wondered when the Merchant Lord nic Cartaí departed the system without a security detail."

"She didn't want one."

"Yet you have decided that she needs one."

"I'm in possession of information she didn't have. Circumstances she wasn't aware of."

"You do not question her judgement."

"Of course I do. Just as I question my own."

"Then you and Young are different in two respects," Old said. "He did not question his own judgment. And he is dead."

"I'm not defying the merchant captain's wishes. I'm doing what she would have done had she known what I know now."

"And keeping it secret from her."

"Keeping it secret from everyone."

"Because you do not know where to lay trust. Excepting upon this agent whom you trust like a father."

"That's right."

"We do not have fathers," Old said. "Or we have too many, depending upon how one views the process of our creation. One wonders at the nature of such trust, being unable to gauge its measure from experience."

"It varies from father to father. This agent is the best I can do under the circumstances."

"Then we will make it work, Merchant Lord. Death and pain to our foes."

20

Pinion System, Imperial Ojinate

They took it low and slow into Pinion system, Hess at the helm, a textbook insertion below the orbital plane of eight of the nine planets surrounding the star, and on the far side of the star from the primary world and its extensive orbital structures.

"No local traffic," Ko Shan said. "And no sign of a system picket." She floated, suspended inside the amber fluid of the full-immersion sensor rig. The viscous, oxygenated goop filling her lungs made her voice sound distant and uninflected.

"We are very deep in the Ojinate," Swan said. "Look for fixed orbital defenses and a few light mobile units."

"You're acting like we're here for a gunfight," Ciarán said.

"We're an unknown ship, of an unknown configuration, and we have just appeared out of nowhere in the Ojin Empire's back garden. There will be guns, and they will be aimed at us."

"We're being hailed," Ko Shan said.

Swan tapped on the arm of her command chair, and a stern Ojin Eng face appeared on the ship's main display. "Heave to and prepare to be boarded."

"How do you wish to respond, Merchant-in-Charge?"

"Is that a real person?" Ciarán said.

"It is likely an expert system."

"Do we have an expert system ready?"

"We do."

"Let's see it."

The captain split the display so that both systems were shown side by side.

Quite Possibly Alien's expert looked like Ciarán's dad in a merchant captain's day dress. It took Ciarán a moment to realize that the image was meant to look like *him*, only, older, wiser, and much more dangerous.

"Make it look like me and add Wisp to my right. Lose the overseer's rod and merchant captain's greatcoat."

The image changed.

"How'd you do that?"

"The ship did it."

"Thank you, Ship."

"You are welcome, Merchant-in-Charge."

"The rules are no boarding under any circumstances," Ciarán said. "Quote the precise sections of the Non-Aggression Treaty word for word. Be firm but polite. We expect to be treated like any other Freeman merchant in any other Ojin port, no better and no worse. Greetings from the People of the Mong Hu to the People of the Book, and all the usual pleasantries.

"We won't be docking at the station but sending a longboat over. We have business on the planet and will ride the commercial shuttle down and back. No goods to declare, a buying trip only, and the first of many successful transactions, profitable for both parties. A demonstration of continued amity that does honor to the Pinion system, to its people, and to our mutual ancestors. Replace Pinion with whatever they call the system."

"Fir, with Wren Nesting."

"That's what they call the system?"

"It is, Merchant-in-Charge."

"That's weird."

"It is unusual in the taxonomy of Ojinate system names. Is that all for directives?"

"Not quite," Ciarán said. "Don't reveal the nature of our business unless absolutely necessary. It's not secret, but it's consistent with cultural stereotypes for us to act like it is.

"Neither offer nor pay bribes. If a bribe is asked for, note the ask and haggle some before saying you need to consult your purser. Be noncommittal without appearing furtive. Have Wisp appear to follow the conversation. If they are being unreasonable, have Wisp show displeasure instead of me. But don't overdo it.

"They can tell us where to park and ask us to follow the system rules for filing longboat flight plans and so on. But no boarding and no forwarding of manifests or customs inspections either. We're from Trinity Station where Ojin and Freeman breath the same air. We know the rules on both sides of the line. All we're asking is that they follow the rules their bosses and our bosses agreed to. Because that's what we're going to do.

"End directive, commit and execute."

"Confirmed," the ship said.

Ciarán watched and listened while the facsimile of some Ojin potentate and his own facsimile dickered. His facsimile kept mispronouncing proper names.

Ciarán glanced at Swan. "Do I really sound like that?"

"According to Natsuko, you sound exactly like a Kyo news announcer."

"So not like that."

"The ship and I agreed. It is best if others continue to underestimate you."

"Well, thank you both for your forethought."

"You are welcome, Merchant-in-Charge."

Swan smiled, all teeth. "Just doing my job, Freeman whelp."

21

P inion Station sprawled across the longboat's forward viewing ports, a jumble of spars and spans without ring or spindle, as if someone had dropped a box of drinking straws sized for human habitation, and rather than impose order on the resulting chaos, simply set up home-making wherever the straws fell. There didn't seem any order to the docking facilities as well, and they were following directions to a dock that lay "underneath" the bulk of the station, if one assumed the station's "bottom" faced the planet it hung above.

The Eng were engineered for life in free fall, and no telling what they considered up or down, top or bottom. Generations had lived and died aboard slowships transiting between stars. This adaption for space proved the greatest difference between the Eng and not-Eng, regardless of the apparent differences between present-day cultures. The ruling Eng piloted and maintained the slowships while the not-Eng rode in cryogenic stasis, safe within heavily shielded hulls. Those stations first built by the Eng reflected this lack of concern for gravity or gravity generators. The design of Pinion Station alone proved it ancient beyond measure. It was pleasant to look at, though, if one appreciated engineering artfully disguised as chaos. That the station had grown old certainly wasn't evident in its maintenance. Every external surface gleamed. Even the fleet of automated maintenance drones weaving in and out amongst the spars appeared new, or nearly so.

Hess rolled the longboat up to the dock and settled it nicely. Ingress and egress locks connected with a thunk. Once the pressures normalized Ciarán worked the egress hatch. The familiar scent he associated with the Ojin Sector of Trinity Station wafted in. Ciarán glanced toward the stern, where Natsuko remained belted to her seat. She'd seemed very uncomfortable on the ride over, and Ciarán couldn't decide if she disliked riding in longboats or if something more serious disturbed her about this trip. The sole member of the crew born in the Ojinate, Natsuko seemed... unenthused about this homecoming. She'd chosen a party mask wearing the scowling face of an elderly Ojin Eng for her atmosphere supply.

Ciarán thought that an odd choice, as she had many more attractive masks. She knew far more about what she was doing than he did, though. Surely she had a reason for her decision.

He carried two spare atmosphere supply bottles for her mask, thick walled and surprisingly heavy for their size. Heavy enough that he'd asked Mr. Gagenot to find one of the large string bags they used when transporting fresh comestibles from the boat bay to the galley.

Natsuko looked very proper in her dark-blue ship's utilities, her golden skin, amethyst eyes, and striking physical beauty notwithstanding. Not-Eng, she hailed from Low Brasil, a distant frontier world yet in the early stages of terraforming. She and her kin were engineered for life in the high-carbon-dioxide atmosphere of the planet's deadly lowlands, and about as far as an Ojin citizen could get from places like Pinion. He wondered if she would stand out, or if Pinion might resemble Trinity Station, where citizens from the Ojinate's many worlds could be found mingling.

Pinion system had turned out to be far larger and more populous than they'd expected. Perhaps Natsuko simply felt out of her place, just like Ciarán would amongst the sophistication and wealth of Columbia Station, hub of the interstellar wheel of commerce and heart of the League.

There might be another reason for her upset. A Kazuki Ryuu fangirl, Natsuko might feel nervous about meeting the famous actor.

Ciarán didn't want to disappoint her, so he'd said maybe when she'd asked if they would meet Kazuki Ryuu. In truth, the likelihood of that was astronomically slim. The actor's agent managed all financial arrangements, and this was purely a financial deal. If they met Kazuki Ryuu, it would be by accident.

Something bothered Natsuko, and if he asked she'd just deny it. Politely, of course, but denial nonetheless.

Ciarán hefted the string bag. He traveled light besides that, just a general-purpose handheld linked to the ship and his identification wallet. No weapons allowed on Pinion Station, which Ciarán was glad to hear. Natsuko carried a small backpack and nothing more.

"Natsuko," Ciarán said. "It's time to go."

She nodded and unbelted, the grim old man's mask nodding with her.

"Got something for you, before you go," Hess said. "Let's see your handhelds."

Hess did something to the devices then handed them back, along with one black coin each. "Pocket the coin and open up the Trinity Station Public Library app on your handhelds."

"There is no such app on my..." Natsuko flipped through the displays. "I beg your pardon. There now appears to be such an app."

"Now, look at the books you've both checked out, and scroll down until you find the one titled *Making Sense of Sensors: Theory and Practice.*

"Find it?"

"Found it," Ciarán said.

"Now go to page one hundred and look at the picture of the old Todd-Armison luggable. The one with the big honking display."

Natsuko huffed. "Erik, I see no point to this."

"Trust me, Nat, you'll like it."

"All right, I'm looking at the picture," Natsuko said.

"Click it."

Ciarán clicked the picture, and it expanded to fill the handheld's display. It didn't look any different at first, just larger, and then three dots appeared on the picture of the display and one of the dots... moved.

"Hey." Hess had moved to the stern of the longboat. "See what it does?"

Ciarán stepped to the bow of the longboat and two of the three dots seemed to move further away from him.

"You've hidden a scanner in an e-book," Ciarán said.

"If I'm being cashiered, I figure I need to bone up on stuff like this. It's a prototype, but it works."

Natsuko's brow wrinkled as she stared at her handheld. "Yes, but what is it detecting?"

"The coins," Ciarán said. "I'm guessing they're made of the same stuff as *Quite Possibly Alien*'s hull. And you've made a coin for each of the crew."

"Making," Hess said. "Since you're the ones going out on your own, you're getting the first ones. It's a simple, low-power design. The coins themselves are fully passive. It won't work on the ship, of course, and it only works at close range. But the only thing it detects is second-epoch League hull composite, and I don't expect you'll stumble across any of that around here. Steer clear of pickpockets, and you'll be good to go. We won't lose any *Quite Possibly Alien* needles in this godawful jumble of a haystack."

Natsuko pulled the coin out of her pocket and stared at it. It had what looked like a large eye embossed on one face and a leaping mong hu on the other.

"That's the ship's boat-bay iris and the ship's cat," Hess said.

Natsuko peered closely at the coin. She held it up to the light. She lowered her mask, and touched it to her lips, and then... she swallowed it.

She moved away from the airlock. "I can see me. Can you see me?"

"I can see you fine," Hess said. "That's a good idea. Ciarán, you need to swallow yours too."

Ciarán flipped the coin in his hand.

"It is medically safe," Natsuko said. "If there are complications, I will attend to them. But there won't be."

"I wasn't thinking about that." As merchant-in-charge, he'd be off the ship a lot. Swallowing the coin the first time wasn't very appealing. But tomorrow, or the next day, when he had to swallow it again?

"I'll carry this beauty in my pocket, thank you very much."

Natsuko frowned. "But—"

"The important thing is that if you get separated now Ciarán can find you," Hess said. "Finding him is easy. He sort of stands out in a crowd, coin or no coin."

Natsuko bowed, and smiled at Hess. "As you say, Engineer."

"As I do, Medic." Hess stepped up to her and took the mask from her hand. He lifted her chin with a finger, forcing her to look him in the eyes. "If anything happens to Ciarán, I will find you. And I will take you home."

Ciarán watched as Natsuko nodded and wiped her eyes.

As Hess handed her the mask.

As she touched his sleeve.

His fingers.

She donned her mask.

Hess glanced up to notice Ciarán watching.

And then he donned his own.

"Let's do this, merchie man."

22

Pinion Station proved a maze. Every corridor had the same white walls and deckhead above a pale silver deck. Hatches were spaced at regular intervals, and corridors intersected other corridors, though never at right angles, and all but a few of the hatches were unlabeled.

They hadn't seen another soul since they'd left the long-boat's dock. The locals appeared to have built a giant honking space station and then abandoned it, not years ago, but right before Natsuko and Ciarán had stepped through the docking bay airlock. The whole place had the usual pleasant Ojin-sector odor, *jasmine*, according to Natsuko, and the heat was on, but it was deadly silent, and their footfalls echoing along the long, straight corridors seemed not just odd, but fake, like sound effects in a thriller drama. Stations were meant to be alive, with people shouldering past one another, talking, and now and then shouting, and strange, random scents coming from Arcade shops, and the deck rumbling, and clattering air-handler fans. Ciarán had only been on two stations, Trinity and Ambidex, but they were both like that, noisy, and odorous, and flashy, and crude. Pinion Station was the opposite of all that. *Unnatural*, and downright unnerving.

He'd figured out that any time he saw a label he'd better read the tiny thing, because only public hatches were labeled, and then just barely. All the unlabeled hatches he'd tried were locked. The labelled ones weren't. The hatch in front of him had a label that said, "Up and Down Vessel to Wren, Nesting."

He glanced at Natsuko. "I think it's the commercial shuttle to the planet through there."

"It seems possible. Perhaps even reasonable."

"None of this is familiar to you?"

"This station is very old. Very *Ojin Eng*, like in storybooks. It is familiar, but also like a storybook."

"So nothing like this at home?"

"Nothing." She ran her finger along the bezel surrounding the hatch controls. "No dust. No wear. And no pleading."

She meant the way Ojin hatch locks noticed when someone stepped nearby and begged to be of service. Most Eng-made stuff worked like that. The Ojin stuff seemed a little less obsequious than the Huangxu stuff and, in general, prettier to look at. It rarely worked as well as the Huangxu equivalent, though. Almost all the medical supplies on Freeman vessels, for example, were Huangxu-made, even though the Ojin versions were cheaper and easier to get.

"I say we go in."

"Let's do it." Natsuko didn't seem excited about doing it.

Ciarán chuckled as he worked the hatch controls. *Let's do it* was a Hess-ism, like *Have you tried power cycling it*, and *It's supposed to do that*. That Natsuko and Hess weren't just ship-mates but friends surprised him, and he wondered why that was. He also wondered if they were more than friends and if, as merchant-in-charge, he was supposed to do or say something about that, or if, as a Freeman and a decent human being, he was supposed to pretend he hadn't noticed, and leave it at that.

There wasn't anything he could do, not while on an away mission, but he'd think about it. Maybe something would occur to him. For now he needed to pay attention, not just because it was his job, but because Natsuko wasn't paying attention. Something bothered her, bothered her big time, and he didn't know what.

THE COMPARTMENT APPEARED to be a debarkation and arrivals lounge, one with benches lining the interior bulkheads. Two airlocks on the exterior bulkhead flanked a tall counter with a display unit atop it. The display unit appeared powered down. All the benches were deserted but for one, where an old man in stained brown utilities sat eyeballing them.

Natsuko stiffened at the sight of the old man. He wiped his grubby hands on the front of his utilities before he ran his fingers through his lank black hair, greasy hair so long it stained the shoulders of his utilities. He unfolded from the seat and stood, back bent, and grinned, his teeth blackened nubs. He carried a patched backpack and leaned on a length of stiff wiring conduit as if it were a cane. He began to hobble toward them, and as he grew near his odor grew near as well, an unclean scent, part body odor, part something that didn't have a name, but a scent every spacer knew, a moldy, fungal reek of moist, exhaled air, and overcrowded compartments and overstressed scrubbers.

When he spoke it was in Ojin, but with a distinctly archaic accent. "Pardon me, my feet grew weary." He pointed at the bench. "One does not presume." He stood, leaning on his makeshift cane, and leered at Natsuko. "You are returned, great lord." He dropped to a knee and looked like he might abase himself before her.

Natsuko stood frozen to the spot, her mask obscuring her expression.

It felt like he'd seen this man before, but if so, he couldn't place him. It took Ciarán a second to process what the man had said. "Please, sir," he said. "Take a seat, and be at your ease." Dressed like some sort of menial worker from the bowels of the station, he appeared to have mistaken them for important people. "Do you know, sir, is this the shuttle to the planetary surface?"

The man leaned on his makeshift cane and stood. "It is."

"And the attendants?"

"There are no attendants. You pay your fare at the terminal." The man pointed.

"Will it be long before the shuttle arrives?"

"It is out there, waiting. Present your ticket at the hatch and it will open. Enter, and the shuttle will take you to the surface."

"You are waiting for a friend, or family?"

"I am waiting for a miracle," the man said. "I have business on the surface and no fare."

Ciarán crossed the compartment to the terminal the man had pointed to. He touched the display and instructions appeared. The man's overwhelming odor seemed to flood the compartment.

Ciarán followed the instructions on the display. The fare for a seat appeared in Ojin local currency, ridiculously cheap, a few pingins only, after he'd done the math in his head. The unit accepted his ship's credentials and debited the ship's account for two tickets. He glanced at Natsuko, who still stood motionless, her masked face aimed at the man. Ciarán wished he had a rebreather like the one built into her mask. His eyes were beginning to water from the man's overpowering reek.

"How big are these shuttles," Ciarán said.

"Very small," the man said. "Tight. Three seats, and elbow to elbow."

"I see." Ciarán touched the display once more and committed the changes. A flimsy strip of magnetic material ejected from a slot.

"Natsuko," Ciarán said. "Let's go."

The man grinned. He flicked his earlobe, like Ojin stationers sometimes did, a gesture that could be interpreted as an insult, or as a silent warning to friends, depending upon whether the Freeman in question was meant to see or not. "I suppose it is true, then, what they say."

"That a Freeman never gives?"

The man shrugged.

Ciarán inserted the strip into a reader beside the hatch. The hatch cycled with a whisper. Ciarán swung it open. "Natsuko."

"Yes." She glanced at Ciarán, lowering her mask so that he could see her eyes. "I will pay his fare."

"Already done," Ciarán said. "Now come on, before I change my mind." Ciarán bowed, and held the hatch wide. "Are you coming, wise master?"

The man glared at him. "I will come."

A simple control surface in the shuttle prompted him, and Ciarán chuckled as he responded to the system prompts, entering their destination, the Doru Spaceport, Nesting, Minori Prefecture, Fir, with Wren Nesting, Imperial Ojinate.

"What?" Natsuko said.

"A lot of data entry for a place with only one spaceport."

"Do you have business at the spaceport?" the old man said.

"We don't."

"Then why would you go there?"

"Because that's where shuttles go."

"They go where they are told."

"So you're saying I could enter any address here and the shuttle would take me there?"

"Any address."

"So if I told the shuttle to take me to the business offices of Kazuki Ryuu's agent it would take me there."

"You could tell it to take you to Kazuki Ryuu and it would take you to her."

"I need to think about this," Ciarán said. "Where do you want the shuttle to take you, wise master?"

"What difference does that make?"

"If it's not too far out of the way, we'll drop you and take ground transportation from there."

The old man crossed his arms and stared out the viewport. "Wren, Minori Prefecture, Fir, with Wren Nesting, Eight Banners Empire."

Ciarán worked the terminal. "Got it. Belt in."

"Wait." Natsuko placed her hand on Ciarán's sleeve. "There is no such place as Eight Banners Empire. It is a myth."

"The shuttle thinks there is such a place." Ciarán nodded to the old man. "As does he."

The old man gazed out the viewport. "If it were not a myth, would you wish to go there?"

"I would not."

The old man turned his gaze upon her. "Show me your face."

The mask she held to hide her face quivered. "This is my face."

"That is the death mask of Sato Atomu, the man who designed you. Who made you. Whose heirs yet own you."

"No. The emperor surrendered Brasil system to the League, and all its people with it. We are League citizens now, and no part of the Ojinate any longer."

"Yet here you are, and you wear Sato's face, and not that of the League's queen."

"I wear this face out of respect for the emperor."

"You wear that *mask* because you are compelled to by your nature. Do not lie to me."

"She usually wears other masks," Ciarán said. "The mong hu one is particularly striking."

"Ciarán, please," Natsuko said. "You don't understand."

"I understand," Ciarán said. "This man just called you a liar, and he is mistaken. I respectfully ask that he take that back."

"And if he does not?" the man said.

"Then I'll know he's no gentleman and plan accordingly."

"No," Natsuko said. "It is true. I wished to do otherwise but could not. Not here. Here this is all I am."

"And so we agree," the old man said. "You are Sato's slave and nothing more."

"That's not what she said. She said that in the *Ojinate* that's all she is." Ciarán pressed the commit control and the shuttle began to vibrate. "If this Eight Banners Empire isn't a myth, then we'll know soon enough."

"How can it not be?" Natsuko said. "It exists only in stories."

23

T he shuttle swept toward the planet, descending in a curving arc. As they passed the terminator between the day and night side of the planet, Ciarán squeezed Natsuko's hand. She squeezed back, and Ciarán smiled. When he glanced up he found the old man staring at him. The air handler in the shuttle seemed to keep the wicked stench ponging off the man at bay. It was easier to stare back at him now that Ciarán's eyes weren't watering.

The old man flicked his own earlobe. "Where is your earring?"

"Gave it to the ship's captain. She took the Oath a few days ago."

"You don't need an earring?"

"She needed it more."

"Huh."

Ciarán gazed out the viewport. Few lights shone on the planet's nightside, but those that did shone in a circle, with blocks of light spaced around the circumference, like teeth on a gear. The center of the circle gazed back at him, black and empty. "That's why we call it Pinion."

"We call it the spider," the old man said.

"What's in the middle of the circle?"

"A hole in the earth," the old man said. "Where a stump used to be. Before that, a tree. Before that, a seed."

"And before that, a hole in the earth," Ciarán said. "And around the hole, space for a forest, and stars for a crown, and..."

"Hope," Natsuko said.

The old man stared at him.

"It's a quote from a play," Ciarán said. "One we watched recently."

"And how did this play end?"

"Tragically," Natsuko said. "But with hope."

Ciarán watched the old man's face. "We'd like to license similar material."

"We wish to speak with Kazuki Ryuu about this." Natsuko gazed out the viewport. "We're descending rapidly."

The shuttle plunged into a dense layer of cloud.

"License for your own use?"

"For resale."

"And for our own use," Natsuko said.

Ciarán chuckled. "I had a list of titles the customer liked. I needed to view a few of the titles to be able to identify similar material. They were good enough to share, and the crew like them, so on the way here we watched them after meals."

"How many of them?"

"Thirty-five."

"Over the course of how many days?"

"Three days," Ciarán said.

Natsuko slapped his arm. "Liar."

"A month, standard," Ciarán said. "But it would have been three days if Natsuko had been in charge."

"They are very good stories," Natsuko said. "And Kazuki Ryuu is pretty."

"Someone told me they were fantastic stories. And Kazuki

Ryuu the most spectacular woman ever born." Ciarán tapped Natsuko's sleeve. "Maybe I should have brought *her* to meet Kazuki Ryuu instead."

"Maybe you did bring her. And maybe she wants you to strike a good bargain."

"Then the ship and I thank her for her concern. But if we really do get to meet her? You should tell her how you truly feel."

"As if my opinion on anything is important," Natsuko said.

"It's as important as anyone else's." Ciarán pointed out the viewport. "Look. The clouds are thinning."

Natsuko rested her arm on his shoulder and craned her neck to share the view. "Is that the city?"

"It's huge," Ciarán said. There were hundreds of buildings, each one taller than the next, and all clustered together. A wide, straight highway led to a glassfield in the distance.

Natsuko shivered. "Incredible."

"That is the Doru Spaceport," the old man said. "The city is further east."

They swept over the spaceport and on toward what Ciarán had mistakenly thought was a distant mountain range. "That can't be real."

Natsuko shoved against him. "There are thousands of buildings!"

"There are tens of thousands of buildings in Nesting," the old man said. "And many more outside the city."

"How many people?" Ciarán asked.

"Many."

They watched in silence as the city passed beneath them, and when it was gone from view they settled into their seats.

"You must think we're a pair of country rubes," Ciarán said.

"Are there no cities where you are from?"

"None," Natsuko said. "We don't even have a functioning atmosphere yet."

The old man gazed at Ciarán. "And you, Freeman? Have you no cities?"

"There's not enough of us to fill a city that size. And even if there were..."

"Yes?"

"You'd probably have to pay people to live there."

The old man stared at him.

"At first, I mean. Not that people wouldn't like it in the long run."

The old man stared at him.

"We have some planets. Two fairly nice ones."

"One fairly nice one," Natsuko said. "And Unity."

The old man continued to stare at him.

"I'm from the fairly nice one, so she can say that, but I can't. Not without being accused of punching down."

The shuttle began to slow its descent.

"Do you know of the Eight Banners Empire?"

Ciarán nodded. "It's all over those plays we watched. Not the empire itself, but talk of it. Lots of people trying to escape to it, and others trying to find it and destroy it, and others still vehemently denying its existence."

"The old folks used to talk of it," Natsuko said. "To frighten children into obeying."

"I figure it's a starship," Ciarán said. "And that's why no one can ever find it when they want to."

"I was told it was a great deep pit," Natsuko said. "One that parents throw the bad children down. But in the plays it was described quite differently."

"In what way?" the old man said.

Natsuko's brow wrinkled. "It seemed more a pit one would leap into, rather than live another day as a bad child."

The shuttle bumped to a halt.

"The Eight Banners Empire is neither of those things," the old man said. "And it is both."

The hatch telltale glowed green, and he reached for the lock and turned it.

"And now we are there."

Bright sunlight streamed in through the opening, and mercifully, fresh air.

"Show me your face," he said.

Natsuko lowered the mask. A tear ran down her cheek.

"I was mistaken. You are a person. Throw that mask away."

"I need it or I will die."

"You need to throw it away or you will never live."

He disappeared through the hatch.

Ciarán followed him out, and then Natsuko. The shuttle rested atop a grassy knoll, a large white orb in a field of green. The sky arced blue overhead, without a cloud. A gravel road ran at the base of the knoll. The old man already hiked along it, toward a vermillion gateway in the distance.

"Wait here," Ciarán said, and ran after the man. He caught up with him in seconds. "Kazuki Ryuu. Where may we find her?"

"The other way, and over the brow of the next hill. If you get lost, ask directions to the Wren."

"May I ask you one other question?"

The old man stopped and gazed up at him. "Go on."

"If a space station had a *kami*, what would it look like?"

"That would depend upon the space station." The old man flicked his earlobe and pointed over Ciarán's shoulder. "And who was looking. Best you hurry. I hear it gets dark fast in the country." He turned on his heel and began walking toward the shrine gateway in the distance.

Ciarán shouted. "Are you moving in?"

The old man shouted back without turning. "Visiting relatives!"

24

They walked along the gravel road under the bright sun. A light breeze cooled them and the walking felt easy. Natsuko had a ground-eating stride and an elegant swing to her arms, her back straight, her head high. From a distance she would appear a pretty woman out for a stroll in the country, one with a hulking bodyguard in tow.

Seen up close, one would note first the mask she needed to survive, and the golden sheen of her skin, now dewed from exertion, and were she to peer over her mask, those amethyst eyes, slit like a cat's, though horizontally, more like a goat's eyes than a cat's. He'd never liked goat's eyes and often found them unnerving, until he'd met her. Now he always found them unnerving when he looked up to find her watching him. He had no idea how she saw him, or saw the world, for that matter.

"May I tell you something terrible," she said, as they walked along.

"How terrible?"

"As terrible as it gets."

"Do you want to stop?"

"No. Walking helps. It's harder to glance at your face when I tell you."

"Go on."

"When I was a little girl, an Eng lord and his family visited our home. My father was at the weather station, and my mother busy analyzing seismology data, but she dropped everything and *attended* to these people.

"They had a little girl, and she somehow latched onto my brother and began following him around. I was trying to help my mother with her work, and not paying much attention, and then I heard this *slap*, and the girl began to cry, and the lord began shouting, and mother began weeping, and *prostrating* herself at the lord's feet, and all but kissing his boots, apologizing, and begging for his forgiveness.

"I didn't understand. *Forgiveness for what?* Children fight. They make up. What was the problem? Of course I didn't say that. Children didn't speak to adults, but I thought it.

"And then my father came home. And my mother told him what had happened, and he began prostrating himself at this stranger's feet, and apologizing. It was *humiliating*, and him a proud man, and a local leader.

"I asked my brother why he'd hit the girl. He said it was because she'd wanted to look into his eyes and see if it was true. That Sato Atomu's creatures had no souls. So he let her look, and she laughed and said it was true. He would never be Eng because he was not even alive. So he hit her.

"The lord asked which of us had hit the girl, and I lied and said I had. At that age I was bigger, and more used to beatings. I was caned, and made to apologize to the girl, who didn't really care who was punished, so long as she could watch, and then they left.

"Afterward my father caned me for lying and my mother caned me for leaving my brother unattended.

"The next morning, my father told me that what the girl

said was a lie, that we had souls, and that the reason we couldn't sense the beauty of the world was because it didn't exist yet. That we had to work hard and make the world before we could experience it as one was meant to. I heard him out, and I thought he was lying. I knew the girl was right. I'd seen images of grass and I knew in my heart I was less alive than the tiniest blade.

"That evening my mother told me that before she'd been sent there, to Brasil Surface, she'd passed through Brasil Station—what they call Low Brasil now, but the only station then—and she'd cried herself to sleep, and woken in the middle of the night to find an old woman staring at her from the bunk across from hers. The old woman had taken her hand, pressed a flower into her palm, and smiled, and kissed her forehead, and told her all would be well. She showed me a lab notebook, a very old one, and pressed inside the cover was a flower. It was flat, and faded, but she let me touch it, and I did, and it felt like paper, only not so rough, and for a moment, it truly did seem that some faint sense of faded beauty reached my heart. She said the flower was a gift from the station's spirit, it's *kami*, and she had seen the *kami*, and spoken with it. That proved she had a soul. And if she had a soul, then her daughter had a soul. That girl was a liar.

"She asked if I believed her, and I nodded yes, but I knew that girl was right. And after I'd stolen a scrap of the 'flower' and run it through the mass spectrometer, I had proof the girl was right. It was my mother that was the liar. It was my father. It was everyone except the brave Eng girl who looked at us and told the truth, if only to add to our suffering.

"I knew in that moment. I have no soul. I would never sense the beauty and wonder of the world around me. I would walk through the world as if blind, and when I died it would be as if I had never existed. My spirit would not leave any lasting mark on the world because my spirit did not exist. I was a husk in the shape of a girl, and one day I would be a husk in the shape of a woman, and one day a husk in the shape of a crone, and one day not even that, but the wind of time blowing across my bones and sweeping on without so much as an eddy in my wake.

"When the fighting broke out, and the planet and its people changed hands, I thought nothing of it. When the most heinous acts of barbarity became commonplace I fought back, but only to preserve my life and that of my friends. It was as if I had died the day I'd watched my parents not just *kneel* before a stranger but *crawl*, and kiss his hem. The sole advantage of being born a soulless science experiment was that the bootlicking gene had been accidentally bred out of me as well."

She glanced at Ciarán as they trudged along. "You're still awake."

Ciarán nodded. "Like a boiling pot, I am. And you're telling me this because something has changed."

"When we entered this system. I could feel it."

"Everyone feels it."

"No," she said. "Not the translational nausea. The system itself. I could feel the system. Like it was alive. Like it was watching me. Judging me."

"Huh. That's strange."

"Strange indeed. And this mask. I could choose no other. It isn't even mine, but my mother's. I'd completely forgotten about it. I hate it, and yet—"

"You felt compelled to wear it."

"As if my fingers were another's. Like I was *watching them* disobey me. And when the old man asked me to remove the mask—"

"You couldn't take it off."

"When I first saw him, it was as if time had stopped, and run backward. I *felt* the station's *kami*. I saw the station's *kami*. And yet—"

"You felt the spirit and the flesh weren't quite aligned."

"You felt it too."

"I didn't, not in the way you described. But I know the feeling."

"If I can feel the station's *kami* then I have a soul. And the girl was wrong. *I* have been wrong all my life. The choices I have made... I have *wasted* a precious gift."

"That's a lot of change all at once. Wait a while longer before you make any decisions."

"I will wait until we speak with Kazuki Ryuu."

Until we speak with Kazuki Ryuu again.

The reason that old man looked familiar was that Ciarán had seen him in a *Noh* play. One with Kazuki Ryuu behind the mask.

Ciarán glanced at the sky. "Come on, it's getting dark."

THEY ARRIVED at the little cottage at dusk. The shadows of distant mountains framed the curving roofline, its extended eaves seeming to hover above the earth. A thatched roof crowned the simple lines of a wooden structure, a broad porch and wooden columns framing paper-glazed windows, and beneath them, lines of shadow disappearing into deeper shadow as the light faded. The corner of a flower garden peeked out from behind the building. The cottage appeared rustic at first glance, but the closer they grew the more it appeared the builder had chosen the roughest local materials and proceeded to elevate them to art through hours of painstaking craft.

"It's very Ojin," Ciarán said.

Natsuko glanced at him. "Beauty over function, you mean."

"You heard that." That had been what he'd been thinking. But he needed to amend his thoughts if he were to successfully negotiate with Kazuki Ryuu. Whatever she, or he was, it was more than an actor. Like nearly everything Ojin-made, the closer one looked the more one could see.

"You speak like a Kyo newscaster."

"By that you mean well."

"Well, in the sense that your words are easily understood. Not well, in the sense that your words reveal the unspoken sentiments behind them."

"So it's an insult to say someone speaks like a Kyo newscaster."

"It is an instruction to do better."

"You could have said."

"That is what I did. You could have understood. The merchant captain would have."

"And how would she have instructed me to change my words?"

"She would not have done so. She would have instructed you to examine your sentiments."

"I see."

"Perhaps you do, and perhaps she is right. But her way seems very difficult to me, and unnecessary." She lowered her mask and peered at him over the top of it. "I think you are a good friend. I would like others to think you are a great man, and worthy of respect."

"And?"

"No one honorable respects a Kyo newsman."

"I mean, what do you suggest I do?"

"Empty your mind of sentiment."

"Is that what you're doing now?"

"In large part, yes. I do not wish to force my unexamined opinions on Kazuki Ryuu. I'd rather she sees my body in a state of undress than my mind."

"And our talk, on the way here?"

"Oh." She fluttered her mask. "A presumption on my part. I beg your forgiveness."

"For what? Letting me ogle your naked thoughts?"

"For forcing such intimacy upon you."

Ciarán gripped his left little finger between his right thumb and middle fingers and lightly wiggled it. "Oh, Natsuko, you brute. Don't. Stop."

She laughed. "I am not so strong as that."

"Yes," Ciarán said. "That must be true."

Of all the Ojin words he knew, *yes* was the most alien, both because no exact equivalent in his native tongue existed, and because, said like that in Ojin, it didn't mean what it said. The measure of a hull wasn't how well it held vacuum *out*. It was how well it held pressure *in*. If there were stronger women made, he hadn't met one.

She tapped his sleeve. "Much better. Your words are a still pond."

"That's grand," Ciarán said, the phrase a distant cousin in kind, if not meaning, to the Ojin *yes*.

25

Ciarán's hullwalkers had barely touched the porch boards when he noticed the woman sitting in the shadows. She sat cross-legged on a cushion and appeared to be carving something. Wood shavings lay scattered around her, and an assortment of slender knives rested at her side. She dressed in a simple yet elegantly patterned silken robe, belted with a sash. Not the sort of outfit one wore on Trinity Station's Ojin Arcade, but according to his textbooks, nothing extraordinary for an Ojin planet.

He'd studied Ojin culture at the Academy, and had done all the lab work like a good little rule follower. It was a lucky thing he had. He recognized much of what he saw. If there were goings on here out of the ordinary, and it certainly seemed like there were, he might have enough knowledge to recognize the snake in the woodpile before it bit him. Or Natsuko might, and warn him.

"Greetings," Ciarán said to the woman. "We were told we might find Kazuki Ryuu here."

"You might," she said. "Who told you that?"

"A man on the station."

She snorted. "There are no men on the station. They are all dead."

"The men are all dead?"

"Those on the station," she said. "It's a mausoleum."

"There are no people on the station at all?"

"Now and then. For maintenance. For funerals. People are quit of that place, and no loss."

"A maintenance man, then," Ciarán said. "We didn't get his name."

"It doesn't matter. You are here. Would you like some tea?" She ran her gaze up and down him. "This cottage lacks a foreign room."

"Tea would be lovely," Ciarán said. "We would be honored."

She groaned, and stood and stretched her back, and placed her workpiece on the pillow. It looked like she carved the sort of mask Natsuko used. "What would be lovely is for someone young and flexible to serve."

Natsuko bowed. "Truly?"

"Are you young and flexible?"

"Young enough. Flexible enough."

"Then truly, yes." She shoved a paper-glazed panel aside and entered the cottage. "This way."

"I am honored." Natsuko placed her hand on Ciarán's sleeve. "This is tea cult, not tea and biscuit. You have experienced this?"

Ciarán stepped into the cottage and removed his boots. He wiggled his toes before sliding his feet into the largest of the three pairs of slippers provided. The slippers were very tight.

"I took a class at the Academy."

"Did you excel in this class?"

"I didn't burn the tea room down, if that's what you mean."

"Comforting."

"Just caught it on fire a little."

Natsuko chuckled. "Don't do that here."

"I'll try not to. But no guarantees."

The woman beckoned them inside. The tea room seemed identical to the practice lab at the Academy, though everything he could see was of much higher quality and in much better condition. He recalled that he should say something complementary about the decor. A lovely tapestry hung in an alcove, and the mats on the floor were equally lovely. Even the woodgrain of the timber used in the room's construction seemed spectacularly notable. And on the ceiling—

"That luminaire is very unusual."

"The carving? It is the traditional Eight Banners. Every home has one."

It was indeed a carving, and not a lamp, and made from wood, not second-epoch hull material, and that meant it likely wouldn't drop to the floor and shove a force blade through some part of him without warning. But it appeared identical in form to *Quite Possibly Alien*'s luminaires, so much so that it couldn't have been passed down from generation to generation as an idea, one that would soften or grow stylized as it worked its way into the minds and out of the hands of subsequent artists. Rather it looked milled from a pattern in a directives file and subsequently polished, or otherwise carved by hand from an original artist's template.

"Exquisite." Ciarán bowed to the woman. "Certainly no home could have finer. Does your... carving... possess a history you may relate?"

"Sit, and I will tell you while your young lady prepares the tea."

Ciarán began to say that Natsuko wasn't anyone's young lady but her own when he glanced at her and she held her index finger upright in front of her mask. Freeman merchants had a hand-talking language, one with gestures both subtle and unmistakable. That Natsuko knew this language surprised him. That she could simultaneously display the universal symbol for 'silence' with one hand, while also ordering him to 'keep her busy' in merchant's sign with the fingers holding her mask surprised him more.

Ciarán sat on the pillow provided. The woman, who might or might not be Kazuki Ryuu, watched him.

"You are quite nimble for such a large man."

"I have to be, unless I want the ship's crew to beat me silly. They take their workouts seriously." Ciarán grinned. "I also grew up on a planet, so this is like coming home. Gravity's a little lighter here, but everything else feels familiar."

"Does it?"

"Mostly. But we don't have anything nearly as refined, which I guess you're used to hearing. We certainly don't have anything as nice as that carving."

"Nothing that nice on an entire planet? You are flattering me."

"If I could I would," Ciarán said. "But it's a fact. My people are mostly spacefaring, and that's where all the nice stuff is. On the stations, on the family ships, and so on. Planet's full of practical stuff. There are a couple of big landowners, with big houses, but they're all quantity over quality. Luxury goods, but mass produced. Nothing made by hand like that carving. I'd love to hear more about it."

"Why do you think that is? This lack of handwork on your world?"

"It's not for lack of appreciation," Ciarán said. "It's mostly a lack of resources, and time."

"The Earth Restoration League lacks resources?"

"No, I don't think they do. Why do you ask?"

"Because you just said they do."

"I said *we* do. The Freeman Federation."

"But the Freeman Federation is simply a substate of the League."

"Well if that's the case, then someone better tell the League. And the Federation."

"You are genetically identical to League citizens."

"Some of us are. A lot of Freeman were born in the League, and took the Oath afterward."

"And your 'First Families'?"

"Likely they are genetically similar to many in the League. But why would that make them part of the League?"

"They share ancestors. They share a history. They are one."

"Up to a point, that's right. But only up to a point."

"And what would that point be?"

"The point at which the League broke its word and abandoned our ancestors on Earth."

"That is a myth."

"That is a fact. And if it weren't for the Huangxu Eng agreeing to ship my ancestors in cryo with their livestock, I wouldn't be here today. And if *their* descendants hadn't forgotten about my ancestors, and waited two thousand years to defrost my ancestors, and then decided they owned my ancestors like breeding stock, I might be prancing around in a red-and-gold skinsuit and cooing over fancy bulbs that only bloom on certain days of the year. And I'd be fine with that, so long as I wasn't a master or a slave."

"You Freemen actually believe that a hundred pregnant teenagers and a dozen house cats led a successful slave revolt against the Huangxu Eng? It is absurd."

"That does sound absurd," Ciarán said.

"And?"

"It was a hundred and twenty women and twenty-four mong hu. And most of the women were no longer pregnant by then. But I'm wondering what this conversation has to do with that pretty carving up there?"

She glanced up.

Natsuko pressed a woodcarving knife to her throat. "The tea is drugged."

"And you know this because?"

"Because I'm a medic, and I brought my test kit."

"Oh."

"Now tie her up."

Ciarán exploded from his seat and slammed his fist into the woman's face.

He kicked the nerve disrupter from her limp fingers and toed her kimono open the rest of the way. "There's a whole arsenal in there." He scooped the ugly weapon up, flicked the safety on, and tossed it to Natsuko.

She caught it one handed. "I didn't think to look. How did you know?"

He pocketed the man's razorgun and folding force blade. "I asked a wood carver about wood carving and all they want to do is slag my family?"

"Oh."

"You're mocking me."

"I'm not."

"Okay. How about this for a plan," Ciarán said. "You make the tea, and I'll force it down him."

"And then we find Kazuki Ryuu."

"Right. Unless we already have."

"I don't think we have."

"Me neither, and not just because this one's sporting the wrong team's kit."

"Because man or woman, Kazuki Ryuu inhabits the role."

"You really do admire her."

"Very much so."

Then let's find her."

"THAT WAS EASY," Ciarán said.

Kazuki Ryuu lay bound and gagged on a palette in the next room.

Natsuko began to untie her.

"It's customary to take the gag out first. It gives the captive a feeling of agency."

Ever since finding Seamus in the slave pen on Gallarus, he'd been reading up on abductions and their aftermath. Not that he could do anything for Seamus, but next time...

Natsuko worked on the gag. She had it out.

"Behind you!"

Ciarán ducked and pivoted as a sword blade scythed through the air above him. He dropped to his seat and lashed out with a left foot to the tackle room, and the swordsman huffed, dropping to a knee, and Ciarán swept his ankle, sending him sprawling. Ciarán planted his heel on the back of the swordsman's hand, and twisted upright. The swordsman pulled his hand free, and Ciarán dropped his weight onto the swordsman's spine. He hammered the man's temple with clenched knuckles and put him down hard. If he'd landed on him any harder, he would have driven him through the floor.

That was the sort of dirty fighting Mrs. Amati swore by, and Ciarán reluctantly embraced. He had wondered if he could do it in real life.

"I thought you said the tea was drugged."

"I thought you said you gave him all of it."

"Anyway, that's the other reason you take the gag out first." Ciarán kicked the grip of the long sword into his palm. "This guy is packing more hardware than the Black Fleet."

He tested the balance of the blade. It was similar to the practice blades he and Ko Shan exercised with, though obviously much finer, and sharper.

"That's mine," Kazuki Ryuu said.

"It's nice," Ciarán said.

"It ought to be. I stole it from the emperor."

"What'd the emperor think of that?"

"He hasn't noticed yet."

"I think maybe he has." Ciarán could hear an air car kicking up dust outside.

"Those are local thugs," Kazuki Ryuu said. "The emperor would simply drop a rock on me."

"Kinetic bombardment of a planetary surface is proscribed by a dozen international treaties." Ciarán swept the sword in a flashing arc. "Plus, he would risk nicking the blade."

Kazuki Ryuu laughed. It sounded just like the laugh in the *Noh* plays.

"Do you keep a lot of money on you?" Ciarán asked.

"That's rather personal."

"It is. I'm just trying to figure out why anyone would send one person to tie you up, and then a bunch more later."

"That's easy. They would tie me up so they wouldn't have to kill me. And they would call for the rest of the team when they knew the package had arrived. But that logic doesn't apply in this case."

"Were you expecting any deliveries?"

"She means us," Natsuko said. "We're the package."

"Oh."

"As I said, that logic doesn't apply here."

"Does this thing have a scabbard?"

"It did when I stole it."

"How about lately?"

"Look in the wardrobe." She pointed at a tall cabinet.

The wardrobe held nothing but a pile of masks.

Kazuki Ryuu rose and began massaging her limbs. "There's a sack in there. You may need to dig for it. Put all the masks in it and bring it. I'll go talk to them."

"That doesn't seem very sensible."

"Do you have a better idea?"

He stuffed all the masks into the sack. And then he found the scabbard.

"As a matter of fact," Ciarán said. "I might."

26

The man on the floor groaned and shook his head. "Whatever it is, it is a stupid idea." He'd managed to make it to his hands and knees. "They are not my compatriots. And they are not locals. And they are not here for you. She asked me to tie her up."

"He is lying," Natsuko said.

"Indeed," Ryuu said. "I rarely *ask* for anything."

"Believe me or not," the man said. "But you can't outrun them, and if you fight them, you cannot simply kill them." He jerked his chin at the sword in Ciarán's hand. "You must... defenestrate them."

"Cut their heads off," Natsuko said.

"Even a nerve disruptor only slows them down."

"Interesting," Kazuki Ryuu said. "What are they?"

"They were hounds," the man said. "But now—"

Ciarán laughed. "Dogs that can operate an air car?"

"Silence," Kazuki Ryuu said. "Whose hounds?"

The man's face twisted into a bitter grin. "Mine."

Footsteps sounded on the porch outside. Heavy boots, pacing. Then another pair. And another.

"How many," Kazuki Ryuu said.

"Four."

Ciarán listened for a fourth pair of boots.

"Get up. Quietly."

Kazuki Ryuu glanced at the man's feet. "Where are your shoes?"

"I don't know."

"Get on the bed. Quickly."

The footsteps drew nearer, their steps muffled. They were in the tea room.

And then one was in the doorway.

He looked like an Ojin merchant, the sort of solidly situated spacer whose utilities were always pressed and whose hull-walkers were always polished. He smiled a merchant's welcoming smile, and nodded his head minutely. The plasma rifle in his hands seemed brand new, and if not for the stench of pre-heater oil, might have been mistaken for a showroom specimen, one powered down and meant for a customer's inspection.

"In here."

And then three of them stood in the doorway, Ojin merchants, not just similar, but identical.

One of them glanced at Ciarán. For an instant something black and bottomless flickered behind his eyes.

He turned away from Ciarán.

And then *it* turned back.

"Plowboy."

Then all three glared at him, any semblance of humanity wiped from their night-black eyes.

"We will save you for last," the first one said.

"Don't move," Kazuki Ryuu said.

The things glanced at her.

And laughed as one.

"Not you." Kazuki Ryuu pointed. "The plowboy." Her lips

twisted into a smile. "You are free to dance."

A white light flared, and arced, and the reek of ozone and roasting meat flooded the room.

Kazuki Ryuu gripped a small black box in her hand.

They were all three down, and twitching on the floor, sparks arcing between the plasma rifles clamped in their rigid fingers and whatever lay beneath the charred rush mats now swaddling the floor.

Kazuki Ryuu thrust the box into her pocket and hammered her palm into Ciarán's shoulder, rocking him back on his heels as she swept the sword from the scabbard.

Ciarán glanced at the scabbard still in his hands.

He glanced at Kazuki Ryuu.

The shop merchants, or hounds, or *whatever* had stopped twitching and were beginning to mutter.

"Diediediediediedie—"

"Find the fourth one," Kazuki Ryuu said as plasma fire roasted through the wall centimeters from his elbow.

"Found it," Ciarán said.

The mask cabinet exploded toward him and an arm thrust through from behind it, and a leg, and then it was there, swinging the plasma rifle up. Ciarán rammed the scabbard into its gut until his fist felt meat.

Something wet splashed his face. Natsuko dropped the woodcarving knife and tossed him a towel.

The fourth hound lay muttering and gurgling, throat slashed ear to ear.

"You must finish the job," the man said.

Ciarán scooped up the woodcarving knife and tossed it onto the bed. "Be my guest."

Kazuki Ryuu yanked the scabbard free from his grip and sheathed the sword. "We must hurry. Follow me."

"Hang on." Ciarán dashed out to the porch and retrieved

their belongings. He handed Natsuko the heavy atmosphere canisters. "Can you carry those?"

She nodded.

Ciarán studied the wreckage of the hounds as he weighed the string sack dangling from his fingers.

He had to do this, but the idea of carrying around four severed heads in a sack didn't just seem nasty, but unnecessary.

He glanced at Kazuki Ryuu. "Do you have an axe, or a stiff knife, or something? Ideally, I'd like an overseer's rod, but—"

"I have one of those."

"Oh."

"Would you like me to fetch it for you?"

"Sure."

"I'm joking. Do I look like someone who fetches?"

"You do not."

"It's in the cabinet. In a secret compartment in the base."

"This won't take a minute."

The cabinet lay in splinters, but she really did have an overseer's rod. Ciarán flicked the monomolecular whip out a few centimeters, what he'd begun to think of as "scalpel mode." He glanced up to find them all staring at him.

"If you're squeamish you might want to look away."

When he was done, he pocketed the four powered-down riders. He didn't know what else to do with them. He needed to get them back to the ship for analysis as soon as possible. He didn't want to panic anyone, but this sort of situation could easily end up with every man, woman, and child in Pinion System getting pulverized to atoms and sucked into a brand new *Quite Possibly Alien* black hole.

And who knows how many more of these things were out there, either here or elsewhere. He thought the problem had been contained. That they were handling it. And now the first system they visited, the *very first*, crawled with these things. This was a mess, and he needed time to think it through.

"We have to hurry," Kazuki Ryuu said.

"Right." Natsuko and he paused to put on their boots.

Natsuko touched his sleeve, and at first it didn't register that her fingers were tracing out merchant hand-script against his skin.

This is not right.

He rested his hand on her thigh.

Agreed. Stay close.

"We must go," Kazuki Ryuu said.

"Can I keep these slippers?" Hess would love to reverse engineer them. They had to be the world's best insulators.

"Fine. Now come on."

She led them along the gravel road for a few hundred meters then plunged into a dense wood. The shadows grew darker, without a moon. Branches clawed at them. Their pace slowed as they fought through the thickening underbrush.

"Here," Ciarán said, taking the sack of masks and the sword from Kazuki Ryuu. "We'll move faster."

"We must hurry," she said.

The man they'd mistaken for Ryuu had taken the lead. He shoved through the underbrush, clearing a path.

They burst out of the woods and into a clearing. A blocky building in the center of the clearing loomed before them, one with a shape Ciarán recognized. He put on a burst of speed, tapping Natsuko's sleeve as he passed. She fell in behind him as he slowed.

The Ryuu imposter darted through the building's darkened doorway.

"Quickly." Kazuki Ryuu ducked inside.

Ciarán stuck his head and shoulders in, just to be certain.

Slave pen. Just like on Gallarus.

He yanked the barred door closed and made certain it had locked.

Kazuki Ryuu gripped the bars and glared at him. "What are you doing?"

"Locking you in and calling for backup."

"Both of you," Kazuki Ryuu hissed. "Get in here right now."

"You're joking, right?"

"This is not a suggestion. It is an *order*."

The sound of a light flyer's engines passed overhead.

"Do I look like someone who follows orders?"

"You look like a fool." She turned her attention to Natsuko. "Do as I ask."

Natsuko shouldered Ciarán aside. She tried the lock. It wouldn't open. "Give me the key."

"I don't have a key."

"Too late," the man said. "The all-consuming flame comes. We must go deeper in."

"Oh, my sweet child." Kazuki Ryuu reached her fingers through the bars to touch Natsuko's sleeve. "I'm so sorry."

And then Kazuki Ryuu disappeared in shadow.

A second later the sky flared white.

Ciarán glanced at Natsuko. Her mask had dropped and her eyes were wide, focused on the mushrooming pillar of fire rising in the distance.

"Natsuko."

She gazed up at him.

The sky darkened. A distant roar began.

Caught out in the open they had no chance.

He glanced at the lock.

Even if he had a key, there wasn't time to work the lock.

He had to shout to be heard. "Forgive me!"

He didn't know if she heard. Her lips were open in a scream, her gaze fixed on the terror racing toward them, the moonlit tree line behind him reflected in her eyes.

One instant the trees were standing and then they weren't.

The roar of the wind shredded the sky as pebbles danced at his feet.

A cloud crossed the moon.

There existed only roaring, and shaking, and darkness.

Until even that nightmare ceased.

27

Trinity System, Freeman Federation

As far as interrogation cells went, this one was pretty nice. Macer guessed it had been a conference room, with large tables suitable for a half score of people around them, and another score seated around the walls, all in the industrial-looking wheeled office chairs you'd only find on planets and aboard fixed-position orbitals.

They'd brought him through a hatch facing one long side of a table, one set perpendicular to another table, and parallel to a third, so that the tables created three sides of a rectangle, the fourth side being open and backed by a deck-to-deckhead display wall. On the table directly facing the displays rested a placard in front of a slightly-taller-than-the-others chair, and that placard said *Stationmaster* in all four languages of Trinity Station.

A holo tank in the center of the tables projected the in-system traffic as measured from the tens of thousands of sensors spread throughout Trinity space. The display wall presently hosted hundreds of smaller displays, each showing some aspect of the exterior of the station, from spindle to the ring. It wouldn't surprise Macer if they'd come up with some sort of smell-display as well, and when the stationmaster appeared they'd switch it on so he could get a whiff of the fear, or relief, or whatever other emotion ponged around the station at the moment.

Most of the sensors were surplus Hundred Planets kit, and nearly state of the art. The Huangxu Eng constantly upgraded their own systems and sold off the lightly used surplus. The stationmaster was a big one for knowing what was going on, and a reliable customer. Macer didn't like the stationmaster much. He was a crony of his dad's, and married into the family, and a blow-in, not that there was anything wrong with being a blow-in. Truxton was a blow-in, and he was changing those things that needed changing. The stationmaster was a blow-in, and he was ruining all the things that shouldn't change.

Macer and his guards were the only ones in the compartment. They didn't fashion themselves guards, but "escorts," and maybe they were right. If he'd wanted to escape he could have at any time, and maybe he should have, and headed down to the planet, and let them try to dig him out. He wasn't keeping his job, not the way things ultimately went down, and no way he was keeping *any* job in Truxton Engineering, or any of the other Truxton companies, for that matter. He wasn't certain, anyway, that he wanted to stay in space service for anyone, if this was how it worked. Your boss stabbing you in your back, your captain turning out to be an idiot, a self-destructive maniac, and the sort of imbecile that could snatch defeat from the jaws of victory, all while feeling proud and virtuous.

The lead escort, a skinny guy who would snap like a twig in *Four-Squared*'s punishing gravity, ordered him to sit, and when Macer didn't, looked like he wanted to do something about it. His two other escorts stepped closer, pinning Macer between them and the table.

"Go ahead," the skinny guy said. "Try something."

Macer glanced around the compartment. He locked gazes with the lead escort.

There was no percentage in trying something with a man he could break in half one-handed. And if he was going to try something, it would be with the stationmaster, who actually had some authority, and thus something to lose. Maybe he would try something, but when he did it would be on his own terms, and the price his own price. Until then—

"Back off."

All three of them backed off.

And Macer took a seat.

His dad had once told him that people weren't mind readers. But even the most gormless imbecile could grasp a headline if it was stamped on your face. You had to be willing to spell out the rest of the story, though, one bloody syllable at a time. And you had to keep on keeping on, even if it took a novel to hammer out all you had to say.

His dad wasn't often right, but he was right about that.

The stationmaster entered through the hatch behind the head table.

He wasn't wearing court robes, and that was good.

Lucan mac Tír appeared average. Average sized for a spacer, and average height, with average looks, neither League nor Ojin. The only thing about him that didn't look average was his apparent age. He appeared positively ancient, which he might well be, with white hair and beard, both station length, and icy blue eyes that looked like they'd stared into the void, sized the void up, and invited the void to take up residence inside him, to peer back out from behind those eyes. The ancient pendant spire dangling from his drooping earlobe seemed positively youthful next to his creased face.

There were lots of explanations about why they'd made mac Tír stationmaster. The only one that made any sense said that he was the only candidate the League, the Ojinate, and the First Families could agree upon. They each detested him equally, and expected that he would screw them over, which he would inevitably do. But when he did screw them over, he'd screw their neighbors over even more.

Macer found nothing to fault in that logic. Lucan mac Tír was a man exactly like his own father. He looked out for his own interests first and foremost, consistently and without mercy. By making mac Tír stationmaster, the great powers of Trinity space had lashed his interests to theirs. So long as the station prospered, he prospered, and so long as he prospered, he did not interfere in their business.

The stationmaster took a seat.

He turned to Macer.

He didn't look happy, and that was bad. "Do you know why you're here?"

"Because I'd rather be here than hurt these three guards on your station."

"You're dismissed," the stationmaster said.

Macer began to stand.

"Not you. Sit down."

Macer sat.

The stationmaster waited for the hatch to close. "How's your father?"

"Still pumping air, last I heard."

"You sound disappointed."

"Not disappointed, sir. I do not wish him ill. It's only..."

"Go on."

"I had a lot more fun when he was dead."

The stationmaster grinned. "Didn't we all."

"We did, sir."

The stationmaster pressed a button and the holo tank in the center of the table retracted into its base. He used a handheld to brush through the patchwork of smaller displays until he found the one he wanted. He expanded the view of the nic Cartaí orbital yard and zoomed in on a single vessel in a repair dock. Truxton's *Golden Parachute*.

"That's a confusing sight."

"It is, sir."

"I can't decide which I find more disturbing. The sight of a Truxton superluminal in a nic Cartaí yard, or the idea that there's been an unregistered Templeman drive lashed to my station time and again over the last twenty years."

"Which is worse is for you to decide, sir."

"It is, and to decide I need facts. According to my people, you have not been supplying any facts."

"They're trying to wake the dead, sir. And it's not my place to answer. What I could tell them I've told them, and what I could show them I showed them. But according to nic Cartaí, the sensor logs from *Golden Parachute* are their property by right of salvage. And the log nexus on *Four-Squared* has been slagged, and the local sensor logs wrapped by now."

"Who slagged the nexus?"

"I can't say. I didn't see it done, and I don't have proof one way or another."

"But you have suspicions."

"I know I didn't do it and that's all."

"You're protecting Singh."

"I'm protecting us all. Accusing people without proof hurts everyone."

"That's a pinhole you're focused on. We're talking about a

gash in the hull torn stem to stern if that drive breached containment."

"But it didn't, sir. And in time a pinhole can kill you as dead as a blowout."

"Your father would tell me."

"He would, sir."

"And that's the engine idling beneath your skin, isn't it, son?"

"Sir?"

"Anything Luther Gant would do? Macer Gant will do the opposite."

"That's not true."

The stationmaster drummed his fingers on the table. "That's not true. Sir."

"As you say, sir."

The stationmaster pressed a button. "I've disabled all sensors in this compartment. If you have anything you want to say to me off the record, you may do so."

Macer only had the stationmaster's word for the disabled sensors. The stationmaster might still be recording their conversation and just saying that he wasn't.

"Nothing off the record, sir."

"Here's a word of advice, and it isn't free advice. It's the sort of advice one has to pay dearly for, and I'm offering it to you in trade, simple terms, payment due in full at a future date mutually agreed upon."

"I'm listening, sir." It seemed like he hadn't been lying. They really were having a private conversation.

"The easiest course to steer is a reciprocal. And the least profitable."

"Thank you, sir. That's..."

"A statement. And not advice."

"Um... Agreed, sir."

"I don't want nor require your agreement. I'm not senile,

you heaping lump of planetary meat."

"Noted, sir."

He held up a finger. "If you wish to be considered wise, you must consider your words before you speak."

"Thank you, sir. That is good advice."

"It's a bromide, you dolt."

"It is, sir. Although it sounds a lot like advice I've heard before."

The stationmaster sighed. "Here is the important part to remember. When you wish others to consider you foolish? You must appear to reply without thought."

Macer nodded. "And then?"

"Were you dropped on your head at birth?"

Macer pretended to think about it. "I don't recall, sir. I was pretty young back then."

"Macer Gant, you have been and remain a fool." He tapped the table to get Macer's attention. Then he pressed another button. "But you are a special kind of fool."

Macer's handheld chirped. The compartment sensors weren't just "off." They were powered down and disconnected from the station nexus.

"Now, do you understand me?"

"I have a tell regarding my father, one that others will attempt to exploit to manipulate me. This is a weakness, and I should fix it. And I should fix it without revealing that it is fixed. Then, when I realize I am being manipulated, I can use this secret self-knowledge to project a false face and turn the tables on the manipulator or manipulators."

The stationmaster stared at him. "And?"

"And I'm not there yet. But I'm working on it, Uncle." Macer grimaced. "I mean, sir."

"Was that so hard?"

"It wasn't, sir."

"We're done here. For now."

Macer stood.

"Where do you think you're going?"

"You said we're done here."

"I am done here. You are just getting started."

28

T he stationmaster abandoned him in the compartment without a backward glance.

Macer didn't know what came next, but he assumed he wouldn't like it. He watched the wall display, where hardsuited nic Cartaí yard monkeys were beginning to crawl over the surface of Truxton's *Golden Parachute*. They'd peeled back the force window and wrenched the boat bay doors open already. A crew of six were beginning to carve up the longboat wreckage into lift sled–sized pieces for removal.

The hatch across from him opened and a short, blocky man stepped in. He wore a red skinsuit patterned with gold Imperial lions in the loose-fitting Huangxu style. Over that he wore a woven antiballistic jumper, the sort that fastened from neck to navel. It was presently open, as if he wasn't too worried about being shot in the front anytime soon. Fast on his heels came the largest mong hu Macer had ever seen.

The pair were instantly recognizable. Merchant Captain Thomas Truxton and Crewman Thorn, ship's cat of the merchant vessel *Rose*. Macer's boss's boss's boss's boss. A living legend.

Truxton dropped into the seat across from Macer. "What are you staring at?"

Macer started to rise.

"Don't move too fast. Thorn's coming to check you out."

The mong hu's nose appeared from under the table next to him. Macer extended his hand, palm up, and allowed the big cat to inspect it.

"You know mong hu."

"I do, sir."

"Drop the honorific. We don't know each other. And you don't work for me as of now."

"I understand." He'd figured he'd be cut loose. But now that it was real, he felt sick to his stomach.

"It's hot as blazes in here. Can you turn the heat down?"

"The controls are at the stationmaster's seat."

"I didn't ask where the controls were. I asked you to turn down the heat."

"I don't work for you anymore. If you'd like to turn the heat down, you now know where you may do so."

"Listen to you. Mister Formal Freeman. I give you one little bit of bad news and your back's up like I've filed intent. Just because I can't order you around anymore doesn't mean you can't help me out if you want to. It's called being polite."

"And if I don't want to be polite?"

"You don't have to be."

Macer heard the rest, spoken or not. "But?"

"But if you were, it would be good for us both. Word of a merchant."

Macer stood and walked to the stationmaster's seat. He adjusted the thermostat.

"Take a seat. I'm sure Uncle Lucan won't mind."

Macer glanced at the stationmaster's seat and the control arrayed in front of it. The stationmaster had disabled the room sensors and forgotten to turn them back on.

Macer glanced at Truxton and found him watching. So far, this entire conversation had taken place in private. Unless Truxton had a recorder hidden on him.

"So you see how it is," Truxton said. "Off the record, and nothing under the table. An honest and private conversation with the stationmaster's permission. On second thought, come over here and slide in next to Thorn and me. You look so terribly inconsequential over there."

Macer did as asked.

Truxton tapped his sleeve. "I scare you."

"It's a weird feeling," Macer said. "Maybe this is what being scared feels like."

"You don't know?"

"If I thought about it, I could know. But then you might say or do something important and I'd miss it while I was thinking."

"Okay, then I won't tell you not to be scared. I just want to chat and get some idea of what sort of mess I'm in."

"Mess *you're* in?"

"Sure. I have a captain with a vessel with an unregistered Templeman drive getting ready to jump out of the system, and another captain that appears to have turned pirate and attacked a nic Cartaí daughter, and the stationmaster ready to kick me out of the system for putting the station in danger by not doing maintenance on the unregistered Templeman drive, and a giant line of credit ready to get pulled by the Freeman Merchant Bank when my formerly productive collateral drops off the long-range sensors. Plus I just had to mothball a repair dock and lay off its crew for lack of work. That's just for starters."

"That's a lot," Macer said. "I wish I could help."

"I think you can," Truxton said.

"I *know* I can," Macer said. "But I need to concentrate on looking for work."

"Suppose I gave your old job back and paid you for your time."

"You just said that *Four-Squared* was outbound, so there goes my job."

"How about I just pay you for your time."

"Time is what I haven't got. Do you have any idea how hard it is to find an associate engineering gig?"

"Hard. But you'd have a gig with me."

"Until you got what you wanted and didn't need me anymore. Then I'd be back here again. Looking for work."

"But I could make it harder to find work. Or easier."

"My face. It's in the news stream," Macer said. "I don't think you can do anything either way."

"You underestimate me."

"Never," Macer said, and meant it.

"What do you want?" Truxton said.

"Some surplus gear. A fresh engineering handheld, a used drone, a hardsuit with a hole in its visor and a replacement visor, used or new old stock, doesn't matter so long as it holds pressure."

"You're setting up freelance."

"Who's going to have me on their payroll after this fiasco?"

"I can think of one guy."

"Singh."

"The obvious choice."

"Up until he pulled rank and took my place on the liberty boat, I thought he was a solid citizen. It still seems unreal to me. Given what I know now? Working for Singh is not an option."

"Given what you know or what you suspect?"

"What I know."

"And the price of this knowledge is the stuff you just named?"

"All that stuff but the replacement visor is on board *Golden*

Parachute. I got the feeling Aoife nic Cartaí has decided anything Truxton she can touch is hers. So the price of what I know is you signing a quit claim that says I can have that stuff if nic Cartaí agrees. Plus a replacement visor."

"What's the catch?"

"It's a nice drone."

"How nice?"

"Very. Nice."

"You didn't have to tell me that."

"I don't want to cheat you."

"Why not? I just canned you."

"It's complicated."

When he was a kid, he'd wanted to go off planet because that was where the future was. And he wanted to work for Truxton because Truxton was the one making the future Macer wanted to live in. If he helped Truxton out, even if Truxton really was abandoning the system, Macer wouldn't be abandoning his dreams.

When he had the kit and could go out on his own, maybe he'd be the one to pick up the torch and carry it forward. It wasn't likely, but it wasn't impossible. And if it wasn't impossible then it was worth thinking about, and deciding if it was worth mapping out and planning, just to see if it might work.

It really wasn't all that complicated, but it was more than he wanted to tell anyone else, even Truxton.

Not without thinking it through first.

"Okay," Truxton said. "It's a deal. Draw up a contract and I'll sign it."

"Do we need a contract?"

"I don't. But you're delivering first."

"I'm willing to trust you."

Truxton looked him up and down. "I haven't heard that line in a long time."

Truxton pulled a pen and paper from inside his sweater. He scribbled on the paper for a while and slid it along the table to Macer. "Just in case I'm tempted to cheat you later."

Macer pocketed the paper without looking at it. "What do you want to know?"

"How close are you with the stationmaster?"

"He's my mother's sister's widower. He gives me advice now and then, and tries to look out for me if it's not too much trouble for him."

"And has it been? Too much trouble?"

"Not until now. But then, I've never done anything... notable until now."

"Is there anything I should know that won't keep until later?"

"You could stop worrying about *Four-Squared* and tell your bankers to get off your back."

"Because?"

"Because I put the superluminal drive in diagnostic mode before I went across to *Golden Parachute*. And since Captain Violet hung me out to dry, it will still be in diagnostic mode. No one is jumping out of the system on that vessel. Not without a Templeman-rated power engineer on board."

"Wait here," Truxton said.

"There's more."

"Tell me."

Macer fished around in his mouth with a finger. He popped the data crystal loose. He polished it on his utility sleeve before passing it to Truxton.

"Complete logs from the *Golden Parachute* since it underwent total system wipe in Gallarus space. Salvaged logs from the vessel prior to its capture by Aoife nic Cartaí. Select logs from nic Cartaí's *Quite Possibly Alien* that nic Cartaí says will be of interest to you. And select sensor logs from *Four-Squared* showing the assassin that turned up and details of the bomb he planted."

"Is that all?"

All, but for some nice footage of Sensors Operator Lizzie Teal in a Truxton skinsuit, but Truxton wasn't asking about that. "I think that's it. The stationmaster would like a copy of the logs."

"You didn't give him a copy?"

"I was a Truxton hand when he asked. They weren't mine to give."

"And now?"

"If I wanted to start a riot, I'd show them to him. But that's entirely up to you and nic Cartaí. I'm just the messenger. So don't shoot me after you've reviewed all that."

"You didn't keep a copy?"

"Just the parts I'm in, excepting those parts where I'm naked or unconscious."

Truxton stared at him.

"I'm in a skinsuit in those parts I might need to keep out of prison. I wouldn't have kept those either, except the situation still seems fluid to me."

"Fluid."

"Right. I didn't have time to even look at the stuff from before I stepped on board *Golden Parachute*. Aoife nic Cartaí said to tell you to look at those first."

"What do you think of her?"

"She has nice ankles. "

"That's it?"

Macer shrugged.

Truxton started to stand and changed his mind. "A lot of my drones are bank financed."

"Not this one," Macer said. "I checked."

"Give me that note."

Macer passed the scrap of paper over.

Truxton scribbled on it, folded it, and passed it back.

"Oh," Macer said. "I forgot. Can I keep these utilities? It's just until I see my tailor, and then I'll send them back."

Truxton laughed. "Sure, kid. You do that. Now get out of here."

29

A bell rang as Macer entered the tailor's shop in one of the older, and thus dingier, parts of the Arcade. Mr. Pearse had been his father's tailor, and his grandfather's before that, and while the tailor's given name might change, his surname did not. The current Mr. Pearse appeared to have been born Ojin Eng, and he might indeed pass for such, if not for the pendant spire dangling from his earlobe, and the fact then when he spoke it was as if he'd just stepped off the Trinity Surface shuttle.

"If it isn't the former and future Gant, a pleasure to behold your face. But as for the rest of you? What can I say?"

"'Tis a shame to hide a star beneath a bushel." That was what the previous Mr. Pearse and the present Mr. Pearse had said to him on each and every visit, ever since he'd first set foot on the station as a pudgy and sullen boy-child.

"Aptly put, my young friend."

"It's not very original." That too, was part of the tailor's timeworn script.

"If you want originality, best to look elsewhere," Mr. Pearse said. "Here we deliver—"

"Elegance," they both said at the same time.

"Would you mind bringing out my funeral suit, and my evening wear?" It was traditional for planetary customers without station apartments to maintain a wardrobe at their tailor's. It saved boosting their station kit out of a gravity well again and again, and no place on the planet to use it, anyway.

"On it," Mr. Pearse said, and returned with the two garments. He stretched them out on a scarred but spotless cutting table.

"Behold!" they both said at the same time.

Mr. Pearse eyed him up and down. "You've gained weight."

"I have? Where?"

"Everywhere a man wants it. Are you frequenting a gymnasium?"

"Serving on a high-gravity vessel."

"They must have kept you hopping, else you'd be a kilometer wide and a meter tall. Now what are we wanting with such an incongruous pair?"

"I've a job interview, and I'm trying to decide which to wear."

"Well, one makes you look like a pallbearer. And the other makes you look like a gigolo."

"So if I showed up in the funeral suit, I couldn't be mistaken for a prosperous businessman?"

"You could, if you were a prosperous businessman on your way to bury your mother."

"I see." Macer glanced out the shop window. It was a typical workday, with regular, but light, foot traffic passing. Perhaps this had been a mistake.

"She was a sweet and beautiful woman, and much beloved. If you'd like me to alter this suit, it can be accomplished."

"But?"

"But it will cost you."

Macer glanced at the tailor. "How much?"

"Only the finest garment Mr. Pearse has ever made." He ran his palm across the fabric, his fingers lingering. "I'm not saying my boy, or his boy, couldn't better this work one day. But she was a rose amongst briars, your mother, and you *her* finest work."

Mr. Pearse flicked a speck of lint away. "And for one dreadful day, at least? You looked it."

"The evening wear, then."

"It can't be done," Mr. Pearse said. "There's not enough material to work with."

"You misunderstand," Macer said. "Change of plans. I'll take it as is."

"You'll look like some relict pauper's boy toy."

"How so?"

"It's too tight in the shoulders and too loose in the waist, even for a... I mean..."

"Even for an Arcade-slinking nightcrawler like me."

"You have been reported to cat around, it's true. But it's an ill-fitting garment now, and not the sort of attire an otherwise respectable man would be seen in."

"A man with money, you mean."

"A gentleman with means and taste."

"We can't have that."

"That's the first sensible thing you've said, lad."

"Suppose I *wanted* to look like a rich and elegant woman's plaything?"

"I'd take in the waist, and rework adjacent areas."

"And the shoulders?"

"Leave them as is. The current fashion is to advertise in all things. Subtlety is out, and with it, dignity."

"How long would that take?"

"To dress you like a shameless hoor?"

"To dress me like a man with considerable means but insufficient judgement."

"Not long. I've been dressing your father all his life. Put your arms out and hold still."

Mr. Pearse ran the measuring scanner around him. "I'll be back."

Macer peeled out of his Truxton utilities while he waited. Except for emergency alterations for ancient Trinity-system families, Mr. Pearse's had little walk-in trade.

He squeezed into the outfit under Mr. Pearse's critical eye.

"Ach," Mr. Pearse said. "It fits, for shame. Where shall I send the bill?"

"To my father."

"He'll never pay it."

"Here." Macer struck a pose. "Take a still image and send it along with the bill. Explain that some newsies have been hounding you for dirt on your customers and you wanted his advice."

"That's blackmail."

"Not quite. But if you wanted to ask him to do more than pay my bill it would be."

"What if I asked him to pay all of his own bills as well?"

"That would be smart business. Mention I was on my way to a meeting with Fionnuala nic Cartaí and see if he doesn't order a dozen new shirts."

"You're making that up."

"About the shirts? Maybe. It might be two dozen."

"About Nuala nic Cartaí."

"I wish I was. Now work quick. I'm losing feeling in areas I'd rather not name."

Mr. Pearse grabbed his handheld. "Smile, and try not to split your trousers."

MACER TOOK a deep breath and steadied his nerves. *In for a pingin, in for a crown.*

He plunged into the crowded flower stall. Someone pinched his ass. Someone cupped his... assets. Bloom's was the largest and most popular flower stall on the Arcade, and its cashier the station's most reliable gossip.

He'd never understood flower shops. A flower or two on their own smelled nice. A thousand thousand flowers, each competing for a single nose, wasn't just distracting. It was an assault.

Macer lurched as he was pinched again. He'd made it to the counter.

"Back off, the lot of you," the young woman behind the till said. "Walk of shame, is it now?"

"You mean the way I'm dressed?"

"It's hardly business attire for this time of day. I've nothing but sympathy for you, pet."

"I imagine you have something more than that for me."

She glanced up and her gaze narrowed. "Do you *imagine* that?"

"I'd like a flower." He looked her in the eye. "For my lapel."

"Well, as you might have noticed, we have many flowers. Is there any particular *floral unit* that strikes your fancy?"

"I'm not following."

"You don't remember me," she said.

"Of course I do."

"What's my name?"

"Ellen Kirwan."

"So you can read a name tag? I'm impressed."

"You asked me your name. I told you."

"What sort of flower is it you're wanting?"

"As I said, one for my lapel."

"It's called a *boutonniere.*"

"All right."

"Say it."

"Boutonniere."

"It's a technical term. Like *Templeman damper*, and *flux wand* and *wideband scanner correction.*"

"*Scatter* correction."

"Do I look like I give a rat's ass?"

"You look angry."

"Well, there's where you're wrong. What sort of boutonniere are you after, sir?"

"One that says I'm off the market and in a relationship with an older woman."

"That figures." She pinned a flower to his lapel. A big, ugly, smelly flower. "It's on the house."

"Ellen—"

"You know, my ould wan warned me about engineers, and I didn't believe her."

"I thought we were having a good time," Macer said. "And then you—"

"Got a call. About a *flower-shop emergency.* That didn't seem like a clue to you?"

"A chiller might have experienced a pump failure. There could have been a leak in the hydration spray system. A—"

"It was two in the morning, Macer, and you prattling on endlessly about *work.* And it's not *my* flower shop. I'm only the cashier."

"So?"

"So my ould wan was right about you lot. Shag first. Talk later. "

She looked him up and down and shook her head. "What a waste."

"Ellen—"

"Look, just go."

"I will," Macer said.

"What?"

"Thanks."

"This old bitty of yours. Is she deaf or just gormless?"

Macer leaned across the counter and whispered, "I wouldn't let them hear you say that on the nic Cartaí dock."

He reached out and pushed her mouth closed.

She blinked as he brushed his fingers against her neck. He kissed her earlobe and breathed into her ear. "I didn't realize I was boring you. Maybe try a little honesty next time."

He made it back to the Arcade with only a few more bruises and nine-tenths of his dignity still intact. He had a thick skin, and very little shame, but some of what Ellen said very nearly hurt.

He dumped the floral unit into the first waste receptacle he passed and kept on going.

30

The bog-standard Freeman longboat slowed as it approached the merchant vessel. It bypassed the boat bay and docked with a battered FFE mounted to the mast directly aft of the boat bay. Macer didn't know why, when the rest of these FFEs on the mast were shiny and new, that ring of containers was ancient and scarred, or why one had been modified to sport docking clamps and an airlock. He had a guess, though. Nic Cartaí was all about tradition, and somebody's great-great-granny had probably been chained up in there, and the rows of slave chain and cargo seats still intact, a visible lesson for the younger generation as to just how good they had it.

He didn't need a lesson. He knew he had it good, and he didn't understand the obsession with looking backward. But he'd agreed to meet Aoife nic Cartaí at a place of her choosing to retrieve his stuff, and she'd chosen here, the former slave compartments of *Invisible Hand*, flagship of Fionnuala nic Cartaí's merchant empire, and personal conveyance of the Cartaí herself.

He and the nic Cartaí pilot were the only ones on board,

and the pilot not inclined to talk, so when the pilot heaved the airlock open, he said thanks and stepped through.

The woman standing in the compartment didn't look like Aoife nic Cartaí. Related, maybe, but nothing remotely gene-modded and leveled-up about her.

She looked like a knife blade shaped into a woman's form and honed sharp enough to slice through a hull. She had some cycles on her that didn't show as wear, but as a burnishing of the grip and shimmer to the water-blade from honest work at the business she was forged for. She wore a nic Cartaí skinsuit and a merchant captain's greatcoat over that, and an overseer's rod jammed beneath her belt. A merchant's ring adorned her finger where a wedding band would go, and all he could think at first was how much he'd like to see her unsheathed.

Macer felt his lip curl. "You're not Aoife nic Cartaí."

"Not hardly." She watched him mercilessly. "One of those are you? A cutlery fan. And a smirker."

"I know art when I see it."

"Well, you're direct, I'll give you that." She swept her arm in an arc, like merchants did. "How do you like the frame?"

The bulkheads were covered in Alexandrian rosewood. In the center of the compartment stood a live-edged table capable of seating two score guests, one shaped from a massive cross-section of lacewing ebony, black with contrasting patterns in orange. Around the table stood nearly forty chairs, each one unique and made of wood, but wood as hard as ceramic composite, and each chair the product of a single tree, pruned and urged into the shape of a chair. It took decades to grow a single chair.

Any tech installed seemed largely hidden and entirely state-of-the-art; the carpet white, trackless, and centimeters deep; the lighting warm and diffuse—the general impression of immense wealth and unstoppable power.

At the far end of the table stood a single chair that didn't match the rest. A common ship's mess chair, battered and scarred, made from cheap extruded plastics in a garish orange, blackened as if it had been charred, the entire mess immersed in a pool of light brighter than the light in the rest of the compartment, as if the chair were on display. On the far bulkhead pranced the symbol of nic Cartaí, a leaping stag in red and white with gold antlers. It looked like it might race the length of the table any minute.

"I expected a slaver's deck."

"It's there, beneath it all."

Macer nodded. This was what incredible wealth looked like. It took a merchant empire to feed the beast that vomited out such luxuries, an insatiable monster that would forever be rattling the chain for more. Imagine a life lashed to that, even in such a lovely setting.

He could rescue her and take her away from all this suffering.

He let his gaze rest upon her.

"I meant that underneath this fancy carpet the slaver's deck is still there. I yank all of this out now and then just to remind myself."

"Oh. I thought you were making an analogy."

"You mean speaking metaphorically."

"Right."

"You can shove the genie back into the bottle. But you can't erase its smoke."

"That's an analogy."

"It's a message about where we stand. I thought you were a merchant captain yourself for a second. Who taught you to project your thoughts like that?"

"It came naturally. It was learning to turn it off that took training. And practice."

"Same here."

"Do you really think of yourself as a sword?"

"I do, when meeting someone I might have to cut down to size."

"But what about when you met me just now?"

"It's good you can joke. Do you know why you're here? And why my daughter is not?"

"Your deck, your rules."

"And yet you came."

"I'm unemployed. And you have my stuff."

"I have Truxton's 'stuff.'"

Macer passed her the note Truxton had scribbled. She unfolded it and read. "You are either very clever or very stupid."

"I could be both," Macer said.

"What did you think I would do when I read this?"

"I didn't think anything. Does it say something bad?"

"You haven't read it?"

"It wasn't addressed to me."

"It wasn't sealed."

"I could have read it if I wanted. But what would be the point? Regardless of what it said I was bringing it to you. And if it said something bad I might get worried. And if it said something good I might get hopeful. This way I'm paying attention to *now*, and ready for whatever happens."

"If you'd read it you might have made preparations."

"Preparations for what? I'm delivering a message from the most powerful man in Trinity space to the richest woman in all creation. Short of elevating me to a god or damning my soul for all eternity, there's not much that can be done that the pair of you couldn't do, working together. I'd need a carryall the size of a planet just to bring every tool I might need to fight you, let alone raw materials and other consumable supplies."

"You might have run away, and not delivered it."

"And the pair of you hunt me down for knowing you've

conspired. That wouldn't be very smart. In addition, you have my stuff. And I want it."

"You seem convinced Truxton and I are in league."

"It was on your face, just now."

"Was it?"

"No question."

"And if someone asked you about this conversation what would you say?"

"What conversation?"

"And if they held your feet to the fire?"

"I'd say whatever they wanted me to say. Just like anybody else."

She handed him the note. "Read that."

Give the kid whatever of mine he wants. He's Lucan mac Tír's nephew ~~and Luther Gant's son. If you want to s~~Show him the airlock ~~I understand.~~ Make sure you aim him first.

Truxton

Macer felt the blood drain from his face. "I guess I should have brought a weapon."

"You did." Nuala nic Cartaí slid open a hidden drawer in the big conference table. She pressed a button and spoke in a language he didn't understand.

Seconds later a hatch opened and a pair of armed men stepped in.

A third man wheeled a fast-pallet in.

Nic Cartaí pointed. "Put it over there."

Macer wondered if they were going to kill him first and strap his corpse to the fast-pallet or just stun him and strap him to the fast-pallet so that when they spaced him he'd feel it.

"Attend me," nic Cartaí said.

He turned to face her.

"A shield is a weapon." She pressed a control and the big wall display burst to life. She tapped on a control pad and three images appeared, two men and a woman. "Do you recognize these people?"

"I recognize her." Aoife nic Cartaí, Fionnuala nic Cartaí's daughter, though younger, and sporting an Academy buzz cut.

"And the men?"

"Never seen them."

"The foppish one calls himself Hector Poole."

She meant the guy in a League Home Guard uniform holding a cocktail glass and chatting with an elegantly dressed woman. All he could see of the woman was the wedding ring on her finger and the sequined sleeve of her evening gown.

"Sensor images might help."

"They would indeed. But we work with what we have."

"Are you going to kill me?"

She glanced at him. "Not today. But later? Perhaps. Though not by my own hand."

"That's a relief."

She frowned. "Not as much as you might think. Now look at the other man."

The man was tall and handsome by Freeman standards. He was dressed in black, in what might be a military uniform, but if so, not one Macer was familiar with. He seemed distinctly foreign, even though he wore the pendant spire like he was born to it.

"If I'd seen that guy I think I'd remember."

"He calls himself Commodore Olek."

Macer snorted. "Commodore Evil? Seriously?"

"Olek, not Olc."

"That's an unfortunate choice of name for a blown-in."

"He claims to be Freeman born."

"Then some name chooser up the family tree deserves a serious beating."

Nuala nic Cartaí chuckled. "Agreed. Kirill Olek is master and commander of the vessel *Sudden Fall of Darkness*. He's an unknown unknown, if you follow me, and I need him turned into a known unknown at the very least."

Macer studied Olek's face. "He's not even related to anyone I know."

"You remember faces."

"My father's a politician. A pretty wife and a healthy boy are useful props for a family man on the campaign trail. There wasn't much else to do but look at people, and wonder about their lives."

"And this is salient because?"

"I was expected to recognize everyone and greet them by name should I ever met them again." *Or else.*

He was also expected to remember their birthdays, the names of their spouses and children, all *their* birthdays and wedding anniversaries, and so forth. He'd developed a system as a boy, and it worked, but it demanded he *pay attention* to the moment. By the time he'd gotten an implant, he hadn't needed one. He'd had it removed less than a month later because it kept trying to distract him.

He turned away from the display. "I doubt Olek is from Trinity Surface."

"He's not from Trinity or Unity Stations, either."

"Unity Surface?"

"Possibly. Or Cordame."

"You don't sound convinced."

"There is one more possibility."

"I can't think of one."

"That's because your people are blow-ins."

"Three hundred years ago."

"Nonetheless. Here's what I'd like you to do. Are you listening?"

"I'm listening."

"Keep an eye out for these characters, my own daughter included. If you do by chance spy one, get as close as you dare, and learn as much as you can without being found out. Don't let on your motives, and don't bother trying to seduce Aoife. She's not your type. But if you fancy either of the others—"

"I don't."

"You have the look that you might."

"I like to be presentable when meeting with potentates."

"I might like you better if you weren't so shiny and new."

"Maybe if someone experienced buffed the sheen off me I wouldn't be."

"Maybe you have a jumped-up opinion of your appeal."

"If I don't, who will?"

"A fair point. You broke a lot of what Truxton had set up with your antics. The fallout is going to be extensive but short lasting. There will be chaos, and a lot of eyes diverted, but after that passes they'll be looking for a scapegoat, and there's no more convenient scapegoat than you. So in that sense you have a vast appeal, but to all the wrong people."

"That isn't what I meant."

"I know what you meant, and not just what you said. Now, consider you this, Romeo, what drives away bad news?"

"Worse news."

"Not worse news. More *sensational news*. Imagine the flap if Nuala nic Cartaí showed up in public with a spanking fresh Truxton engineer on her arm, and word got out it wasn't just in public they were consorting, but between the sheets."

"No one would believe that."

"You're missing the point entirely. I'm stating the deal. You do what I ask, and if it ends up with you in the frame, that's the story I'll put around. But only if you manage to produce *results*."

"It would only be a story?"

Nuala nic Cartaí laughed. "You've the neck on you, there's no denying." She looked him up and down. "We'll see."

He couldn't read her at all. It was as if she peered out at him from within a fortress of calm indifference. A fortress that hadn't been there an instant ago, one so strong that he couldn't begin to imagine what effort it had taken to erect it, or what need would drive anyone to do so in the first place.

"You're lying." He didn't know if she was lying or not, and that worried him. The way she was examining him like a specimen worried him. She'd flushed his thoughts out of the present and into the future, and it wasn't a future he was certain he wanted, nor was it one he was certain he didn't want. He was in the open, without cover, and he knew then what he hadn't known in the stationmaster's office.

This was what fear felt like.

He forced himself to meet her gaze.

"I could be lying. But there's one sure way to find out." When he spoke his voice cracked. "By delivering results."

She laughed again, and pinned him to the deck with her gaze. "By delivering *spectacular* results."

She smiled, all teeth, and everything snapped into focus.

She didn't have a mong hu beside her because she didn't need one. She *was* one.

And she'd been toying with him all this time, and him believing he had the upper hand.

"No one sensible will believe that story you're putting around as it sits," she said.

"I need time to think."

"I bet you do. You're not a bad workman, and you've devised a fair distraction. I dare say it might have even worked if I was cut from the same cloth as the cronies you're familiar with. But you misunderstand my nature entirely, and I assure you, those whose opinions matter don't."

"Ma'am."

"Look me in the eye."

He did as she asked.

"Good. I'm not a ma'am. I'm a merchant captain. If you wish

people to believe we've met, you'll address me as such to my face. You can call me anything you want behind my back."

"Understood, Merchant Captain."

"Now, your plan might yet work, and my offer stands. But for it to work it must be *believable*. And anyone who is anyone knows Nuala nic Cartaí has no interest in *boys*."

"Understood, Merchant Captain."

"Is it?"

"Not entirely. But enough that I can act."

"Good." She pointed at the fast-pallet. "Take that. Get your kit and go do what I want."

"Just to be clear..."

"Grow up, you ignorant child. Now get out of here. And put some decent clothes on. At least *appear* to be made of something more substantial than meat."

31

The downworld shuttle was packed. More than a score of League children filled the seats.

The pilot jerked his chin and Macer followed him forward to the longboat's flight deck, which in truth was nothing more than the longboat's usual piloting station, just walled off from the rest of the hull so that inebriated passengers couldn't lurch into the controls.

"Macer," the pilot said.

"Rafe. What's with the throng? Field trip?" Macer scanned the length of the longboat. There didn't seem to be an open seat.

"Contract farmhands, believe it or not. From an orphanage for deaf and dumb kids."

"That sounds hazardous."

"It sounds insane. What's with the backpack? You usually travel light."

Macer had looped by Mr. Pearse's and a luggage shop on his way to the station-to-surface shuttle. That Rafe hadn't commented on his civilian stationer's utilities was good. That the nosy pilot had commented on the backpack was bad. So long as he didn't get a look at the contents, everything would be fine.

"Extended stay. Thought I'd check in on the family."

"It's a full flight. You can take the flight engineer's jump seat."

"Thanks."

The copilot squeezed past.

"Janie."

"Piss off, Gant." She buckled in.

"I've been meaning to call."

"And I've been meaning to crater this bird. Maybe this is a lucky day for both of us. Preflight."

"I'm the pilot here," Rafe said.

"That's what I'm saying." She punched a display and the preflight checklist popped up. "So stop your jawing and act like it."

Rafe winked at Macer. "It's that time of the—"

"Don't you even. You and this *amadán* both. Attend the altimeter. If you feel a breeze coming off it, you'll know I've had it with youse."

"Think of the children." Macer elbowed Janie and aimed her attention at the passenger cabin.

She jerked a thumb at Macer. "To the cheap seats with you."

"It's a full flight, Janie." Rafe began running through the checklist. "He can ride there."

"I swear, if the pair of you start droning on about... *drones*... again I'll—" Janie shouted. "You kids back there! Sit down and belt in!"

"They're from a deaf school," Rafe said.

"Well, they're following orders, unlike some I could name. There are twenty items on that preflight checklist and you're on number three."

"I'm the pilot," Rafe said. "I give the orders."

"Well then give them. You see the rubbish I have to put up with, Macer?"

"I do, Janie."

"You might have called. I brought in breakfast and everything."

"I don't know why I didn't."

"There," Rafe said. "Twenty. Are you happy?"

"Do I look happy?"

"You look about like you always do."

"Grand," Janie said. "Everyone belted?"

Macer glanced into the cabin. One of the older kids gave him the thumbs-up sign. "All buckled and tight."

"Grab your guts, lads." Janie toggled the main drive hot.

Macer belted in. "Does your father know Rafe's letting you pilot?" Janie Byrne's father owned the shuttle, and she was a proven maniac and hazard to navigation.

"There's no need for him to know. He only pays the insurance premium. He doesn't underwrite the coverage."

"My father underwrites it," Macer said.

"Luther Gant can sweat while he makes us bleed. That's what I say."

That was one of his dad's many get-richer-quicker schemes. Insurance for the uninsurable, with no intention of paying out. There weren't many rules in Trinity system, and what rules there were were new. If people could cheat the rules they would. The stationmaster demanded that public conveyances provide proof of insurance. Any insurance sold by the stationmaster's own brother-in-law had to be good, right?

Macer glanced at Rafe. "And what does the pilot say?"

"Cross your fingers and hope she doesn't hit anything this time," Rafe said.

Macer began to unbuckle.

"I'm joking," Rafe said. "Sit down, else you might distract her."

"Might distract me more." Janie ran the copilot's control yoke through its motions.

"Ignition in five.

"Four."

She swiveled in her seat so she could look at him. "You should have called."

Her gaze narrowed.

"One."

Her lip curled.

"Ignition. You bug."

A COUPLE of blond-headed League kids towered over him. He was flat on his back, but the sky above him seemed to be moving. His head felt like it might have split open, or if not, was preparing to. His left eye didn't seem to want to focus.

"That's far enough lads, and thank you," Janie said. "Dump him off here, and hurry on with youse. The island boat's about to be leaving."

They pitched Macer off the fast-pallet without slowing. Janie dropped his backpack next to him.

"I never took you for a thief, Macer Gant."

"What?" He rolled over on his stomach and lurched to his hands and knees. A calf-length flight boot pitched into view. He was gaining an encyclopedic knowledge of women's footwear and all after having the snot beaten out of him. "Help me up."

"Rafe says that's a stolen drone in your backpack."

"Where's he gone?"

"To call the authorities."

"We have authorities now? Whose bright idea is that?"

"The stationmaster's. So long as you're on the glassfield, there's people to enforce the law."

'There's laws?"

"That's what the authorities are telling us."

"That's daft."

"Agreed."

Macer managed to get one foot under him. "Are you going to help me or not?"

"I already did. I had those kids dump you in the car park."

"We have cars now?"

"We don't. But 'car park' is what it says on that sign over there. It's where I land my flitter. And it's not on the glassfield, so you're safe from the law."

"I'm not a thief."

"Rafe says that a drone like that costs more than a family ship earns in a year. I don't know how much that is, but he made it seem like a lot."

"It's a stupid measure." He was standing. "There's lots of different families and lots of different ships." He brushed the dust from his utilities.

"Well, is it more than an associate engineer makes?"

"A thousand times that, at least."

"Is it more than the Gant takes in over the course of a year?"

"Gross or net?"

"Net."

"Above board or below?"

"Combined."

"Ten times that, at least. And I didn't steal it. I bought it."

"With what?"

"My virtue."

She laughed. "You don't have any of that."

"My reputation, then." *And likely my future.* "What did you hit me with?"

"It was you doing the hitting. Your bony head assaulted the shuttle's inner hull."

"There's stops on the throttles for a reason."

"I took 'em off. They kept chipping my nails."

"You what?"

"I'm joking. And I'm not an idiot, Macer. I hadn't been at the helm since you were last down for a visit. No one told me you'd given the main drive a tune-up."

"I had to get out of the house." He touched the bandage on his head. It made a cooing sound. "The shuttle was just sitting there, and your dad asked if I'd give it a once over. Surprised he didn't tell you."

"He told Rafe. Because he's the pilot. And I'm the daughter."

"And a maniac."

"Takes one."

"That's fair."

"Why didn't you call me?"

"It's complicated."

"So you don't want to tell me."

"I mean that literally. It would take a long time to explain."

"Here comes Rafe with the local bullies."

"You said the law ended at the glassfield."

"They have legs on them, and I think the three of them could toss you onto the glassfield from here, the state you're in."

"Maybe."

"Supposing you don't want to send me into spasms of admiration with a demonstration of your pugilistic prowess."

"Supposing I don't."

"You've missed the ferry to Clear Island."

"I have."

"What you may not recall is that I have a flitter."

"I do recall that."

"I'll race you to it."

"What's this flitter ride going to cost me?"

"A long explanation."

"And what do I get if I win this race?"

"You get to open the canopy for me like a gentleman."

Macer scooped up his backpack and began to run.

"Didn't you forget something?"

"Go!"

32

The little flitter rocketed along just above the crests of the waves. Macer's head still pounded. At the current speed and heading, it would be two hours before they so much as spied Clear Island on a good day.

It was a good day, so far, though out here on the open ocean, the weather was variable, and the closer they grew to land, the more unpredictable it would become. He wasn't counting on sunlight the full way, but he'd take it while he had it. He leaned back in the copilot's seat and let the sunlight slashing in through the canopy warm his face and turn the inside of his eyelids translucent red.

"Wake up," Janie said.

He wasn't sure how long he'd slept. An hour and a half by the flight-deck clock. They'd climbed to three thousand meters.

"What's wrong?"

"Nothing. But you owe me an explanation, and you said it would take time."

He closed his eyes again. "Give me a minute."

The problem with the explanation he owed her was that she'd want something linear, *I thought this, and I did that, then this other thing happened*, and it wasn't like that at all. It was a mesh of ideas and emotions, like a net, though tangled, so even if he smoothed it out and spread it onto the deck for her to look at all at once, it would still be full of knots, ones he hadn't tied himself, but that he'd inherited along with the individual strands of the net as well.

"Okay," he said. "This is a story about a boy we'll call Ace, and a man we'll call Bernie, and his daughter. Let's call her Jamie."

"I don't want one of your *seánachie* stories. I want the truth."

"And I don't want to wake the dead." *Seánachie* stories were how you delivered one without causing the other.

"There's just the two of us here. I won't tell anyone if you don't."

"There's more than us pair in this story."

"I promise to not file intent over anything I hear."

"You can't make that promise. Not until you've heard the story."

"Do you think I'd want to file intent against anyone if you told me their names?"

"I don't. But I don't know what other stories you've heard, or if there's something I'd be revealing that alters your mind about anyone in general."

"Let's risk it."

"But—"

"So there's you, and my dad, and me in this story. And you asked me out on a date because—"

"Because I didn't want your father to vote for my father in the upcoming election."

"What?"

"I told you it's complicated."

"But I thought you liked me."

"I more than like you, Janie. That's why I decided to start my crusade with you."

"Your crusade?"

"To turn the county against my father."

"By asking me out on a date."

"Not just you, but every age-appropriate daughter in the county. You know the story of the vagabond and the farmer's daughter, right?"

"I know that story."

"Well, I figured your father would be pretty upset if he thought I'd gotten a ride off you and then hightailed it, pardon the language. And if he was furious with me, he wouldn't vote for my father."

"And you thought I'd go along with that."

"I'm very convincing when I want to be. And anyway, it wouldn't have mattered whether you wanted to go along with it or not."

"Oh, wouldn't it have?"

"I told you it was complicated. Anyway, I figured to test out this hypothetical on your father and you, and if it worked, ramp up my output and vagabond my way across the county. I'd made a list, and I figured I could finish the job in sixty days or less, with time off for Sundays. It was a tight election if you remember."

"So I wasn't the only girl you were planning to take advantage of."

"The first of many, but I wouldn't call it taking advantage of. You said yes in a big hurry if you recall."

"Is that all?"

"Not by half. I was also intent upon turning Rafe against you."

"I don't believe you."

"He wanted to play the part of the bridegroom, with you the bride."

"And you stopped that."

"Did I ever. With me and that story around, he'd never be

sure we weren't going behind his back. He's the jealous type, first and foremost. He'd rather starve than eat if eating meant sharing a crust."

"And that's the story."

"All but the parts you were there for, and afterwards."

"There wasn't any afterwards. We watched a movie in, and you droned on so much about *attitude-thruster maintenance* I fell asleep shortly after the opening credits began to roll."

"You fell asleep during the coming attractions. So I sat around for a while looking at you, and when you were good and asleep, I carried you into your bedroom and tucked you in. Then I watched the rest of the movie, which was actually pretty good. Once it was suspiciously late, I picked up my shoes and crept out the door."

"And scarpered."

"I would have if a shotgun barrel hadn't lifted my chin up just as my nose cleared the doorframe."

"My father doesn't own a shotgun."

"It was your mother."

"She has one."

"Don't I know it."

"Then what?"

"She shot me."

"She did not."

"She said she wanted to, but instead she interrogated me. So I told her about Ace, and Bernie, and Jamie, and the rest of my scheme."

"And then what?"

"She shot me."

"She did not."

"She said she wanted to, and she called me an idiot. So I told her about *Raul*, and how he was a low dog, and sniffing around Jamie, not because he loved her, but because he coveted her dowry."

"Bernie's shuttle business being Jamie's dowry that Raul coveted."

"Precisely. She didn't believe me, but I told her I could prove it. She went out to the hangar and woke Rafe up while I slipped back into your apartment, and when I heard some clattering outside I knew it was time to go, so I stuck my head out, and looked both ways, and then I stepped out. My knees would have been shaking if I'd been in my right mind.

"I plastered myself to the wall, and crept to the corner of the hangar, and peered around the corner, and saw my flitter gleaming in the moonlight. I took off loping toward it and then your mother shouted, 'Macer Gant,' so I sped up. I was ten strides from my flitter when a shotgun roared."

"She shot you."

"That was the plan. She'd shoot *at* me, and miss. Except she didn't. Rafe yanked the shotgun from her grip at the last minute and unloaded on me."

"Go on!"

"He did, and it blasted my flitter's canopy to splinters. I climbed in, and toggled the drive hot but forgot to switch on the blower. I'd just bent to reach the toggle when he unloaded again and shredded the headrest. I lifted like no tomorrow."

"I wouldn't have slept through all that."

"You can sleep through a shuttle launch. I've seen it."

"You let my mother shoot at you for what?"

"So Rafe would believe it when she told him you were crazy for me and couldn't ever get enough. That we were a package deal, though you were yet on the market. I wasn't the marrying sort, and that was a good thing."

"You're making that up."

"I wish I was."

"That's insane."

"You're telling me. I figured even if she hit me I could make it home on autopilot. We had a fine new autodoc in the hangar that could patch up just about anything, excepting if I'd had my head blown off. Of course if that was the case, then I wouldn't have cared either way. I was in a bad temper back then and feeling quite fell if you recall."

"But you and Rafe are friends."

"I'm not his enemy is what you mean. He missed, and it takes two to make an argument."

"I don't believe you."

"Ask your mother."

"It's true, she won't hear a word against you. And she doesn't like Rafe one bit. But this is unbelievable."

"It's because of that night. And because if any of your family badmouthed a Gant and my father heard about it, he'd cancel your insurance. It's not me he cares about, mark you, but the family name. The only thing unbelievable is that I'd thought the whole scheme a good idea at the time."

"I had no inkling."

"Nor did I, but your mother explained it to me, later, when I came to see you and you were out. She said my plan was a good one if I wanted to get myself killed and ruin a county's worth of girls' reputations, but their fathers wouldn't vote against my father either way, because it wasn't a matter of preference, but a matter of business. So I gave up my meticulous plan.

"She suggested that if I really did like you that I'd leave you be, because you needed someone steady who would ground you, and that I was a maniac, and as you were also a maniac, we'd end up plastered across some rocky crag's face or our bones washed up beside a pile of wreckage on some distant strand, and nothing to show for our lives but a few good laughs and a cautionary tale starring Jamie and Ace."

"And that's why you didn't call."

"It's as simple as that."

The rocky shoreline of Clear Island hove into view.

"Can I show you something?" Macer said.

"If you want."

"Give me the yoke."

"What yoke?"

"The yoke yoke."

"It's yours."

Macer aimed the flitter's nose up and increased main thrust.

"One year while you were away at school, your father had the bright idea to advertise during the holiday parade of lights. The only problem was he didn't have a boat, and if he flew a shuttle overhead it'd just make an irritating roar and boil the ocean if he hovered, and it would disappear over the horizon if he didn't. So he decided to use this flitter, only it had a similar problem. It would either outrace the fleet or stall and fall out of the sky.

"Since I was mooning around the glassfield anyway, he asked if I wanted to help him make modifications. I didn't want to, but he said he'd let me ride along if I did, so I helped him, and it worked, sort of, but the mechanism he'd devised ended up being so large that only one person would fit. He'd have to take it up alone.

"Except he'd made a deal, that I would get to ride, and a deal's a deal. So it wouldn't be him behind the yoke but me, and I could tell he was gutted. Not just disappointed, but utterly destroyed. He'd been planning for that flyby since the last year's parade.

"So I thought about it, and couldn't sleep, and went down to the hangar and just got to work."

"What for?"

"This." Macer cut the main drive. The flitter's nose dropped. The flitter began to plummet like a stone.

"What are you doing?"

"I'm falling out of the sky. What are you doing?"

She hammered the main drive ignition. Nothing happened.

Macer reached under the copilot's cowling. "How's the breeze off that altimeter? Cool enough for you, Jamie?"

"Macer!"

"Ace."

"This isn't funny!"

"No, but this is." Macer pressed a button beneath the cowling.

The flitter flared and began to rise as great spun-fabric wings sprouted from the fuselage and filled. And emptied. Filled. And emptied.

The flapping was nearly deafening inside the cockpit. It was doubly so outside, from below, where you wouldn't have any choice but to look up, and see the ungainly contraption rise and fall. There was practically no controlling it. It would pitch up and rise, then slow, and stall, then pitch down and gain speed, then pitch up and stall, again and again. It made forward motion, just barely, and it lost altitude, just barely, but it didn't fall out of the sky.

Macer shouted over the racket. "You can't read it from here, but it says, 'It takes Byrne to lift' underneath!"

"It's mad!"

"It's brilliant!"

"You made this?"

"Your dad came up with it!" Macer shouted. "I just miniaturized the control module!"

Macer retracted the wings and lit the main engine. "The yoke's yours. Do you see the runway there?"

"I do," Janie said. "Did you and my dad have a falling out?"

"Never," Macer said.

"But you were willing to have him think the worst of you."

"Everyone else already does," Macer said. "All I wanted to do was use a bad reputation to do good."

"By getting your father defeated in the election."

By getting Rafe to back off without having to drag his carcass to a bog and weight it down.

"It's complicated," Macer said. "You can come up to the house and say hello to the family if you want."

"I'd like that."

"Grand," Macer said. "I'll refuel your makeshift ornithopter while you're gone. If my dad is there, tell him I'm headed up in twenty. If he still doesn't want to see my face in his house he'll need to clear the way, because I'm bringing it."

33

During that brief year when his father had been declared dead and Macer had been the Gant, he'd tried to do an inventory of all the improvements on Gant land, and specifically those that weren't leased to tenant farmers but rather his own responsibility for repair and maintenance.

Besides the working hangar where he kept his flitter and his tools—and the boat docks where they kept the boats, and the storage hangar where they kept the flyers only used for special purposes and occasions—there were a dozen barns and silos in various states of disintegration, cow sheds, and sheep sheds; garages for the ground transportation and stables for the horses; and a couple bunkhouses, one halfway between the hangars and docks, and presently vacant, and one farther upslope in the next valley over, on the far shoulder of a ridge that ran from the mountain in the heart of Clear Island. The tall spiny ridges were natural dividers, and it was a hike up to the far bunkhouse, but he'd head there if things at the house went ill.

Macer kicked a stone across the gravel drive and gazed up

hill. He couldn't see the house yet but it lurked there, behind the copse meant to hide the lower bunkhouse from the view. It was built by his grandfather's grandmother to look out over the bay to the east and all the working guts of the place to the southeast, and downslope. The house itself stood on a promontory rock, one that limited how many wings and appendages could be added, else it would look like an old woman's idea of a castle of old, and her son's and her grandson's tacked on expansions leaning against it as if they were too lazy to stand on their own.

As it was, all but the tower house itself had the hint of a slow slide down, every swaybacked ridge beam and patched slate roof losing a war with the inevitable gravity that too much pride and property and not enough cold hard cash exerted. The Gants weren't First Families, but early adopters, and they'd farmed this valley for three hundred years, and the next valley over for nearly two hundred. That his father had nearly lost it all in less than thirty years of adventurism and get-richer-quick schemes wasn't widely known. The wolf was no longer at the door, and Luther Gant might have learned his lesson, but if he had it would be a surprise to Macer.

Still, seen from a distance the house remained impressive, the second largest on the island, though nothing like the size of the great houses on the mainland. It hadn't been home for going on five years, and even before, not so much home as a transient slip, one with a hot meal and his laundry done, and a shower of shiftless cronies to navigate around and over, as his father and his pals schemed their way into the state house and the poor house at the same time. That scheme had worked, and now the money flowed in again, but it wasn't from mountains of butter and lakes of milk but from a wink, and a nod, and credit chits passed under the table.

The land behind the house fell away to reveal a sloping parkland framing a lake. A gravel road ran down from the house and past a folly ruin disguising the lake dam's overflow, and from there beneath some willows, and back up the further hill and down again. A dairy barn loomed over the brow, the biggest and oldest on the property. A constant stream of self-powered carryalls plied their way up and down that gravel road from the house's kitchens and back. That could only mean one thing. A party planned for tonight, one too big to fit in the house, and that meant a political do.

Macer hitched his backpack higher, climbed the hill, and swung the big entry door open. The entry hall was one big room, the largest in the house, and what furniture that might be useful to break up its cavernous expanse squared away against the four walls. The stone tile floor might have been black-and-white herringbone back in olden times; it was now an uneven patchwork of overlapping wine stains, the bulk of which were blackened with age.

A slender blond woman and two six-year-old boys stood in the center of the empty room. The woman stared at him. She had her arms around the boys like she was penning them up. They were also blond, a blond so blond it seemed white. He glanced around for his father.

"I take it Janie sounded the alarm." He looked her up and down. "Hello, evil stepmother." He smiled at the boys. "Hello, replacement heir one and replacement heir two."

"Hello, major disappointment," the twin on the right said. The twin on the left just stared at him.

"I guess we know which one of you is Luther Gant, the younger. What's wrong there Sam? Cat got your tongue?"

"Leave him be," Shayna Gant said. That's what she called herself now. Shayna Gant. Up until five years ago, she was a mystery, a city wife and family that his father kept separate and hidden from island view. But then it had all come out like a thunderclap the night his father had died. Since he'd been declared alive again, his father had decided no additional shame accrued from piling his mess up all in one place than from having it spread out over the face of the globe. That was Macer's theory, anyway.

"I will leave him be," Macer said. "So long as he leaves the cat be." The pair of boys were psychopaths, and they got that from their mother. "Run along now, lads. I saw some flies down the stable, and I'd swear there were one or two still had their wings on."

"He's seen us." Luther the younger wriggled. "Let us go."

Sam, the other boy, remained still as a statue, and staring at Macer.

"Go to your rooms," Shayna said.

The boys bolted.

She began to walk toward him.

She wore a bright floral print sheath that would look lovely in a garden. Here, in the semidark of the hall, it seemed as if the entire world were in monochrome and her the only color in it.

She knew how to work a dress, and she knew how to work a room.

She stalked toward him, his gaze glued to her, like to a roadside disaster viewed in passing. It wouldn't surprise him if she simply brushed his sleeve on the way out the door, and he'd turn, like a gawker who couldn't look away, and follow her with his gaze. He could see precisely what his father, and any other man, for that matter, saw in her, and it was all on the surface and seemingly pristine and inviting, like a freshly frozen lake on the first morning after a cold snap.

She stopped in front of him, close enough that he could touch her hair. She wasn't leaning on him, trying to get him to back up, but rather stood a comfortable distance from him, in city terms. They'd gotten off to a bad start when first they'd met. He'd stepped back then, to a country distance, and she'd mistaken settling in for a decent chat as sign of weakness.

She gazed up at him and smiled. "You're not welcome here."

"If I had a pingin for every time I've heard that." He reached out and brushed the strap of her dress, where it dropped across her collarbone. "You've given yourself a bob."

She took a step back.

He made a scissors motion with his fingers. "Cut your hair." She'd had shoulder length hair every other time he'd met her. Like a city woman. Now she looked like she might have stepped right off Trinity Station's Arcade, minus the dress.

He ran his gaze up and down her, imagining her minus the dress.

"Luther!" she shouted. "Your pervert spawn is undressing me with his eyes!"

"He's a loud thinker," his father said from behind him. "He gets that from his mother."

He imagined her wriggling into a Truxton skinsuit. He walked around her, considering. Something remained missing.

"Stop it," she said.

He imagined a long, slender force blade in her hand. He had her swipe it through the air.

"It's not a good look on you," he said. "The stationer's cut."

"Macer," his father said. "Stop looking at her like that."

"Like what?"

"Like you're ready to file intent, that's what." He clapped his hands "Wake up, son."

"What? Oh, sorry, Pop. What were we talking about?"

"You, being a pervert," Shayna said.

"No, that wasn't it. You've been up to the station."

"She took the boys up for the shopping," his father said. "I'm still getting the bills."

"That explains it, then."

"Explains what?"

"She looks different." He needed to think about this.

"Speaking of bills," his father said. "I got one from Mr. Pearse's."

"I didn't take them to that stuffy old rathole," she said.

"Why would you? It's a men's shop for the gentry."

"They'll be men soon enough," she said.

"And we'll find a suitable shop for you to take them to, my heart."

Shayna took another step back. Her gaze darted to Macer. She had eyes the color of winter ice. And she'd heard the same thing he'd heard. Mr. Pearse's wasn't fit for her sons, not because they weren't yet men, but because they'd never be gentry.

"I'm standing in your way," Macer said.

A muscle in her cheek twitched.

"You look like you need some air." Macer stepped to the side. "The door's that way."

"If you're going outside, my heart, you might as well check the preparations at the barn."

"I'm not going," she said.

"If you don't mind," his father said. "There's this matter of the bill, and it's not every day a man's son comes home. Take the boys with you, and have a Bridget pack a lunch basket."

"But..." She glanced from face to face. "You ordered him to never show his face in your house again."

"I did, and it was a hot moment. Upon reflection? It's as much his house as mine."

Macer snorted.

"I mean it, son. Now come into the office, and let's get this Pearse invoice sorted."

34

His father's office was in one of the newer parts of the house, a large single room with three work desks each with their own display, and a jumble of papers and boxes of file folders and cabinets of file folders, and shelves of paper books and binders of papers that halfway resembled books and halfway resembled files. Some of the materials seemed as if they were printed that morning, some yellowed and layered in dust.

Most of the paperwork hailed from his grandfather's time, when the old man had thought to exploit the vast tract of pine forest his own father had planted with a pulp mill and a printed literary revival.

The ancient art of recording the past in opinionated detail hadn't caught on with the locals. Writing down "histories" wasn't just waking the dead, it was putting words in the mouths of the dead and building an army from their shambling corpses. The practice hadn't turned a profit, but it had taken hold in his father's mind. He liked the idea of an army that followed orders and didn't talk back. He was an apostate by nature and practice, born into a family that wasn't afraid to trot out the past when it gave them a handle on a man, or a woman.

Doing so wasn't precisely illegal, very little was, but it wasn't thought well of—like being a bigamist and having one family on the island and a secret other family in the city wasn't thought well of, but might have been tolerated by itself, if not for all the other transgressions. His father wasn't a pariah because of any single mortal sin, but because of a never-ending accumulation of venal ones.

The votes kept rolling in, though, because for nearly three hundred years the Gants had been lenders of last resort, and accumulators of promises to pay, and keepers of secrets. For most of his life, he'd believed his father to be the top of the food chain on Trinity Surface. It wasn't until his father had died and Macer became the Gant for a time that he discovered the truth, quite by accident. The Gants weren't petty merchant lords.

They were clerks for an organization called the Consortium, and before that, vassals of the Huangxu Eng. And for three hundred years they'd been skimming.

That was indeed a crime, the sort that called for a match-making if it were noticed.

That crack about the house being as much Macer's and his own was the tell.

They'd been found out and called to account. Seen in that light, his father's death by paperwork and subsequent resurrection through drawn-out legal wrangling made more sense. He had thought his father had been killed on paper by his neighbors, those who'd finally grown tired of his shenanigans.

But it might have been a convenient suicide, one that seen from afar, on a workstation's display, would appear real, and the accounting for sins of the father passed on to the son. Once paid, well, what can one say? It was a paperwork snafu. Now, let's get back to business.

His father plopped into his chair and put his feet up. "Take a load off, son, while I pull up the invoice."

He didn't look to be doing any sort of thing, but then he wouldn't look it. Though his office seemed a shamble, his mind was anything but, and since he'd upgraded his implant, he'd been sharper than ever.

Macer wondered if it wouldn't be easier to just pick his dad up by the collar and beat the truth out of him. That was the sort of conversation he'd understand.

"Rafe was piloting the shuttle today," Macer said.

"Was he? How'd he look?"

"Rested." When he wasn't piloting, Rafe picked debtors up by the collar and beat money out of them for Luther Gant.

"It's been a wet spring," his father said. "I think the drought is behind us."

"Mr. Pearse says it hasn't rained in ages. He's expecting showers."

"Who are you? His rainmaker?"

"He didn't send along a note."

"Just a bill for alterations for your prancing frock, and I'm expected to pay."

"He's meek, I see."

"Well, one day he'll inherit. But until then—"

"Uncle Lucan sends his regards."

"When you see him, send them back."

"Were he to call—"

"He has. Repeatedly."

"And?"

"And what? I'm busy. I'll get to him when I get to him. There's a big affair tonight, and it's timely you're here. I expect you to attend and be on your best behavior."

"Why?"

"Guests from out-system. Friends of the family."

"Which family? The island one or the city one?"

"Get over that. We're all one and the same."

"Do you not follow the news at all?"

"I knew you were on the shuttle."

"Rafe told you."

"It's his job to keep me apprised of important goings-on."

"News from the station, I'm talking about."

"No one owes me money on the station."

"You should access the stationmaster's messages."

"Since you're so connected, why don't you give me the executive summary."

"I don't know how much he's figured out."

"Figured out about what?"

"About you being a tout."

"An informer? Who am I supposed to have informed on?"

"That's what you're going to tell me now."

"Or what?"

He hadn't been sure until that moment. His father knew what was going on. Might even be behind it.

"Do you know how I met Shayna?" his father said.

"I don't. And if you're going to wake the dead—"

"I'll do what I want in my own home. And it's a matter of record. A fair number of legislators were getting death threats, myself amongst them. So I went to mac Kenna—"

"The family solicitor."

"The barrister, his brother. Here's the point. I said I needed security, and others as well, and he said he'd take care of it, and he did. He contracted for actual licensed bodyguards, not just thugs, I'm telling you, but skilled people, the best of the best. And from that moment, it felt like a great weight was lifted from me. I hadn't known how draining always looking over my shoulder had become. I could relax for once, and see the world around me, not as a dark wood to be feared, but as a garden to be enjoyed.

"Your mother and I, that was an arrangement, and the

paying of a debt. When she lit out and never came back, I wasn't heartbroken, as she'd left the only thing I'd wanted out of the bargain, though in truth she cheated me. It was a mistake allowing her to raise you, and ruin you. But I was busy at the time, and the dark wood always in my mind."

The door to the office burst open.

Shayna stood framed in the doorway, a projectile weapon in her fist.

"She was your bodyguard," Macer said.

"Still is," his father said. "Macer's going to his room to think and rest up before dinner."

"You said she was a licensed bodyguard." *So why was she framing herself in the doorway?*

"She'd like you to try something, son. Now go to your room and don't give her the pleasure."

"I can see that she'd like me to try something," Macer said. "But there's no such thing as a licensed bodyguard."

"According to mac Kenna there is on New Sparta." His father rapped his knuckled on the desk. "Now, darling, I need him alive, so no accidents."

SHE OPENED his bedroom door and motioned for him to enter. "In."

"And if I don't go in there. Would you shoot me?"

"I said go in."

"It's a strange thing, having conflicting orders and limited resources. One, you're to keep me alive, and two, I'm to do as you say, and three, you don't have anything to compel me but deadly force, so four, that leaves you with a bit of a quandary."

"You don't think I'll shoot you."

"I think you want to."

"Get in there."

"Make me."

She looked very much like she wanted to shoot him. Like she was thinking about it.

"It's too much force, a pistol, for the job. And it's inconvenient, having it in your hand. Maybe if you put it down you could make me. And then again, maybe not."

She aimed the pistol at his knee.

"Like that will work. I admit it'd hurt. But anything short of killing me, I'm jamming that pistol down your throat, and if you think I'm kidding just try me. Then I'll crawl to an autodoc and pull myself in. Did my father not warn you?"

"He said you're brave."

"Not in a million years would he say that. He said I'm *fearless*, which is another thing entirely. One is a virtue. The other is a mental condition."

She looked him up and down, maybe trying to figure out what part of him she could shoot that would render him unable to reach her without killing him. Had she been standing at the end of the hallway she might have figured something out. But she'd gotten too close and could see it now. He watched her make a mental note. It wouldn't happen again.

"Here's what I suggest," Macer said. "You walk away, and we never mention this conversation to anyone."

"And what will you do?"

"I'll go in there because I want to."

She glared daggers at him, willing him to suffer, and kneel, and die, die, die.

Macer laughed. "I thought I was a loud thinker. Now is it a deal or not?"

H is bedroom appeared exactly the way he'd left it. A bed, a nightstand, an armoire, all heavy wood, all made in a local factory. A threadbare carpet over warped wooden floorboards, the carpet machine-woven, the floorboards made from the same stand of timber the pulp mill had processed into paper. No pictures on the wall, no personal items, just the essentials, like on the station, and aboard *Four-Squared*. He had his workshop in the hangar if he wanted to work or relax. His bedroom was for sleeping. And for thinking.

He parked his backpack in the corner, slipped off his boots, and stretched out on the bed. It was just as lumpy as he remembered.

He got out of bed and padded to the door. He pressed his ear to the door, listening.

He cracked the door open, peering out into the hall. She was gone.

Macer crept down the hall to the bathroom. He ran cold water from the sink tap and splashed it across his face. It was one thing, staying anchored in the present when considering an interesting technical problem. It hadn't even been that hard when she'd aimed the gun at his kneecap. But when his father's mare had considered gelding him, and unconsciously grinned? He'd nearly fallen into the future then. It had taken all the self-control he could muster to stay anchored in the present and stand his ground.

Maybe his father was right, and Macer's reckless disregard for consequences was a result of a defect in his mother's genes. But if that was the case, why did it seem like so much work? He could feel his hands shaking. But when he held them out in front of him, they were still.

Weird.

He averted his gaze from the mirror, dried his hands, and went back to his bedroom to think, long and deep.

His first inclination was to begin at the beginning and order his thoughts chronologically. The difficulty with that was when to begin the timeline. Was it when he'd discovered that *Four-Squared* possessed an unregistered Templeman drive? Was it earlier, when he'd been posted to the vessel? Or earlier, still, when he'd been made the Gant, at least temporarily? Or earlier still, when he'd been born into a loveless marriage, and raised by a mother that didn't dislike her husband so much as strive to negate his very existence.

No, a timeline wouldn't do. What he needed was an inventory, or a cast list.

A cast list had the advantage of being a bounded inventory. There were only so many people he knew, and only so many linkages between them. And that was the important aspect, wasn't it? Not the names and faces of the drama that was his life, but the relationships. And while he could not easily list all the characters, it would be much harder to annotate the mesh of their interrelationships, and he'd end up drowning in data.

Again, how far back should he go, and how wide a net should be cast were fundamental questions, and ones he didn't have the answers for. In addition, he was missing data, since he only knew of those relationships he had personally witnessed, or had been told of, or read about, or otherwise had discovered. He could see the tip of the iceberg. But as to the overall shape beneath the surface? He remained ignorant.

Here was perhaps a way to bound the problem, and that was to begin from the moment he could now perceive as the beginning of his utility in whatever scheme he was enmeshed in. He was being used by others. This use had been going on for some time. He needed to work forward and backward from that point, cataloging just those relationships he'd discovered, and just those preconceptions he'd been disabused of.

Begin, he told himself, and he began.

Singh. He'd seemed a competent and conventional engineer. He was clearly more, and he'd used Macer toward some ultimate unknown end, but the proximate use appeared to be to cause a public record documenting the existence of an unregistered superluminal drive on Truxton's *Tractor Four-Squared*.

Who was hurt by this action? Truxton, obviously, and the ship's captain and crew, who were hiding the secret, and who were all, excepting Singh and Macer, from Sampson and New Sparta, systems banned to Freeman trade for some reason he didn't know.

So, potentially those systems would be hurt by association, though they were already pariah societies, and thus largely immune to further harm. If he wanted to be a completist, he should probably also list rival footie ball teams, and anyone with personal enmity toward any individual crewman, who might also indirectly benefit. Given all that, the biggest loser by a large margin remained Truxton. It made sense, then to say that the harm of the action accrued to Truxton. Of course there might be more to the footie ball angle, as he had no idea how big a deal these finals were, either purely as a matter of prestige or of remuneration. He would feel pretty stupid if he constructed a map of causality and it turned out that he'd been used to throw a sports game and nothing more.

The big question, part two. Who was helped by this revelation? Truxton's enemies, and potentially, enemies of the crew, including enemies of Macer. Of course Macer was a nothing, and vulnerable to much easier methods of harm, ones closer at home, and more likely to cause him suffering and grief. Similarly, rival footie ball teams, individuals with personal grudges against the crew, or Sampson and New Sparta, or, now that he thought about it, the stationmaster, who wouldn't want an unregistered Templeman drive in the system. Or anyone else, for that matter, that knew about the drive and didn't want it kept secret, although who that would be he couldn't imagine, unless it was whomever Captain Violet was buying black-market parts from, or whomever Singh was then selling them on to, assuming he wasn't simply discarded the parts without installing them, which was crazy, and unlikely.

Assume Singh is a rational actor unless proven otherwise.

Macer spent much of the afternoon lying in bed, staring at the ceiling, and thinking through everything he'd experienced, their possible implications, and winnowing those down to several plausible hypotheses. In the end, he hadn't drawn any conclusions, but he did have a list of *things I know now that I didn't know then* that he could mull over later.

For example, he knew that Singh wasn't what he appeared, and that he'd manipulated Macer into revealing that *Four-Squared* possessed a superluminal drive. Singh doing that was inconsistent with Singh planting a bomb on the vessel. The simplest explanation for Singh not installing Captain Violet's black-market parts was that he was selling them on and pocketing the money, all the while betting that an idling drive was unlikely to fail. Singh simply bugged out before the inquiry began, and was now safely elsewhere, living off his black-market profits. Except if that was true, why did he blind internal sensors before leaving?

Captain Violet was obviously a numbskull, and his Sampson and New Sparta crew simply useful idiots. Their days of utility were over. He wondered what would happen to them but didn't really care. They'd abandoned him on an out-of-control plague ship.

Rik Severn and his murderous identical twin were an enigma. They were working for someone by Severn's own admission, and had planted the bomb, also by Severn's own admission. But here the trail forked, because Severn also said his orders were to kill the chief engineer, which would have been Singh, if he'd been on board, and which was Macer, since with Singh away he was acting chief engineer.

Macer had believed that Singh was the target because no one outside of him and Singh himself were aware that Singh had left and put Macer in charge. Except that wasn't actually true. If Singh worked for someone else, then they could have known Macer was acting chief engineer. And they could have aimed Rik Severn at him. Which hadn't made any sense until he'd seen Shayna with her stationer's hair bob. She and Rik Severn might well be brother and sister. The resemblance was uncanny and required further investigation.

What if he'd been the target all along?

Everything after that, the events aboard *Golden Parachute*, the meeting with Truxton, the meeting with Fionnuala nic Cartaí, the order that he keep an eye on her daughter and two strangers he'd never met, that all had to take a backseat to finding out if Rik Severn had been sent to kill him, and if so, who sent him. It could have been Shayna, but that seemed implausible. More likely it was whoever Singh worked for. Or his father.

Could Singh work for his father?

He wouldn't get a straight answer if he asked.

What he needed to do was find out for sure who had fina-gled a Truxton berth for him, and how that berth ended up being on Truxton's *Tractor Four-Squared*. A Truxton gig was what he'd wanted straight out of the Academy. He hadn't expected it. And he certainly hadn't earned it. His grades were average at best, and while his instructors liked him, they liked their own kind better, space-born Freemen whose families endowed the Academy and who could offer jobs and promo-tions to their own station-born children.

But that was it. The thread to pull. And the beginning of the timeline.

The day he put his credentials into the posting computer.

And a miracle occurred.

LATER THAT AFTERNOON, Macer stopped by the kitchen for a snack. The kitchen was in one of the newer wings of the house, the one closest to the gravel drive that led to the meeting barn. All the Bridgets were on duty and cooking, but it was Bridget Three that interrupted him on the way to the refrigerator. She was the youngest of the trio and two years younger than he. She was also the talker of the crew, which was what he was after, in addition to a snack.

Years ago the kitchen had been just like any other kitchen on the island, excepting the kitchen at Ellis Park, which was more like the kitchen on a luxury cruise vessel than a regular house. Macer's father could have simply expanded the kitchen and bought groceries locally, but the Ellis had a macrofab and so the Gant needed a macrofab, it was simple as that. The Ellis had walk-in refrigerators. The Ellis had searing stations, and fast chillers, and sonic scrubbers, or whatever they called the things you put dirty plates and glasses inside and they came out clean, like a refresher for crockery. Maybe they called it a refresher, he didn't know, because he only came to the kitchen for two things: chow and chat.

Bridget Three's mother and her grandmother glanced up from the macrofab display and eyeballed him before going back to their work. For family gatherings, something garden fresh would be in order, and there were no finer cooks on the island. That the Bridgets were cranking out patterned chow in mass quantities was unexpected. Whatever his father had planned for tonight included a monster of a meeting.

Bridget Three planted her hands on her hips and took up a defensive stance between him and the refrigerator. "You shall not pass."

He picked her up and shifted her out of the way.

She giggled and followed him into the refrigerator. They'd been playing that game since he was nine and her seven.

She stood on her tiptoes and kissed his cheek. "Welcome home, Your Horribleness."

That was new. He ran his gaze over her and she blushed.

"I mean—"

"I know what you mean, Bridget Three." He kissed the crown of her head. "I hadn't really felt home until this very moment."

She started to remove items from the shelves and hand them to him. Hand-stuffed bologna sausage from the mac Owens, artisan cheddar from the Keanes, mayonnaise and pickled cucumbers from the Bridgets' own farm.

"Looks like they've been feeding you in space."

"There's eight different flavors of tubed paste and an all-you-can-squeeze policy. Plus, any vermin we catch we get to keep."

"You're pulling my leg."

"I am. There's only four flavors of paste."

"Get out with you and take that lot to the table."

He did as ordered. She followed him out and disappeared

behind the macrofab only to return seconds later with a pair of knives and a crusty loaf.

"From Murtagh's?" Macer asked.

"The one and only." She began sawing at the loaf with a serrated knife. "They'll all be here tonight, rain or shine."

"What's the occasion?"

"Prodigal son's return it isn't," she said. "Though now that you're here, there'll be a lot breathing a sigh of relief and bending your ear after."

"Over what?"

"Over these blow-ins, and the buying up of all the land."

"Who are they and what are they doing?"

"Buying up, and at top price. Bridget One was sorely tempted to sell, and it wouldn't surprise me if old man Keane hasn't done so already."

"And why are they buying?"

"No one knows. According to Bridget One, the offer was to buy the land and lease it back for a pittance, with the lease to run five years, and after that we're to move out."

"To where?'

"To the mainland, and anywhere we want. There's a threat under it all, according to my mother, that if we don't sell they'll force us off anyway."

"Where would Bridget Two get that idea?"

She sawed into the bologna with the second knife. "From your father. He says that these people doing the buying have connections, and that if we don't go along, they'll get a law passed and just take the land from us."

"Who would enforce the law if they did?"

"That's what Bridget One said. We're not like spacers breathing someone else's air. They can have whatever laws they want on the station but they're not welcome here. We have no need for them."

"Who are these people?"

"You'll see them tonight." She shoved the sandwich toward him. "There. I think it's disgusting, but it's tradition."

The food wasn't any worse in space than what Bridget One and Bridget Two were cranking out of the macrofab. In fact, it was identical, which was the entire point of using the macrofab. But a bologna, cheese, and pickle sandwich with mayonnaise, every bit from his home island, was another thing entirely.

"Start at the beginning and tell me everything you know about these people and what they're doing."

"I have work to do."

He picked up the serrated knife and sliced into the sandwich, dividing it. "I have three-fifths of a sandwich to eat. What say we work together?"

He shoved a portion of the sandwich toward her.

She pulled out a chair and sat down. "Looks more like you have three-fourths of a sandwich to eat."

"Maybe that's so."

"It is." She bit into her part of the sandwich.

He waited until she'd finished.

"How was it?"

She grinned. "Disgusting."

"I'll have to see for myself. Now talk."

36

Macer stopped by the working barn to pick up a
herder's cap and sticks before hiking up to the
high pasture. He stuffed a couple of lopers into
his pockets, not that he thought he'd need them.

He opened the pasture gate and swung it wide. Nearly all
the valley lay below him, the rambling house on its promontory
rock, the big meeting barn, a couple of working barns, and
further to the south, the hangar and landing strip and below
them, the little harbor and boat house where he'd misspent
most of his childhood. It was a pretty place, far more attractive
than productive, and even then, richer and better land than
most of the island. He wondered what foreigners had in mind
with buying up the land. Bridget Three hadn't known, and no
advantage to speculating.

He clicked the sticks together and began walking toward
the herd. These were beef cattle, not the milking kind, and as to
why they were in this pasture only mac Manus, the herder,
would know. They needed to be moved because where they
were grazing hadn't always been pasture, and it was the most
level land in the valley.

This herd belonged in the next valley over, and they knew it. They began walking toward him, and he let them pass. He had a herder's natural disposition according to mac Manus, placid and unthreatening. Today the herd seemed to agree. They passed through the gate without any stragglers and he took up position in their wake, clicking the sticks together now and then when they seemed inclined to grow distracted.

The herd proceeded at a slow walk because that was how mac Manus had trained them. If Macer let himself think about it, he could feel the anticipation of the herd. The next valley over was their usual grazing area because it was marginally dryer over there, and the turf in better shape as a result, all but for a high boggy hectare partitioned off from the rest. At this rate, it would take all afternoon to move them, and all his concentration to keep on top of them, but that would give his subconscious time to chew on all that Bridget Three had told him.

It was a clear day at first but turned soft a kilometer or so from the pasture. It was general practice to leave the gate open so one man could move the herd, but then it was also general practice to leave the herd in the valley as well. Macer fished the lopers out of his pocked and tossed them to the turf. They were autonomous drones of a sort, though without much intelligence. They extended spindly legs and puffed up to about the size of a border collie, smaller than a wolf, which would have sent the herd off and running. Mac Manus had a border collie and it was brilliant. The lopers weren't even in the same league, but they'd keep the herd moving together while he ranged forward and checked the gate was open.

It wasn't open, so he opened it, and moved well away from the gate, leaning against the fence twenty meters south of the opening and watching the herd progress. When he was a boy, he'd liked this kind of work because it was outdoors, and because mac Manus had a thousand stories, and because of the dog. Nowadays mac Manus mostly worked with the sheep, which were more of a handful, mostly because of the terrain upslope, and the general wildness of the island's interior. Macer supposed that was where the herdsman was now, as the work was never ending.

Once the herd was all through the gate, Macer closed it and pressed a button on one of the herder's sticks. The lopers headed toward him at a trot. He powered them down and pocketed them. It would have been more of an accomplishment if he'd been able to move the herd without them, but still and all, it was done, and a good day's walk.

He checked his handheld and found no signal, so it was uphill for him, and when he got to the fence around the boggy hectare he stopped, and leaned against the stacked stones, and checked his handheld again.

He had signal, and he had an id addy for Fionnuala nic Cartaí, and he had something to say, thanks to Bridget Three. He executed the command.

Nic Cartaí's icy voice drilled into his ear. "What?"

"This is really your personal address?"

"We're an item. Do you think I want my assistant or *anyone else* listening in?"

"Got it." She was reminding him that anything he said could be overheard.

"Spill the cargo. I'm late for a meeting."

"My father's having a big party tonight in honor of some visiting foreigners. Commodore something or other and some Erl history professor. It's a big affair, and I've never seen anything like it."

"You're telling me this because?"

"Because I don't have a date. It's so boring here without you. I need a *distraction*."

"Don't be an idiot. I'm busy, and that's the back of beyond."

"We have a glassfield."

"You don't."

"It's on the old surveys. I could send you the coordinates."

"Do it. And mind you, no promises."

He sent the coordinates. "Done."

"Now is that all?"

"Almost. Why are Sampson and New Sparta closed to Freeman trade?"

"Because Sampson was knowingly trading with the Enemy. And New Sparta was harboring a nest of them."

"I don't understand. We're neutral. We don't have enemies."

"Not an enemy. The Enemy. And I don't have time for a history lesson."

"If I met the Enemy, what would they look like?"

"They could look like anyone. Why?"

"How would I know one if I saw one?"

"By what they do. Why are you asking all of this?"

"You haven't spoken to Truxton."

"Getting ready to."

"Ask him."

"I will. Now I really have to go."

"I understand, my pet."

The connection went dead.

SOMETHING WAS SPOOKING THE HERD. Macer glanced toward the tree line and saw it.

A wolf.

Wolves were everywhere up on the mountain, but they were rare down here. That would explain why the herd had been moved.

And then he saw the second wolf, and he was certain that was why the herd had been moved.

He'd have to figure out what to do about this, because he

wasn't moving the herd back to the glassfield. He liked a good steak as much as the next man, but if Nuala nic Cartaí really did decide to drop from the sky, he'd rather not barbecue the entire herd.

He fished a loper out of his pocket and fiddled with the controls. He tossed it to the ground, and it set off toward the tree line in jumps and starts. He'd limited its apparent size to that of a mountain hare. He did the same with the second loper, aiming it to cross paths with the second wolf.

When the wolves ignored them, he knew what he was dealing with.

"Laura."

A pair of disembodied eyes seemed to float in the air beside him. He wasn't sure if they were human eyes or not. They were the exact color of willow bark.

"Do you have a sweetheart now, Macer?"

"I wouldn't call her that."

"You called her 'pet'."

"That was to get her to ring off."

"You never called me 'pet,' and we were engaged to be married."

"You're no Nuala nic Cartaí. Now peel out of that getup. It gives me the shakes."

"I might be naked underneath."

"Aren't we all? Take the hood off then, so you at least have a face."

Laura Ellis was a neighbor, and the daughter of his father's greatest rival. Their respective mothers had arranged a marriage for Macer and Laura when they were just little children. That was the fashion amongst mothers back then, but Macer knew from the get-go it wasn't going to happen. There was only one man for Laura and it wasn't him.

She took off the ghillie suit's hood. Her father, the Ellis, was a big collector of antique Erl military gear, and that suit was just one of a thousand weird artifacts he'd collected over the years. It wasn't common knowledge that Laura liked to slope around the countryside in that getup, but he'd been spying on her one summer and he'd seen her put it on and disappear. And no question that she was naked underneath that day.

"Those wolves aren't doing you any favors."

"They follow me around all the time now, whenever I wear the suit. It's only recently that they've started crossing the Willow Bride and following me down the mountain."

"Maybe you ought to think about staying home then." She wore a black-and-silver outfit that looked like a cross between a skinsuit and a military uniform, with none of the formfitting attractiveness of a skinsuit and none of the dignity of a uniform. "That's an ugly frock."

"It is."

"How's your father?"

"He's dead."

"That explains the frock."

It was traditional to dress in black after the death of a loved one. How long you had to dress that way was a function of the deceased's relationship to the wearer. A complicated set of rules applied, rules Macer and Laura's mothers could have recited cold. He'd have to look them up, and he was pretty sure Laura would have to look them up as well, if she hadn't already looked them up for amusement. She was a scholar by nature and easily the smartest person Macer had ever met. She was also the most mentally unbalanced person he'd ever met, excepting Ciarán's mother, and she was dead. "Have you ever thought about killing me, or hunting me for sport?"

"Not until I met you."

"But you haven't decided to."

"I'm still thinking about it."

"That's good. I'm sorry about your father."

She stared at him. "Is that it? He treated you like a son."

"He treated me better than that." The Ellis had treated him like a man, or someone who might grow into one, and taught him how to act like one, so that he might.

Years ago Macer had asked the Ellis why Laura was so easily upset all the time, and weepy, and was there something wrong with her, or with him. The Ellis said only one letter separated the mountain from the fountain. Whether you showed what you felt was entirely one of convention, or of utility, depending. Laura could appear soft because he appeared hard. And vice versa. There wasn't anything wrong with Laura or with him. They were two faces of the same coin, and more similar than different beneath the surface.

He hadn't believed the Ellis but he'd decided to act as if he did, and to wait, and to see who was right.

"I expected you'd have more to say."

"I'm shocked, is all. I hadn't even known he was ill."

"He wasn't. He was murdered."

"Who did it?"

"I don't know."

"Are you planning to find out?"

"I am."

"Suppose you do."

"I will."

"When you do. Do you have a matchmaker in the family?"

"I'm all that's left."

"There's your mother."

"She's dead."

"She's *missing*."

"We attended a funeral, Macer. For both our mothers."

"One without bodies."

"Believe what you want."

"It's not waking the dead to speak of her. They're out there, in the wider world, and one day they're coming home."

"What's the point of talking to you?"

"There's this. Until Ciarán mans up and decides to fight me for you, we're still betrothed, right?"

"Only if our mothers are yet alive and the deal yet alive between them. And now that we're of age, only if we both want to be bound by the agreement."

"You can think of your mother as dead all you want. But the fact is, the *Thinker's Dame* remains listed as overdue and missing. I have a trigger set up on the stationmaster's log for any change in status. There's been none."

"So what? Are you proposing to me? Do you imagine I'll accept?"

"I'm explaining to you something I know and you don't."

"Well, educate me then, Professor Macer Gant. What is it *the Ellis* is so *ignorant* of?"

"That's right, with your father dead you're the Ellis now."

"That's the way the world works."

"It's one way the world can work. I hope you do a better job as the Ellis than I did as the Gant."

"You're ten times the man your father is. Everyone says so."

"Ten times zero is still zero."

"That was supposed to go over your head."

"Pretend it did, Lorelei. It's what *I* do most of the time."

"You've changed."

"I don't think I have. I think it's the weather that's changed."

"The weather."

"You know how on a soft day you can't see the mountain, but the mountain's shadow, if even that?"

"I do."

"Well, if you've lived a life of only stormy days, you wouldn't know the mountain was there at all. On the first clear day, you'd think the mountain appeared out of nowhere."

"So?"

"You're a naturally morose and glass-half-empty person.

You expect the worst of people and they generally live up to your expectations."

"I know that."

"It makes you easy to fool."

She crossed her arms and gazed into the distance.

"Here's what I know and you don't. That when you wake up and look in the mirror you only appear to be alone."

"That's not how it feels."

"Then turn around, and open the window, and look out." Macer pressed the recall button for the lopers. "The mountain is there. Behind the clouds."

"And you're the mountain."

"I'm not. Are you coming to this get-together tonight?"

"Absolutely not."

"That's good to know. I expect there will be fireworks. I'll come up to your place when I have a chance, and you can tell me whatever you want about your father's death and what needs to be done."

"Fine."

"We'll act as if the contract is in force even if we both know it isn't. And if you need a matchmaker I'll do it."

"But you'd rather not."

"That's a feature of me, and not a bug." Not much matched one killing but another.

"I suppose everyone must has one redeeming feature."

"That's another thing you're wrong about."

37

When Macer returned to the house he found Shayna waiting.

"You said you'd stay in your room."

"I said I'd go in there, but I got hungry. So I got a snack and went for a walk and called my girlfriend. Now I'm back."

"You have a girlfriend."

"I think I'd know if I did."

"What's her name?"

"Nuala nic Cartaí."

"Fine, don't tell me."

"Don't ask questions if you know you won't like the answer. I'm going to my room now. Would you rather wrestle me across the threshold or take my word for it?"

"Like the word of any Gant is worth a pingin."

"I never said it was. But that's a missed opportunity. You should have opted for the wrestling clause. We both might have learned something."

"I already know what wrestling with a Gant feels like."

"Not the new and improved version, you don't. I'll be upstairs if you change your mind, Shayna *Gant*."

MACER PEELED out of his boots and flopped onto the bed. He pulled out his handheld and punched in the id addy from memory. He needed to do this now, while he was still keyed up for a fight.

"Be brief," the stationmaster said.

"I will. Who would know how I ended up with a Truxton posting?"

"Truxton, obviously."

"Besides him."

"Me."

"Oh. How was it then?"

"I asked him to give you one. As a favor."

"In exchange for what?"

"A favor. And you know better to ask that on an open line."

"Sorry, Uncle. Did you ask for a posting in general, or for one with *Tractor Four-Squared* in particular?"

"In particular. Your father said you were dead set on working that hull."

"How would he know that?"

"Ask him yourself."

"What exactly did he say. Do you recall?"

"Of course I recall, you imbecile. I'm not senile. It wasn't him that called but that shiny new toy of his."

"Shayna?"

"Herself. What kind of name is that?"

"New Spartan, I've been led to believe."

"He's going to be the ruination of this family. We were better off when he was dead."

"Yes, sir, though I doubt he sees it that way. Do you know any reason someone would be buying up Clear Island properties?"

"There's a proposal to put in a new spaceport there."

"On this island?"

"I don't know, does it look like I have extrasensory powers? Where in the world are you?"

"I'm at the house."

"With your father."

"Co-located with him, roughly."

"Well, tell him to stop ignoring my calls and to ring me back."

"I will. But I don't get it. Why would anyone want an island that's mostly mountain for a spaceport?"

"You're asking the wrong man, lad. I don't know why anyone would want to live on a ball of dirt at all. Now is there some point to this conversation?"

"Do you want me to get a message to my father? In case he remains uncommunicative."

A long silence hung between them.

"Uncle?"

"I'm thinking."

"Take your time."

"Like I need your permission, junior."

"No, sir. I mean, yes, sir."

"You don't know what you mean. Fine, here's what you can tell him. That his eldest son remains under investigation for mutiny, and that new evidence has come forward linking him to the murder of the ship's doctor. At this point, it's all circumstantial but it looks bad for the boy."

"I see. What's the new evidence?"

"Testimony by a crew member that overheard Macer Gant threatening to kill the ship's doctor prior to the murder of the ship's doctor."

"That never happened."

"According to this witness it did."

"Well it didn't."

"Don't you want to know who the witness is?"

"There wasn't any conversation, so there wasn't any witness."

"The accuser, then."

"Sure, why not."

"You seem to be taking this very lightly."

"It's a bald-faced lie. What difference does it make who's telling it?"

"If someone was telling lies about me, I'd want to know who it was."

"What for?"

"So I could make them stop."

"Tell me, then."

"Ares Adonis."

"I don't know who that is."

"You served on a vessel with him for six months."

"So?"

"There's only twenty people on the vessel."

"Fewer than that, if you consider that most of them were in cryo."

"What?"

"Turns out there were ever only about eight of us awake at a time, except during footie ball game tournaments. Did I not mention this?"

"You did not. Now listen to me, son, it's bad enough my own nephew is six months aboard a vessel with an unregistered Templeman drive, and him an engineer, and no maintenance done on the drive, and not a word out of him to me about these flagrant violations of station protocol. But now you're telling me Truxton's been cold-crewing the vessel as well, and you not saying a word?"

"I didn't know any of this until the day Singh made me acting chief engineer."

"No one sensible would believe that."

"It's the truth. I had no interaction with the rest of the crew until that day. And if I'd known the drive was unregistered, why would I have put in a parts requisition for it?"

"I don't see any way of proving a single part of that."

"It's trivial. Someone slagged the sensor nexus. They didn't slag the recordings. There are only three missing days from the logs. Not only that, all you have to do is ask Singh."

"You'd trust him not to lie."

"Why would he lie? I followed orders and stayed in engineering. I did a competent job. I didn't install that drive, and it hadn't had any maintenance in seventy years. I'd only been there six months. Lying about my involvement wouldn't let Singh of the hook."

"Maybe he has it in for you."

"We got along. We were a good team. Why would he have it in for me?"

"Why would he plant a bomb on board and leave you to die?"

"That wasn't Singh, it was Rik Severn."

"Who is Rik Severn?"

"The person who planted a bomb on board. He came on board from the liberty boat. There were three replacement crew arriving and Singh and one other crewman leaving. I was distracted at the time on account of Singh taking my place, so I didn't note the odd count."

"Three for two isn't usual. Why am I only hearing about this now?"

"I gave the recordings to Truxton. You might ask him."

"What recordings?"

"The ones I got from the ship's sensors before the buffers wrapped."

"And you didn't think to give these to me?"

"I thought about it. But I read my contract with Truxton and decided I couldn't. They weren't my property to give."

"You could have slipped them to me and no one the wiser."

"And violate an employment contract? Then I really would be guilty of something."

"All the time I've known you, I thought you were just pretending to be an idiot."

"I guess you didn't know me very well."

"Wait, and don't go anywhere."

"I will."

Macer could hear the stationmaster giving orders in the background. After a while he came back.

"Two replacement workers on, two off, no record of this Rik Severn."

"I don't know what to tell you. He was there."

"You could have given me those logs."

"Merchant Captain Truxton could have as well."

"Well, he's not family is he? I don't expect him to have my best interests at heart."

"Your best interests?"

"Lad, have you no concept of how this entire fiasco makes me look?"

"But nothing bad happened."

"Purely by happenstance. I'm not paid to be lucky, Macer. I'm paid to protect the lives and property of three different nations, and each one of them more distrustful than the next. Now it looks like there's been a Freeman-flagged bomb I've let lash itself to the station now and then, and two out of three of those nations are asking themselves if the *Freeman* station-master turned a blind eye, or is he just incompetent.

"Not to mention that it just appears a matter of providence that a superluminal vessel didn't plunge through the heart of the nic Cartaí shipyard and murder over a thousand workers and their families, many of whom are citizens of the League and the Ojinate. I appreciate that you stopped the runaway, but it's easier to imagine that you hadn't than that you had. And that's what they're all doing. Unless they're imagining I knew about the tug's superluminal drive all the time and just didn't tell anyone. That I had family on board, ready to use it or not at my command."

"But none of that is true."

"You and I know that. But that's not the way it looks. And the way it looks is all that matters."

"According to Aoife nic Cartaí, she was always in control. She was just in a hurry."

"I've seen no evidence of that."

"She has logs to prove it."

"Have you seen these logs?"

"She gave me copies of them. But I didn't look at them."

"And you didn't think to tell me this?"

"I thought about it, but—"

"They weren't yours to give."

"Right."

"Send them to me now."

"I don't have them."

"Who does?"

"I imagine she does. She and Truxton."

"I hope the pair of them paid you handsomely for selling out your old uncle."

"It's not like that."

"It looks like that to me."

"I'll call Truxton—"

"Don't bother. I'll do it myself. And nic Cartaí as well."

"It's no bother."

"You didn't have to give me the logs. All you needed to do was warn me of their existence."

"I can see that now."

"You know, every time your mother and that Ellis woman hared off, she made me promise I'd look after you while she was gone. I like to think I did that when I could. But you're a man now, and not my sister-in-law's little boy any longer. And I am done with Macer Gant the child."

"Understood."

"Good. Now are we through here?"

"You said there were two listed as getting off the liberty boat and two getting on."

"I did."

"Who besides Singh is listed as leaving *Four-Squared*?"

"A navigator registered under the name of Ares Adonis. New Spartan, hasn't taken the Oath."

"Previous postings?"

"None, according to the Registry."

"What's a navigator doing on an in-system tug?"

"That's a good question. If we could find him, we'd ask him."

"I'll find him and ask him."

"That's the first sensible thing you've said."

38

Macer showered and dressed for the party, or meeting, or whatever exactly it was. An island-man's suit hung in the wardrobe, one that was a little loose in the waist and tight in the shoulders, but that style of suit was cut loose to begin with, and he wasn't planning on any heavy lifting tonight, where he might pop a seam. He shouldered his backpack and headed for the hangar, where he dropped it off, and from there to the docks just as the first of the early arrivals rounded the point and turned toward the little harbor. They'd be rafting up tonight, for certain, but the first few boats would tie directly to the docks.

Macer held his hand aloft and Rufus Murtagh tossed him a bow line. He cleated it off and caught the stern line when the island's best baker tossed that, too, and he tailed the line while Murtagh walked the stern in. Macer cleated the line off, and then Murtagh had the boat on the spring lines and was step-ping off lightly, his three children behind him, all in their Sunday finest, and no sign of the missus. You'd think a baker would be all fat and jolly, but they were each skinny as rails.

"Thought you were in space," Murtagh said as he shook Macer's hand.

"I come down for a sandwich, and a sheaf of loaves to go."

"Sure you did, you remember these three."

"James, of the strong arm, and Samuel, of the fleet feet, and oh, your poor daughter Susan, still as homely as ever."

"She is that," Murtagh said. "All the boys come around just to gape at her."

"I doubt that's all they come around for. You should have named her Helen, after her mother."

"There's enough of that going on around the island. It's hard to keep the accounts receivable straight with all the Ones and Twos and Threes around."

"That's true, but if someone asked who's the prettiest woman on the island, I wouldn't have to think so hard. I could just say Helen and be done with it."

"You're making herself red in the face, and her at home with the pups."

"Apologize for me when you see her."

"I'll do that."

"There's something else you can do for me, if you've a moment."

"Run along kids," Murtagh said.

"They can stay if they want. The more minds the better on this."

"What is it?"

"First off, I'm looking for a fellow called Ares Adonis. Have any of you heard of him?"

They looked at each other and shook their heads.

"That was a long shot, but this one's sure to hit closer to home. I've heard that some foreigners are making offers to buy family land here on the island, and I've heard they're offering top dollar."

"I've heard that," Murtagh said, his expression now wary.

"Well, that's fine, if people whose families have been part of the community for hundreds of years decide it's what they want. If it's in their best interests to take the money and move to wherever, the mainland, the city, even the station. But if they don't want to take the money but feel pressured to do so, *for whatever reason*, I think that's not right, and ought not to happen."

"Go on. "

"I'm on a crusade, Mr. Murtagh, and I'd like you and the whole Murtagh clan to spread the word. There's no reason in the world folks who live here and want to stay should leave. So I'll top any cash offer for any islander, and all they need to do is tell these foreigners they'd got a better price from Macer Gant."

"Do you have that kind of money?"

"That's hard to say. But no one can fault a Freeman for refusing one offer for a better one. If these foreigners or *anyone they're working with* don't like it, they can take it up with me. Those folks under the gun can hold firm and with a good and sensible reason to do so."

"We can fight our own fights."

"Now that is why I'm glad your young men and your young lady stayed to be part of this conversation. Mark that, you boys in particular, because that is what sets an island man apart from men on the mainland, and in the city, and even on the station. And that's why I wanted to speak to your father first.

"He's a successful businessman, and respected in the community, and in better shape than most of his neighbors, some of which are less industrious and frugal, it's true, but many of which are simply less fortunate, through no fault of their own. It's not for you, Mr. Murtagh, I'm worried, but for those who might owe more than they could afford to pay, should their debts all come due at once."

"Does your father know you're doing this?"

"Do you know everything James, and Samuel, and Susan get up to?"

"He doesn't," Susan said.

"He'll murder you when he finds out."

"He'll want to, that's true. But if anyone murders me, it won't be him."

"What do you get out of this?"

"I'm trying to make the right people mad."

"What for?"

"So they'll come and see me."

"Well, I hope you know what you're doing."

"I hope that too. There's the Powers's boat, and it looks like they need a hand with the lines. Will you excuse me?"

Macer was on the move without waiting for an answer. He caught the lines, and worked them, and helped Peg Powers and her mister onto the dock.

"I thought you were in space," Peg said.

"I come down for a new pair of boots or three."

She glanced at his feet. "Who needs four fine pairs of boots?"

"Someone who wants something from the cobbler," Bill Powers said.

"As a matter of fact, I do. Have either of you heard of this fellow Ares Adonis?"

"That's two fellows," Bill said. "One's a god of war and the other's a pretty boy."

"In this case, it's just one fellow. He's listed in the Registry as a navigator from New Sparta."

"Why are you looking for him?" Peg said.

"I owe him, and I'd like to make sure he gets paid."

"We don't know him," Peg said.

"It was a long shot. Anyway, I've heard that some foreigners are making offers to buy family land here on the island, and I've heard they're offering top dollar."

"That's true," Peg said.

"I figured you'd of heard about it, and that's why I wanted to talk to you about it first..."

MACER LEANED against a piling and scrubbed his hands through his hair. It was full dark, and the little harbor likewise full with boats lashed to the docks, and to one another. It seemed as if nearly the entire population of the island had arrived, women, men, and children. The last of them were beginning to wind their way up the hill and past the hangar, handheld torchlight bobbing in time with their steps.

He had a good memory for names and faces, and but for a few small ones born in the five years he'd been away at the Academy and on the job, he'd recognized them and been able to do his duty as a son born to privilege. That he generally liked and respected most of his neighbors made it easier, and that he wanted them to think well of him, and of his family, made it important. Life on the island wasn't like on the station, with people coming and going as they pleased and reputations, both good and bad, disappearing along with them.

There was no raising of the dead, not in this community, but there was no rest for the living, either, as every word and glance, every acknowledgment and slight, was constantly being summed and subtracted, so that one didn't need to recall the past to know the measure of a woman or a man. He hadn't realized any of this until he'd seen if from a distance. Some people were like birds, and some like fish, but he was the flying fish, who, knowing the sky, would always find his course plunging back into the ocean, unless it was into the jaws of some leviathan lurking just beneath the surface.

He didn't want his father to be the leviathan, and hoped that he wasn't, but he couldn't be sure. He'd been away most of the time, and when he hadn't been he'd slept in the hangar, or the bunkhouse in the valley over, or at the mac Diarmuids', and not so much as two paragraphs of words between him and his father in five years, until today. Luther Gant might have grown sharper teeth in that time, but if so he'd have had to change. The father he knew was a canny man, and a conniver, and entirely centered on his own desires. It made no sense for him to be part of a... *disassembly* of the community unless that something profited him, profited more than he could get out of the present situation, where he could gouge and ride the backs of his neighbors and never have to work an honest day of his life.

It made more sense that he wasn't the beast itself, but more like a fin, or a tail fluke of something bigger. Something that had him by the short hairs like he had every mortgage-paying farmer, and receivables-factoring business owner and every over-extended salaryman on the island by theirs. And whatever this bigger beast was, it wanted title to some part of the island, for some reason Macer didn't know. He could spend weeks asking around, or trying to squeeze a drop of truth out of his father, and it would be like dangling a worm in a whirlpool, all spinning and no bites. He accepted more risk this way, considerably more, but if you wanted to come face-to-face with a shark, no surer way existed than opening a vein and plunging into the depths.

And so he had. And now he'd wait and see what showed up. He was on his home turf, and whoever these foreigners were, they weren't. No one was sneaking up on him on Clear Island, and that was a fact. He'd see them coming, and once he sighted them, he'd know how to prepare.

Someone cleared their throat beside him. "Pardon me, but I couldn't help overhear."

Macer felt the hairs on his neck stand straight. *So much for that plan.* He felt his fingers knot into fists as he turned his gaze upon the speaker.

The man grinned and stepped back. He was a Leagueman, no doubt, dressed in the traveling outfit their leisure class adopted. He was average in height and size for a Leagueman, which meant thicker and taller than most space-born Freeman. He had a pleasantly forgettable face and might otherwise be forgettable, if not for the fact that he'd snuck up on Macer unaware—and the fact that Macer had seen his still image aboard Nuala nic Cartai's flagship, only in that image he'd been wearing a League Home Guard major's uniform, chatting with an attractive arm, and holding a cocktail glass.

"I'm guessing you could have and chose not to," Macer said. "I'm Macer Gant."

"A name I've heard you called over a hundred times tonight."

"People like saying it. Do they like saying your name?"

"Far more of them than I like."

"If one of them was to utter that name now, what would it be?"

"A mistake. As I was saying, I couldn't overhear your asking after Ares Adonis."

"Do you know that fellow?"

"Ares Adonis is an entertainer's handle. A pseudonym, or a character's name. You might as well ask people if they know Prince Rigel Templeman or Lord Varlock the Destroyer."

"Everybody knows who those people are."

"Do they? Then why isn't Prince Rigel sitting on the Emerald Throne?"

"He does, in season three."

"That is an actor in a recorded drama, not the real Prince Rigel."

"There's a real Prince Rigel?"

"And a real Lord Varlock, though not at the present time. If you wish to find this Ares Adonis, you need to ask in the right places. The name is a cultural reference. To find Ares Adonis you must first find his *people*."

"That's something to think about."

"You're welcome." He stood staring at Macer, hands behind his back, rocking on the balls of his feet like he needed to go somewhere but was waiting for Macer's permission.

"Run along now."

"I beg your pardon?"

"You interrupted my thinking, and you told me what you wanted to say. I think we're done here."

"It's customary to exchange information for information."

"It's customary around here to exchange handles. If a fellow won't tell you his name he's either up to no good or Folk. You don't look like Folk."

"Hector Poole."

"Nice to meet you, Mr. Poole. What can I help you with?"

"I'm trying to find a man named Seán mac Diarmuid. I thought I might find him here."

"I'd try the mac Diarmuid place. It's two valleys over, that away." Macer pointed along the coastline.

"So he won't be attending tonight's presentation?"

"There's a presentation?"

"Regarding the buyout. For the spaceport."

"Is that something you're involved in?"

"Not at all. It seems outlandish to me, the idea that one would build a spaceport on an island that's largely a mountain."

"We agree on that."

"Mr. Mac Diarmuid?"

"What about him?"

"I was told you and he are friends."

"That was true last time we talked."

"Would you be willing to introduce me to him?"

"That wouldn't do you any good. If you want to talk to Seán, just go see him. Unless you come in guns blazing, he'll listen."

"I was led to understand that it is customary to..."

"Oil the oiler?"

He grinned. "In a word, yes."

"Is that the custom where you're from?"

"In certain circles, yes."

"But not amongst your own kind."

"It's how one does business with foreigners."

"Well, I'm a native man. And I'm willing to treat you like a native, so long as you behave like one."

"And that entails?"

"For starters, going to see what this presentation is all about. During the intermission you can tell me about your business. You've already heard all about mine."

"I'd be happy to explain. It's nothing nefarious, Mr. Gant."

"Spoken like a native, Mr. Poole."

Every native man knew you didn't judge a man by what he said.

You judged him by what he did.

And if sneaking up on a man and spying on his business wasn't nefarious, Macer didn't know what was.

39

Ten minutes into the presentation, it was clear that the idea of turning Clear Island into a spaceport was utter rubbish, and a front for something else entirely. The expert brought in from the mainland projected chart after chart on a large portable display set up for the purpose, and even showed an animated short of longboats arriving at a glassfield and terminal that was now the Ellis place, and a burgeoning city along the coastline from there clear past the mac Diarmuids', and high-speed hydrofoils running back and forth to the mainland, all on a clear day, with flat seas, which raised a wisecrack or two from the gathered throng.

Macer tapped the Leagueman's elbow and led him outside into the cool night, crabbing their way past the outstretched legs of the watchers inside, most of whom had nodded off, and those remaining passing a flask back and forth and whispering quietly. The serious party would begin once the presentation was over, and it was clear now, the party at Luther Gant's expense was what these folks were here for.

Macer could hear shouting coming from up the hill, and his heart stopped beating for an instant. He'd cleared out the upper pasture to use as a glassfield, and it hadn't occurred to him that some youngster would find it ideal as a playing field. He glanced skyward in reflex and begin trotting up the hill. The Leagueman trotted along beside him.

They were two dozen of them and playing some sort of game that involved a ball the size of a man's head and a lot of kicking, and punching, and swearing. Bill Powers had his elbows hooked over the top rail of the fence as he puffed on a pipe and watched.

"It's not safe," Macer said. "We need to shoo them out of there."

"Footie's not about safety," Powers said. "They're not hurting nothing but each other."

"It's a glassfield under that turf," Macer said.

"Aye," Powers said. "Used to be a great amount of comings and goings. Make it ideal for the play, though a little hard on the elbows and the knees."

"I moved the cows to another pasture, Mr. Powers, because I'm expecting an incoming."

"An incoming what?"

"Longboat."

"Ach, you can hear one of those coming from ten clicks away."

"A nic Cartaí longboat, Mr. Powers, and you know how that lot plummets."

"I'll warn them to watch the sky, and scatter at the slightest."

"And if one of them trips and falls while scattering?"

"When did you become such a nervous nanny?"

"After seeing what a longboat's main drive can do to a boat bay."

"Only a fool would light up a main drive inside a hull."

"And what sort of parent would let their children play on an active glassfield?"

"You should go find them and ask them."

The Leagueman whistled, loudly.

The kids came running over. They seemed to be all ages, though mostly boys. The largest ones, including the Murtagh lads, were noticeably winded.

The Leagueman pointed at the ball. "May I?"

James Murtagh handed him the ball.

The Leagueman tossed the ball down the gravel road, toward the big barn. "Fetch."

The throng of children swarmed through and over the fence, chasing the ball like a pack.

"They won't be back," he said. "Provided there's level ground closer by."

The Murtagh boys began climbing stiffly over the fence.

"Glassfield." Macer pointed skyward. "Can the pair of you keep them downslope?"

"I'm not going anywhere near them," Samuel said. "We were practicing our kicks and the next thing you know, we were mobbed."

"Footie's a popular sport," Powers said. "Now the clinic has an autodoc."

"According to my dad, it's not a sport," James said. "It's a game."

"At the amateur level of play, I'm inclined to agree. But in the pros? It's a sport, lads."

"What's the difference?" Macer said.

"In a game one can be injured," the Leagueman said. "In a sport one can die."

Powers tapped out his pipe. "In a sport you will die, if you stick at it long enough."

"So life is a sport," Macer said.

"For most." Powers aimed the stem of his pipe at the boys. "If the pair of youse weren't a year apart, there'd be no telling you from Ares and Adonis. Fair play to you, and I thank you for the exhibition."

"Hang on," Macer said. "There are two footie players, one named Ares and the other Adonis?"

"Identical twins," Samuel Murtagh said.

"They're monsters," James Murtagh said.

"Why didn't you say earlier?"

"You said you were looking for one man," Samuel said.

"And Dad doesn't like to hear footie talk," James said.

"Ares and Adonis, they play around here?"

"On the station," James said. "They're starting ruckmen for Max Violent's Offenders."

"Low-G footie," Powers said. "Punishment in three dimensions."

"Is that their real names, do you know?"

"No idea," Powers said. "But you should ask your father's city acquisition. She hails from the same neighborhood."

"How do you know that?"

"Because she sounds just like them when she talks," Powers said. "All baah and oyt, and datso, if you take my meaning. Come on boys, I'll buy you a round." He winked at Macer. "Royster's Limeade, the soft drink of hard men."

When they were gone, Macer leaned against the fence and watched the sky. "Thank you for that whistle. Do you have children?"

"I teach at the Home Guard Academy on Cordame," the Leagueman said. "Many of the students are childlike."

"When they arrive, you mean."

"And when they leave. It's as much a reform school as military academy. We have an excess of hereditary elite, and little to do with them between wars."

"The League appears to be solving that problem," Macer said.

"Or making it worse. It's too soon to say. As civil wars go, this appears to be more serious than most. Which partly explains why I'm here, and why I wish to speak with Seán mac Diarmuid."

"Because of the League civil war."

"Because every two thousand years or so, we don't just have a squabble, but a score settling that consumes all it touches. War so total that our civilization is reduced to rubble and our society all but erased."

"And then you rebuild."

"We have, twice now. But that was before we discovered we had neighbors, and our neighbors discovered us. This time it will be different. We won't simply pick ourselves up and dust ourselves off. Others will watch, and wait, and when we have exhausted our resources and torn ourselves asunder? They'll pick our bones clean and plow them under."

"And Seán mac Diarmuid can stop that."

"Hardly," the Leagueman said. "Nor can I. But what I can do is investigate and analyze the events leading up to the last League-spanning civil war and its earliest years. And I believe Seán mac Diarmuid can help me with that. I understand he has recovered several second-epoch artifacts. I'd like to examine them. And my sponsor may wish to negotiate for the purchase of some or all of them."

"Your sponsor?"

"Commodore Kirill Olek. He's a collector and captain of the *Sudden Fall of Darkness*. It's a second-epoch survey vessel and a sort of... mobile museum of second-epoch League technology."

"And you want me to introduce you to Seán mac Diarmuid."

"Introduce both of us. Commodore Olek is here as well."

"I see." Macer gazed upward.

"Whom are you expecting to arrive in this longboat?"

"No one. It's more like a wish than an expectation. Let's go back down and see if they've finished up. Tomorrow, if you're up for it, I'll run you and the commodore over to the mac Diarmuid place. I expect Seán will talk to you all he wants, but I wouldn't get my hopes up on buying anything."

"Why is that?"

"It's mostly debris. Bits and pieces of stuff."

Growing up Macer had spent more time with Seán mac Diarmuid than anyone else on the island. Seán had the biggest boat around, and he was always willing to help clear a field for plowing anywhere on the island, so long as it wasn't just stones that needed clearing, but junk. More junk than stones blanketed a third of the island, and some of that junk weighed hundreds or even thousands of kilograms.

What Macer realized, and maybe he wouldn't have realized at all, if he hadn't been Luther Gant's son, was that you could have a conversation with another man, or woman, and when the pair of you had your shoulders against a piece of fallen metal big as a boulder, and both of you grunting, and pushing, and rocking the nasty beast free, that the words spoken didn't matter. It was the sweat that told the story, the mud you kicked off your boots, the jug you passed around.

His father had one sort of hold on folk, money-debt that could be multiplied and divided, and summed up to some calculable total. Seán mac Diarmuid had another sort of hold, a debt of shared pain, and shared curses, and at the end of the day, the sort of shared satisfaction that only came from a hard day's work building something together.

Seán mac Diarmuid wasn't just collecting space junk and stacking it up in his farmyard because he might be able to sell it on one day. He was clearing away the past, and not even their own past, and cementing together the future, one clean furrow and one firm handshake at a time. Three summers he'd worked beside Seán. In that time they must have hauled off the mass of a longboat one wheelbarrow after another, and that with a lot of the debris being small enough to plow under.

He'd never thought about putting all that junk back together into something recognizable, and now that he did think about it, he didn't think it could be done. Most of the bits were alien, even to an engineer's trained eye.

"I don't think you'd be able to make anything out of that junk but smaller pieces of junk."

"Perhaps some of the pieces will prove instructive," the Leagueman said.

"Anything's possible. Let's go on down now and see what's up."

THE MAINLAND EXPERT had been replaced on stage by Macer's father, who was going on about how there wasn't any work on the island for young folk, and there wasn't any work on the mainland for island folk, not unless they wanted to get with the times, and that meant adopting modern ways.

"Like this new implant I got last time I was over there," Luther Gant said. "It's a miracle, the way it works, and it opens up a vast array of possibilities. There isn't a League citizen over the age of ten without one, and that's the competition, whether we like it or not."

Peg Powers shouted, "We're not made of money like some!"

"I'm glad you brought that up, Peg, because I was just getting to that. I've been talking to these Consortium folks that are here tonight and telling them about our plight, and here's what they agreed. That for anyone who wants to sell, here and now, they'll pay for an implant for each and every member of the family, in addition to the honest offer they'll make you, or have already made you.

"And if that's too much to ask, and you need time to think, they'll still pay for an implant for each of your children, provided you make your mind up within the week."

Peg shouted. "We don't have no children!"

Macer's father made a production out of listening to someone talking to him via his implant. There weren't many on the island that had them, but everyone recognized that distracted look, either from their time on the mainland, or the station, or from recorded dramas.

"Seven days," Luther Gant said. "For the childless, husband and wife both, and for bachelors, and widows or widowers living alone. But any longer, it's still the generous offer, and hard cash money the moment you make your mark. Now Rafe there, by the entrance, has a sign-up pad, and he'll take your particulars, and even if you're just inclined to think about it, he'll take that down and get the pump primed for when you do decide to move forward.

"It's time we step up and join the rest of the wider world."

He held a single finger aloft, and again looked like he was distracted by his implant. He tilted his head and touched the finger to his ear, and it was clear this time he was faking.

"One more thing before I forget." Luther Gant looked from face-to-face across the room. "The bar is open!"

A great roaring cheer went up, and underneath it another roar.

Macer stepped outside.

The night sky was screaming. Macer took off in a run for the upper pasture.

"A longboat," the Leagueman at his elbow said.

Macer glanced at the man. He'd managed to keep up with Macer in a panic run and he wasn't even breathing hard.

"A Truxton longboat."

"How can you tell?"

"The burn regulation. It's rock solid. A family operation can't pull that off."

"Nic Cartaí or Kavanagh could."

"They tune for efficiency. That's cracking ninety without a leash, and that's one of ours. I mean, one of Truxton's."

"It's not slowing."

"It will. It's a Truxton hull with a nic Cartaí pilot at the helm. Has to be."

"Because?"

"Because if it isn't, it won't matter. We're both fast runners but not that fast."

"He needs to start braking."

"She will."

The Leagueman stared upward as the descending star of a longboat's main drive plummeted toward them. A sonic boom shattered the sky.

"If there are stupider ways to die, I can't think of any."

"Huh," Macer said. "I can think of several."

Being blown up by a Templeman drive failure. Being murdered by an Olympian assassin on a starship's hull. Being abandoned by a maniac captain on a plague ship. Being hung for mutiny. Being hung for a murder you didn't commit. Being assassinated by your evil stepmother.

"It's not slowing."

"That's disappointing." He'd been hoping it was Fionnuala arriving fashionably late.

Instead it looked like she'd sent her insane daughter in her place.

Either that or she'd decided an aerial bombardment of the Gant place would solve whatever problems she was having with Hector Poole and Commodore Kirill Olek.

"I'm going to run," the Leagueman said.

"I'm going to stick. I'm pretty sure that's Aoife nic Cartaí."

"Please, god, no."

"Sounds like you've met her." Macer glanced at his hand-held. "She's terminal in three... two... one."

The main drive blinked off. A constellation of tiny suns

ignited as the retros boiled atmosphere and the longboat's hull plates begun to change from cherry red to blazing white.

The screaming sound of a longboat at maximum deceleration washed over them seconds later.

"It's her," Macer said.

"Kill me now," the Leagueman said.

40

Pinion System, Imperial Ojinate

A white light appeared in the distance and Ciarán felt drawn toward it. He lay in a white room, on a white operating table. He swung his feet over the side of the table and sat up. A loose white robe covered him from neck to ankles. The sleeves of the robe were long enough to hide his hands. He glanced at the floor. It was silver.

He had it in his mind to stand when a door opened, one he hadn't seen, a white door in a white wall, and a woman in a white robe like the one he wore entered. She looked familiar but he couldn't place her. She appeared to be concerned about something. He wanted to tell her not to worry. That everything would be all right.

When he tried to speak, he found he couldn't.

She didn't appear to see him, or if she did, she ignored him. She walked toward the light.

He wanted to follow her.

She switched the light off.

The world went black.

A man started to scream.

"Ciarán, wake up."

He gasped and opened his eyes.

He was in a white room, on a white sheet. He was wearing a white robe.

Natsuko smiled at him. "You are like the mong hu. Only eight more lives for you."

He licked his lips and tried to speak. She handed him a glass with a drinking straw and held it to his lips one-handed. Her other arm hung in a sling.

"How—"

"You broke my arm when you threw yourself atop me. Only one autodoc was available and you needed it more."

He swallowed. "How—"

"You used the overseer's rod to generate a force shield to protect us. It worked well but not perfectly. The all-consuming flame is a fission weapon. You received extensive radiation burns. We were able to stabilize you and get you to the station, where they have precision medical equipment."

"How—" She placed the straw between his lips so that he could drink. "Is... ship... crew?"

"They are well and aware of the situation. You will require a final treatment and another day of bed rest."

"Rest... on ship."

"Here, in the medical facility."

"That's... order."

"You've been temporarily relieved of command."

"Who."

"Swan."

"Ack."

"There's a sedative in the water."

"Hu..."

"You saved me, Ciarán. Everyone is safe. Now get some rest. They say the last treatment is the most painful. You must be strong."

"K."

HE WOKE AGAIN in the merchant apprentice's berthing compartment aboard *Quite Possibly Alien*. He lay on his side and twisted into a comma shape. Wisp had commandeered most of the bunk. When he elbowed her she rolled onto her back, stretched all four legs, and began to purr. He lifted the covers and looked. He appeared to have all his appendages. Just not any clothes to cover them. He slid out of bed and opened the hanging locker.

"Your clothes are over here," Agnes Swan said.

She sat in his workstation chair. She had a hot cup of caife and a breakfast roll. She watched him as he dressed.

"You seem to be over your initial shyness around the crew."

"I've seen you naked. What's good for the swan..."

"Is good for the drake."

"Seems to balance out, anyway." He strapped into his hull-walkers. "I'm back on the job. So whatever of my duties you've taken upon yourself to shoulder?"

"Yes?"

"I want them back right now."

"Done."

"Fill me in."

"We are prepped and ready to depart."

"I need to finalize our agreement with Kazuki Ryuu."

"Unnecessary."

"Why's that?"

The hatch opened and Kazuki Ryuu walked in. "Because I'm coming with you."

"Nice entrance."

Ryuu nodded. "It's an art."

"Fine," Ciarán said. "The more the merrier."

"I expected an argument."

"I need to go down to the surface."

"Impossible," Ryuu said.

Swan chuckled. "And so it begins..."

AFTER SOME GREAT WRANGLING, Ciarán ended up returning to the surface alone. He'd suspected that Kazuki Ryuu was a person of importance in the system before she had taken over communications with the station. Afterward he was certain. She could get whatever she wanted in Pinion space, which meant that she was more than a *Noh* actor of international acclaim.

He asked Hess to meet him in the boat bay with enough worn or damaged ship parts to fill the copilot's seat of a second-epoch shuttle. The engineer did, and he helped Ciarán load the jumbled carton of junk into the shuttle.

"What's this for?"

"An experiment."

"You don't want to tell me."

"I don't want you to think I'm crazy. If it works, I'll tell you."

Ciarán settled into the pilot's seat and began to run through the preflight. When he was finished, he instructed the shuttle to lift and aimed it toward the boat-bay iris. He noticed motion to his right, and when he turned to look found Mrs. Amati sprinting toward the shuttle. She waved and shouted.

He took the boat through the iris.

"Sxipestro," Ciarán said.

"I am here."

"Please advise the ship's armsman that I'll be fine. It's just a *quick down and back*, and not to worry."

"She advises that you're still under medication and in no condition to be operating heavy machinery."

"Tell her the objection has been noted. Mac Diarmuid out."

The little two-person craft followed the flight path outlined by Kazuki Ryuu. So long as he stuck to it, he was assured, no one would fire upon him. She hadn't wanted to reveal the location of the crater where her cottage once stood, but he explained that he was only interested in saving time. Both Natsuko and he had been wearing trackers and the ship could find the location with some small effort. He wasn't so much interested in the location of the cottage as he was of the nearby temple.

It remained difficult, telling what was real from what was a dream. He had realized sometime during his treatment that the woman who turned the light off and plunged him into darkness was the woodcarver from Ryuu's cabin, who'd turned out to be, at least physically, a man. That was at least how he remembered the events of that day, though much of what he recalled seemed scrambled.

Below lay the crater where the cottage once stood and the flattened forest surrounding it. He passed over the slave pen where he'd very nearly gotten Natsuko killed. In the distance he caught a flash of vermillion. The temple gate.

According to Ryuu, the bombardment of her home was an automated response, one triggered by the assault on her person. It was determined that under no circumstances could she be abducted and the knowledge she possessed fall into enemy hands. A plasma weapon discharging near her signaled the beginning of the end. Since ascending to head the Diplomatic Service, she had lived under threat of annihilation not simply from foe, but from friend as well. Now that the die was cast she was free again, to travel and to take the fight directly to the enemy.

The blast radius of the all-consuming flame extended past the temple. There were trees flattened all around it, yet it appeared entirely untouched. A circle ringed it, as if etched into the earth. Inside that circle nothing had changed. He settled the shuttle to the ground outside the gate and popped the canopy latch. He hoisted the carton of junk out of the copilot's seat and carried it up the hill and through the temple gate. The day was warm, the air close and still. He grew winded by the time he'd reached the base of the temple stairs. He rested the crate beside the other offerings there. It looked crude and artless beside the elegant architecture and intricate carvings of the temple. Carvings that were lovely, but entirely unlike the carving of a second-epoch starship's spidery luminaire.

He really wasn't recovered yet. By the time he'd climbed the temple stairs, he felt lightheaded and sick to his stomach. He'd yet to see another soul. He thought about ringing the large bell in the center of the temple, but before he could, someone appeared. She was wearing a white robe like in his dream, or nightmare, and today, at least, she appeared to be a man.

"I wondered if you might find your way here," he said. "Come, let us have tea."

"I'd rather not, if it's all the same to you. I'm looking for the man from the station."

"The station's *kami*."

"I don't think so. The station's maintenance man. And the man who maintains the equipment here. You were very evasive about the wood carving at Kazuki Ryuu's."

"It's not a proper topic of discussion."

"Then you make something up about it. You don't change the subject and insult a visitor's lineage. You didn't want me to even *think* about the carving. Getting me boiling about the past would do that. But that's not all."

"No?"

"It wasn't your tea. You were visiting Kazuki Ryuu, and on foot. The only places close enough to walk from was the shuttle landing spot and this temple."

"And thus you found me."

"It wasn't hard."

"So I am discovering. Ryuu and I have a relationship. We share information. You were expected to contact her factor in Nesting, who would send you to her at a time of her choosing. Instead you arrived prematurely on her doorstep. Such an interruption was unexpected.

"I didn't comprehend at first who you were. And by the time I did, events had escalated beyond my control."

"It was you who had bound and gagged her."

"She is of the artist class. They have peculiarities of taste. In matters of love, one strives to be accommodating."

"And those people who attacked us?"

"They aren't people. They only appear to be."

"They were very convincing."

"That is their purpose. Come, I will take you to Hoshi."

"Who or what is that?"

"A relic of years gone by."

Hoshi was the name of the maintenance man from the station. The grubby man was clambering over the matte-black surface of a second-epoch League macrofab.

"Ryuu draws her inspiration for the *Noh* masks from life," the monk said.

"And you carve the masks."

"Sometimes. When I need a break from more physical activities. Kazuki Ryuu believes that practice makes perfect in all things. She can be quit demanding."

"You were wearing her kimono at the cabin."

"These white robes are very hard to keep clean."

"I'm sorry we drugged and bound you."

"You should be. You aren't very good at it. And I apologize for trying to murder you. I was drugged, and not in my right mind."

Hoshi noticed them and waved. Ciarán waved back. "I need to know where those people got their implants."

"We don't call them people. We call them hounds."

"Okay. Where those *hounds* got the implants."

"You would have to ask the people I made the hounds for."

"You made them?"

"I wasn't always a monk."

"Who did you make them for?"

"Some very bad people. I heard they were angry, and looking for me, and there could only be one reason for that. So I hid where they would least expect to find me. Or so I thought."

Hoshi lumbered up to them. "It works again, though I fail to see the point. Everything else has been repaired as well."

"This macrofab makes the Eight Banners carvings," Ciarán said.

Hoshi grunted, "It makes machines of wood because all they feed it is wood."

"There's a crate of second-epoch castoffs outside. You might try feeding it that."

"Why would I do that?"

"To learn what happens when you do."

He flicked his earlobe. "What's in it for you?"

"I want to learn what happens when you do."

"Ungh. It will take some time."

"You can show me around while we wait." He turned to the monk. "And you can tell me about these very bad people. And where I can find them."

41

While Hoshi worked, the monk led him through a doorway that led to a stairway leading downward. The steps were cupped with age and the lighting dim. It was instantly cooler once past the door. They headed downward for what seemed like a very long time.

A maze of caverns stretched deep beneath the shrine. The caverns might once have been natural, but they had been expanded in size, not with machinery, but by hand.

"Are these pickaxe marks?"

"They might be. Fir, with Wren Nesting was the second of the Ojin worlds colonized," the monk said. "These excavations were here when they arrived."

The monk, who said his name was Brother Alexi, reminded Ciarán that the Ojin Eng, like all the Eng, had traveled to their respective planets by slowship. The Ojin travelled longer and farther than the Huangxu and Alexandrians, and as a result were the last to settle upon planets.

The League, however, had developed superluminal technology long before the first Ojin set foot on a single planet. It was therefore quite logical that League technology might be found on a newly discovered planet. What was unusual, though, is that there were no Leaguemen to be found, and no nearby League worlds.

"It was this discovery that led the Ojin to search the stars for their neighbors. As they did not have superluminal technology, this took some time, and they were the last to stumble upon the League."

All Eng superluminal tech was derived from stolen League designs based around the ubiquitous third-epoch Templeman drive. He wondered, if the Ojin Eng had discovered the wreckage of a second-epoch vessel, why they hadn't reverse-engineered second-epoch drive technology.

Ciarán recognized most of the equipment. One of the largest devices was a starship's impact-shielding generator. "That's how the shrine survived the all-consuming flame."

"You recognize this machine?"

"It is quite familiar."

"Even Leaguemen don't recognize it."

"I'm not surprised. It's ancient tech." The League had bombed itself into the stone age twice in the last four thousand years. A vast amount of what they once knew had to be rediscovered each time.

"What is this object?"

Ciarán ran his fingers across the matte-black surface of a sphere that was taller than he was. "It's the housing for a computational core." It looked nearly identical to the images in the technical manuals he'd translated. Other than a couple extra black wires lashed to the sphere's wiring loom, it seemed identical.

"What should the inside look like?"

"It's powered off. So it should look like a sphere filled with fine-grained black sand."

"And it if were powered on?"

"The surface of the sand would appear roiled, like boiling water."

"Why is that?"

"I don't know."

"This sphere is empty."

"There are usually two such spheres on a second-epoch survey vessel. A sphere this size would normally house the vessel's operating system."

"So a computer."

"Like a computer, only sentient."

"Then a synthetic intelligence, as on the League warships."

"Similar, though unrelated. This sentience would have been engineered for a specific purpose. The intelligences found on third-epoch League starships are general-purpose and thought to have achieved sentience independently."

The monk led him deeper beneath the shrine. Eventually they arrived at what looked like an airlock. He worked the lock and stepped inside.

Ciarán followed him in.

The chamber was crammed with equipment, all of it third-epoch League gear, including a pair of macrofabs and supporting modules. All the gear had a thick layer of dust on it.

"This is where hounds were invented. This equipment was first devised as an instrument of torture."

"I don't understand."

"This system is home to the Ojin Diplomatic Service. This facility was once their principal research laboratory. There is a hatch at the far end of this chamber that leads to a corridor, and that corridor leads to the slave pen you unfortunately refused to enter. Prisoners were brought in that entrance and escorted here. They were interrogated, and if they lied, they were placed into the first of these paired manufacturing chambers. This chamber is configured for disassembly and pattern recording."

"You shoved living people into the supply side of a macrofab."

"I did not. I am not Ojin, and this facility was last used long before I was born."

"But people were murdered here."

"They were *disassembled* here, one atom at a time, and their pattern recorded. It was discovered that by disassembling a living being, not only could the composition and arrangement of their constituent matter be recorded, but some baser operations of their physiology patterned. Their constituent elements could be reassembled from this extended pattern in the second chamber. While lacking consciousness, the resulting hound could be imprinted with rudimentary urges and made to operate remotely. Over time the technology advanced, so that it was possible to create higher and higher functioning hounds. It was believed that ultimately it would be possible to disassemble a human being in one chamber and recreate the same human being in the other."

"That seems farfetched."

"It does. But consider the process of a selective brain wipe."

"I'd rather not."

"A typical layman's reaction. However, if you do consider that to conduct a surgically precise erasure of memories one must be able to identify those memories and only those memories, it follows that one can map the structure of all memories. These adjunct processors that you see here are the ones used in that procedure. It became possible to extract enough of a prisoner's memory that one could pick and choose those most useful skills and motivations for a particular task. In effect, if one knew ahead of time how one might wish to use a hound, one could *program* it simply by choosing to retain those select higher-order functions and memories necessary for it to carry out its mission.

"In practice, this didn't work as well as the theory suggested. The process was hardware constrained. It was thus posited that if one had enough computational power and storage, one could transfer an entire human's consciousness from the disassembled original to the reassembled hound. And once one had a functional pattern, one could do this repeatedly, effectively producing multiple copies of a single person. One truly could be in more than one place at one time. The implications for the Diplomatic Service were profound."

"And?"

"Such profound secrets are impossible to hide. In time, the Ojinate's neighbors learned of this technology and began to experiment with it. Even the League ran an experimental program until the existence of the program leaked to the press, and the practice was outlawed. But the Huangxu Eng and the Alexandrian Eng continued to experiment. It was eventually determined that the process would prove too costly, and the programs were terminated. That was the official story. Unofficially the programs continued. One day an Alexandrian scientist hit upon a process they believed would work.

"If they repurposed a sentient starship's processing core for computation and storage, they would have enough resources for the process to complete. There were two remaining problems with turning theory into practice. First, there were no such processing cores in the Alexandrine. And second, any core used would accommodate only one sentience. To store a new pattern, the existing pattern would need erasure.

"A plan was devised and executed. A League starship containing a sentient core was captured and the process attempted. The process worked. It was repeated. And worked again."

"The process would kill the synthetic intelligence."

"Indeed. Some unfortunate sacrifices needed occur. On the third attempt, the process succeeded again. And the third human to step from the reassembly chamber ordered the first two executed and their patterns erased. He could do this because he was emperor.

"Again, such a technological breakthrough could not go unnoticed. The Huangxu Eng stole the procedure, and ran their own tests, and accomplished the same. Their emperor, after running the experiment on two prisoners scheduled for execution, entered the disassembly chamber as a man and emerged from the reassembly chamber as an immortal.

"Consider the implications. The use of a sentient core was only required to produce the pattern. If the emperor were to die, a new copy could be made of him from the pattern. Any new instantiation of the emperor would lose all accumulated experience, but death would not be permanent. I am told that both emperors employ staff, ubiquitous surveillance, and other means to document their every hour in order that, should an accident occur, their renewed selves might benefit from any experience gained since the pattern had been made. Their immortality is assured so long as their patterns remain safe.

"The Ojin emperor was not so lucky. By the time his scientists had learned of these advancements, the League had learned of the procedure as well, and that six starships had been captured and six sentient cores had been murdered, all for the benefit of two men."

"The League considers synthetic intelligences citizens."

"Once they did. But now synthetic intelligences consider themselves an independent polity and bound to the League solely through a mutual defense treaty. It is these synthetic intelligences that refuse to end the war with the Alexandrian and Huangxu Eng, and who might yet declare war on the Ojin Eng."

"Why?"

"Because the present Ojin emperor hasn't given up on this quest for immortality. And he's ordered the Diplomatic Service to locate a synthetic intelligence while his body remains young enough to make eternal life enjoyable."

"That sounds—"

"Monstrous, I know. You should not trust her."

"Ryuu?"

"She knows there is a synthetic intelligence on your vessel."

"Thanks for the warning." Ciarán wasn't too worried about anyone capturing *Quite Possibly Alien*. Not so long as the ship's monster was on the job. "Those all sound like very bad people. Which are the ones that put the implants in the hounds that attacked us?"

"None of them. Even though the patterns of the test subjects were ordered destroyed, that did not happen. A young Alexandrian scientist spirited away a copy of the second test subject and subsequently resurrected her. This second test subject persuaded a Huangxu scientist to preserve hidden copies of both Huangxu test subjects. She subsequently convinced the Alexandrian scientist to resurrect them. These are the people who wish me dead, and who sent these hounds against me. These are the people who placed the implants into the skulls of the hounds. They call themselves the Consortium."

"Where can I find them?"

"The Consortium operations are based in the independent polity of New Sparta."

"How would I recognize these people?"

"The Huangxu subjects were male. One was large and powerful. The other quick and clever. Both were psychopaths and sentenced to death by the Huangxu Eng. Look for identical twins. Find the Consortium and you will find them."

"And the Alexandrian test subject?"

"Much more discrete. She changes her name as often as I

change robes. An image of her would prove more useful. I have one in my sleeping chamber."

"How do you know all of this?"

"It should be obvious. I'm the Alexandrian scientist who resurrected them."

42

Brother Alexis's sleeping chamber was at ground level in the temple. It was large, and airy, with a view of the temple courtyard. He rummaged through the contents of a jumbled travelling case. "Here it is." He handed Ciarán a printed image, one showing a smiling Brother Alexi and a tall woman with an athletic physique and a shaved head. They were both standing in front of a mechanism nearly the twin of the one he'd examined below. A computational core's containment sphere dangled from a truss system overhead, a thick hydra of cables sprouting from the sphere's access port and spilling down the legs of the truss system to disappear into the blocky equipment crowded behind the pair.

"Is this before or after the transfer?"

"No one smiles before the transfer."

"How long ago was this image taken?"

"Sixty years ago."

"You look younger in the image. But not sixty years younger."

"That isn't me in the picture."

"It looks just like you."

"Yes, well. It isn't."

"Unless you performed the procedure on yourself."

"Here," he said, and pawed through the contents of the travel bag again. He pulled a handheld weapon from the bag and aimed it at Ciarán. "I wish you hadn't said that. I'd hoped to aim you at them."

"So they'd leave you alone."

"They'll never leave me alone. But you might have distracted them while I ran."

"I still could. I don't see the problem."

"The problem is that the instant someone reviews this conversation it won't just be Vatya sending hounds after me. It will be Ryuu."

"I don't understand."

"Of course you don't, you ignorant bumpkin."

Ciarán had never seen another weapon like that. "Is that an Alexandrian sidearm? Because if it is and you shoot me, it won't be that hard to figure out who to blame for my murder."

"Shut up."

"I'm a Freeman merchant. If I turn up dead, the locals are going to investigate. And then my people will come gunning for you. And if you think this Vatya is a nasty piece of work, wait until you meet Seán mac Diarmuid. I have three brothers, each of them bigger than me, and—"

"I said shut up!" He seemed to think for a moment. "Turn around. Now march."

He ordered Ciarán to return to the torture chamber deep in the heart of the caverns. He held Ciarán at gunpoint while he powered the system up.

"Open the disassembly chamber and get in."

"You already explained how much that would hurt. I'd rather you just shoot me and try to wrestle my body in there."

"Do as I say."

"I don't think so. Do you think I'd come here alone? My

crew knows exactly where I am. There's no escaping them. While you're lugging my bulky carcass around, my crew will be locking and loading. And when they drag you out and hang you for murder, you'll be good and finally dead."

He pointed the pistol at Ciarán's forehead. "Get in the chamber. I promise I'll put you out of your misery first."

"I don't see what murdering me and then disassembling me gets you. You should just start running now. If you want, I'll help you carry your stuff to your getaway ride."

"Get in."

"Oh. You don't have a getaway ride."

"I said get in."

"I have a getaway ride. You let me go and I'll help you get away."

"Shut up! You can't help me. Now get in or I'll frag you here."

"Okay." Ciarán opened the hatch and climbed in.

"They'll waste time trying to save you."

"Even so, that isn't going to solve anything for you. Your pattern will still be here, in that computational core sphere out there. If what you tell me is true, you're the last Brother Alexi, no matter what you do to me."

"My *pattern*?"

"The primary processing-core sphere on a second-epoch League vessel is much larger than the secondary sphere. But the secondary sphere is large enough to hold a third-epoch computational core."

"I told you. That sphere's empty."

"I know you said that. But why bring it up at all, unless it was to prevent me from looking inside and discovering it wasn't? In addition it had two nonstandard leads. The pair of black wires are likely hooked to a remote power supply."

Brother Alexi's face seemed like a *Noh* mask, one frozen open-mouthed in sudden realization.

"I get it now. This is a surveillance state. I should have said all of that earlier, and gotten it on the record. And you couldn't know that I'd notice the extra leads. I'm not exactly the technical type. But I have translated more second-epoch technical manuals than anyone you're likely to meet. You were still thinking you could run, and send someone back later for the sphere."

Ciarán kicked the chamber door closed. There were riders loose in the world. Finding them and stopping them was all that mattered.

Brother Alexi dogged the hatch from the outside. He began firing up the equipment.

Ciarán shouted, "You should just run!"

Brother Alexi ignored him. He had a plan, and wasn't ready to admit he'd already lost.

Ciarán had a plan too.

He had his handheld out.

The comms system didn't work.

The messaging system didn't work.

The lights in the cavern began to flicker as power began to flow to the macrofab console.

His skin began to itch.

He flipped to the Trinity Station Library app. He opened the *Making Sense of Sensors* book. He flipped to page one hundred. He touched the black coin in his pocket. He wanted to make sure it was working. He wondered how long it would keep working as it was torn apart along with him. Long enough that someone would be able to find his remains, he hoped. Maybe it would keep working even after it was disassembled because the tracker was based on the materials in it.

He glanced at the display. It looked like it was already broken. He shook the handheld and nothing happened. He tapped the screen.

Now it worked.

His skin was really itching now.

The handheld broke again. It had been showing one coin. Now it showed two. Could the disassembler work that fast?

It felt like his palms were beginning to burn, but maybe he was imagining that.

He needed to find some way to make sure the crew got all the information he had. He opened the handheld's system menu. He checked the local network settings. This wasn't going to work. A local network mesh existed, but he couldn't join it.

His throat was dry. His eyes felt like they were on fire.

He put his handheld into mesh initiator mode.

It asked for a seedname.

VatyaFemaleRingleaderRiderSource

He created an open network and began advertising it.

He tore it down and created another.

IdenticalTwinsMaleNewSpartansBeware

He created an open network and began advertising it.

He tore it down and created another.

ConsortiumNewSpartaFrontOrganization

He created an open network and began advertising it.

He tore it down and created another.

BrotherAlexiKilledCiaránMacDiarmuid

And left it running.

He sat on the floor and waited. Waited to die. Waited for rescue. Waited for something.

No one was going to examine the network security logs in real time. But when he turned up missing they would. He had to believe that. This place had been a Ojin Diplomatic Service facility. Surely it had network security. It would have been studded with sensors back in the day.

He opened a note-taking app on his handheld and typed out all he'd learned from Brother Alexi. He'd thought it pointless to do so, since the handheld would be disassembled along with him. But a pattern would be made, and while reassembling the pattern wouldn't resurrect him, it would re-create his dead body and the handheld. And if memories could be recorded, maybe the contents of the handheld's memory could be as well. When an investigation began, they'd re-create whatever had been disassembled from the pattern buffer. Unless Brother Alexi wiped the pattern buffer.

When he was done typing, he flipped to the Trinity Public Library app.

Now his coin had split into three coins.

He closed his eyes. There were incredibly dry.

He opened them again, glancing at the handheld's display.

One of the coins began to move. *Fast.*

Something large and midnight blue passed in front of the cracked viewport. He clambered to his feet and gazed out the viewport.

A fanged monster stared back. It took him a moment to realize it was a League exo with a monster's face crudely painted on the helmet.

Ciarán pointed at the console and shouted, "Turn it off!"

Mrs. Amati's armored fingers gripped the controls and twisted.

Ciarán screamed. "Off! Not up!"

The disassembler hatch swung open. Armored fingers gripped his collar and dragged him out.

Amati dropped him on the deck. "A simple down and back. Natsuko!"

"Coming!"

"Bring the fast-pallet!"

"I have it!"

Ciarán tried to speak.

Amati toed him. "Save it."

43

He woke in the white room again. This time he wasn't dressed in white robes but in a fresh set of dark-blue utilities. He didn't hurt at all, which probably meant he was still drugged. When he tried to stand, he found that he could. He found a new set of socks and hullwalkers by the hatch. He pulled them on and tried the hatch release.

It was locked.

He fished in his pockets. He didn't have a handheld, but he did have his identification wallet and the black coin.

He couldn't find any comm equipment in the compartment.

He hefted the black coin. He tossed it across the compartment.

He retrieved it and tossed it again.

After the eleventh toss the hatch opened. Natsuko skidded to a halt in the compartment, med kit in her hand. Hess was right behind her, and behind him, Ryuu and an Ojin guardsman.

"Why am I being held against my will?" Ciarán said.

"You aren't," Ryuu said.

"The hatch is locked."

"Private compartments do that. If you'd checked your wallet you would have found an access card inside."

"Where are my clothes?"

"They fell apart, as you might well have. What were you thinking?"

"That Brother Alexi had the drop on me. That I could get a message out if I had time to work my handheld, but he wasn't going to give me that time unless I complied. And I knew Mrs. Amati would come after me. I just didn't know how long it would take."

"And how precisely did you know this?"

"It's how she's built."

Keep your buddies alive. Do your job. Let others do theirs. And never surrender. That was Amati's secret recipe for winning a war. And "a simple down and back" was what she called one of the training exercises she was constantly drilling him on. One where she gave him a head start before hunting him like prey.

"You took a great risk."

"I took a series of calculated risks. I wasn't sure if Brother Alexi—"

"Fyodor Durst."

"That's not the name he gave me."

"That is fortunate. If he'd given you his real name, you can be certain he meant to kill you."

"He didn't intend to kill me at first. He wanted to use me to distract the people trying to kill him so he'd have time to escape. He told me how to find them, but I made a mistake and said something aloud I should have kept to myself."

"You could have simply told me what you wanted to know and left the job to the professionals."

"I wasn't sure if you were in league with him or not." He still wasn't certain.

"Come along then. It has been many years since I've performed in front of a live audience."

44

R yuu led them to a compartment and ushered them in. There were three long rows of theater seating, each one raised taller than the next proceeding backward from what Ciarán at first mistook for a display, but which proved to be a window. It overlooked a compartment one deck below, a compartment that was nearly empty, but for a single straight-backed chair in its center and a rack of equipment at its far end. At the near end lay a single hatch. Directly across from them, and on the same level as they were, was a long mirror, which Ciarán decided was also a window like the one they looked out through, both windows constructed so that one could see out but no one could see in.

The compartment across from them might be empty, or there might be others watching from there. He tried to imagine just who would be there watching, if anyone. He had no idea. He wasn't even certain what they were there to watch. He glanced at Natsuko and Hess beside him. They had their heads together and were whispering quite expressively.

"Tell him," Hess said.

Natsuko tapped Ciarán's sleeve. "Engineer Hess wishes you

to know that sensors have picked up a great deal of second-epoch hull material on the planet."

"From the shrine, near where the shuttle let us off," Ciarán said.

"There, and also from the center of the vast gear-shaped device the station's *kami* called the Spider."

"Why doesn't the engineer want to tell me this himself?"

"Because he thinks it's rude to talk in the theater."

"There's no one in here but us."

"Indeed. He has also reason to believe you are angry with him for not noticing this earlier. That he was distracted from his duty by personal concerns and has failed the ship and crew."

"Tell him we're fine. And I already knew about the equipment at the shrine, and figured there had to be something at the Pinion. A second-epoch survey vessel set down or crashed on this planet, and the main drive is missing. So is the primary computational core. Those could have been destroyed in a crash, or they could have been stripped out and moved.

"I'm guessing they're both there, at the center of their Spider, unless these people have figured out how to use the ship's drive as a weapon without the help of a ship's minder."

The hatch to the compartment below opened and an Ojin woman in formal dress entered. She placed a mat on the floor and knelt upon it. She tapped the deck beside her, and a plinth arose from the deck before her. She pulled a scroll, a pair of brushes, and a dark bottle from her sleeve and arrayed them on the plinth.

Hess whispered to Natsuko.

"Court reporter," Natsuko said. "Very old school."

"That's ridiculous," Hess said. "The compartment's studded with recording sensors."

"The official transcript will be devoid of any imagery that might inflame passions."

Hess snorted. "Like that's going to happen in a courtroom."

An Ojin man dressed in equally formal robes entered, pushing a portable projection rig. He arranged it so that it could be seen by whomever ended up in the chair and by whomever was watching from the galleries above.

He checked that the rig worked and left the compartment

Seconds later the same man returned with Fyodor Durst, alias Brother Alexi. The man wasn't dressed as a monk now, but in simple stationer's utilities. He was barefoot.

The Ojin man shackled the prisoner to the single chair, his wrists lashed together behind him. He didn't struggle or attempt to escape. Durst glanced from one viewing gallery to the other, and it seemed to Ciarán that for an instant, their eyes met. Durst glanced toward the hatch as the man left.

The hatch closed.

The court recorder dipped a brush into the ink bottle.

She held the brush above the scroll.

The hatch opened.

And Kazuki Ryuu entered.

She was dressed in the standard shipboard skinsuit of the Ojin Navy, white with orange piping, and over that the golden full-dress robe of an Ojin admiral. The grip of the sword she'd claimed was the emperor's own projected above her left shoulder. A matching honor blade depended from a clasp on her belt. In her left hand she held the handle of a mask, and on that mask was a grim face, one with the corners of its mouth turned down.

"The first emperor," Natsuko said. "Like in the story books. This is incredible."

She circled the prisoner slowly.

When she was directly behind him, the sword whispered from its scabbard, the light in the chamber dancing along its water blade.

She rested the tip of the blade lightly on his shoulder and completed the circle.

"I, Kazuki Ryuu, a servant waiting upon the Emperor of the Eight Banners, accuse you, Fyodor Durst, of crimes against the empire. How do you plead?"

Durst glanced up at her. "What difference does it make how I plead?"

"The record will show that the defendant answered a question with a question."

The court reporter nodded and returned to her work.

Ryuu sheathed the sword. "The judgement of this court is held in abeyance of an answer to the defendant's question."

The court reporter gathered her possessions and disappeared them beneath her robes. She knelt and rolled up her mat, tucking it beneath her arm.

She approached Kazuki Ryuu and bowed.

Ryuu handed her the mask. She removed the robe and passed it to the court reporter. She kept the sword. The court reporter left through the hatch.

She turned to face the prisoner. "I am Kazuki Ryuu, Diplomatic Representative of the Imperial Ojinate, and you will answer whatever questions you are posed."

"Or what?"

"Bring the prisoner in."

The hatch opened and a bound man was led in. The man appeared to be a younger Fyodor Durst. He blinked as if drugged.

The guard stepped back, and the man blinked again as Kazuki Ryuu drew the emperor's sword in one fluid arc, and blood splattered the viewing window and the man's headless body slumped to the deck. His severed head bumped against the bound man's bare toes.

Kazuki Ryuu stepped forward. She cleaned the emperor's blade on Durst's sleeve. She sheathed the sword.

"Do you think we are fools? We *invented* the technology you and your like have perverted. You cannot lie to me. Shall I make another of you and question it as well? Surely after a dozen or so of you are made to speak, some pattern of truth will arise."

Ciarán was out of his seat.

Natsuko's hand on his sleeve stopped him. "You cannot stop her."

"I'm not sure I want to. But I can't sit here and watch as she murders people."

"It's a fake," Hess said. "I watched them make it in a macrofab."

"Listen," Natsuko said.

"I am done with your lies. Here is the truth. You are not the scientist who created these abominations. You are one of the abominations. You are no fugitive but a tool of Vatya Zukova's designs."

The bound man didn't seem to be able to drag his gaze away from the headless corpse. "If I tell you what I know?"

"You already have. Many times."

He looked up at her.

"Here is what our scientists say. That the pattern that re-creates you also sustains you. That were we to power it down you would cease to live."

"That is a lie."

"Is it? Observe the display."

The display they'd brought in earlier blinked to life. It showed the cavern beneath the shrine, and the containment sphere there, the one Durst had said was empty, but which in truth contained the pattern used to re-create him again and again.

The lights in the cavern went out.

"You see?" Durst said. "Lies. All lies."

A handheld torch began to burn. Its light traced the thick cables jutting from the sphere's access port. The torchlight followed the cables meter by meter. All but two of the cables disappeared into a conduit. Those black cables snaked into a crevice, the display blanked, and the cable reappeared coming out of another crevice, and ran across the cavern floor to a portable power supply.

"Switch it off," Kazuki Ryuu said.

"Wait." The bound man had begun to sweat. "What do you want to know?"

"Everything."

45

"Keep watching," Ciarán said. "I'll be back."

He opened the hatch and glanced into the corridor. He had the gnawing sensation that this was entirely a show trial, and the show wasn't for Natsuko, or Hess, or him.

The corridor remained deserted. Ciarán hiked along it until he came to a hatch.

He tried the hatch controls. It was locked.

He knocked.

If he was correct, this hatch led to the viewing compartment on the opposite side of the theater, courtroom, torture chamber, whatever the compartment below was. Perhaps it was all three.

He knocked again.

The hatch opened and he stepped inside.

The compartment mirrored the one he'd just left. Two people were inside: a young Fyodor Durst and Hoshi.

Durst watched the proceedings intently, not even glancing toward Ciarán.

Hoshi grunted and flicked his earlobe. "You are here to collect your debt."

"What debt?"

"Of knowledge. What happens when the Eight Banners machine is properly fed."

"I'd forgotten about that."

"Yes. Sit and watch. Hoshi will translate."

"I understand the words."

"Yes. There is no shortage of such understanding."

The man bound to the chair continued to speak. Much of what he said corresponded with what he'd told Ciarán, the principal differences being those that Ryuu had already declared in her opening remarks. It was Vatya Zukova and her team that performed the experiments. It was Vatya Zukova that used the second-epoch League core to insure her immortality.

Durst had long been her favorite until recently when his position had been supplanted by another. He had stolen his pattern and escaped Vatya's grasp, fleeing with nothing more than the clothes on his back and his own pattern.

He bribed the locals to smuggle him and his pattern out of the system aboard a merchant vessel. He was not on that vessel, however. Instead he arranged for another merchant to bring him to another system, where he was able to book passage on an Ojin vessel, and through a series of transfers, arrived on Pinion.

"She's not pressing him on particulars," Ciarán said.

"She's heard all of this already," Hoshi said. "These statements are for the official record."

Once on Pinion Fyodor Durst resumed a role he had played once before, as Brother Alexi at the shrine near Wren. He did not think Vatya would look for him on the Diplomatic Service's homeworld. And even if she did, he would be safer under the Ojin Diplomatic Service's kimono than skulking about from world to world.

"And?" Ryuu said.

"And I was mistaken. Vatya found me and tried to kill me."

"I will offer an alternative explanation," Ryuu said. "That you were sent here, and with you were sent four hounds. That when you learned of the Freeman merchant's arrival in the system, and that Kazuki Ryuu meant to do business with him, you panicked. In your mind only one thing Kazuki Ryuu possessed was worth trading for. And that possession was the very one you were meant to steal, or safeguard until such time that your allies could arrive in force and take it."

"She means the second-epoch superluminal drive," Ciarán said.

Hoshi grunted.

"What is the spider aimed at?"

"Kyo."

"The Ojinate's seat of government?"

"Yes. Watch now. This is the moment she strives for."

"You conspired to redeem yourself," Kazuki Ryuu said. "Only to discover there could be no redemption."

"But I warned you of the hounds."

"Because they were sent *with* you, but not under your control. They were Vatya's vassals through the implant devices. You were her prisoner, and saw your chance to free yourself of her leash. You hoped to aim the Freeman at Vatya to distract her while you fled, taking your pattern with you.

"Imagine our surprise to find such an abomination hidden in our midst. Has it not occurred to you that we might *use* this monstrous device to pare truth from lie?"

"It occurred to me that without my help you lack the skill."

"Suppose we possessed the skill. What strange truth might we uncover? What dreadful epiphany might we reach?"

"I have no idea."

"Perhaps the most transcendent attribute of sentient intelligences is the linkage between minds of common heritage. This ability of kinship groups to communicate instantaneously at any distance."

All the color seemed to drain from Fyodor Durst's face.

"Vatya Zukova's process works, not because it reuses a synthetic intelligence's hardware, but because it *enslaves* the sentience, overwriting its will and its *identity* with another's. Vatya's hounds are no longer with you. But *they* are. The two Huangxu experiments. Their voices are in your head, and yours in theirs."

"That is a lie."

The Fyodor Durst in the compartment with Ciarán spoke. "It's true. I can hear them."

"There is more," Kazuki Ryuu said. "They are not alone. The Alexandrian emperor. The Huangxu emperor. They are there with you. Watching. Whispering. Nudging. Only Vatya herself remains apart, because the sentience she enslaved is not of the same kinship group."

"Lies. All lies."

"You are no longer human. You are a parasitic disease. One that invades the body of the host and infects its mind. That *destroys* its mind."

"No."

"Look at me when I speak!"

The bound man gazed up at her.

"You are with them even now. You betray us to them! You betray me!"

He looked away. "There is nothing between us to betray."

Ciarán was roughly shoved aside as the Fyodor Durst in the compartment pushed past him. He worked the hatch and left it open. His sprinting footsteps echoed along the corridor.

The hatch in the compartment below opened and the young man rushed in and without so much as slowing, pulled the emperor's sword from the scabbard in Kazuki Ryuu's hand.

"I am not this man! I will never be this man!"

The bound man looked up and grinned. "You were born this man."

"No!" He swept the blade downward in a killing blow.

Kazuki Ryuu flowed forward, catching the blade between her palms, the muscles of her neck bulging with the strain. "Control yourself."

The pair stepped apart.

The young man gazed wildly about the compartment. He seemed to bounce from foot to foot as his gaze swept over the mirrored glass of the viewing windows, the utilitarian glow of the portable projection equipment, the place on the floor where the court reporter had spread her mat and knelt. Everywhere, he looked everywhere, but where he dared not.

Kazuki Ryuu watched in silence. She might have been carved from stone, so still she stood, and so set the features of her face. Ciarán recognized the set of her shoulders, the tilt of her head, from a role she had played in a *Noh* drama he and the crew had watched together. She was judge and executioner, though the verdict was not her own, handed down in a court she ruled, but one she'd inherited, from the judge that judged her. She was the hand that held the sword of empire, and she knew her duty. That it was her lover who faced his death would not stay her hand. What was love without honor? Without duty? One needed first be worthy of love. To accept less was treason, not to the emperor, but to the empire, and to the self.

There is no joy here.

There is no future.

There is only ash in the air.

And a black rain on the tongue.

He bowed to her and held the sword, hilt first, toward her. "A thousand apologies." A tear ran down his cheek.

She took the sword and sheathed it. "Leave us," she said, and proceeded to ignore him.

"The time for lies is past. You are *known* to us. *All of you* are known to us now."

The court reporter returned. She handed Kazuki Ryuu the

cape and mask, spread her mat, and arranged her writing materials in silence. When she was ready she nodded.

Kazuki Ryuu placed the sword on the floor between the bound man and her. She moved behind him, and using her honor blade, sliced his bonds. She returned to face him.

His gaze darted to the sword.

"The Ojin emperor may notice, upon reviewing this record, that I have his sword. His majesty may come and retrieve it at any time."

She donned the cape in one fluid motion. She held the mask in front of her face.

"I, Kazuki Ryuu, a servant waiting upon the Emperor of the Eight Banners, hereby sever all ties between the people of the Eight Banners and the Ojin Empire.

"Further, the people of the Eight Banners demand the surrender of the Alexandrian emperor, the Huangxu emperor, and those acting on their behalf to us, or to our agents, for crimes against the universal family of sentient beings. A list of individuals and charges will be forwarded upon the completion of this examination of fact."

She glanced at the display, which was still showing a dim cavern, and a portable power supply, and a thin cable snaking from it to disappear into a crevice. A gleaming shadow moved into the light, and then another, and another, eight spidery limbs clacking against hard stone. A force blade flared blue on the end of one spider limb. It hung motionless above the cable.

"I, Kazuki Ryuu, a servant waiting upon the Emperor of the Eight Banners, ask you again, Fyodor Durst: How do you plead?"

Fyodor Durst leaned forward in his seat, his face white. His gaze remained glued to the display.

"Guilty," the younger Fyodor Durst said.

"So noted. This court is adjourned."

The court reporter gathered her things and dashed from the compartment without taking her mat.

Kazuki Ryuu stalked from the compartment, slamming the hatch behind her.

The elder Durst glanced away from the display. His gaze fell upon his younger self, and shifted to the sword lying on the deck, and from there back to his faster and more nimble incarnation.

Fyodor Durst was alone in the compartment with himself.

And an emperor's sword.

Blue light flared on the display and then the cavern was plunged into darkness, the only sounds the clicking of eight metallic limbs against stone.

Both men slumped to the deck as if switched off.

"As you see," Hoshi said. "The machine performs well when properly fed."

46

Ciarán watched the station recede through the longboat's viewing port. He had a cache of data crystals in his pocket, a formal handoff of licensing rights from Kazuki Ryuu as well as several additional documents he hadn't reviewed, transcripts of the interrogations of a dozen iterations of Fyodor Durst, a contract for the supply of scrap second-epoch hull material, and a personal note, expressing her regrets that she could not accompany the crew to meet those persons in Contract system that held her work in such high regard. The note included a recorded statement by Kazuki Ryuu to her fans, one he'd not yet had time to view. Ryuu had also sent personal gifts for each of the crew.

There was no such thing as a good coincidence, and he had wondered about the strange fortune that had brought them to Pinion, and which had set in motion the division of the Ojinate and a war between the Eight Banners Empire and the Alexandrian and Huangxu Eng, not to mention the discovery of a missing survey vessel's fate.

"Your coming here was preordained," Kazuki Ryuu had told him. "All who experience my work will eventually find their way to the Eight Banners Empire. Such art is our greatest weapon. That you experienced three decades of work over the course of thirty days, and that Watanabe Natsuko was with you, made your choice of destination a certainty."

He didn't see how that could be true. He hadn't felt influenced in their choice of destinations, and he'd made the call. She had laughed, and bowed to him, and sent him on his way.

Ciarán glanced across the aisle at Natsuko. She wasn't looking out the viewport. Rather, she sat staring at him.

"What?"

"I was thinking that you are either a very good merchant or a very lucky man."

"I could be both."

She smiled. "You could be."

"You're in a better mood than when we arrived."

"I had a long talk with Ryuu. She explained everything."

"And?"

"And what?"

"Are you going to tell me what she said?"

"Ryuu said that before there was the emperor there was the law, and before there was the law there was the Book. Her people, the first diplomats, have an original copy of the Book, as does the emperor. She showed me the book, and let me touch it, and showed me a copy of the emperor's book as well. They are quite different.

"The emperor's Book is about this thick." She held her fingers apart to show him. "It is beautifully made, and filled with wisdom, and truly a wonder."

"And their Book?"

"A cover only, scuffed and water stained. She said that it was a family Book, from the provinces, and carried beneath a warrior's armor, above his heart, for many decades of campaigns. It was then handed down, from generation to generation, sometimes skipping a generation, when an ancestor felt their offspring unworthy, but always finding its way into the hands of someone willing to live its words and carry it forward through time. A son or daughter of the Book.

"This went on for many generations, until the Book found its way into the hands of Junh, three generations after their arrival at Fir with Wren, Nesting. He had many adventures, and barely escaped dozens of times with only his skin and the Book, and one particularly bitter winter found himself snowed in, miles from anywhere, with no escape or hope of rescue.

"So he burned the Book, page by page, over the course of a long winter. As he grew thinner and thinner so did the Book, until nothing remained but leather, and emptiness, and ash."

"And Junh," Ciarán said.

"And the Book. You have heard this story?"

"I haven't."

"This is what Kazuki Ryuu told me. That the Eight Banners Empire broke from the Ojinate over the work of Sato Atomu. That the foundation of the Ojinate, and its reason for being, was so that all Ojin might strive for advancement and thus win elevation to Eng, and their genes judged worthy of propagation throughout the fabric of the empire.

"Sato proposed to create a class of people suitable for dangerous and difficult work, people whose genetic makeup would be so divergent from that of the Eng that these people would eternally be judged unworthy of elevation, regardless of their contribution to the empire.

"Kazuki Ryuu's predecessor argued that not only was this immoral, and contrary to the Book, but it was impractical, because without hope of elevation within society such people would revolt.

"Sato said that was untrue.

"Ryuu's predecessor reminded him that this was precisely what had happened with the Alexandrian and Huangxu Eng, whose natures were so altered to accommodate the long journey that upon waking their charges, the Eng chose to enslave them rather than reunite with them in blood. Master or vassal, the result would be the same. The empire's strength was its homogeneity. The Book spoke to every heart.

"Sato said that he would make these people without the capacity for affiliation. They would not hope for elevation, but rather rejoice in their separateness. Over the Diplomatic Service's objections, the emperor agreed to let him try. Sato was a trusted ally to the emperor, and in addition to his own projects, responsible for the emperor's immortality project.

"Ryuu's predecessor charged Ryuu with infiltrating the project and discovering a way to counteract it. She discovered that while Sato's genetic modifications were effective at producing differentiated workers, those intended to reduce affiliation were not. Rather, these desires were repressed through social conditioning.

"Ryuu proposed a plan to subvert this social conditioning. And when the emperor approved Sato's project, and it moved from prototype to production, she did just that, and the Eight Banners Empire was born."

Natsuko beamed at Ciarán. "Ryuu says that we are each a citizen of the Eight Banners Empire now. That we were destined to be, by our birth as children of Earth, and by our nature as sentient beings, inevitably allies."

"Because we watched some *Noh* plays."

"Because we followed the way of the Book, and it led us to her."

"I've never even read the Book."

"She said you would say that. Then she said you would ask if, as citizens, we were subject to conscription."

"I was going to ask that. As a joke."

"She said to tell you that, as Freeman are neutral, Ciarán mac Diarmuid is exempt from conscription."

"That's good to know."

"She said that Charles Newton is exempt as well, as he's already enlisted."

Ciarán jerked forward in his seat, his mind racing. "That woman. Vatya. I know where I've seen her before."

"Where?"

"In a still image I found on Trinity Station." His gaze darted to Natsuko. "How long have these people been using me?"

"Ryuu said you would say that."

"And?"

"And she laughed."

"Like a villain or like a regular person?"

Natsuko peered over the top of her mask at him. "Yes. Like that."

47

Q*uite Possibly Alien* plunged into the photosphere of Pinion system's star.

Ciarán reclined in the pilot's seat as Ko Shan began reading out the ever-rising hull temperature.

Agnes Swan leaned forward in the captain's seat. She projected the boiling surface of the star on the forward viewscreen.

Ciarán chuckled.

"What is so funny," Swan said.

"I was just thinking how relaxing it was, being home."

"All done," Maura Kavanagh said.

Ciarán jumped the ship a safe distance from the star.

"There are three possibilities, all three of which probably move us closer to our destination. Two of the systems are uncharted and one is a Huangxu sector hub."

"Which sector," Ciarán said.

"The one closest to Contract space," Maura said. "Sweet Olive Blossom."

"So we can jump into a system where we might get trapped and possibly die," Ciarán said. "Or we can—"

"Jump into one of the unoccupied ones," Swan said. "Your humor is growing predictable, Merchant-in-Charge."

"I aim for consistency, Ship's Captain. Any objections to this Huangxu world?" Ciarán stood and glanced around the bridge as Hess entered and took the pilot's seat. "Erik, a jump into the unknown or into the lion's den?"

"A den with or without lions?"

"With," Ko Shan said. "Once we arrive."

"I say go with what we know."

"Ask the rest of the crew, Ship's Captain?"

"Not on my account."

"Ship?"

"I am here."

"Do you have a preference?"

"I do not."

"And the ship's monster?"

"Says it does not," the ship said.

"Tell us about this system. Briefly."

"Sweet Olive Blossom, the hub system of the same name. Four planets, six uninhabitable moons, a single station with spindle, redundant superluminal nodes, ten orbital manufactories."

"Ten?"

"The system borders the Outer Reach," Ko Shan said.

"So?"

"Forward placement," Swan said. "In anticipation of expansion or annexation of contested systems."

"Such staging systems are often heavily patrolled," Ko Shan said. "And always very congested."

"Could we get parts for a superluminal node there?" Ciarán said.

"Sweet Olive Blossom Station is regional manufacturing and distribution center for the Glorious Voice of Empire Corporation," the ship said. "The probability is high that they will have parts. The probability that they will sell parts to a Freeman merchant is low."

"They haven't heard our offer yet. Try to bring us in with the star between us and the bulk of their sensors, Captain Swan. Let's try to get our exit plan in place before we answer any hails this time."

Maura Kavanagh began working the navigational plot. "I could lay a course to jump us directly into the photosphere of the star."

"Is that safe?" Ciarán said.

"If you wanted safe you should have stayed on Trinity Surface."

"It is not safe," Ko Shan said. "It is borderline insane."

"Captain Swan?"

"Ko Shan is correct."

"But you want to do it anyway."

"Maura will run the calculations for both methods of system entry. If you're needed you'll be sent for. Until then—"

"I know," Ciarán said. "Get off my bridge, Freeman whelp."

Ciarán stopped in the hatch and glanced around the bridge. If he'd stayed on Trinity Surface he wouldn't have met a one of these people. He wouldn't have learned the truth if he'd stayed at home, safe on the farm.

Some things in life were worth any risk.

He'd sent a message to Aoife via Pinion's superluminal node. He didn't want to say much for fear of being overheard. There'd been no incoming for the ship, which was to be expected. It would take her time to sort things out and she wouldn't want to send an update until she had something significant to report. And even if she wanted to, where would she send it? Communications was a one-way channel for now. Until Aoife met them in Contract space they would just keep on doing their jobs and live up to the contract. It was comforting to think that every threat he faced out here was one less danger to his friends and family at home.

"Close the hatch," Swan said.

"I will, Ship's Captain."

And he did.

48

Trinity System, Freeman Federation

Tiny grass fires ignited as the longboat settled onto the pasture. Little plumes of dark smoke rose into the night sky. The smell of burning turf warred with the odor that was as much heat as scent, of the cooling hull, pinging and groaning in the chill night air.

The sounds of people shouting and stomping up the hill like a herd drowned out the noise of a hatch opening and a cooltube licking out from the opening.

The kids were the first to arrive, jabbering excitedly, crowding the fence. The youngest ones had likely never seen a merchant vessel's longboat, or any conveyance, for that matter, larger than a trawler over from the mainland or the county's book barge tied up to the schoolyard dock.

The drink was on a fair number of the adults, and they were weaving their way up behind their little ones. Bringing up the rear was none other than the Gant himself and the bodyguard he'd married.

"I wager it will be Aoife nic Cartaí first out the tube," Macer said to the air where the Leagueman had been just a moment before. He spied the man's back heading down the hill, and a dark shadow of a man waiting below, hands stuffed into his pockets and gazing past Macer, to the big hull and the smoldering turf, and the fused soil of the once-again glassfield.

No one came out of the cooltube.

The parents had made it to the fence, and they were plucking their little ones off it, and dragging them back, and away, and no small number of them headed back down the hill, kids in tow, toward the Gant's open bar.

A longboat was news to children, but many of their parents had served on merchant vessels and longboats were thick as seagulls over a fish-cleaning table in Trinity space. There was nothing new to see that wouldn't look better with a liter more of the Gant's generosity in them, not that they weren't paying for that open bar themselves, but indirectly.

No one came out of the cooltube.

The Gant shoved in next to Macer, leaving his beloved bodyguard to fend for herself. "You expecting someone?"

"My girlfriend, though I don't think that's her."

"You have a girlfriend? Anyone I know?"

"Nuala nic Cartaí."

His father laughed. "Don't tell me, then. That's a Truxton hull. There won't be a nic Cartaí inside there."

"Did you not return the stationmaster's calls?"

"I've been busy."

"That was Aoife nic Cartaí behind the yoke just now. She's taken a Truxton hull by right of salvage. That's the longboat from the prize vessel."

"You're joking."

"You should have called the stationmaster."

"Because of some dustup between a nic Cartaí brat and Tom Truxton? I think not."

"I think so. Because your wan there has got you tangled up in the same net, and you'll be flopping on the deck soon, and me along with you. I don't know who these people are she's lashed you to, but I'm going to find out. It would save time and effort if you tell me now, while she can't overhear."

"I don't know what you're talking about."

"You're bent, and I let it slide. That ends tonight."

"You *let* it, did you?"

"Did you have to bring your rubbish home with you?"

"She's not—"

"I'm not talking about your second wife, and your second life. This Consortium business. I won't have it. Not on my island."

"Listen to you. You have no idea who you're dealing with."

"Then enlighten me."

"It would be the death of me."

"Do you want out, or is it nice in there?"

"There's no way out."

"There's nothing between us but blood, I've known that all my life. But I'm asking as one Freeman to another, if there were a way."

"Your grandfather and I had a talk very much like this one."

"Don't wake the dead."

"I don't know how to make you believe me, without telling you what he told me."

"Go on, then."

"He said, 'Son, there is no way out. Give up your trying before you get us both killed.'"

"So you gave up."

"I didn't. Because I loved him. And they made me watch as they tortured and killed him."

"And then you gave up."

"And then I found the smartest, most independent woman I could and paid her to have a son and raise him. Because life goes on."

"It was a mistake, telling me that."

"A man's entitled to one mistake." His father leaned on the fence rail and gazed up at him. "We were always going to fight, you and I. Lying down and letting you win was never in the game plan."

"I see."

"Not yet, you don't. The stationmaster is calling to say that someone has filed legal documents in my name on the station. Documents disinheriting Macer Gant and stripping him of all family property and connections. Additional documents have been filed naming Luther Gant the Younger as my heir and Shayna Gant as his guardian. He wants to know if the documents are real."

"Are they?"

"That's hard to say. I'd fight them if it was me."

"I'm not you."

"And you never will be." His father pointed. "Looks like your date has arrived."

"You can't avoid the stationmaster's call forever."

"A truer word has never been spoken," his father said. "All a man can do is try."

At first Macer thought it was a child walking away from the cooltube, so short and slight they were. Then he thought it was an old woman, the closer they came, because they walked with a cane and a bent back; and then he thought it was an old man, because they hobbled like an old man, and because their head was shaved, like a convict, and bandaged, like an invalid, and one arm in a sling, and bandaged from the elbow to where a hand ought to be.

By the time he was close enough to recognize, he was close enough the see the shock on Macer's face, which Macer wiped away with a thought. Then Macer was up and over the fence rail, and there just in time as Seamus mac Donnacha's cane slipped out from under him and his knee hit the ground.

Then Macer had him in his arms, and carried him toward the fence, and he shouted for them to open the gate, and they did. Seamus rocked in his arms, and Macer thought at first he was laughing, until he felt the moisture against his neck and realized his roommate from the Academy was crying.

Macer wasn't sure which he was more of—relieved to find Seamus alive, or horrified at the shape of him.

Relieved, he decided.

He shouldered his way through the crowd and was surprised again when he heard the longboat's thrusters engage, and the main engine ignite overhead, and a bright pillar of fire split the night sky.

He couldn't take Seamus to the barn, or to the house, not without drawing a crowd or a raft of questions, so he carried him down the hill, and past the house, all the way to the hangar. He elbowed the man door open, stepped inside, and made his way to the right rear corner, where he'd set up an old settee and a couple of cast-off loungers and a low table. He lowered Seamus to the settee and took one of the chairs for his own sitting.

"Thanks," Seamus whispered.

"I can turn the lights on, if you like." Macer could navigate the hangar blindfolded.

Seamus sniffled. "Either way."

"That was Aoife nic Cartaí behind the yoke just now."

"It was."

"She strikes me as a person in a hurry."

"She is that."

"Would you like a drink, or something to eat? I've a small kitchen in back."

"Macer—"

"I don't want to know, Seamus. You know how I am. It's enough you're here and still largely upright."

"I've done some unforgivable things, Macer."

"That's between you and whomever. You haven't done them to me or mine, as far as I know."

"I haven't."

"Then you're welcome to stay as long as you like. I have to run some foreigners up the mac Diarmuid place tomorrow, but I'll be back by nightfall. You're welcome to come along if you're feeling up to it."

"My father wouldn't allow me aboard *Tell Me Another*," Seamus said. "It wasn't what I'd done that set him off, but my lack of utility. He said I belonged down the gravity well, where a cripple fumbling about couldn't get innocent people killed."

"He has a point."

"And where my talent for failure wouldn't rub off on anyone that mattered."

"I can hear him saying it." Seamus's father was a piece of work, and about as unlikable as a man could get away with in public.

Macer sat in silence while Seamus sobbed. It was tough, being space born and rendered useless, or worse, dangerous. A Freeman station or family ship had no room for dead wood. It was either down the gravity well or to a noncommercial orbital, and there weren't any of those in Freeman space. He'd have to move to the League or the Ojinate, or get used to the punishing gravity of Trinity Surface, and the ugly reality that every studied competence he'd developed since childhood was useless on a planet. He hadn't inventoried the extent of Seamus's injuries, but even if they weren't debilitating, he'd have a hard time finding all but menial work.

On Trinity Station Seamus had been the rising heir of a moderately successful merchant family. On Trinity Surface he was a blow-in, and one without an extended family to anchor him.

"I'm sorry," Seamus said.

"Don't apologize to me. I'm just glad to see you. I thought you were dead."

"I wish I was dead."

"I'm glad you're not."

"I deserve to be."

"It's a good thing none of us get what we deserve. How's the gravity feeling?"

"They gave me meds on the station. Said I won't feel anything until tomorrow."

"But you kept up with the exercises, on account of being a merchant apprentice, and having to go planet-side now and then."

"I did until... Until..."

Macer thought while Seamus sobbed. He didn't like pulling his attention out of the present, but he needed somewhere to keep Seamus safe, and it wasn't here. He'd bumped the shark, and he was going to keep on bumping it until it turned around to snap and he could judge the size of it. If Seamus was in good mental and physical health, he'd be glad for his help. Seamus mac Donnacha in fighting trim was the most dangerous man Macer had ever met. But broken Seamus was a liability and a distraction.

"I promised a friend I'd stop by and chat. I'd like you to come with me if you're up to it."

"I'll try."

"They have a variable-G exercise room. I was thinking maybe we could sack out in there tonight, and that way when the meds wear off, you've a way to ease into the full load."

"I don't want to be a burden."

"You are a burden as you are," Macer said. "There's no use sugarcoating it, because we both know it."

"Coming here was a mistake."

"Maybe. Shall I show you my scar, from the through and through?"

"I've seen it."

"You've only seen it when it was a new hole in me, and you holding a tourniquet above it, and me bleeding out all over the place. It's much prettier now. I'll turn the light on and you can look."

"I'll pass."

"It's no *burden* to show you. I'm rather proud of it. It reminds me I once had friends."

"If you knew what I'd done, you wouldn't want me as a friend."

"Then what are you doing here, Seamus?"

"I was told the commodore was here."

"Commodore Evil?"

"Olek."

"That's what I said. He's one of these foreigners I need to run out to the mac Diarmuid place tomorrow."

"You don't want anything to do with him."

"But you do."

"I want to kill him."

"I don't think you could kill a fly right now, Seamus."

"I have to try."

"Have you filed intent against him?"

"I have."

"You have, not Truxton?"

"I don't work for Truxton anymore."

"And that's why your father cast you out. Because as head of the family, it'd be his name on the filing, and his neck on the line."

"He's more afraid of Olek than he is ashamed of me."

"Well, then maybe you ought to be afraid of Olek as well."

"I'm terrified of him."

"That's because you're not in your right mind. So I want you to sit right there while I make you some caife, and while you drink it, I'll preflight my flitter, and we'll go to my friend's and get some rest in you, and in the morning you may be your old confident self."

"I don't want to be my old self."

"Then a new, confident you."

Macer fiddled in the kitchen, in the dark, and it didn't work out, so he turned the light on, made a pot of caife, and brought a cup to Seamus.

Then he switched the lights on in the main part of the hangar and went over his machine's checklist. It was time consuming, doubly so because he found a problem. Eventually he was ready though, so he shoved the two-person machine out onto the runway and went back inside to retrieve Seamus, who insisted on hobbling out to the flitter under his own power. Macer had to help him belt in because he hadn't learned how to do it one-handed yet, and that led to another sobbing jag. Macer left him there, went back into the hangar, shut off the lights, and closed the overhead door.

Once belted in, Seamus stared down the runway and out to sea, where the moon was just rising.

"There's a problem," Macer said, "And I need a pilot's expert opinion."

"Are you asking me?"

"Do you see any other pilots milling around here?"

"I'm not a pilot anymore. I'll never fly again."

"But you're not denying that you're listed in the Registry as a qualified pilot, and one of the best."

"Not one of. As the best."

"Well then, that qualifies you as an expert."

"I suppose."

"We agree. Now, supposing you had two choices. In the first choice you could fly over a mountain ridge but you might fly so high that you blew up and your guts scattered the length and breadth of the county. And in the second choice you could fly out over the ocean, but you might run out of fuel and plummet into the sea and drown. As an expert pilot, which choice would you prefer?"

"How could anyone blow up by flying too high?"

"They might have found a bomb strapped to their flitter

during preflight, for instance. And the bomb might have an altitude-triggered fuse."

"I'd remove the bomb before takeoff."

"I didn't ask for your opinion as an engineer. I asked it as a pilot."

"I'd get another flitter."

"There isn't one."

"Then I wouldn't fly."

"Even if a friend's life depended on you flying?"

"What altitude is the fuse set for?"

"I don't know. High as you'd usually fly a flitter going over a mountain ridge, I'd guess. You wouldn't want it going off on takeoff."

"Then I'd stick to the deck and go over the ridge."

"Not out over the ocean?"

"I wouldn't fancy drowning."

"Me neither."

Macer fired the engine up.

"I'd stick to the deck unless it was at night," Seamus said.

"Too late. I've already made my mind up. Now keep your eyeballs peeled and shout out if it looks like we're going to hit anything."

Seamus laughed. "There's a bomb on this flitter."

"A big one. Whoever lashed it on wasn't trying to hide it."

"Did you search for a second, hidden bomb?"

"That's why it took so long. Whoever put the bomb on here thinks I'm the sort of reckless maniac that would skip a preflight."

"What would give them that idea?"

"They don't know me, that's what, so that narrows the list of miscreants down." Macer glanced at Seamus. "You're the one said you wished you were dead. Here's your chance to prove it. Anytime you want the yoke all you need to do is ask. If you decide to aim for the stars you'll get no arguments from me."

"But you'd rather I didn't."

"I have work I'd like to finish. It sounds like you do too. I'm not tapping out, but if you feel like you need to, I'm along for the ride."

Seamus nodded, his eyes moist.

Macer revved the throttle and released the ground brake. "It was not a mistake to come here, brother."

50

The little flitter bounced along the grass runway fronting the Ellis place. Macer taxied to the end of the runway and left the engine idling while he clambered out, opened the hangar door artfully hidden in the cliff face, climbed back into the cockpit, and motored the small craft inside.

He powered down and closed the hanger door, and all the while Seamus slept in the passenger seat. He'd nodded off about halfway through the hair-raising flight, and that told Macer all he needed to know about Seamus's condition. He was done in, not just to look at him, but in fact. He lifted Seamus from the passenger seat and carried him to the lift, which took them up one floor, and he hiked down a long hall to the exercise room and shoved the door open with his hip. He rested Seamus on a stack of workout pads and went looking for a pillow and some blankets.

"House," Macer said.

"I am here."

"Please set the exercise room to zero point five gravities."

"Done."

"Where's Laura?"

"Away."

"Pillow and blankets?"

"Follow the yellow line."

Ellis House was the opposite of his own home. From offshore it looked like a flying saucer had crashed and buried itself halfway into the rock high atop a craggy headland. Where the Gant place was all blocks of mossy stone and rough-hewn weathered wood, the Ellis place was glass, and gleaming metal, and curving lines, all shining and spotless, and gazing out to sea.

The Ellis was a strange man, had been a strange man of strange passions and seemingly limitless wealth. Macer followed the illuminated yellow line that had appeared in the floor, glowing up through a centimeter of translucent deck material. The line stopped at a door made to look like an exterior hatch, one that led, not to space, but to a linen closet. Ellis House towered ten stories over the headland, and burrowed as many stories beneath the ground, and as far as Macer knew, only three people had lived there in recent memory: the Ellis, his merchant captain wife, and their adopted daughter.

Now with the Ellis dead and his wife missing along with Macer's own mother, only Laura lived there alone. Tenants worked the valley's land, and a vast crew of gardeners and maintenance workers, far more than even such a large place needed, but that was the Ellis's way, looking out for his people when times were tough, and making sure they shared in the bounty when they weren't.

His way of thinking had agreed with Macer, and when he wasn't with Seán mac Diarmuid, Macer was as likely to be here as anywhere else, because the Ellis knew more about machines and how to make them do a man's bidding than anyone Macer had ever met, including at the Academy. And he had a tremendous amount of kit, knew how to use it, and wasn't shy about teaching a boy that would rather gouge a chisel into his palm than go home to the cold and loveless pile one valley over.

That said, he hardly knew the man. The Ellis wouldn't wake the dead, not even a night, and he answered every question with another question. Or his favorite phrase: "Why don't you try that, and see what happens." And Macer would try it, and fail, whether it was rebuilding a small engine or turning a fast-pallet into a surfboard, or a pair of them into a glider. And then the Ellis would view the wreckage, or call someone to help load Macer into the autodoc, or often both, and later he'd say, "House, what went wrong here?" and the house would explain what Macer had done wrong in terms even a boy who could barely read could understand.

Macer carried the pillow and blankets back to the exercise room. Zero point five Gs felt pretty light, and Seamus already looked more comfortable.

Macer thought about it for a moment and made up his mind. "House."

"I am here."

"The person inside the exercise room answers to Seamus mac Donnacha."

"Noted."

"Lock the exercise room and notify me when he wants out."

"Understood."

"If I'm not here when he wakes, notify Laura."

"Understood."

Macer took the lift to the top floor, a compact room that was far wider than it was deep, and the wide wall all glass, looking out over the panorama of dark waves and craggy headland. The wall behind him was composed entirely of display panels that didn't display images, but ever shifting hues. The room was sparsely furnished in the Ojin style. In the very center of the room sat a low table, and cushions around it, and on the table a thin leather-bound book.

He sat, ran his fingertips across the leather, and woke the dead.

"ARE YOU A SCHOLAR?" Mrs. Ellis asked. He hadn't heard her enter.

"I'm not," Macer said. Words and numbers swam before his eyes, and he couldn't pin them down.

"I think you will like that book," she said. "I found it in the Ojinate, and brought it home, thinking Laura would enjoy it. But she did not."

"She's a scholar."

"She is, and I am proud of her achievements. But..."

Macer shivered. Laura was so clever, and quick, and brilliant. He was like a lump next to her, and he was always next to her, or Ciarán at school, and Ciarán was almost as bad as Laura at showing him up. No one ever said a bad word about Laura. Laura never got in trouble. And here was her own mother, about to say something bad about Laura. That's what everyone did after a "but".

"But what?"

"Pick it up. Look inside."

The book was very thin, and very light. He opened it and it only had four pages. And all four pages were blank. But it was easy to see that it had once had many more pages, and someone had torn them out.

"What happened to all of the other pages?"

"That is a strange story. Would you like to hear it?"

"I would."

"House," she said.

"I am here."

"What is the most exciting story you can recall about Junh, son of Kalh, grandson of Linh?"

"That is difficult to say. There are so many."

"Junh was a great warrior," she said. "He did many exciting things, and had many amazing adventures, and all because his father thought him a poor scholar."

"Really?"

"Men of action like Junh don't learn like clerks. They learn by doing, and seeing, and touching. They learn by hearing and being an active part of the world. I'd hoped Laura might be able to understand the Book of Junh and explain its lessons to me. But no."

"I could try to understand it," Macer said.

"Would you? For me?"

"I will, Mrs. Ellis."

"Lakshmi. We are family in this house, young warrior." She smiled at him. "House, what is the first adventure of Junh you recall?"

"That would be 'Junh and the Wolf That Nearly Ate the World.'"

"That sounds interesting," Macer said. "Though I think I can guess the ending."

"Can you guess all the things the wolf did eat?" House said.

"Well, I know he didn't eat Junh."

"You don't know that," House said. "Because the wolf did eat Junh."

"No way!"

"Yes, way," House said.

"Okay, I'd like to hear that story."

"I'd like to hear that story too, but I have work to do," she said. "Would you listen to it for me and tell me about it later?"

"I will."

"Better yet, you could draw a picture, and House could show you how to write the names of all the people and places of the story on the picture. Including everything the wolf ate.

Then I'd have something to think about tomorrow, when you're at school."

"Ugh."

"If the picture is excellent, and all the names spelled right, and you remember the story *word for word*, I might be able to convince you mother to let you come here instead of school tomorrow."

"Would you?"

"I would, but only under those conditions. Word of a merchant."

"I can do it."

"That's nice."

"I will do it."

"I'll believe it when I see it."

He worked hard but in the end hadn't done what he'd said he would do. His drawing was a mess. The words were spelled wrong. He didn't remember the story and couldn't repeat it.

So he went to school the next day, and the next, and the next, and every afternoon he came to this room, and House told him a story, and he got it wrong, again and again, and again. Until one day he'd had enough.

"My life is an endless series of failures," he moaned.

"So says the Book of Junh," House said. "You are now ready for module two."

HE PULLED his gaze away from the book, and from the past. He gazed out to sea.

"House," Macer said.

"I am here."

"Did Laura say when she would be back?"

"She didn't."

"Take a note, then, regarding Seamus. He, Ciarán, and I

were roommates at the Academy. He's a friend, and I'm in his debt, and even if I wasn't I'd feel a duty to care for him till he's on his own.

"You wouldn't know to look at him now, but he's an extremely competent man; quick, and clever, and reliable when he gives his word. He's also bent. She's not to trust him with the silverware or her virtue. Scratch that. She's not to trust him, period.

"I have to run some foreigners up to the mac Diarmuid place, else I'd stay. I'll be back as soon as I can. Seamus needs to remain in the low-G room while he heals up some more. I'm not sure he's in his right mind and is likely to harm himself. Don't let him do that if you can convince him otherwise. Whatever you do, don't try to force him to do something he doesn't want to.

"Oh, by the way, he's filed intent against this Commodore Olek fellow, so don't let the two come together unless I'm there. That shouldn't be hard to accomplish, since Olek is one of the foreigners I'm taking to Seán's tomorrow. Or today, depending upon what time it is when you get this.

"I came by so Seamus could use the exercise room but mostly to talk about the Ellis, and your claim he'd been murdered. As I said, I'll be your matchmaker if it turns out to be true, and if we can find the culprit. I don't want you to think I forgot or am backing away from my promise.

"Gant out."

"Noted."

"House, what can you tell me about the death of the Ellis?"

"He was murdered and his body cast onto the rocks below the cliff outside."

"Laura said the coroner ruled it suicide."

"That is true."

"But you don't think it was suicide."

"I know it wasn't."

"How do you know that?"

"Because I witnessed it."

"And you didn't tell Laura."

"I was waiting to tell you."

"Because if you told Laura, she'd try to do something about it."

"She lacks self-control in matters of honor."

"I take it you have evidence."

"A sensor log with attachments."

"Give me a minute."

"Waiting sixty seconds standard."

Macer closed his eyes and emptied his mind.

"Sixty seconds has elapsed."

"Show me."

There were five men standing at the top of the stairway that wound up the cliff face from the docks in the little cove below. He recognized all five.

The Ellis, looking older but still in good health, shook his head no, and pointed down the stairway.

Commodore Olek said something back.

The Ellis again shook his head no, and pointed down the stairs.

The Leagueman, Hector Poole, said something and Olek replied. Poole held both hands out, palms upward and took a step back.

A long force blade erupted from the third man's fist. And from the fourth man's.

The Ellis pointed down the stairs again.

Rik Severn stabbed the Ellis in the heart. His twin planted a boot in the Ellis's chest and sent him over the cliff edge. Or maybe it was the other way around, with the twin stabbing and Rik Severn shoving. It didn't matter.

"Show me the boat they came in."

The image changed.

It was Macer's boat.

Shayna was at the helm.

"Is there anyone else on the boat?"

"No one I could see."

"Using?"

"A wide-spectrum scan, ultraviolet to infrared."

"Is there any way to send that log to the authorities without revealing your existence?"

"Still images. But there would be an on-site investigation. And then—"

"We don't want that. Run it again."

The Severn brothers had four hands between them. So when he'd met Rik Severn, he and his pals had already murdered the Ellis.

"I know all of these people. Leave it to me. Keep this to yourself."

"Without this evidence you can't file intent against them."

"I could. I'd just end up hanging for whatever I did."

"Then it ends here."

"On second thought, delete that permanently before Laura sees it."

"Too late." Laura tossed her riding jacket onto the table. She carried the cold odor of an island night into the compartment with her.

She glared at Macer. "The pair of you, conspiring again. I should have known."

"Protecting you."

"I can take care of myself."

"In most things, that's true. But this is matchmaking business now, and I'll advise you to steer clear of it, and of those people."

"But you just said you weren't going to do anything."

"No, House said the investigation into the murder ends

here. And I said if I filed against anyone without evidence I'd hang."

"So what, we just go on with our lives?"

"So you and House do. And I make it my life's work to gum up whatever these people are after. It shouldn't be hard to crank the pressure up. I've already started the boiler."

"And then what?"

"And then they'll get tired of me, and maybe they'll file against me."

"It's more likely they'll simply try to kill you," House said.

Macer grinned. "I think they already have, once, if not twice. I'd be disappointed if they didn't try again."

"You need backup," Laura said.

"Do you know how in the recorded dramas the hero says, 'Stay in the flitter,' and then the love interest doesn't stay in the flitter, and gets captured by the villain, and then the hero spends the whole second act trying to rescue the love interest, and half the audience groans when she gets out of the flitter, because she isn't acting like a smart and independent woman, but like an airhead who is too stupid to live?"

"What's your point?"

"Stay in the flitter."

"Am I your love interest now?"

"If our lives were a recorded drama you would be. Right up until the big reveal."

"Because you're the hero in not just your own drama, but mine as well."

"You know what I mean."

"I know what you said."

"Why are you always like this?"

"Because you're always like that." She pointed at the book. "All cover and no content."

Macer stared at her.

"Don't bother trying to dream up a comeback." She scooped up her jacket. "You don't have it in you."

"Wait," Macer said as she stepped into the lift.

"Get stuffed." The lift began to descend.

"House."

"I am here."

"You'll tell her about Seamus."

"I will."

"If she leaves the demesne, I'd like to know it. Make it look like the message was sent from Seamus's handheld."

"Understood."

"I'm going to refuel and head back home. I'll let you know when the job is done."

"Understood."

"I could be ten meters tall and able to crush boulders in my fists, and the hero of her story would still be Ciarán mac Diarmuid."

"You are mistaken. The hero of her story will always be Lorelei Ellis. And the difference between Macer Gant and Ciarán mac Diarmuid is that Ciarán mac Diarmuid knows it."

"I'm glad for them both."

"Understood."

51

He cut the flitter's engine a kilometer from the landing field. It was a balancing act, trying to decide how high he dared fly with the bomb still aboard and how far from the field he needed to cut the engine to arrive silently in the predawn hour.

The flitter had been sluggish the whole way and it was sluggish now, and it touched down at the far end of the runway. He'd sweated through his utilities by the time he'd shoved the little craft to the hanger. He racked the fuel nozzle and wiped the sweat from his brow.

He glanced up hill toward the house. It was quiet. Too quiet. "Stay in the flitter," he said.

A pair of willow gray eyes stared back at him from the copilot's seat. "How long have you known?"

"I didn't know until now. But I suspected the minute I pulled back the yoke on takeoff and barely cleared the trees."

"You didn't say anything. We might have talked on the way."

"I needed to concentrate. What did you do with Seamus?"

"House is watching him."

"Please stay in the flitter, Lorelei. There is something very wrong here. I need to remain in the present and I can't do that around you."

"Because you love me."

"Because you're a knot of probability. When I look at you I see a thousand possible futures. I don't have the cycles to think about them all right now."

"How many of these futures are we in, together?"

Macer glanced up the hill. "None of them. Unless—"

"Unless I stay in the flitter."

"Right. I'll be back."

NO SMOKE ROSE from the kitchen or from the house. No chime of halyards against stays. When he passed the harbor, he noted that every boat that had been there last night was still there this morning.

All but for one. His own runabout.

Not a breeze stirred. Not a footfall echoed across the glen but his own. He eased the big entry door open and stepped inside the house. The place looked deserted. Felt deserted.

He started a grid search beginning in his father's office. The room proved empty. The entire house appeared empty.

He pushed the door to his father's bedroom open. Luther Gant sat on the edge of the bed, leaning over, and staring at a full glass on his nightstand.

"That's my lucky milk glass," Macer said. "From the kitchen."

"Don't I know it. I've been staring at it the whole night through trying to decide whether to drink it or not."

"Because it's full of poison."

"That, and because it's your glass, and it's got your fingerprints all over it."

"So it will look like I poisoned you."

"That's how it looks to me. And that wasn't the deal. They were to leave you out of this."

"Where is everyone?"

"Probably on the mainland by now. They had a flotilla of boats ready to ship them off. If anyone investigates, it'll look like they sold up and scattered. But no one will investigate. They'll be off world before the cock crows again, and from there I don't know where they'll take them."

"Why?"

"No one told me, and I didn't ask."

"I mean, why would anyone want to carry off our neighbors?"

"Two reasons I can think of. One, because this commodore thinks some could be descended from a second-epoch League pilot, and two, because they're isolated, and observant of the old ways."

"So?"

"He wants to try out some sort of experiment on them to find out if his theory is true. And if it isn't, he can hand over the survivors to the Enemy for a fee."

"Why would he hand over anyone to his enemies?"

"Not his enemies. The Enemy. That's what the People of the Mong Hu call those of their kin that didn't want to rebel against the Huangxu Eng. That chose to betray their sisters, and side with the emperor of their own free will."

"You're saying that the commodore works for this Enemy."

"He works for himself, and for the Consortium. Haven't you figured it out by now, son?" His father picked up the glass, and touched it to his lips, and drained it. "We're the Enemy. Three hundred years we've lived amongst these people, and done the Huangxu's bidding, and now this Consortium's bidding, generation after generation."

He shattered the glass against the fireplace. "Now here's what I want you to do. Torch this place and everything in it.

Get off world and never look back. You might still get free of them."

"What you just did. All of that before. They're both a coward's way out."

"And so we go out the way we came in. By choosing the chain over the lash."

"Who brought you that glass?"

"Bridget, from the kitchen."

"Which one?"

"The young one. Rafe's girlfriend."

"Bridget Three."

"If you say so. But don't go looking for her. There's no antidote, and I wouldn't take it anyway. It's over, son, and you free and clear of them if you just do as I ask, and then let it lie. Take another name, keep your head down, and stick to the shadows. You're not a smart lad, but you're strong and loyal. You'll make out fine if you pick your friends right."

His father stretched out on the bed.

"Like you did."

"I inherited my friends. You do as I say, and you can pick and choose. Now get out."

"Seán mac Diarmuid says that the surest way to get a Freeman to do something is to order them not to."

"I hate that man."

"I was to take the foreigners out to Seán's this morning."

"They left already. In your boat. I thought they'd be happy with last night's catch and be off with the fleet. But the commodore has a grudge against mac Diarmuid. I'm not sure what it's about."

"There are two ways to judge a man. By the quantity of his friends and the quality of his enemies."

"That sounds like something your mother would say."

"It's from a book."

"Sure it is and tell me another. Go on with you now, I never had more use for you than you had for books."

His father's face twisted into a mask of pain. He began to pant. "They said it would go easy." He cried out and wept. "Oh, what have I done. Leave me now."

"You've very nearly forged a sword. That was your plan, wasn't it?"

"Her plan. Your mother's. She used me."

"If I didn't love you like you loved your father. If only blood lay between us. Whatever they did to you wouldn't touch me. My indifference would make me immune to your pain. I would be free of them. I could walk away and not look back."

He nodded, unable to speak.

"You waited until I returned. Not so that I could witness your suffering, but so that you could judge your own handiwork."

He moaned.

"Do I appear indifferent?"

He nodded. Flecks of white began to crust his lips.

"Then you've won, haven't you?"

His father didn't answer.

Macer knelt and closed his father's eyes. He kissed his forehead.

And heard a sob.

"I *asked* you to stay in the flitter."

MACER HEARD RUSTLING as he passed his father's office. Laura was in there, looking like a floating head and neck with her second-epoch ghillie suit on and the hood thrown back. Papers were shuffling about as if on their own as she rummaged through the Gant's desk.

"What are you doing?"

"Looking for a lighter, or a match. He told you to burn this lot."

"It wouldn't do any good. I made copies of it all when I was the Gant, all but for the time since he's been back in charge. Leave it, and let's go."

"It was his dying wish you burn all this, and him with it."

"That was to destroy evidence and hide the frame job they'd tried to pull on me for his murder. Leave it, I say."

"It was his dying wish."

"And he'd expect me to ignore it. I'm going to the mac Diarmuids with or without you." Macer pulled his father's handheld from the top right desk drawer and entered the id addy from memory. He pointed toward the door. "Go on with you."

"What?" Stationmaster Lucan mac Tír said.

"I want you to close the Trinity Surface glassfield."

"Like hell I will. Who is this?"

"It's the Gant, that's who. Macer Gant."

"Quit messing. Put your father on."

"He's dead."

"For real this time?"

"For real."

"Then I'm not sure you're the Gant. There's some documents been filed says you're disinherited."

"They're fake."

"They look it."

"Because they are. Now close the glassfield, Uncle. I'll explain later."

"It can't be done, even if I wanted to. There's a rush on to leave the station, a shower of merchants all pulling out at once, and half the Ojinate seems to be gunning the other half down on the Arcade. There's a Home Guard cruiser docked at the League Sector and at liberty, and more fistfights and busted barstools than you ever did see. It's just a matter of time before the gunfire breaks out."

"You have to close the glassfield. No flights up from the planet."

"I don't have to do any such thing. Look, I'm too busy to chat. Today has been one long series of failures and I don't need to add to the list."

"Then you're ready for module two. Please, Uncle. I don't have time to explain."

"What did you just say?"

"I said please."

"No, before that."

"It's just a saying."

"No it isn't. Wait one."

"Waiting."

"Back, and I'm already getting calls from the city. The port's closed on my order for twenty-four hours. This better not be a lark of yours."

"It isn't. Thank you."

"I can't stop anything lifting from private fields."

"Understood. Gant out."

Macer thumbed through his address book.

"Byrne's."

"Mrs. Byrne, is Janie there?"

"I thought we'd agreed you'd keep away from her, Macer Gant."

"We did. But I require a lift."

"Where?"

"On the island. At the mac Diarmuid place."

"There's no place to set down there."

"There isn't for a shuttle. I need her to come in her flitter."

"I'll send her father."

"You could do that. Just don't send Rafe."

"How could I? He quit and moved in with his bint on the island."

"That's news."

"Good news, you mean. When do you want that lift?"

"Right away."

"Watch the skies."

"Will do, Mrs. Byrne. Gant out."

Macer began trotting toward the hangar. One more call and he'd be done. It, too, was an id addy he couldn't forget.

"Talk fast," Nuala nic Cartaí said. "I'm on my way to a meeting."

"Are you ever not on your way to a meeting?"

"It doesn't seem that way. Get to the point."

"Your daughter. I need her."

"Those aren't words a mother often hears. Does this mean we're breaking up?"

"A hiatus, I think they call it. We talked about three people, all together, when we met."

"We did."

"Well, I can bring them together or I can keep them apart. Which would you prefer?"

"Apart."

"I see. Well, never mind, then. I just thought, from what one of them said, that bringing them together might prove *illuminating.*"

"What I want and what my daughter wants are two different things."

"That's shocking."

"Isn't it. The same place as last time?"

"The very one. She can slag whatever's on the glassfield should she need to clear a spot."

"You don't say."

"I do say. Is our agreement still in force?"

"It is. Nic Cartaí out."

Macer slid under the flitter and began running through the preflight inspection.

"You were talking to a woman just now," Laura said.

"How can you tell?"

"Your tone of voice changes. It gets all... syrupy."

"Would you like me to go all syrupy when I talk to you? I could, you know. I can turn it on, and I can turn it off."

"Macer—"

"I asked you to stay in the flitter, Lorelei, knowing you wouldn't, all right? I'm not so stupid as everyone thinks I am."

"I don't think you're stupid."

"No you don't think it, you know it. I need to get my kit."

Macer trotted into the hangar and came out with his backpack. He glanced at the copilot's seat. "Are you in there?"

"I am."

"Hold this."

The backpack looked like it was floating in midair.

"I hate your getup."

"At least I don't have grease on my sleeve."

"I put that there on purpose. So you'd have something to complain about."

"It worked."

"It always does. Now belt it and let's do this."

"Maybe you could try flying a little higher this time?"

"Don't tempt me."

"Like I ever could."

52

Macer's runabout was tied up at the mac Diarmuid dock, along with Seán's big salvage barge and a couple of other battered hulls belonging to the mac Diarmuid clan. He overflew the farmstead, which consisted of a weathered single-story farmhouse roofed in green tin and a large barn, also roofed in green tin, and looking like it hadn't seen a lick of paint in twenty years. The field was empty, and no one in the farmyard to be seen, not without a wide-spectrum pass, and he hadn't thought to bring the equipment for that. "I can set down on the barge, but I don't fancy doing that with the bomb on board. So I'm thinking it's the yard, between the house and barn, which I don't fancy, either, or the long acre beside the boreen, or the road itself, to the upper pasture."

"There's a bomb on board?"

"Didn't I say?"

"You didn't."

"Altitude triggered, but I'd hate to jar it on landing."

"The lane itself, then. The grass beside it is crossed with

ditches. Can you not see the difference in color between the wet ground and dry?"

"I can, now that you mention it." He aligned the flitter with the boreen. "Lorelei."

"What?"

"I'd ask that you stay in the flitter until you see me pass over that footbridge safely. These men that killed your father are certified world-class marksmen, and if they're hiding in the hills up there, they might take a shot at me and hit you by accident."

"If they're such good shots how could they do that?"

"I think they're mad enough at me to spray and pray."

"Then they might shoot while we're landing."

"I think they will if they can. I aim to drop us like a stone and catch them unawares."

"If they're shooting from up in those trees, they're on the wrong side of the Willow Bride."

"The minute they murdered the Ellis they were on the wrong side of the Willow Bride."

"You know what I mean."

"I'll put my faith in forces I can see and touch. Will you do as I ask?"

"I'll do you one better. I'll wait in the flitter until nightfall, and then I'll come out."

"That's overkill. Just wait a while." He jammed the yoke forward. "This won't take that long."

MACER SCOOPED up his backpack and took off at a sprint. He'd nearly made it to the Willow Bride footbridge when the fire-fight began. He kept his head down and kept running. Someone was firing down the hill above him while a whole mess of someones else were firing uphill from inside the farmhouse.

He was over the bridge and nearly to the house when he juked right, toward the barn, and a projectile kicked the dust up exactly where he would have been if he hadn't turned. A few tense strides later and he had the house between him and the shooters, and then he was in the barn and peeling out of his backpack. He hoped that Seán still kept his fast-pallets in here, and not on the barge.

And he did. Macer manhandled one up onto the workbench and began to strip it down.

Half an hour later he heard footsteps outside, but only because the walker wanted him to hear.

"Macer."

"Seán."

"What are you up to?"

"I'm making a weapon."

"I'll leave you to it, then."

"Thanks."

And then he had the repulsor strips off, and then he had the control circuitry out, and then he had the drone out of the backpack, and the maintenance panel open; if he screwed this up, he'd brick the drone, and any chance of a future as a freelance engineer was over. It was a very nice drone, and it would be a sin to break it, but not as much of a sin as not trying to do what? Avenge his family? Protect his community? Impress Laura Ellis?

Maybe all those things, and then some. He'd had no idea that the mess he'd found himself in didn't start with something he'd done, or even at the instant of his birth, but was the residue of a self-inflicted stain of his forebearers, women and men who'd sold out their own kin. He was born a traitor, a tout, a grass, and lived under the roof of another. That he hadn't so much as suspected didn't change the fact. He knew his father was bent. But he hadn't comprehended the shape of the curve, or where it began. But he knew where it ended.

Here.

Today.

He picked up the handheld and flipped to the drone-control application.

Right now.

He pressed the 'up' glyph.

The drone rocketed upward, hammered against the tin of the roof, and punched its way through.

It was night outside.

That had taken longer than he'd expected. And worked better than he'd imagined.

He flipped the drone's sensors to a wide-spectrum sweep. It autolocked on infrared when it picked up several heat sources on the far side of the Willow Bride. There were two solids, men or women bellied down behind boulders and watching downslope. That would be the Severns. But there were eight more heat signatures further upslope, much smaller, and moving fast, and behind them a shimmer on the sensors that barely registered at all, like a ghost that came and went.

He pressed the drone forward as the eight smaller shapes doubled their speed downhill. One of the men watching downhill didn't notice their approach, and by the time he did, Macer could already hear his screams.

The other man broke cover and ran exactly the wrong way. Or exactly the right way, depending. Macer rummaged through Seán's tools until he found a pipe-fitter's wrench, the sort of crude and heavy kit Seán used on the junk barge's ancient boiler, as long as his forearm and heavy cast iron.

Macer walked out into the cold night air and gazed across the silver water of the Willow Bride. It was much too early for any moon to rise. He heard a motor overhead and had to jump backward into the barn as a flitter plummeted from the sky. It flared at the last second and set down with a metal-shredding lurch. Its engine cut off abruptly.

"Ouch," Janie Byrne said.

"Right on time," Macer said.

"You could have moved your own flitter off the landing strip. Or turned a light on."

"You could have landed on the barge."

"That hunk of junk? I was afraid I'd punch through the deck."

She climbed out and circled the machine. "My da is going to murder me. Saw a pack of wolves over there on the recon pass. Is it normal they come this close to the farm?"

"Who's to say what's normal, that side of the Willow Bride."

"That why you left your heap parked in the way? To save me from the Folk?"

"The truth is, I was distracted." He flicked the drone control to autoreturn and tossed it onto the workbench. Seconds later the drone hammered through the barn roof and waited, hovering a millimeter above the workbench.

"Is that good for your machine, running it through Seán's barn roof?"

"It isn't. But again, I was distracted."

"That's not like you."

"Go inside the house and get you something to drink. I thought it was your father coming."

"He's in an uproar and playing mediator between his paying customers and the station. The idiot stationmaster has locked down the glassfield. So I got the last-minute call, and my mother fuming. She says I'm to tell you to stay away from me. You're like a gateway drug for female hellions."

"I wouldn't say that."

"I would," Laura Ellis said. She was out of her ghillie suit and back into her ugly mourning frock.

"Laura," Janie said. "My condolences on your father."

"Janie," Laura said. "Thank you. Mr. Mac Manus sends his regards and asks how young Rigel is getting on."

"There's a name I haven't heard in a while," Macer said.

"Nor have I spoken it," Laura said. "I ran into himself on the mountain a month ago, and we shared a meal."

"Rigel's brilliant," Janie said. "Everything a girl could want. Affectionate. Attentive. Even keeps my toes warm at night. I love it when he licks me."

"Rigel is a dog, I hope," Macer said.

"A pup," Janie said. "Out of the mac Manus's border collie. Laura's offered to help me train him when he's old enough. Mac Manus says she's a dab hand with the pups."

"No doubt. About that drink..."

"That sounds grand, so long as you're buying."

"Laura is," Macer said. "Set one up for me."

He glanced at Laura. "I'll be back."

MACER CROSSED the footbridge at a steady, ground-eating walk. He wasn't a woodsman, that was more Ciarán's sort of thing, but he didn't need to be. Blood of the Enemy or not, he was island born, and the Willow Bride looked after her own. She'd lead him where he needed to go, if only he could clear his mind of what-could-have-beens and what-might-yet-be, and simply concentrate on the moment.

He couldn't though, not with so many thoughts spinning around in his head at once. The day he'd finished the Book of Junh he'd been surprised. He'd thought there'd be more to it. Some deep philosophy.

Accept your failures.

Learn from them.

Do better.

Don't wait for tomorrow.

Don't start today.

Start now.

That's all the Book of Junh said.

Lakshmi Ellis said there wasn't one text of the Book of Junh, but as many as there were hearts in the wider world. Just like there wasn't any one way to learn, or to live, or to love. You had to listen for it. You had to watch for it. You had to feel the wind against your face, the earth beneath your feet, hear your own breath, your own heart. Learn patience. Be silent. Think slowly, and deeply. Be one with yourself and with the world. Find the Way.

It settled his mind, thinking about the Book, and the Way.

A pack of wolves passed him, heading up slope toward the Clearing, their paws silent, their muzzles bloody. The moon had risen, washing the forest in silver light.

Laura and Ciarán had shown him the Clearing one summer. Laura had said that if he ever got lost in the Willow Bride's demesne, all he had to do was keep walking and he'd end up here.

"There or the Source," Ciarán had said, meaning the crater lake at the top of the mountain.

Macer hadn't believed them, but it proved to be true. True, and inexplicable. Like a puzzle written on the face of the world. Like a challenge.

He returned with some instrumentation and a datalogger.

Turned out it wasn't inexplicable after all.

He found Rik Severn at the Clearing.

"This side of the mountain is a bowl," Macer said. "One big impact crater. Compasses don't work here, and the woods are dense. You think you're running up hill but you're not.

"If you're not paying attention, your body does the work for you, and your body wants to walk downhill, even though your brain is telling it to climb higher. So you fight it when you notice, and your body takes over when you don't, and you can tell yourself you're gaining ground all day, but unless you stop your daydreaming about the future or reminiscing about the past, and place each footfall *consciously*, there's no escaping the Clearing."

Rik Severn glanced at his handheld.

"Communications and navigational systems work, but not at ground level. If you climbed one of those tall trees, you could get a signal. But you don't look made for that sort of honest work."

The moonlight gleamed from Rik Severn's prosthetic hand. It shied away from the muzzle of his gun.

"Guns don't work here either, according to some," Macer said. "That's why I brought this big honking wrench. You're above average with that long force blade, I'll freely admit. But I think your brother was better."

"He isn't," Rik Severn said.

"He looked better with a blade when he was shoving it into the Ellis. But you did get a boot in afterward. That's how you won all those multipart Olympic competitions, wasn't it? You doing the long-distance murdering and him with the blade work, and the organizers thinking there's just one of you. No wonder you needed the practice, up there on *Tractor Four-Squared*."

Rik Severn glanced at the rifle. And placed it on the ground. He clasped his hands together before him, and a long, wicked force blade sprouted from his mechanical fist.

"Steev does the distance work. I do the blade work. Up close and personal."

"Huh. I can't believe that just worked."

"What just worked?"

"Me getting you to put the gun down like in a recorded drama. Just by jawing at you."

Rik Severn glanced down at the gun.

Macer pressed a button on his handheld and tossed it next to the gun. "Don't look up."

53

"I still can't believe it." Macer wiped the blood off his handheld. "All this time I thought that gag was rubbish." Rik Severn was looking straight up when the drone slammed into his forehead.

Macer shoved the hovering drone aside and knelt next to the wreckage. He had a wicked face wound that would have killed a lesser man. The weaselly little psychopath wasn't quite dead. He kept muttering the word *die* repeatedly.

His eyes had gone all bottomless and black.

Macer tapped Rik Severn's forehead. "Can you hear me in there."

Blood bubbled on his lips. "Diediediediedie."

A mechanical hand gripped Macer's neck and squeezed.

That's an affirmative.

Macer hefted the pipe-fitter's wrench and smiled inside.

He hated dragging along a tool he didn't need.

MACER HAD to lug the drone out of the clearing before it would lift on its own. He sent it winging back to the barn.

Whatever had controlled Rik Severn's dead body and augmentation just wouldn't quit until Macer landed a lucky blow and split its carapace open. He dug the silver-and-blue thing out of the gore and studied it. It looked like a League-standard cranial implant, only larger and more curved.

Whatever it was, the similarities paled in comparison to the differences, because a standard implant didn't stare out of a dead man's eyes and mutter *die* over again until you'd crushed a corpse's voice box, and certainly couldn't control a dead man's limbs, or replacement hand. And he'd been incredibly lucky with that blow, because the thing housed a tiny shaped charge, one packing enough punch it could have blown a crater knee-deep in the rocky soil, and murdered Macer Gant as a side effect. He wasn't sure which was its primary purpose, cranial implant, or cranial bomb. The only thing it hadn't been able to do was turn on the force blade locked in the mechanical hand's death grip, but only because Macer kept batting its other dead hand away from the power toggle.

Once the drone was away he hiked back into the Clearing and searched Severn's pockets. They were empty.

He wrenched off Severn's augmented hand and after a while gave up on trying to free the force blade from its grip. The best he could do was yank the power supply. He carried the gun out as well, and with Seán's pipe-fitting wrench and all that mess found himself wishing he'd brought a sack to carry it in. It wasn't that far a hike back to the mac Diarmuid place, though, and he wasn't going all the way there in one jog, anyway.

Macer plopped his load down next to the mess that used to be Steev Severn. The wolves had been at it hard, but it was still muttering and one of its arms was still clawing at the dirt beneath it. Its eyes were open, and he could see whatever it was inside the dead man's husk glaring back at him.

He used Rik Severn's force blade to slice the blasted thing out, powering the weapon on and off using a small stud located just where the cuff of a sleeve would fall. It seemed a silly design, and not one he would have implemented, but then he would have made the force-blade grip removable from the hand.

And now that he thought about it, the force-blade grip had to be removable, else Rik Severn wouldn't have been able to use the gun. Macer just didn't know how to remove it, and he'd have to work on it in the shop to find out. Some sort of interface surrounded the cuff where it fit over the stump of Rik Severn's arm, but it wasn't any sort of interface he'd run into before.

He'd salvaged the part thinking that he could adapt it to fit Seamus, but even a casual inspection made it clear the work was over his head. He wished Singh was here, because it was exactly the sort of ultracompact, fiddly work the *Four-Squared*'s former chief engineer excelled at.

He gathered up the wrench and prosthetic hand and reached for the implant.

The implant moved away from his fingers.

He drew his hand back on reflex.

The implant stopped moving.

He moved his hand toward it again.

It moved again, toward his fingers this time.

He pulled his hand away.

The implant stopped moving.

"Weird," Macer said.

"I should let it take you," a voice said. "But I need it for another."

54

"Rafe," Macer said. "I sure am glad to see you."

Luther Gant's principal henchman laughed. He held a razorgun in his fist, a shipboard weapon that was deadly up close but not so much from a distance. "Not as glad as I am to see you. Now kick that slug thrower over here. And keep back from the rider."

"The rider? Is that what you call this silvery yoke?"

"Spare me the phony island talk," Rafe said. "I've heard you on the station."

"It's called fitting in. It's like camouflage, only better, because you're not trying to blend into the environment, but live in harmony with it. You wouldn't know about that, being one who likes to stand apart from the common man."

Rafe bent and picked up the rider. "Don't move." He used both hands to manipulate the device. He had a loose grip on the razorgun and his attention on the device in his hands. Macer tensed his muscles and prepared to leap up and risk it when he changed his mind and settled back down. He'd heard footsteps on leaves. Very light and very faint.

He shifted his weight and rustled the leaves beneath him.

Rafe pocketed the rider. "There's been a break in our supply chain, else I'd watch as it drilled into your skull."

Macer shifted his weight again. "You know you're on the wrong side of the river here. It's not safe for foreigners. Just ask your man there, and his little master."

"The riders aren't masters. They're allies. They make it possible for us to do things we've only dreamed of."

"Like murder my father. How did you convince Bridget to go along with it?"

"I didn't need to convince your little pet. Not once she let me put the rider inside her."

"You're a liar. She wouldn't do that."

"She hates you, you know. Deep down. She hates all of you."

"Who all is it she hates?"

"You, and your big houses, and your boats, and your flitters, and farms, with your shuttles, and starships, and the rest of us scraping by, and not even a chance to rise. Not because we're less, because you got there first, and took it all for yourselves. But that's all over. Now we're taking it back."

"You're an educated man. A pilot on an orbital shuttle. Were you born that way? Or did you pull yourself up to there?"

"I pulled myself up as far as your lot let people like me go."

"And that's what Bridget told you. That we're all of us conspiring to keep you and her down."

"It is."

"Again, that's a lie. That might be what a stupid and jealous man might think. But Bridget's a baker from a long line of bakers, and a sensible girl.

"I asked my father about you one time, because I couldn't square the idea of a shuttle pilot and a gombeen man's heavy being housed in the same man's body. He told me that there's some people that would crawl over the corpses of their kin to reach the light. And that there were those that just like the feeling of the dead beneath them, and of the crawling."

"And which one am I supposed to be?"

"I asked him that same question. He said there's only one person who can answer that. The man in the mirror."

"He deserved to die."

"He certainly thought so. I asked him what sort of man was he, a riser, or a crawler?"

"What did he say?"

"He said he was a settled man, and necessary, and resigned to his lot."

"I hated him."

"That's more than I ever did for him. Let me talk to this rider now."

"What?"

"I know it can hear me. I can see it behind your eyes."

"You can't."

"It knows I can."

And then it was there.

Rafe's eyes were black, bottomless voids, and in that void, something utterly inhuman gazed back at him, and saw him.

When it spoke, it spoke with Rafe's voice.

"We are here."

NOTHING ABOUT RAFE seemed to have changed except his eyes. He remained far enough away from Macer that Macer couldn't grapple with him, and close enough that the projectiles from the razorgun in his fist would slice Macer to ribbons.

A moon was fully up and the shadows of the boulders and the trees around them long in the silvery light.

"If you let Bridget go, I'll let you keep Rafe," Macer said. "You can leave Clear Island and never come back. I won't file intent against you, and we'll be quit of each other. If his people want to file on you that's their business."

Rafe's face bent into a grin. "Here is our counteroffer. We will kill you last."

"Huh." Macer scratched his chin. "You're not a synthetic intelligence. I thought for sure you were."

"We are Ixatl-Nine-Go."

House was a synthetic intelligence, and he would have taken the offer. But then House wasn't emotional. Supposedly only humans were, and that had been an emotional response. Ixatl-Nine-Go might not believe Macer could hold up his end of the deal, but that counteroffer wasn't an offer to explore that possibility. It was an insult and meant to provoke.

"Do you have your own sensors, or do you depend upon Rafe's mainland perceptions for all of your environment information?"

Ixatl-Nine-Go stared at him.

"Rafe's obviously." He wouldn't know if an elephant stood behind him or the Willow Bride. "You should leave a note for Ixatl-Ten-Go to the following effect: if you're entirely dependent on the help for results? It's best to hire for quality."

Rafe shook his head, and then he was back in the driver's seat. His gaze darted to the razorgun, and then back to Macer. "I've wanted to do this for so long."

"There's no time like the present."

Rafe aimed the razorgun at Macer.

Macer closed his eyes.

Rafe screamed and kept on screaming.

Macer cracked an eye open.

Rafe was gripping a bloody stump where a hand was meant to be, and hopping around and screaming, and from the looks of it, bleeding out.

Macer scooped up the pipe-fitter's wrench, and clocked

Rafe over the left eye. Rafe dropped like a sack, and after a few seconds, Ixatl-Nine-Go was back in charge.

"You took your time, Lorelei."

"I couldn't find the on switch for this bloody butcher machine."

"It's on the butt end, like on a torch."

"Not on this yoke, it's not. Let's do this before he bleeds out."

"No hurry. Ixatl-Nine-Go's not going anywhere. Not until I dig it out and switch it off."

"Do you even know how to switch it off?"

"I watched Rafe do it. If we can find some way to safely extract it, we might yet save Bridget from its malevolent influence."

"The Bridget that poisoned your father."

"Fair enough. But this devil machine is poisoning her mind, and I can do something about that. There's no resurrecting the Gant this time, not that I know of. Now are you going to say the words or am I?"

"I will."

"Wait until his corpse starts muttering *die* over and over again. You'll know by the darkness staring back from his eyes."

"It's there," Laura said.

"Then tell it."

"I, Lorelei Ellis, being the Ellis of Clear Island, and daughter of the Willow Bride, hereby file intent against Ixatl-Nine-Go and its kin. Ixatl-Nine-Go is banned from the island, and trade with the island, until such time as a match has been made and balance restored. I appoint Macer Gant, the Gant of Clear Island—"

"Stop," Macer said. "Peel back the hood of that nasty outfit so I can at least see your whole face. And start again. I'm not the Gant. My father's filed the paperwork on the station, and now that he's dead, and the Ellis is dead, I don't see the point in fighting to make it so. The lie can die with them if it suits you."

"Does it suit you?"

"You know I don't care what the neighbors think."

"So long as they think well of you."

"So long as they respect me and trust my judgement. So long as I deserve it."

"You're going to hand over your land to Shayna and her brats."

"I'm going to hand over nothing. I'm going to fight them. But I won't claim a victory I haven't won, and I won't claim a title that's yet in question. Not in a blood oath, I won't. I never saw the point of the whole lie, and I don't now."

"That's because you don't know how women think."

"Maybe you'll explain it to me some time."

"Maybe I will."

"Good. Until then, stow it. Let's get this done with. I have a shuttle to catch."

"Fine. I, Lorelei Ellis, being the Ellis of Clear Island, and daughter of the Willow Bride, hereby file intent against Ixatl-Nine-Go and its kin. Ixatl-Nine-Go is banned from the island, and trade with the island, until such time as a match has been made and balance restored. I appoint Macer Gant, free man of Clear Island and son of the Willow Bride, as matchmaker and champion, and charge him with the duty to see balance restored, on this island and in the wider world."

"We're supposed to have witnesses," Macer said.

"We'll get them and repeat the words. But it's heard them, I can see it in its dead eyes."

"What now?" Macer said.

"Switch it off," Laura said.

"Give me that force blade then, and I'll try to carve it out neatly. You may not want to watch."

"I watched a man being eaten alive by wolves. Are you planning on doing a messier job?"

"I'm not, but I work better without an audience."

"Fine. I'll stand over here. Near this other butchered corpse."

"Thank you."

Digging Ixatl-Nine-Go out and switching it off proved fairly easy. It would have been cleaner if the blade of his scalpel wasn't a meter and a half long, and nowhere to grip it but at the far end.

Macer surveyed the wreckage. "Does that wound look familiar?"

"It reminds me of your friend Seamus."

"It does."

"Whoever worked on him went to a lot of trouble to keep him upright."

"That means we have a chance with Bridget Three. You'll see it done, right?"

"I don't like her."

"That's grand. She doesn't like you, either."

"Shush," Laura said. "Do you hear that roaring?"

"It's a longboat."

"There's nowhere to land a longboat here."

"Whoever's piloting doesn't seem to know that."

"Maybe they know something we don't."

"What do you mean maybe? You could write a book about all the stuff I don't know." Macer scooped up his mess of metal and began to jog toward the mac Diarmuid place. "Come on! Race you to the next disaster!"

55

"It looks like they're going to land on the house," Laura said. She'd left the hood of the ghillie suit peeled back so that she just looked like a head and neck floating in midair as she gazed upward.

"You'll want out of that getup," Macer said. The longboat was still a ways up, and while the roaring of it through the atmosphere was loud, it wasn't any louder than a high-flying jet. It just seemed loud, out here in the middle of nowhere.

"In a minute. Shouldn't we warn Seán and the others?"

"It won't land on the house. Not unless it's a plague ship. And it's not."

"In the water, then."

"I hope not. You can do that once or twice and then you have to replace the outer hull. It's expensive, and bad form."

"Even in an emergency?"

"Even then, if there's a relatively flat spot nearby."

"It's flat over by the barn," Laura said.

"It's not big enough."

The longboat seemed to hang roaring in the air straight overhead. Its main drive glowed like the boiling heart of a star.

"It's as big as the pasture at your place if you imagine it without the barn."

Macer pulled his gaze away from the descending vessel. He glanced at the barn. Laura was right. It was big enough, without the barn.

Oh no. "My precious is in there."

The main drive cut off, and then it was just the scream of atmosphere against the hull overhead.

Macer took off running for the barn.

Macer grabbed his backpack and the drone and scrambled for the door.

He tripped over his own feet and fell.

The tin overhead began to curl and blacken.

The rafters began to weep smoke.

He was on his knees when strong fingers grabbed him by the collar and yanked him upright.

Seán mac Diarmuid hoisted him onto his own broad back and strode across the farmyard.

He dropped Macer beside the farmhouse door.

The barn didn't just burn, it exploded as the heat off the hull and the force of the lift bands compressed the material and incinerated it at once.

Seán mac Diarmuid fished a bandana from his pocket and scrubbed it across his forehead. He squinted into what was now a white-hot glow. "I've decided to sell up."

"To the commodore?" Macer said.

"To the Ellis."

"Oh." Macer climbed to his feet. "What for?"

A cooltube licked out from the hull.

"Lack of privacy. It's like Columbia Station around here now."

veritable throng milled around Seán mac Diarmuid's farmyard waiting to see who or what came out of the cooltube.

There were more than two score League children, and Macer recognized them. They were the contract farmhands he'd ridden down on the shuttle with, what was it, two, three days ago? He couldn't remember.

And Janie Byrne, whose flitter was now in danger of catching fire.

And Laura, dressed in her ugly mourning frock, all wild hair, and ashen eyes, and swaddled in coal-black from head to toe.

And Seán... "Where's Seán off to?"

"Checking on the prisoners, I imagine," Janie said.

"What prisoners?"

"Shayna, and that Leagueman, and Bridget Three. They're all tied up in the parlor."

"Is anyone watching them?"

"Seán was, until he glanced out the window and saw you dart into the barn."

Oh no. Please, no.

Seán mac Diarmuid lay stretched out on the parlor floor. He'd taken a razorgun round. Bridget Three appeared to have been tossed up on the kitchen table, stripped bare-chested, and carved on for a while before the devil in her skull had drilled its way out. The carving knife was buried in her own chest, and whoever had done it had wrapped her own bloodstained hand around the hilt.

The Leagueman and Shayna were gone.

Macer dropped to his knees beside Seán. He felt for a pulse. *This can't be happening.* He couldn't feel it. What was he going to tell Ciarán? That he'd been more worried about a *toy* than the lives of his people? That he was responsible for all their deaths? He was responsible. Macer Gant was responsible. He wasn't just the Enemy's spawn. He was the Enemy's helpmate.

What have I done?

Rough hands shoved him aside. "Stand off." The Leagueman dropped a blocky device next to Seán's body. He quickly unspooled some wires from it and attached them to a flexible sheet of what looked like black cloth. He draped the cloth over Seán's body, head to toe.

"What's that?" Macer said.

"Portable autodoc."

"Are you a doctor?"

"I'm accident prone. I had to go to the boat to get this." He glanced up at Macer. "I can't do anything for the girl."

"But you can save Seán?"

"We'll see. She was right on top of him when she fired."

"This is all my fault."

"A man's entitled one mistake." The machine beeped. "He has a pulse."

"Can you save him?"

"I can read the display. If anyone saves him it will be the autodoc."

"But it might. Save him."

"It might stabilize him."

"Where's the implant that was in Bridget?"

"That thing that crawled out of her forehead was an implant?"

"Didn't it look just like a League implant, only bigger, and more curved?"

"Shayna took it."

"After she shot Seán."

"Shayna didn't shoot Seán. Bridget did."

"And then Shayna killed Bridget."

"Bridget killed herself."

"But Shayna's one of them."

"One of whom?"

"One of the Ixatl-Nine-Go people."

The blocky machine beeped. The Leagueman glanced at the display. "He's stable. But we need to get him into a hospitaller's autodoc quickly."

"I'll go commandeer the longboat outside." Macer jerked his chin toward the kitchen table. "Could you put something decent over Bridget Three while I'm gone?"

"Yes."

"And don't run away again. It's not Aoife behind the yoke today. And I have a proposition you'll want to hear."

MACER SHOVED out into the cool night air. The longboat had melted a divot where the barn had been so that the end of the cooltube was now pointed slightly upward. Janie had moved her flitter out of the danger zone, but some of the trees on the far side of the farmyard had begun to blaze. If he hadn't been a spacer and used to the workings of a longboat, Macer imagined it might look like a little bit of hell set down on the countryside, with the stench of a thousand different materials burning, and the soil boiled to glass, and the pitch-fueled torches of the roasting pines blazing twenty meters in the air. The fire wouldn't make it past the banks of the Willow Bride, and if did, so what.

"No one's come out yet," Laura said.

"I can see that. Don't let anyone squeamish in the farm-house. Seán's been shot."

"Is it bad?"

"It's bad. Get the biggest of those boys to help the Leagueman bring Seán down there. Then you tell the pilot to take Seán on board and lift for the station like Lucifer's on his tail. Go with them, and call ahead, talk to Lucan mac Tír, and tell him have a crash cart and an autodoc ready at the ring. Don't let him push you off, and don't let him park you at the spindle."

"Maybe you can order people around like that, but I can't."

"I'm not talking to Laura Ellis, shy and bookish island girl. I'm talking to the Ellis of Clear Island. She can order anyone around she has the nerve to. Don't let anyone tell you different, and don't let anyone stop you. This is on me, what's happened to Seán. I can't fix it alone."

"You should go with Seán."

"I would, but I'm not done here yet. I need someone I trust to do this, Laura. Someone with good sense and a spine. I'm not inviting you to a dance, but to a brawl."

"I like a good brawl."

"Who doesn't. I don't want to have to tell Ciarán it was me that got his dad murdered. I'd rather tell him it was you who saved him."

"What do we tell him about us, and the big lie?"

"We tell him the truth. The whole false betrothal was his mother's idea. Now go get Seán and get him ready. I need to run."

MACER CROSSED the Willow Bride for what he hoped was the last time that day. He'd been awake and running for going on two days, and he'd taken a fair dose of hard radiation while in the Clearing. The husk of the Willow Bride's ruptured mag bottle was still leaking and would be for another ten thousand years. He wouldn't die from the radiation if he could stay awake long enough to find an autodoc in the next twenty-four hours. Something was dragging him back, and slowing him down, that was for certain.

Shayna had climbed into his flitter. She messed with the controls to no avail.

"You need to switch on the blower," Macer said. "It's a manual toggle, down low, on the right."

She stared at him.

He pointed. "It's labeled."

She bent and switched it on. She worked the control, and the flitter fired up.

"Shut it down and get out. There's a bomb on board."

She reached for the canopy pulldown.

"I'm serious. If you want to see your kids again, just shut it off and get out."

She glared at him. "Are you threatening me?"

"I'm trying to help you. Get out and come back to the house. I'll help you find your boys and get them back. They're Gants, and we stick together."

She glanced at the ignition, and her hand moved toward it. She stopped and turned back to face him. It wasn't Shayna looking back, but something else entirely.

"I just needed to be sure," Macer said. "It was a lie, all that rubbish Rafe said. You aren't allies. Shayna wouldn't abandon her own children. You're the horseman, and she's the horse."

"They aren't her children." The thing inside Shayna forced

her mouth into a lopsided grin. "They're mine." It reached for the canopy.

"What you did to Bridget. What you made her do to Seán. Was that meant as a warning or as payback?"

"A down payment." The canopy slammed closed.

The flitter began to accelerate.

It lifted, cleared the tree line, and continued to climb.

Macer was across the Willow Bride by the time a light flared in the sky and, moments later, the sound of the blast echoed across the valley.

LAURA MET Macer on the footbridge over the Willow Bride.

"Why hasn't that longboat lifted?"

"Because it has an autodoc in it."

"Who puts an autodoc in a longboat?"

"Old women and other people who think they might need one."

Macer marched toward the farmhouse and the new glass-field beside it. "That's a nic Cartaí hull."

"The Ancient Hull herself. She's well preserved for being older than our grannies combined."

"You're saying it's Fionnuala nic Cartaí on that longboat."

"So she claims. She came out alone but went back in with that Leagueman by the short hairs. A big old vein in her forehead started throbbing when she laid eyes on him. They had sharp words, and then he came along with her nice into the lion's den."

"I think you should lift with her to the station, and make sure Seán gets all he needs."

"I think you ought to go talk to her first. She seems to have a plan, and it doesn't involve shepherding a slip of a girl around the station."

"She said that to you?"

"Right before I called her a cradle robber."

"Did you tell her you were the Ellis?"

"We didn't get that far in the conversation. She's not a very nice person."

"Neither are you."

"I don't pretend to be."

"Have you ever heard a good word about the nic Cartaí?"

"They say she's pretty."

"How would you feel if that was the best thing anyone could say about you?"

Laura was silent all the way down the hill.

"I wouldn't like that," Laura said.

"Nuala nic Cartaí is the richest woman in Freeman space," Macer said. "And she was born a body slave to the Huangxu Eng. You don't get where she is by being nice. Or by being stupid. We want her on our side. We don't want her neutral to us, and we absolutely don't want her against us. She doesn't have friends. She has interests and she makes enemies."

"Like your father does."

"Like he did, though on a much larger scale, and over a much longer span of time. She has seen everything under this star and a thousand others, but there's one thing she hasn't seen yet."

"What's that?"

"An equal. Don't lick her boots, and don't thumb her in the eye. We have interests, and they're every bit as valid as her own. Don't try to like her or understand her motives. She won't care about yours. Treat her like you would House. Tell her what you want, and wait to hear what she says. Nothing, and I mean absolutely nothing, is personal with her."

"So she's like you are with everyone."

"Like I am with everyone but you and Ciarán. And with Seamus, I suppose."

"So we're exceptions to the indifference of Macer Gant."

"Your good opinion is a reservoir of strength, like a backup battery for my resolve. I don't need it to function, but it's good to know it's there. The knowledge of its existence lets me take risks I might not dare alone."

"You never told me that."

"I never had to kill a man until today, either, and I hope I never do again. Now listen. You know what's important to Clear Island, and Nuala nic Cartaí doesn't have a clue. Nor does she care. Think about what you want and what you're willing to give to get it. Don't think about yesterday, or tomorrow. Think about today, right now. Just talk to her, and listen to what she says. Have your say, and if you can come to some agreement you can live with, do it. And if you can't, walk away. You can ponder what that says about you later."

When they reached the cooltube, Laura rested her hand on Macer's sleeve. "She's a hundred times more experienced than me."

Macer nodded. "More like a thousand, but only in those things that matter to her. However..."

Macer gripped the cooltube hatch and tugged.

"You're prettier."

57

The inside of Nuala nic Cartaí's longboat was unlike any longboat he'd ever seen, all rich wood paneling, and brushed inox fittings, and the latest in workstations and displays. The longboat shipped a head and shower on board, and in a cubby across from it, an autodoc. It looked to be a nice one.

"It's like a palace in here," Macer said. "No wonder you dug a furrow on landing. What's all this kit mass?"

Nuala pointed at a portside settee, one with a table that looked like it might fold down into a bunk if needed. The Leagueman was already seated at it and looking uncomfortable. "Sit," she said.

She didn't look inclined to sit. Neither did Laura. Macer slid in across from the Leagueman. If felt great to sit down. He leaned back and settled in.

"I'll stand, thank you," Laura said. "Would you please explain why you've turned an islander's farmyard into a glassfield?"

"Turned it back into a glassfield, you mean. This entire valley was glass when I was a girl."

"It is Mr. Mac Diarmuid's farm, not yours to do with as you wish."

"It's not much of a farm to speak of. Look around you. There's only one thing you can grow in a place like this."

"Men," Laura said.

"Hard men, if you like them that way, and I do." Nuala nic Cartaí stared at Laura.

"Go on," Laura said.

"I thought you'd blush."

"I will later. What do you want?"

"I have five longboats full of Clear Islanders I caught boosting out of the gravity well. They were in stolen nic Cartaí hulls, and they're now in confinement on a nic Cartaí orbital, eating nic Cartaí food, and drinking nic Cartaí water, and breathing nic Cartaí air."

"They were abducted."

"That's what they say, but things are pretty fluid on the station right now, and anything's possible at the moment. I'm not going to just take their word for it, am I?"

"What did their captors say?"

"I haven't had time to scan through the sensor logs, but I was told it was something like, 'Please Wild Bill Powers, don't shove me out this airlock,' and so forth."

"You've spoken to Peg Powers's husband, and he says the islanders overpowered their captors."

"My people have spoken to him, and others, and the facts speak for themselves. There's five longboats with only islanders on them."

"And you don't believe Mr. Powers."

"He's a native son. I don't believe any of them."

"I don't follow."

"We're all notorious cheats and liars," Macer said.

"And smugglers," the Leagueman said.

"Enough from you," Nuala said.

"That's rich," Laura said. "Coming from you."

"That's the voice of experience, girly."

Laura's grey eyes flashed. She glanced at Macer.

He winked.

"What is it you want?"

"I want to get rid of these people. And to be compensated for doing it."

"So you do believe their story."

"I believe they couldn't have stolen five of my longboats without help. And before I go accusing my own people or opening an investigation, I need to know if they had help."

"And turning the mac Diarmuid farm into slag is the way to do that."

"Talking to Seán mac Diarmuid is the way."

"Because?"

"Because we're acquainted, that's why. Now stop trying to get me to wake the dead, and let's get on with this. I told you what I have, and what I want, and we need to decide on a number."

"She wants island men," Macer said. "And in exchange, she'll send the rest of our people back. She wanted Seán to tell her who to ask for, so she'd be able to bargain for the ones she wants, and not some layabouts. And she wants to know if Seán heard about anyone boosting longboats."

"That's what I said. Standard nic Cartaí terms, honest long-haul work, re-up if both parties agree. Couldn't be fairer, word of a merchant."

"And the men themselves to decide if the contract is agreeable."

"Naturally."

"So all we're really negotiating over is the list of names, and the number of names on the list."

"Well, I don't think I even need the list now. I don't know

you and have no reason to trust your judgement when it comes to men."

"I see. So it's just the number."

"I think I said that half an hour ago."

"Do you have a number in mind?"

"I do. But first, before I tell you. There's another reason I'm here. My daughter Aoife brought home this disturbing story and proof of it. I'm convinced it's true, and that's why she's sitting in a longboat at the Gant place cooling her heels. She asked me to drop everything and come see Seán, on the odd chance yer man was here and detained. The two needs rubbing together made it worth my while."

Laura snorted. "Like anyone could *detain* Macer Gant."

"I'm not the object in question." Macer glanced at the Leagueman. "Sorry, mate. I told them where you were."

"She's on her way here now, and we're to lift in five to clear the glassfield."

"I'd like to come with you," Laura said. "To keep track of Seán."

"He'll get the care he deserves."

"He will because I'm coming with him. You have longboats sitting on two Clear Island glassfields. Do you have *any* idea what the going rate for that is?"

"I'm guessing a lift for a girl to the station."

"A lift for the Ellis and room and board for her as long as Seán mac Diarmuid is there. It doesn't need to be a palace, but it can't be a rat hole."

"Do you want me to throw a party for her, with glass slippers and a coach and four as well?"

"I want nothing for her but the swift return of her neighbors to the island. Once she sees the last one home, she'll be satisfied."

"And what of my men for hire?"

"So long as they sign of their own free will, there's nothing for her to say."

Nuala nic Cartaí's gaze narrowed. "I might have that list off you after all."

"Are we done with the question of the lift?" Laura said.

"We're done."

"Let's hear the number."

"One," Nuala said.

They stared at each other.

Nuala tossed a data chip on the table. "Read that and sign it."

Macer shoved the chip toward the Leagueman.

"Not him, you idiot," Nuala said. "You."

"Me what?"

"He's been awake and active for more than forty-eight hours," the Leagueman said. "And he hasn't looked well since he came back from the woods."

"Macer," Laura said, "did you go to the Clearing?"

"Everyone ends up there eventually, don't they?"

"How long were you there?"

"Long enough to kill a man."

"Hey, kid," the Leagueman said. "Look at your arm."

Macer blinked. And looked.

The Leagueman slapped something gooey and wriggling onto his wrist. It made a cooing sound.

"What's that?"

"It's called a sedative. Very fast acting and very—"

MACER'S EYES blinked open when the longboat's main drive powered up. He was strapped into a standard jump seat bolted to the deck in the standard way. It was a full flight, jammed with League kids in farmer's overalls.

"Is it harvest time?"

"You shouldn't be awake," the Leagueman said.

"It doesn't feel like I am. This longboat isn't anywhere as nice as I remember."

"Just go back to sleep."

"There's a regulation problem with the drive. I can fix it."

"There's nothing wrong with the drive," a woman with nice ankles said.

"It's not perfect," Macer said. "That's what's wrong with it." He unbelted and stood. "I can fix it."

The woman and the Leagueman were arguing. Someone was tugging on his sleeve.

"I thought you said he'd stay under."

"I can't give him much more."

"Well, give him something."

"What's he doing?"

"Where am I?"

"You're on a longboat to Trinity Station," the woman said. "Now sit down."

"Who are these people?"

"A detachment of the Invincible Spear Bearers of Imperial Wrath," the woman said. "Now sit down."

"I don't feel too good." His guts felt like they wanted to jump out his throat.

"You've been injured," the woman said. "Now sit down."

"Belt in," the Leagueman said. "We're slowing."

Macer belted in. "Good. We're almost there."

"Almost where, kid?"

"Where we're going."

"Where's that?"

"He's out of his head," the woman said. "Leave him be."

"Where are we going, Macer?"

"Where everyone goes in the end. Listen."

"I'm listening."

"That's what it's supposed to sound like. When the drive is turned off."

Something cold and moist slapped his wrist. It made a cooing sound.

"That feels weird. Why does it make that sound?"

"So you know that it's working."

"Huh. People aren't like machines, you know. It's not right to switch them off."

"I know," the Leagueman said. "But when they're broken sometimes you have to."

"Do I make a sound? When I'm switched off?"

"What sort of sound?"

"Like this. *Diediediediediedie.*"

"No," the Leagueman said. "You don't make that sound."

"That's good."

"Where did you hear that sound?" the woman said.

"I'm sleepy."

"Wake him," the woman said. "Where did you hear that sound?"

"Get some rest, kid. Where we're going, you'll need it."

58

They put him up in a big suite at the nic Cartaí orbital shipyard. It had a view the length of the yard. Truxton's *Golden Parachute* was racked in outside the viewport and they were working on it at a feverish pace.

The Leagueman said Macer had been out of commission for three days in the autodoc. Since then it had been a week of sitting around, and answering questions, and sleeping, and answering questions again.

He'd been in a world of hurt, and no shame in admitting it. But he was better now, and not exactly eager to get back to work, given his new job, but as ready as he would ever be.

When Laura and Seán showed up for a visit it cheered him a lot. And when Laura handed him his backpack with his beloved drone packed inside, he couldn't keep from beaming.

"Staying with my boys on the mainland," Seán said. "If you see Ciarán out there, you tell him his old da's still kicking."

"I'll do that, if I do," Macer said.

"How they treating you?" Seán said.

"Like a bug. A new kind, one that they've never seen before."

Laura gazed out the window. "What's taking so long?"

"You're not supposed to light up a longboat inside the hull. And you're not supposed to run up so close to light speed for so long. And you're not supposed to burn out the maneuvering thrusters all at the same time."

"But sometimes you have no choice."

"You always have a choice. And there's always a price. And the price right now is a total refit."

"Nuala should just give you another ship."

"No one's giving me anything. Aoife nic Cartaí's course and mine just happen to be running parallel, and she's offered a lift. When her prize vessel's ready."

"In exchange for what?"

"Whatever I'm good at."

"You're good at fixing things. You should be out there working."

"A monkey could fix that rubbish, and they have a hundred of them crawling over it right now. One more pair of hands would just get in the way."

"The Ellis and the Gant could pool their money and buy you a vessel," Laura said.

"They might, if one of them wasn't embroiled in a court battle for their title, and if together they sold everything they owned ten times over. Wealth on a planet and wealth in space are measured on different scales." Macer stood beside Laura and gazed out the viewport. "Speaking of the Ellis, how is her house guest?"

"Seamus? Moody and mooning about. Like me at thirteen, according to... some. He hasn't killed himself yet, if that's what you're asking."

"It is."

"There has to be a way to get you moving. Unless you don't want to."

"This Ixatl-Nine-Go thing enslaved and murdered our

friends, and according to Aoife we got off light. I gave my word to find a match for the harm, and I'm not backing out. And there's the problem of my missing brothers."

"Half brothers."

"They're kin. I'll not be dividing them into pieces in my mind."

"You'll have to find the offending party to make a match," Seán said. "If you can."

"Aoife thinks she knows where it is. And we have the implants, and people are working on them, trying to reverse engineer them without accidentally setting them loose."

"What sort of people?" Laura asked.

"It turns out that the Leagueman works for someone called Lord Aster, who has people who do that sort of thing."

"I thought he worked for that commodore devil."

"Apparently he's not too particular who he works for. And he seems more connected than the Columbia system superluminal node."

"There has to be a way to get you a ship sooner. Could we lease one?"

"You could steal one," Seán said.

"That's not a very Freeman solution to the problem," Laura said.

Seán snorted. "How do you think Nuala nic Cartaí's mother ended up with a starship?"

"By freeing her people from the Huangxu Eng," Laura said.

"That's what she did *after* she stole a starship."

"We don't need any more enemies," Laura said. "I don't see Nuala nic Cartaí standing for that."

"She would," Seán said, "if she had a ship she wanted to be rid of."

Laura glanced at Macer. "Does she?"

"She doesn't," Macer said. "But I know someone who might."

Macer pulled out his handheld and punched in the id addy from memory.

Seán clamped his gnarled fingers around Macer's hand. "You don't ask for permission."

"I know that," Macer said. "I'm roping in a coconspirator."

"That's different, then. Carry on."

"Thank, you, Seán, I will."

Lucan mac Tír's raspy voice shouted in Macer's ear. "What?"

"Are you familiar with the phrase, 'turning a blind eye'?"

"Of course I am, you noisome brat. I'm not senile."

"I never said you were."

"You were thinking it."

"Do you know what else I'm thinking?"

"I don't want to know. Just do it and tell me about it later."

MACER TOSSED the data crystal onto Nuala nic Cartaí's desk. "I can't sign that."

"It's a standard nic Cartaí contract. Everyone signs it."

"I mean I'm not free to sign it. I've agreed to act as matchmaker for the Ellis and need to find my brothers. I can't take a contract until I finish those jobs."

"I see." She ran her gaze over him. "You're never going to sign with nic Cartaí, are you?"

"I already did if you recall. Off the books, and I held up my end of the bargain."

"The commodore got away."

"You didn't ask me to catch him. Just to watch him and tell you, and turn an unknown unknown into a known unknown."

"And?"

"And I did that. Spectacularly."

"And now you're here for payment."

"Not yet. I'd like to modify and extend the deal. Cover, not just for whatever sins they try to pin on me from before, but protection for whatever sins I might commit in the future."

"That's what signing a nic Cartaí contract will do for you."

"I don't want you to shoulder the blame. I want you to run interference. To gum up the works. Whatever it is you people say."

"You people."

"Long-haul spacers."

"Is that how you see me?"

"Isn't that what you are?"

"It is."

"I'm not. I'm an island man, and proud of it. I'm not interested in seeing what's over the horizon. I'd prefer to live my life amongst friends, and build something meaningful together, and die in my own bed, at home. But I'm not going to get to do that now."

"You're angry because you believe my family brought this pestilence upon your world."

"Not just your family. Truxton. Kavanagh. Every family ship. All of you."

Nuala nic Cartaí stared at him.

After a long while she spoke. "Many sons, upon learning that their mother's merchant vessel had gone missing, would choose to search for their missing loved one. Yet you never did."

"I didn't."

"Why is that?"

Macer didn't answer. He couldn't answer, not without waking the dead.

"Because she told you not to," Nuala said. "When she abandoned you."

"She didn't abandon me. She said she'd send for me."

"Once she was settled," Nuala said.

Macer had already said too much.

"You would, of course need to stay in one place, else you

might miss her message. She needed to be able to reach you. How could she reach you if you were, where? Ambidex Station? Prix Canada? Midpoint? Unity? A merchant couldn't possibly leave messages there. No, that wouldn't do. You, Macer Gant, you can't leave Trinity system. Promise me that. Promise you won't. Promise you won't what?"

"Enough," Macer said.

"A man once tried to sell me guard dogs. Can you imagine? We are the People of the Mong Hu. What use could we possibly have for dogs?

"Many, he said. Consider this. These big, strong, massive dogs have the teeth of a wolf. They have the heart of a wolf. But unlike a wolf, they're loyal. Easy to control. Easy to set to a task. Easy to place between danger and a loved one. They would gladly give their life to save a child.

"I wasn't interested.

"But wait, he said. There's more. They are not only biddable. They love the work. They live for the work. You won't even need a leash. Look closely into his great, proud eyes. Can you not see the wolf beneath the skin?

"I told him that I could.

"Well, he said. What do you think?

"I thought he hadn't addressed the most important question, so I asked him."

Macer looked Fionnuala nic Cartaí in the eye. "How do they taste?"

"You've heard this story before."

"Never."

"The dog merchant sputtered at that. But do you know what he said then?"

"They're delicious."

"Indeed."

"I get it."

"Do you? There can be no misunderstanding between us.

Lorelei Ellis is a woman grown. She doesn't need a protector any longer. Any promises you have made regarding her safety have been met."

"According to you."

"According to herself. And if that isn't enough surety for you, I offer this. She has my protection."

"What? Why?"

"My daughter is dead set on thrusting herself into danger. And you've seen firsthand the nature of the enemy she's likely to face."

"I have."

"The Ellis and I have come to an agreement. Pending two conditions."

"What conditions?"

"That you and Aoife work together."

"And?"

"That you don't get in Aoife's way."

"How would I do that?"

"By pretending to be housebroken when we all know you're not."

"And if I do that?"

"Then I can run interference for you."

"What about our side deal?"

"You and me getting personal?"

"In a manner of speaking."

"I'm considering it."

"That's good."

"Why are you still standing there?"

"You said you were considering."

"Bring my daughter back alive and we're eighty percent there."

"That's bad. They say the last twenty percent of anything is the hardest."

"Ninety percent then, but only because you're persistent."

MACER GRABBED a roll-up and a couple flasks of milk in the orbital's commissary and took his lunch back to his room. He needed time to think. His hands were full but the hatch was ajar, and he didn't think much about that until after he'd plopped everything down on the table and sat down.

Singh stepped out of the shadows and closed the hatch all the way. He walked across the compartment and sat down opposite of Macer.

"How's the family," Macer said.

"I don't have a family," Singh said. "I made that up."

Singh reached into his jacket pocket.

Macer stiffened. He wrapped his thumbs beneath the edge of the tabletop.

"Calm down," Singh said. "I want to give you something. In part, to apologize."

"For what?"

"For nearly getting you killed."

"That wasn't you. That was Rik Severn."

"For lying to you, then."

"I imagine you had a good reason. Or thought you did."

Singh placed a silver box onto the table. "You didn't get this from me."

"What is it?"

"It's an implant detector. Or, more specifically, a rider detector. Or, more specifically still, an *activated* rider detector."

"So, what do I do? Wave it at someone?"

"I'd enable it and carry it in my pocket. It vibrates when it detects a positive."

"How is it for false positives?"

"Flawless. I could explain why, but it doesn't matter. It's more likely to produce false negatives. But if you're close to a rider, and it's in an agitated state, it's accurate to five nines."

"If I'm close to a rider and it's agitated, chances are its mount is already wailing on me."

Singh chuckled. "True. But it's the best we can do right now."

"Who're you working for these days?"

"The name wouldn't mean anything to you."

"Try me."

"Charles Newton."

"You're right, that name doesn't mean anything to me. Is Mr. Newton good to work for?"

"I've never met him. In fact, I don't think he really exists."

"Do his paychecks exist?"

Singh grinned. "They do." He stood. "I need to get back."

Macer started to stand.

"Sit. Eat your lunch."

"I will, boss."

"I'm not your boss anymore."

"I know," Macer said. "I just wanted to see what it felt like saying that again."

"And?"

"I think I'm done with bosses."

"Good decision."

"Hey, does this thing have copy protection?"

"It's supposed to. But someone may have forgotten to enable it."

"Well, make sure you persecute the blameless."

"Already on it. But thanks for the reminder."

59

O ver the course of the following week, Laura and Seamus sorted through her father's collection of second-epoch artifacts for anything that might help Macer when facing down Ixatl-Nine-Go. Every day he'd get a new batch brought up on the shuttle, and every night he'd go through the items.

He was stalling, and he knew it, but the nic Cartaí yard was so close to finishing up the refit on *Golden Parachute* and Aoife nic Cartaí still hadn't rustled up a full bridge crew. She'd even lost her henchmatron and pilot, Helen Konstantine, who was some sort of League reserve officer, and called back to active duty once the League knew she was on the station.

Macer preferred to stay in his cabin, thinking through all the options, rather than go over to the station with Aoife. First, he didn't really like her all that much. She was pushy and entitled. And second, it was an absolute madhouse over there.

The League civil war was continuing to heat up, and even though Trinity Station was officially neutral, the Leaguemen working the docks and the Arcade weren't, and fights were common. And since ships of either side could use the station, there were often Royalist and Loyalist courier vessels lashed to the ring at the same time, and fights between their crews as well, though only one prolonged firefight so far, one that ended with the stationmaster evacuating the noncombatants first and the atmosphere soon thereafter.

In addition, some sort of hidden private war had ripped through the Ojin Sector of the station, with one group fighting the other, and both groups indistinguishable from one another to an outsider. Crime was up as well, since it was hard to tell if a citizen found bled out and stuffed into a recycler was stuffed there for something they'd done, or for who they were, or for the colors they wore.

The Freeman Sector was worse, if that was possible, because all the sensible family ships had taken off for less violent pastures, and the lowest sorts of riffraff had moved in, profiteers who didn't mind selling to both sides of a fight at the same time, and stoking the divisions purely in pursuit of profit. It was cheaper to stay lashed to the spindle and sell to the same yobs over and over again than it was to rustle up an honest deal one station at a time in the wider world.

Macer didn't follow the news, never had, and didn't see any point to it. No one knew the truth, and listening to two one-sided stories and comparing the differences didn't provide enlightenment. He was convinced that the whole process wasn't designed to educate him, but to make him angrier and stupider than he already was. The wider world could be in upheaval on every planet and every polity in the universe and he wouldn't know, and he didn't care. He had all the intel he needed.

According to Aoife nic Cartaí, the Ixatl-Nine-Go hailed from a moon in the Contract system and that's where they were headed as soon as she had a ship. Ciarán was to meet them there, and that would be a nice bonus, but he didn't fancy meeting up with his best mate for a man hunt, or a monster hunt, whatever this turned out to be.

Ciarán was a serious brain, and a choir boy, moralistic and quick-witted, all of which he got from his mother, who was a force of nature and a strange agent of the first order. He figured Seán married her out of pity, because she never seemed all there, and after she got sick she practically floated away on her own cloud.

One time she'd seen Macer working on the drawings he did for House, where he labeled the stuff in the stories, so he could remember the stories and recite them, and as he discovered later, so he could learn how to spell and write things down without the words and letters squirming away from him. She asked him, would he make some drawings for her, forty of them, full color, no words, and in the style of a picture she'd shown him.

If she'd had any sense, she would have told a kid she wanted one picture, and told him again, one picture, forty times, but that wasn't the way she was built. She was straight, and direct, and cruel, and treated everyone the same, child or adult. He'd said yes, but only because she scared him, and he didn't know what she would do if he said no. Forty pictures was a lot of pictures.

It would have been good fun if not for the subject matter: caves with glowing lichen; a dragon you could hear but not see, which had taken him a while to figure out how to draw, without captions; and men and women pushing gears around, and watching the skies at the same time.

And then there was the craziest stuff, like imagining Ciarán as the Knight Commander of the Legion of Heroes, and a starship with Laura's face, and himself as a chariot driver, dragging a wheel of fire across the sky. When she asked him to draw her as a corpse, arms crossed on her chest and sinking into the waters of the Willow Bride, he drew the line and said he wouldn't, and the next day she was dead, and when he woke up in the morning and looked at his sketchpad he found he couldn't look away from it until he'd done what she asked, and handed the finished picture to Laura, who cried.

The pair of them were thick as thieves in those last days, and Laura, heartsick and lower for weeks than her normally heartsick and low self. Macer had worried that he'd come out one day and find Laura floating down the Willow Bride like in Cassandra's dream book, but Ciarán said let her be, you're like her shadow, no wonder she's in a foul mood all the time with you looming over her and drinking in all the sunlight.

Ciarán could be cruel like his mother, not in a mean way, but like Macer's brain was an extension of his own, and he didn't have to edit his thoughts before he passed them along. It bothered Macer at first, but later he realized it was a compliment, and a testament to their friendship. For Ciarán there was no point where he ended and Macer began, except when it came to Laura.

Macer didn't think that was fair, what Ciarán said about Laura and the light, but he did what Ciarán said, and it was true, Laura got better, until by the time he'd left for the Academy she was able to pass for normal most of the time.

He didn't know why, precisely, he was thinking about all this now, but maybe it was on account of the great mass of the Ellis's stuff he was pawing through and stuffing into FFEs for attachment to *Golden Parachute*'s mast once it was ready. Thinking about Cassandra mac Diarmuid meant he wasn't thinking about the Ellis, and all the craic they'd had together, trying to get that old stuff to work, and more often than not, trying to figure out what it was for first, and then trying to get it to do that later. They could often get it to do something, though often not what they expected.

The Ellis was a good man, and a hoot to be around, and 'let's try it and see' the happiest words in the world. Macer knew when he was in the Clearing and smashing the living daylights out of Rik Severn's corpse that just *would not die*, that he was erasing some of that joy from his heart one blow at a time, and he couldn't stop, couldn't stop, couldn't stop, until he saw the silvery glint, and thought what's that, and then he'd dug it out, and held it up to the light, and it was as strange and as alien as the items in the Ellis's collection, only the opposite, because it didn't create joy, and wonder, but extinguished them.

He had never really thought about good and evil much, because that would mean that he'd have to look at his own life, and his own home, closer than he wanted to, living in the shade, over the brow of a hill between darkness and light. His father wasn't evil. He did evil things, sometimes, but mostly he did selfish and counterproductive things, being happier getting it over on a man for a pingin than helping him turn a pingin into a crown. He could have done well by doing good, like the Ellis, but it wasn't in his nature, and Macer had wondered if it wasn't in his nature either, and all his striving to be nothing like his father inevitably fruitless, like a chair wishing it was a table because it didn't like the quality of the asses it had to deal with.

When he'd run out of steam, and looked at the mess he'd made of Rik Severn's undying husk, he'd realized he'd been wrong about himself, and worried about nothing. He was man. He could do bad things if he had to, for his neighbors and his family.

But he wasn't a bad man. He took no joy in what he'd done, and he wouldn't want to do it again.

He would do it, though, because if he did it then others wouldn't have to. He could spare the joy because he'd picked it up where he found it, and stored it away, like charge in a battery. So long as he didn't expend more than he took in, he'd be fine.

Just sitting here, doing nothing, was draining. He was leaking joy charge by the hour.

Resistance wasn't just futile. It was a waste of good energy.

So, then.

He needed to do something interesting. It didn't have to be fun. It just needed to have the potential to be a net positive.

He was tired of waiting for Aoife nic Cartaí to scrape her mess into a pile.

She could come along and help, or she could run after him and catch up later.

Macer Gant was stealing a starship, and he was stealing it tomorrow.

60

Sweet Olive Blossom System, Hundred Planets (Huangxu Empire)

The executive offices of the Glorious Voice of Empire Corporation lay not on the station, but a smaller orbital adjacent to the system's communications hub.

Ciarán and Ko Shan arrived at the appointed time, both dressed in standard utilities and neither of them carrying weapons, other than the overseer's rod that Ryuu had gifted Ciarán, which was largely seen as part of the ceremonial trappings of all Freeman merchants, like the pendant spire and the mong hu. Ciarán had considered bringing Wisp with him as a show of strength but decided he would try this first: a show of casual interest, rather than a formal request for trade rights in the system.

They were led into a waiting room and told to wait until someone could see them. That Ciarán had arranged an appointment before arriving seemed not to matter. He wondered if this decided lack of courtesy was the sort of behavior aimed at all Freemen or if he and *Quite Possibly Alien* were being singled out.

Had this been a typical stop at a Huangxu facility for a Freeman merchant, he might not have been so worried. But Ryuu had not simply implied, but had directly stated, that the Huangxu emperor was in faster-than-light communication with Fyodor Durst aka Brother Alexi, and thus could be aware of Ciarán, the ship, and crew, and could act against them. If an order were transmitted, it would come through this superluminal node, so that those closest to it would be the first to know.

Of course the emperor had bigger things to worry about than Ciarán, including wars with the Ojinate, the League, and now the Eight Banners Empire, not to mention dealing with any internal threats that might arise from Ryuu's declaration, namely that the Huangxu Eng might achieve peace with their neighbors if they simply deposed the emperor and handed him over to the Eight Banner Empire for trial.

That was a lot to deal with, and one merchant vessel and crew low on the list of priorities.

An hour later they were still waiting.

"Is this typical?" Ciarán said.

"It is most unusual," Ko Shan said. "It implies they are waiting for something. Or someone. That, or they wish to insult us."

"Waiting for someone like the police?"

"In the case of foreigners, the military. Or the secret police."

"Well, we've done nothing wrong. Let's give then another five minutes and then bail. If they don't want what we're offering, there's no point in waiting any longer."

"We should go now. A wait of an hour is not merely impolite. It is a pointed insult, one meant to put us in our place. We should not in any case negotiate with such people, as they have already demonstrated bad faith."

"That's a good point. I'll let the Merchant's Guild know to scratch this system off the list." Ciarán stood. "Let's roll."

The door to the waiting room opened, and a young man stepped in. He wore traditional Huangxu business dress: elaborate, draping, with long sleeves that made it impossible to do manual labor, expensive silken cloth, cut in a flattering manner that shouted bespoke tailoring. The outfit reminded Ciarán of his friend Macer, and his mother's and Laura Ellis's mother's funeral. The pair of them, Laura and Macer, turned out in their finest formal dress, like knights armored for battle and no one to fight.

The Huangxu Eng nodded to Ciarán, eyed Ko Shan, and apologized insincerely for the delay.

"Please, sit," he said.

Any doubts Ciarán had about the compartment being monitored were swept away.

They sat and the man perched on the arm of a nearby chair, the sort of seat that indicated he wasn't staying. He didn't bother to introduce himself.

"What is it you wished to discuss?"

"We're going to Contract space, and we understand the superluminal node there is down. We're running light and would like to pick up some additional business. So we thought we'd offer to take whatever parts you needed there, in exchange for something we want."

"We have our own repair ships."

"Well, they don't seem to be getting to Contract space. In addition to trying to wrangle up some work, we'd like a functional node in the system for our own benefit. We plan to conduct a reasonable amount of trade out of there."

"It's a low-priority system."

"Not for us. And like I said, we're going there, and have cargo space. And we're not asking for much in return."

"I'm sorry. It's out of the question."

"Why is that?"

"Because it's not something we do."

"Fix your broken equipment isn't something you do?"

"Use outside contractors."

"Fair enough. Then I'd like to file a complaint."

"That's a different department."

"I thought you represented the repair department."

"I represent the interests of the corporation as a whole."

"So you're like a public relations person?"

"In a sense, yes."

"And it's not in the interests of the corporation to repair the superluminal node in Contract space?"

"We intend to repair it."

"Huh. That's good to know." Ciarán glanced at Ko Shan. "I think we're done here."

"I agree."

"I'll escort you out," the man said.

"Nobody is going to fix the superluminal node in Contract space. So we have..." He glanced at Ko Shan.

"Three weeks and twenty-two hours, standard."

"That long," Ciarán said, "to rustle up some cargo, get to Contract space, and do whatever we want before news of it can get back here."

Ko Shan nodded. "That seems accurate."

Ciarán grinned. "Hooray for bureaucracy."

"Just a moment," the man said.

"We're kind of in a hurry," Ciarán said. "Thanks for the chat."

"W<small>AIT</small>," a breathless older woman said as the entry door closed behind her. She glanced at her colleague, bowed to Ciarán, and blinked as her gaze fell on Ko Shan, but nodded, lightly, an acknowledgment, courteous but without implied respect.

"I am Chen Su, and in charge of the repair department. I'm afraid I only now received notice of your arrival. Please accept my sincere and humble apologies."

"Thank you, Miss Chen, but we're in a bit of a hurry. We understand there's a..."

"Window of opportunity," Ko Shan said.

"Right. A window of opportunity. We don't want it miss it."

"If you could afford me but a few minutes of your time," she said. "Purely as a courtesy."

Ciarán pretended to consider her offer. He bowed. "It would be my honor."

She had used the magic words. He wasn't a salesman with his toe blocking the hatch. She needed something, and he might be able to help her. It was worth exploring. They might not come to an agreement on price, but they'd hear each other out. If she'd offered him a promise of money he'd have run for the door. But a request for help? That was how connections were made, and fortunes built. One handshake, or bow, at a time.

The young man started to crab away.

"You," she said. "Get us tea."

Her office was probably as big as any other executive's office on the orbital, but hers was crammed with junk. Shipping crates, burnt and broken parts, some awards on the wall for efficiency, the most recent one five years ago.

She snatched up a handheld from the desk, and they exchanged particulars via data transfer. That way if they did do business it could move forward faster, and if it didn't, she'd have one more name on her list of merchant shippers. Even if she had no intention of doing business with him, she could use his bid as a negotiating tool with her usual suppliers.

It felt good to be doing what he had trained to do. Helping people solve problems by working together. She wasn't going to pull a nerve disrupter out of her pocket, or try to cheat him at knifepoint, or rough him up so he'd bend to her will. They were going to talk, and see where that led. If it worked out? Great. If it didn't work out, no one was going to get gunned down.

"Please, tell me how I may be of assistance," she said.

Ciarán laid it all out. How they were going to Contract space, how they had room for cargo, how they wanted a functional superluminal node there for selfish reasons, and how they might work together to make that happen.

"We protect our monopoly," she said. "Principally by controlling access to our technology. So the idea that we would deliver spare parts to a third party is not one we have considered."

"I thought the technology was developed by the League," Ciarán said.

"Initially. But we have modified that technology to suit our own needs. Those modifications are what we wish to protect."

"Bonded containers?" Ciarán said. "With tamper seals?"

"Our competitors can defeat those. However, that might be acceptable if we could ensure their security."

"We have unparalleled security aboard *Quite Possibly Alien*," Ciarán said.

"I was thinking more along the lines of providing my own."

"Your own security systems?"

"My own technicians, to travel with the parts."

The young man returned with the tea. He poured three cups and passed them out. The process was entirely informal, more League than Huangxu, and Ciarán wondered if that was the norm in the Hundred Planets now, or something that was unique to those technical areas where the work and the technology was based on League designs.

"We could accommodate that." Ciarán set his tea down without touching it. "Provided we come to agreement on other terms."

Ko Shan also set her tea down without touching it.

"Such as?"

"I represent a number of interested parties who are in favor of emancipation. While they don't believe that this can be accomplished overnight, they are of the opinion that when the opportunity presents itself, they should act. It's come to their attention that several mercenary companies are composed of former soldiers deemed no longer valuable to the Hundred Planets. They wish to purchase these people and free them."

"That's a rather... unusual request."

"You mean because it simply wouldn't work? That regardless of whatever transfer of title might occur these soldiers' loyalty would remain with the empire, and the emperor?"

"I take it you have told them this. That they would be purchasing nothing but meaningless words."

"Meaningless to the soldiers themselves. But one hopes, not meaningless to the emperor."

"I can ask," she said. "Do you have the names of these mercenary companies?"

"I do." Ciarán flashed them from his handheld to hers. There were ten names, the Invincible Spear Bearers' name just one of many, and sandwiched more than halfway down the list.

"That doesn't seem like much to ask," she said.

"We're going to Contract space anyway. And having a working superluminal node will benefit us. We don't need much in return."

"I can't guarantee that we can fix the node until I have people on site. If the entanglement has been severed, we'd need to reestablish the link via slowship."

"Does that happen often?"

"Often in contested areas," she said. "Almost never in populous or long-established systems."

"Do we have an agreement?" Ciarán asked. "Provided your superiors agree to our request?"

"We do. I'm fairly certain I can secure title to these assets."

"Excellent."

"It feels as if I'm cheating you."

"Well," Ciarán said. "There is one more thing we'd like, but..."

"What?"

"It feels petty to ask."

"Let me be the judge of that."

"We'd like this young man to drink the tea he's poured for us."

"And if he refuses?"

"We'd like his clothing."

"And his shoes," Ko Shan said.

iarán glanced across the longboat aisle at Ko Shan. She was gazing out the viewport and running her fingers absently over the fine cloth of the young man's formal, and apparently very expensive, business suit. The massive structure of the Huangxu station passed by outside.

"Why the shoes?" he asked.

"Because he will come home barefoot, and his wife will see."

"And she'll think that's funny? Embarrassing? What?"

"Did you not notice the way he looked at me?"

"He was extra rude, I admit to seeing that."

"He thought I was your concubine. As did Chen Su."

"Why would they think that?"

"Because my genotype is universally recognized in the Hundred Planets. Pleasure slave, designed for men of consequence and their associates. In one sense, my status is far beneath his own. In another sense, my very presence with a man little older than he illuminated the differences between your status and his."

Ciarán could feel his ears heat. "I brought you with me

because I couldn't bring Swan. And because my command of the language isn't what I'd like."

"We both know that. But they do not. They saw it as a statement on your part. That you are a foreigner openly displaying me would be interpreted as aggressive. Alpha male behavior, in simpler terms. He was offended. She was intrigued."

"What else did I miss?"

"She thinks you are a warlord and that your claim of representing a benevolent emancipation organization a lie. She believes you are assembling a mercenary force, and wish to obtain clear title to these organizations."

"But I'm a Freeman. We don't own slaves." He didn't represent anyone but the ship and crew. He just wanted to see if he could free the Invincible Spear Bearers. The rest of the names were on the list so he could hide what he really wanted in the noise and so that if negotiations were required, he'd be able to give something up without surrendering what he really wanted. He hadn't imagined the Huangxu Eng might agree to his proposal without a fight.

"That is why I said *organizations*. The mercenary company leader will be emancipated by the emperor and the rest of the company sold or gifted to him or her. The leader will establish a shell organization with himself as the sole member. He will then sell or otherwise transfer controlling interest of this organization to you. You won't own slaves. You will own shares in a joint corporation with an emancipated slave."

"One that owns slaves."

"Which you could then emancipate. But you won't. Because you are raising a mercenary army. That is what she believes."

"To what end?"

"She doesn't know or care. She told you, Contract system is of no consequence to the Hundred Planets. You, however, might prove useful to her."

"In what way?"

"In defending populous or long-established systems. She thought you were fishing for work. She anticipates that she will have work soon."

"I missed all of that."

"And so did the young man. But Chen Su is experienced. You talk. I listen. It is the way in big business, for a man to bring his body slave for this purpose. Just as you might loan me out to business associates, should you wish to gather nonpublic information in an informal way."

"I wouldn't—"

"Your face is as crimson as these shoes. Every culture has its own mores and conventions. If you wish to do business with the Huangxu Eng, you must understand and accommodate this. What you see as shameful they do not. What you see as virtue they see as vice."

"Emancipating slaves, you mean."

"Who will care for them? Who will give them purpose? How will they know their place?"

"You seem to have adjusted to freedom well enough."

"My father is a spy of the Huangxu Eng. I was raised in an Ojin system and grew to adulthood in the same system under League control. Had I been born in this system? Chen Su might well be proposing that you borrow me for the night. And I would not only be looking forward to pleasing her, but quivering in anticipation of our night of bliss together. And by the morning, Ciarán mac Diarmuid? I would be master, and you the slave."

Ciarán swallowed. "I can see that happening."

Ko Shan smiled. "I can be very benevolent to those who please me."

"That doesn't surprise me."

Ko Shan hid her face in her hands. Her shoulders shook.

"You're laughing at me."

"And at myself. For a moment there, when I saw the look on Chen Su's face as she appraised you. I saw you as she did."

"And?"

"And I have never wanted a man more."

"What about now?"

"Now I think we should leave the Hundred Planets. I am not the person I wish to be here."

"We're leaving. I'm giving it twenty-four hours and we're gone. We're already sticking our necks out just by being here. But a working superluminal node would be worth it."

"I agree. And it was worth it for me personally as well. I wondered what it would feel like, to be judged once more, not for who I am, but for what I appeared to be."

"And?"

"And I am not nearly as evolved as I imagined. When a man does not compensate a prostitute, it is customary to hold his shoes hostage. When that young man arrives at home that is what his wife will assume. Except..."

"What?"

"I don't believe he will make it home unless he's the son of a powerful official. He did poison our tea."

"I assumed he'd spit in it."

"If that were the case, he would have agreed to drink. He is most likely already dead."

"For poisoning our tea."

"For poisoning our tea without Chen Su's approval. And for being caught at it."

"None of that's on you."

"I know. But how I feel about it is."

"And you're glad."

"Overjoyed."

THREE SEALED CONTAINERS labeled as superluminal node spares were waiting on the Glorious Voice of Empire loading dock eighteen hours later, along with a data crystal containing bills of lading, handling instructions, and a note from Chen Su indicating that no technicians were available presently, and that they would be dispatched to Contract system at their earliest availability.

Delivery of the parts should proceed as planned, with receipt of the parts by the corporation's local representative marking the completion of the contract. Because the request for compensation was so small, and in anticipation of a long and fruitful association in the future, payment in full was enclosed.

"I thought she might slow roll it," Ciarán said, as Hess helped him load the containers onto the longboat.

Hess wiped his brow. "Keep us here, you mean?"

"Delay us, while they investigated our background. Do we have a way of inspecting these containers without opening them? I don't like that they aren't sending technicians."

"I thought you said they intend to send them later."

"The purpose of sending them wasn't just to fix the node, but to guard the shipment."

"I can scan them."

"Carefully. As if they were ordnance."

"Sure. But with these people they're more likely to be biologicals. Unless they're just what they say they are."

"If there's one thing I learned yesterday, it's that nothing in the Hundred Planets is what I think they say it is."

THE CREW MET in the mess. Maura Kavanagh was unusually brief. "There's one route out of here, and it's to a League World. Prescott Grange."

"Great," Hess said. "Fleet Forward Headquarters." He glanced at Mrs. Amati. "How are we going to pass through there without checking in?"

"You're not," Ciarán said. "We'll transit into the star's photosphere as we did here. Maura will get her readings, do her calculations, and we'll transit out before you receive a reply. "Unless you've changed your minds, and now believe your being cashiered is a mistake."

"It's not," Amati said. "We had access to this system's superluminal node while you were away. I did some indirect checking."

"You could simply desert," Ko Shan said.

"We don't want the League chasing down deserters," Ciarán said. "We have enough enemies as it is."

"And that's not going to happen," Mrs. Amati said. "We're going to heed the call. If it's simply a matter of affirming loyalties, we'll reenlist."

"But you'll be on opposites sides of the war," Natsuko said.

"The war could be over already," Hess said. "And we wouldn't be on opposite sides anyway. We're both regular Navy."

"Until I resign my commission," Mrs. Amati said. "And join the Guard."

"Which would be stupid," Hess said. "They're not going to let you walk off with all that hardware."

"We'll see." Amati shifted in her seat.

"We could both sign with Aster's Army. That way we wouldn't be actively fighting."

"Stabbing people in the back is still fighting. Now let's move on," Amati said. "Agnes has news."

"Not of interest to the crew," Ship's Captain Agnes Swan said.

"I'm interested," Ko Shan said.

"As am I," Natsuko said.

"My brother has escaped from prison," Agnes said. "He is on the run, according to Peaceful Dawn Platform authorities."

"What was he in prison for?" Natsuko asked.

"That remains unclear," Swan said.

"Start filing our route plan with the Merchant Guild's Registry," Ciarán said. "If he knows where you are, he might aim toward you."

"But we don't know our route plan," Natsuko said.

"File what we know. Contact system by way of Prescott Grange."

"And if he arrives at Prescott Grange and we're no longer there?" Natsuko said.

"He will have made it to League space, and that's the same as escaping. It's a developed, well-defended system, and he can book transit to Trinity space from there, or elect to chase after us. We'll leave a next hop address."

"Unless we're cul-de-saced there," Maura said. "There's only one way in. There might be zero ways out."

"There's at least a way out by conventional means. We wouldn't die of old age trying to reach the nearest star," Ko Shan said.

"I've been thinking about that," Hess said.

"And?" Ko Shan said.

"There's plenty of room to mount a standard Templeman drive. As a backup."

"So even if we do get cul-de-saced at Prescott Grange, we could buy a drive and keep going," Maura said. "I like it."

"Except we can't afford to buy a drive," Ciarán said. "And we don't have time to have one fitted. We do have enough in the ship's fund to buy passage for a few. Some of us could continue to Contract space and fulfill the contract. But let's not borrow trouble."

"It's not borrowing trouble," Swan said. "It's planning for a contingency."

"An unlikely one," Ciarán said. "And I have planned for it."

"Well, in your plan, what of the remaining ship and crew?"

"Contact the Freeman Merchant Bank. Take out a loan for a salvage operation or, now that you mention it, the purchase and fitment of a Templeman drive."

"Secured by a mortgage on the ship," Maura said. "I don't see Aoife going for that."

"Or the ship itself going for it," Ciarán said. "If Aoife owned the ship, it would have been seized by the League ages ago. It's incredibly valuable technology. They'd invent a law to steal it from her. Ship?"

"I am here."

"Are you property?"

"I am not."

"Under League and Federation law, no one can own this vessel. It has the same rights we do. And those rights include starting a business, selling shares, and applying for debt financing."

"So the ship would take out a loan?" Maura said. "Secured with what? Its hull?"

"Its knowledge, for one thing," Ciarán said. "It possesses unique technology, at least until it starts sharing what it knows, and people begin experimenting and rediscovering all that was lost.

"But that could only be sold once, or licensed a finite number of times. What it possesses that is unique and infinitely renewable is its ability to explore. To discover new worlds. To expand the universe of possibilities."

"Until it gets cul-de-saced," Maura said.

"Right. I don't know why Erik's idea hadn't occurred to me," Ciarán said. "But it makes perfect sense. We couldn't get cul-de-saced if we had a Templeman drive on board. We'd be unstoppable."

"So we'd what?" Hess said. "Make new charts and sell them?"

"No," Swan said. "We would discover new frontiers. The possibilities are endless."

"We'll be rich," Maura said.

"We'll be free," Natsuko said.

"Will Gag sees Ciarán mac Diarmuid," Mr. Gagenot said. He spoke so little it was easy to forget he was there.

"What is it Mr. Gagenot?"

"Will Gag sees daylight."

"Indeed," Ciarán said. "I don't know about the rest of you, but I am so tired of being shot at and shooting back. It's not what I want to do with my life. I'd like to profit by making the pie bigger, not by scrabbling for the biggest scrap. And I'd like to start over. To take the best of what the children of Earth have made, and combine those things, and throw the rest away. All the squabbling. All the jockeying for position. We've outgrown the need for empires, and for emperors. The time for change is now."

"You're practicing your pitch for the bankers," Mrs. Amati said.

"I am," Ciarán admitted.

"Keep working on it," Swan said. "While the possibilities are endless, the limits of human nature are not. Less idealism and more balance sheet seems in order."

"But the concept is sound," Ciarán said.

"It is," Swan said. "Now let us endeavor to make it so."

62

H ess wheeled the beacon across the boat bay on a fast-pallet. One more beacon remained in stores, and a pattern in storage, but they were fast running out of materials to fuel the macrofab.

He positioned the device right in front of the boat-bay iris.

"Same frequencies as the others?" he said.

"The same," Ciarán said.

They'd left a beacon in each system they'd passed through, one that would only respond to a broadcast of three naturally occurring frequencies in the properly unnatural coded sequence. The beacons would then transmit a timestamp and destination coordinates for the system *Quite Possibly Alien* would jump to next. The beacons were bread crumbs left behind for Aoife, should Ciarán fail to appear in Contract space by the contracted time. Aoife could begin in Gallarus space and trace their progress, one hop at a time, until they sailed off the edge of the world. And she'd at least know where they'd meant to go when they disappeared, if they disappeared, which seemed unlikely, since they were sticking to known populated systems and not haring off into the wild.

Always before they'd used the beacons alone to mark their passing and advertise their plans. This would be the first time they advertised their intermediate destination in the Registry. Their ultimate destination was well known, having been posted in the Registry when the contract was first made. How they got to Contract space was their own business. It was easier to sleep at night knowing they couldn't be followed, and knowing if trouble did find them, it would be at the end of the journey and not along the way.

If advertising their route plan could help Agnes Swan's brother find his way to safety, though, it was worth the small risk that they could be followed by anyone meaning them harm. They were running out of time, and Maura believed their next jump, or the one after that, would find them in Contract space.

Ciarán certainly hoped so. He did not want to have to tell Aoife that he'd missed the contract window, and he did not want a black mark against his name with the Merchant's Guild on the first contract of his career. If that happened it would be a deep hole he'd have to climb out of, one that might prove too deep for a merchant apprentice, or for a merchant, even. He might end up on the Trinity Surface shuttle with one cruise under his belt and a reputation of one hundred percent failure.

He hoped not, but it could happen.

Hess launched the beacon.

"About our new cargo," Hess said. "Two of them are full of superluminal node spares."

"And the third one?"

"A bomb."

"Not a biological pathogen?"

"A simple, ordinary, everyday explosive device. Set to trigger when we engaged our Templeman drive."

"We don't have a Templeman drive."

"Either the bomber didn't know that," Hess said, "Or the bomb is meant for whoever takes delivery of the spares."

"There's a third option. It was intended for us. But they mistook us for someone else."

"*Sudden Fall of Darkness?*"

"They've been known to run our transponder code. And there is the physical resemblance."

"Maybe. What do you want to do with it?"

"The bomb? Is it safe to store?"

"Yeah. Provided we don't suddenly blast ourselves into a bubble universe."

"With the bomb?"

"By engaging the T-drive."

"That's what a Templeman drive does?"

"Basically? Yeah. It's a big bang that never finishes banging."

"That doesn't sound very safe."

"Safer than jumping into the photosphere of a star."

"Maybe it is safer," Ciarán said. "But it doesn't *sound* safer."

"What's your point?"

"I'm trying to figure out how to sell what we can do. How to downplay the danger and focus on the upside."

"To bankers? Just tell them that you take all the risk and they get all the reward."

"Only if we stay alive long enough for there to be a reward."

"Then you dazzle them with jargon: 'We simply dip our temporal-spacial instrumentation into the Kavanagh probability matrix and select from a multidimensional menu of *n* inviting opportunities.' That sort of thing."

"It's not as sexy as *stardiving*. But it does sound more..."

"Survivable?"

"That's the word."

63

Prescott Grange System, Earth Restoration League

The jump into Prescott system proved bumpy. In addition to the usual translational nausea, it felt as if they were buffeted—by solar winds, by waves of gravity—by something invisible yet capable of exerting force on the hull, or on those parts of him that interpreted the unseen force as acting through the hull.

The hell of the star boiled around them. Ko Shan read off the rising hull temperature. Captain Swan watched the main viewscreen for indications of impending mass ejecta. Maura worked her navigational instruments. Ciarán sat at the piloting console consciously keeping his hands away from the controls. He no longer had to sit on his hands to keep them from straying toward the jump toggle, but he wasn't far past that. Something about leaping into the fiery furnace of a star remained terrifying. Something glandular and lizard brained.

Maura was taking longer than usual at her job.

"The outer hull will begin to boil away in twenty seconds," Captain Swan said.

"Fifteen seconds."

"Maura?" Ko Shan said. She read off another disturbing number, one so large that it made no sense to Ciarán. A human body wouldn't burn at that temperature. It would vaporize.

"Ten seconds," Swan said.

Ciarán licked his lips. There were two hulls, one inside the other. All the outer hull really did was make it so that the inner hull wasn't the outer hull. According to Hess, the inner hull was plenty strong enough to keep the atmosphere in and the heat on. The outer hull protected them from collisions, which weren't all that likely, and from deadly radiation that was everywhere, but which wouldn't kill them instantly. They'd just wish it had.

"Five seconds," Swan said. "Four. Three."

"Get us out of here," Maura said.

Ciarán jumped the ship clear of the star.

"Did you get the data?" Ciarán asked.

"I got it," Maura said.

"Well?"

The collision warning began to wail.

Swan shoved Ciarán out of his seat. She hammered the maneuvering thruster controls and the ship responded.

The alarm silenced.

"Pilot the ship, Freeman whelp. Chat later."

Hess entered the bridge. "I got it, merchie man. Go towel off." He took the pilot's seat and began working the controls.

The collision alarm sounded again.

Hess maneuvered the ship. "There's a lot of junk here for an occupied system."

"We're out of the space lanes," Swan said. "They may dump their debris nearby and allow it to burn up in the star."

"Possibly," Ko Shan said. "Although it seems odd."

"The sooner we are gone the better," Swan said. "Navigator? What is our next destination?"

"There is no next destination," Maura said. "We're cul-de-saced."

64

Ciarán felt as if he'd been hammered in the chest. He'd known that they could jump into a system and not be able to jump out. It just hadn't seemed real. Until now.

"Okay." Ciarán tried to sound confident. "We've planned for this."

The collision alarm screamed again, and Hess juked the ship once more. "That was a big one. It would have hurt."

Ciarán glanced at Swan. "This is why we jumped into an occupied system. For just such an emergency. Captain?"

"Take us out from behind the star," Swan said. "Enter from above the plane of the system. Slowly and unthreateningly, Mr. Hess. We don't want to pop out of nowhere and frighten the natives."

"Not when the natives are the League Navy," Hess said.

"I don't think surprise will be a problem," Ko Shan said.

She slaved the main viewscreen to the sensor display. It was a jumbled and nearly indecipherable isometric projection of the three-dimensional model that a full-immersion sensor rig displayed to a command-net user. It looked like a sea of red arrows and catalog tags, one so information dense that it entirely obscured the station and orbital shipyards, and most of the planet below.

"We're not instrumented," Swan said.

"My apologies, Captain. It's difficult to mask so many layers at once." Ko Shan's hands danced over the controls. "There."

The display resolved.

Hess began to mutter. "Shishihsishishishi..."

"There's no station," Maura said. "There's nothing but a debris field."

"There is half of the station, and it is yet holding atmosphere. That it is operable remains in doubt," Ko Shan said. "Operable or not, it is falling toward the planet."

"Estimated time of impact?" Swan said.

"Not enough data yet."

"Active vessels in the system?"

"A dozen at most."

"Superluminal vessels?"

"Two," Ko Shan said. "Scratch that." She glanced at Maura. "One, not counting ourselves."

"Details on the one?"

"This data is hours old, given our relative positions. We need to get closer. The vessel is in the sensor shadow of the station."

"This is the third largest shipyard in the League." Ciarán stared at the display. "There should be hundreds of vessels here."

"There may yet be," Ko Shan said. "The debris field is immense."

Ciarán asked what Swan would not. "Life pods?"

"Undetectable at this range," Ko Shan said.

"Take us in, Mr. Hess. As if we wished to dock at the station."

"Roger that, Captain. Taking us in."

Ciarán glanced around the bridge. "Do you need me here?"

"If I do I will call," Swan said. "And Ciarán?"

"What?"

"You can't have foreseen this."

"Merchant Captain nic Cartaí would have."

"And the results would have been the same. You made only sensible choices."

"I don't have a plan forward."

"No one expects you to. We are still gathering information. Go, and get some rest. I will call you when we know more."

"But—"

"Get off my bridge, Merchant. That is an order."

"Captain."

"Tell Amati I need her."

"I will, Ship's Captain."

The debris field on the display had continued to resolve. Not a single tagged item on the display appeared larger than a longboat, other than the remains of the station. The League's forward fleet shipyard and every ship in it had been reduced to slag. Nothing appeared on the long-range trace, no system picket, no fleeing survivors, nothing but a ball of debris spreading outward.

Swan aimed her finger at him. "Go!"

65

Ciarán stared at the workstation display in the merchant's day cabin. He'd been able to pipe a dumbed-down and delayed version of the ship's sensor feed onto the screen. The resolution was fine up to a point, but beyond that everything grew fuzzy. Ciarán realized that Ko Shan must have reeled in the vessel's towed array and stowed its tiny constellation of remote sensors. She was using sensors inside the hull, and inside the vessel's impact shielding, and even then, running them on passive alone. It would take forever to get an accurate picture of the system.

They were driving in toward the remains of the station. The debris field was dense and spreading outward. He didn't have enough military or technical knowledge to judge what had happened from the scans alone, or even how many vessels and orbitals were involved in the destruction, or whether whoever had done what was done here was yet in the system or—satisfied with the destruction—had moved on. There might be the remains of two contesting fleets out there for all he could tell, each torn asunder and scattered in interlocking starbursts of shredded vessels, cargo, and crew. Whatever happened,

happened quickly. So far they hadn't detected a single surviving life pod.

What the passive scans were good at detecting and tagging was acceleration. In addition they listened for electromagnetic radiation and gravity fluctuations of the anomalous kind, and dozens of other potential threat signs within their very small detection radius. He had the distinct impression they worked better when stationary though he couldn't remember if Ko Shan had told him that, or if he'd read it while translating the ship's technical documents.

He definitely remembered reading that what they didn't do was give away the ship's position and heading like the active scans did. Captain Swan was proceeding as if in an active threat situation. The upside was that she was keeping them safe. The downside was that they were picking their way slowly through a star-system-sized debris field with the equivalent of a hand-held torch for illumination. They were a mouse creeping silently through an abattoir; one where the butcher might be centimeters away, and raising the cleaver for one swift deathblow.

He couldn't worry about that. Captain Swan knew what she was doing, and even if she didn't, he knew even less. He wasn't any use to the ship or the crew if all he did was worry. He needed to plan. How were they going to get out of this system and carry on with their mission?

One way could be to dive into the star again and collect a second, or even a third, set of samples. The translation into the system had been bumpy, and that wasn't something they'd encountered before. Whatever had happened here might have had some effect on their readings. Certainly they'd never tried to gather data with so much debris being drawn into the star's fiery engine. It could be that the sudden influx of material had masked the correct readings. It was worth a try. Even if they had to dive in deeper it was worth a try. No upper limit existed to the number of times they could try, so long as they didn't push their luck. But it also might be that pushing their luck was exactly what they needed to do to find a route out of the system. He'd need to think about that more.

Another way out of the system would be to find a working Templeman drive and install it, or find the plans and pattern for a Templeman drive and build their own. Certainly enough raw material remained in orbit to feed the macrofabs. He had no idea how hard that would be, or if it was even possible, or how long it would take if it was possible. He'd ask Hess. The engineer would know.

He doubted they would be able to find a functioning Templeman drive in the system. Their initial scans hadn't shown anything conclusive yet. What had seemed like another active vessel hidden behind the station had turned out to be nothing. A ghost on the sensors.

If they needed plans and a pattern, the station remained the natural place to look. Except the station was falling down the planet's gravity well. So if they wanted to look there, they needed to look soon.

Another way out of the system was to wait until someone wandered into the system and convince them to give the crew a lift. Or force them to. That wasn't a very Freeman thing to think about, but it was an option. If it were only the contract with Adderly at stake, he wouldn't even consider it. But the Ixatl-Nine-Go situation made the option harder to ignore. He'd need to discuss that with the ship. It couldn't protect the League from every danger. At what point would it decide it had done all it could to neutralize the threat?

And that brought up another variable to consider. Supposing they found a ride. At what point would they abandon the ship to escape the system? Or divide the crew into those left to look after the vessel and those sent out to find help, or live up to the contract? Not that he could live up to the contract without a vessel ready to shift cargo.

He scraped the sensor feed off the display and brought up the system details from the Registry.

According to the log, Prescott Grange was the League's Fleet Forward Headquarters for the Outer Reach, an administrative center for the contested worlds, complete with orbital repair and refitting docks, a superluminal node, and a redundant superluminal node, both of which seemed to be missing or out of order, not according to the Registry, which listed them as active, but from Ko Shan's sensor readings.

And that was another option. If they could find or fix a superluminal node, they could call for help. Now that he thought about it, that should be the first option they explored. Even if they did find a way out of the system, they needed to get the news out about what happened here. And if they called for help and it turned out they didn't need it, then someone in the system might.

The planet was an automated agricultural world, one with a handful of people cultivating and tending a large percentage of the planet's surface. Ciarán ran his gaze down the list of crops. Mostly grains of varying degrees of climate adaptation, all capable of being planted, cultivated, and harvested by an army of machines, machines largely similar but for the crop-specific outboard gear.

Records showed less than a thousand people on the surface, many widely scattered, a hundred to two hundred in First Landing, the only city on the world, though town or village might be more accurate. More than half of all League worlds had cities named First Landing, and on more than half of those they were the largest city. He scanned the records to make sure. First Landing was the only city.

Ciarán figured the people on the planet had seen what went on overhead and were already taking measures to avoid the fallout. He scrubbed the sensor feed back onto the display. It showed a motion vector and magnitude for the remaining hulk of the station, but the trace wasn't long enough to project the impact zone. He didn't have the technical skills to figure out how to calculate it. He'd ask Ko Shan later. The odds of it hitting one small town on one big planet were pretty low. And even if it was aimed right at First Landing, he couldn't do much about it, except make sure the people below knew it.

This was one of those times when the bulk of what he didn't know towered like a mountain over all he did know. All he could do was wait.

Prepare and wait.

He wrote out what he would say if he had to call for help.

He wrote out what he would say if he had to warn the people planet-side.

He wrote out what he would say if he had to ask a passing captain for help.

And he wrote out what he would say if he had to commandeer a vessel to complete the mission.

He leaned back in his seat. He glanced at the deckhead. He'd have to put a bunk in the merchant's day cabin. He knew he should rack out in his berth, but it was a long hike to his cabin and he wanted to be near the bridge in case something happened.

He closed his eyes and ordered his brain to think about the options he'd discovered, and to search for some more he hadn't thought of yet.

And he waited.

WISP WANDERED in several hours later. He scratched her ears until she purred, and they waited together.

"I'm getting a bunk put in," he told her.

She blinked at him. Slowly.

"I'm putting it in myself, but you know what I mean. There will be a bunk."

Wisp jumped onto his workstation surface without disturbing a single item. She head-butted him.

He cleared the desk surface and she sprawled across it. Her paws dangled off either end. He scratched her chin and her paws flared.

She wasn't a kitten anymore, but there remained a kitten inside her. Just as he wasn't a boy anymore, and yet he was. He could be patient, more patient than most people. But that was when patience was his job. That sort of *waiting* wasn't something that he endured, but rather an act itself. Waiting with a purpose. Waiting with a plan, like a cat stalking a mouse.

Here they were the mouse.

He wondered if mice had a plan.

Know where all the bolt holes were. That was pretty much a mouse's plans.

And that was exactly what he hadn't planned for. What did they do if they couldn't jump out of the system and whatever had torn through a League Forward Fleet facility was still out there, in the system, waiting? Waiting for them to come closer. And closer. And closer.

Ciarán stood and lifted Wisp off his workstation surface. He set her gently onto the deck, all four paws touching at once, her back arching. She remained arched, staring at him accusingly, glancing at the corner of the cabin that could accommodate a bunk, and then stretching tall, and wandering through the hatch, probably on her way back to his bunk in the merchant apprentice's berthing compartment.

Where could they go to hide, quickly, if they were being stalked? He pulled up the Registry database on the system and studied it. There were six planets and seventeen moons, only one planet in the League habitable zone, two in the Ojin habitable zone, three in the Huangxu zone, and no data on the current Alexandrian zone parameters. The newest data on the Alexandrians was nearly seventy years old. It listed the Alexandrian zone as being equivalent to the League's.

He checked the history log. The system had never changed hands. So, unless there were clandestine sites in the system, he was only looking at one habitable planet and two rocky moons, each with small facilities dug into the regolith. Both were listed as inactive yet maintained. He didn't know if *maintained* meant stocked with emergency stores or simply able to hold atmosphere and provide power.

If they lost the ship and had to survive, their only real option was the planet. The planet which was going to be plowed by the wreckage of the station sometime soon. The station didn't have the mass of a moon, but it would slam into the planet like an asteroid strike unless it broke up on the way down. Or unless they made sure it broke up on the way down. He'd have to think more about it, but he was inclined to make sure the station did break up before it entered the atmosphere. If they ended up marooned for a time, he didn't want to do it on a dying planet, under a blanket of airborne dust and ash. If they didn't end up marooned, they would have done the Leaguemen on the planet a world of good, so to speak. If there were survivors on the station, it would be a different story. But according to Ko Shan's preliminary scans, there were no signs of survivors.

Worst case, they had to abandon ship. He now had a solution, and he'd probably come up with more alternatives while he thought through the less dire scenarios. Being wounded and having to hide. Being wounded and having to fight. Being unwounded and having to hide.

He couldn't plan for an attack on an unseen enemy. Not with the data he had now.

But he could plan to hide in a hundred different ways, and more.

The easiest way to hide would be to jump into the photosphere of the star, where no modern vessels could follow. They couldn't stay in there indefinitely, but they might be able to enter in one location and exit in another, a location far enough away from their hunter that they could run and hide elsewhere in the system, going quiet and dark, and waiting until whatever was out there grew impatient and gave up. If they made a series of repeated jumps into and out of the star, they might confuse the enemy. The farther they could jump without being detected, the larger the error between where they really were and where they appeared to be would grow purely based on the propagation delay of their detectable electromagnetic signature. So long as their jumps remained unpredictable, they wouldn't even have to jump into the star. They could hop around the system indefinitely, so long as they remained within their own sensors' range of the stellar mass. Unless they accidentally jumped into the range of an enemy's weapons, they could survive. Until the ship's stores ran out. Which wouldn't happen unless the material collection systems broke down and they couldn't replenish the macrofabs. You couldn't do that repeated jumping about in-system with a Templeman drive. He didn't know why you couldn't, but he knew that if you could, Freeman captains would be doing it, and they weren't. System entry and exit were limited to one superluminal jump in and out and sublight on main thrusters from beyond the tripwire, which he was pretty sure wasn't an artificial safety protocol but a physical limitation of the drives, or space, or something. If he hadn't been born on a planet, he'd know this, but he could only cram so much into his brain at the Academy. If he'd tried to go for engineering track, he'd have flunked out, not just because he wasn't interested, but because he lacked the fundamentals that space-born Freeman learned in primary school.

Maybe his ignorance was a strength, for once.

They'd been going about this all wrong. Thinking like spacers riding a Templeman drive. They shouldn't be going in toward the station. Not yet. They should be going out, away from it.

"Ship," Ciarán said.

"I am here."

"Do we have an estimate yet for when this destruction occurred?"

"Approximately three days ago according to the navigator's calculations."

"Suppose we wanted to jump within the system, but without jumping into the star's photosphere. Could we do that?"

"We can. The navigator has the data necessary to lay in such a course."

"Are there any limits to how far we can jump?"

"The only limits are the navigator's ability to calculate the course."

"Thank you. Will you tell Captain Swan I am coming to the bridge?"

"I have. She says not to. They are busy."

"Tell her they are about to get busier."

"Doing what?"

"Waving to our younger selves." They could move faster than light. If they jumped far enough out-system they could stand still. Three-day old light would wash across their sensors like a wave, or a hail of particles, or whatever the sensors could sense. They could *see* what happened here, and learn *who*—or *what*—was responsible.

And more importantly, learn whether they were still out there.

Watching.

Waiting.

Preparing to strike.

The ship spoke. "The captain requests the merchant on the bridge."

Ciarán leapt out of his seat. "Have they found something?"

"In a manner of speaking."

He slapped the hatch control. "And?"

"And the ship's merchant is required on the bridge immediately."

He paused outside the bridge hatch to compose himself. "Ship? Tell me."

"We have found nothing. However—"

"Someone has found us."

"Not someone," the ship said. "Some*ones*."

"Sxipestro?"

"Someones, or some *things*," the ship's minder growled inside his head. "Now *handle* this, human."

"Before *you* do."

"Before I *have* to. We are quite possibly allied in this desire, are we not?"

"We are more than that."

Ciaran touched the hatch control.

We are as one.

ABOUT THE AUTHOR

Patrick O'Sullivan is a writer living and working in the United States and Ireland. Patrick's fantasy and science fiction works have won awards in the Writers of the Future Contest as well as the James Patrick Baen Memorial Writing Contest sponsored by Baen Books and the National Space Society.

www.patrickosullivan.com

Made in the USA
Las Vegas, NV
14 January 2024

84375474R00267